The Price She Paid

David Graham Phillips

Alpha Editions

This edition published in 2024

ISBN 9789362091307

Design and Setting By

Alpha Editions
www.alphaedis.com

Email - info@alphaedis.com

Contents

I

HENRY GOWER was dead at sixty-one—the end of a lifelong fraud which never had been suspected, and never would be. With the world, with his acquaintances and neighbors, with his wife and son and daughter, he passed as a generous, warm-hearted, good-natured man, ready at all times to do anything to help anybody, incapable of envy or hatred or meanness. In fact, not once in all his days had he ever thought or done a single thing except for his own comfort. Like all intensely selfish people who are wise, he was cheerful and amiable, because that was the way to be healthy and happy and to have those around one agreeable and in the mood to do what one wished them to do. He told people, not the truth, not the unpleasant thing that might help them, but what they wished to hear. His family lived in luxurious comfort only because he himself was fond of luxurious comfort. His wife and his daughter dressed fashionably and went about and entertained in the fashionable, expensive way only because that was the sort of life that gratified his vanity. He lived to get what he wanted; he got it every day and every hour of a life into which no rain ever fell; he died, honored, respected, beloved, and lamented.

The clever trick he had played upon his fellow beings came very near to discovery a few days after his death. His widow and her son and daughter-in-law and daughter were in the living-room of the charming house at Hanging Rock, near New York, alternating between sorrowings over the dead man and plannings for the future. Said the widow:

"If Henry had only thought what would become of us if he were taken away!"

"If he had saved even a small part of what he made every year from the time he was twenty-six—for he always made a big income," said his son, Frank.

"But he was so generous, so soft-hearted!" exclaimed the widow. "He could deny us nothing."

"He couldn't bear seeing us with the slightest wish ungratified," said Frank.

"He was the best father that ever lived!" cried the daughter, Mildred.

And Mrs. Gower the elder and Mrs. Gower the younger wept; and Mildred turned away to hide the emotion distorting her face; and Frank stared gloomily at the carpet and sighed. The hideous secret of the life of duplicity was safe, safe forever.

In fact, Henry Gower had often thought of the fate of his family if he should die. In the first year of his married life, at a time when passion for a beautiful bride was almost sweeping him into generous thought, he had listened for upward of an hour to the eloquence of a life insurance agent. Then the agent, misled by Gower's effusively generous and unselfish expressions, had taken a false tack. He had descanted upon the supreme satisfaction that would be felt by a dying man as he reflected how his young widow would be left in affluence. He made a vivid picture; Gower saw— saw his bride happier after his death than she had been during his life, and attracting a swarm of admirers by her beauty, well set off in becoming black, and by her independent income. The generous impulse then and there shriveled to its weak and shallow roots. With tears in his kind, clear eyes he thanked the agent and said:

"You have convinced me. You need say no more. I'll send for you in a few days."

The agent never got into his presence again. Gower lived up to his income, secure in the knowledge that his ability as a lawyer made him certain of plenty of money as long as he should live. But it would show an utter lack of comprehension of his peculiar species of character to imagine that he let himself into the secret of his own icy-heartedness by ceasing to think of the problem of his wife and two children without him to take care of them. On the contrary, he thought of it every day, and planned what he would do about it—to-morrow. And for his delay he had excellent convincing excuses. Did he not take care of his naturally robust health? Would he not certainly outlive his wife, who was always doctoring more or less? Frank would be able to take care of himself; anyhow, it was not well to bring a boy up to expectations, because every man should be self-supporting and self-reliant. As for Mildred, why, with her beauty and her cleverness she could not but make a brilliant marriage. Really, there was for him no problem of an orphaned family's future; there was no reason why he should deny himself any comfort or luxury, or his vanity any of the titillations that come from social display.

That one of his calculations which was the most vital and seemed the surest proved to be worthless. It is not the weaklings who die, after infancy and youth, but the strong, healthy men and women. The weaklings have to look out for themselves, receive ample warning in the disastrous obvious effects of the slightest imprudence. The robust, even the wariest of them, even the Henry Gowers, overestimate and overtax their strength. Gower's downfall was champagne. He could not resist a bottle of it for dinner every night. As so often happens, the collapse of the kidneys came without any warning that a man of powerful constitution would deem worthy of notice. By the time the doctor began to suspect the gravity of his trouble he was too far gone.

Frank, candidly greedy and selfish—"Such a contrast to his father!" everyone said—was married to the prettiest girl in Hanging Rock and had a satisfactory law practice in New York. His income was about fifteen thousand a year. But his wife had tastes as extravagant as his own; and Hanging Rock is one of those suburbs of New York where gather well-to-do middle-class people to live luxuriously and to delude each other and themselves with the notion that they are fashionable, rich New Yorkers who prefer to live in the country "like the English." Thus, Henry Gower's widow and daughter could count on little help from Frank—and they knew it.

"You and Milly will have to move to some less expensive place than Hanging Rock," said Frank—it was the living-room conference a few days after the funeral.

Mildred flushed and her eyes flashed. She opened her lips to speak—closed them again with the angry retort unuttered. After all, Frank was her mother's and her sole dependence. They could hope for little from him, but nothing must be said that would give him and his mean, selfish wife a chance to break with them and refuse to do anything whatever.

"And Mildred must get married," said Natalie. In Hanging Rock most of the girls and many of the boys had given names taken from Burke's Peerage, the Almanac de Gotha, and fashionable novels.

Again Mildred flushed; but her eyes did not flash, neither did she open her lips to speak. The little remark of her sister-in-law, apparently so harmless and sensible, was in fact a poisoned arrow. For Mildred was twenty-three, had been "out" five years, and was not even in the way to become engaged. She and everyone had assumed from her lovely babyhood that she would marry splendidly, would marry wealth and social position. How could it be otherwise? Had she not beauty? Had she not family and position? Had she not style and cleverness? Yet—five years out and not a "serious" proposal. An impudent poor fellow with no prospects had asked her. An impudent rich man from fashionable New York had hung after her—and had presently abandoned whatever dark projects he may have been concealing and had married in his own set, "as they always do, the miserable snobs," raved Mrs. Gower, who had been building high upon those lavish outpourings of candy, flowers, and automobile rides. Mildred, however, had accepted the defection more philosophically. She had had enough vanity to like the attentions of the rich and fashionable New

Yorker, enough good sense to suspect, perhaps not definitely, what those attentions meant, but certainly what they did not mean. Also, in the back of her head had been an intention to refuse Stanley Baird, if by chance he should ask her. Was there any substance to this intention, sprung from her disliking the conceited, self-assured snob as much as she liked his wealth and station? Perhaps not. Who can say? At any rate, may we not claim credit for our good intentions—so long as, even through lack of opportunity, we have not stultified them?

With every natural advantage apparently, Mildred's failure to catch a husband seemed to be somehow her own fault. Other girls, less endowed than she, were marrying, were marrying fairly well. Why, then, was Mildred lagging in the market?

There may have been other reasons, reasons of accident—for, in the higher class matrimonial market, few are called and fewer chosen. There was one reason not accidental; Hanging Rock was no place for a girl so superior as was Mildred Gower to find a fitting husband. As has been hinted, Hanging Rock was one of those upper-middle-class colonies where splurge and social ambition dominate the community life. In such colonies the young men are of two classes—those beneath such a girl as Mildred, and those who had the looks, the manners, the intelligence, and the prospects to justify them in looking higher socially—in looking among the very rich and really fashionable. In the Hanging Rock sort of community, having all the snobbishness of Fifth Avenue, Back Bay, and Rittenhouse Square, with the added torment of the snobbishness being perpetually ungratified—in such communities, beneath a surface reeking culture and idealistic folderol, there is a coarse and brutal materialism, a passion for money, for luxury, for display, that equals aristocratic societies at their worst. No one can live for a winter, much less grow up, in such a place without becoming saturated with sycophantry. Thus, only by some impossible combination of chances could there have been at Hanging Rock a young man who would have appreciated Mildred and have had the courage of his appreciation. This combination did not happen. In Mildred's generation and set there were only the two classes of men noted above. The men of the one of them which could not have attracted her accepted their fate of mating with second-choice females to whom they were themselves second choice. The men of the other class rarely appeared at Hanging Rock functions, hung about the rich people in New York, Newport, and on Long Island, and would as soon have thought of taking a Hanging Rock society girl to wife as of exchanging hundred-dollar bills for twenty-five-cent pieces. Having attractions acceptable in the best markets, they took them there. Hanging Rock denounced them as snobs, for Hanging Rock was virtuously eloquent on the subject of snobbishness—we human creatures being never so effective as when assailing in others the vice or weakness we know from lifelong, intimate, internal association with it. But secretly the successfully ambitious spurners of that suburban society were approved, were envied. And Hanging Rock was most gracious to them whenever it got the chance.

In her five years of social life Mildred had gone only with the various classes of fashionable people, had therefore known only the men who are full of the poison of snobbishness. She had been born and bred in an environment as impregnated with that poison as the air of a kitchen-garden with onions. She knew nothing else. The secret intention to refuse Stanley Baird, should he propose, was therefore the more astonishing—and the more significant. From time to time in any given environment you will find some isolated person, some personality, with a trait wholly foreign and out of place there. Now it is a soft voice and courteous manners in a slum; again it is a longing for a life of freedom and equality in a member of a royal family that has known nothing but sordid slavery for centuries. Or, in the petty conventionality of a prosperous middle- or upper-class community you come upon one who dreams—perhaps vaguely but still longingly—of an existence where love and ideas shall elevate and glorify life. In spite of her training, in spite of the teaching and example of all about her from the moment of her opening her eyes upon the world, Mildred Gower at twenty-three still retained something of these dream flowers sown in the soil of her naturally good mind by some book or play or perhaps by some casually read and soon forgotten article in magazine or newspaper. We have the habit of thinking only weeds produce seeds that penetrate and prosper everywhere and anywhere. The truth is that fine plants of all kinds, vegetable, fruit, and flower of rarest color and perfume, have this same hardiness and fecundity. Pull away at the weeds in your garden for a while, and see if this is not so. Though you may plant nothing, you will be amazed at the results if you but clear a little space of its weeds—which you have been planting and cultivating.

Mildred—woman fashion—regarded it as a reproach upon her that she had not yet succeeded in making the marriage everyone, including herself, predicted for her and expected of her. On the contrary, it was the most savage indictment possible of the marriageable and marrying men who had met her—of their stupidity, of their short-sighted and mean-souled calculation, of their lack of courage—the courage to take what they, as men of flesh and blood wanted, instead of what their snobbishness ordered. And if Stanley Baird, the nearest to a flesh-and-blood man of any who had known her, had not been so profoundly afraid of his fashionable mother and of his sister, the Countess of Waring— But he was profoundly afraid of them; so, it is idle to speculate about him.

What did men see when they looked at Mildred Gower? Usually, when men look at a woman, they have a hazy, either pleasant or unpleasant, sense of something feminine. That, and nothing more. Afterward, through some whim or some thrust from chance they may see in her, or fancy they see in her, the thing feminine that their souls—it is always "soul"—most yearns after. But just at first glance, so colorless or conventionally colored is the usual human being, the average woman—indeed every woman but she who is exceptional—creates upon man the mere impression of pleasant or unpleasant petticoats. In the exceptional woman something obtrudes. She has astonishing hair, or extraordinary eyes, or a mouth that seems to draw a man like a magnet; or it is the allure of a peculiar smile or of a figure whose sinuosities as she moves seem to cause a corresponding wave-disturbance in masculine nerves. Further, the possession of one of these signal charms usually causes all her charms to have more than ordinary potency. The sight of the man is so bewitched by the one potent charm that he sees the whole woman under a spell.

Mildred Gower, of the medium height and of a slender and well-formed figure, had a face of the kind that is called lovely; and her smile, sweet, dreamy, revealing white and even teeth, gave her loveliness delicate animation. She had an abundance of hair, neither light nor dark; she had a fine clear skin. Her eyes, gray and rather serious and well set under long straight brows, gave her a look of honesty and intelligence. But the charm that won men, her charm of charms, was her mouth—mobile, slightly pouted, not too narrow, of a wonderful, vividly healthy and vital red. She had beauty, she had intelligence. But it was impossible for a man to think of either, once his glance had been caught by those expressive, inviting lips of hers, so young, so fresh, with their ever-changing, ever-fascinating line expressing in a thousand ways the passion and poetry of the kiss.

Of all the men who had admired her and had edged away because they feared she would bewitch them into forgetting what the world calls "good common sense"—of all those men only one had suspected the real reason for her physical power over men. All but Stanley Baird had thought themselves attracted because she was so pretty or so stylish or so clever and amusing to talk with. Baird had lived intelligently enough to learn that feminine charm is never general, is always specific. He knew it was Mildred Gower's lips that haunted, that frightened ambitious men away, that sent men who knew they hadn't a ghost of a chance with her discontentedly back to the second-choice women who alone were available for them. Fortunately for Mildred, Stanley Baird, too wise to flatter a woman discriminatingly, did not tell her the secret of her fascination. If he had told her, she would no doubt have tried to train and to use it—and so would inevitably have lost it.

To go on with that important conference in the sitting-room in the handsome, roomy house of the Gowers at Hanging Rock, Frank Gower eagerly seized upon his wife's subtly nasty remark. "I don't see why in thunder you haven't married, Milly," said he. "You've had every chance, these last four or five years."

"And it'll be harder now," moaned her mother. "For it looks as though we were going to be wretchedly poor. And poverty is so repulsive."

"Do you think," said Mildred, "that giving me the idea that I must marry right away will make it easier for me to marry? Everyone who knows us knows our circumstances." She looked significantly at Frank's wife, who had been wailing through Hanging Rock the woeful plight of her dead father-in-law's family. The young Mrs. Gower blushed and glanced away. "And," Mildred went on, "everyone is saying that I must marry at once—that there's nothing else for me to do." She smiled bitterly. "When I go into the street again I shall see nothing but flying men. And no man would come to call unless he brought a chaperon and a witness with him."

"How can you be so frivolous?" reproached her mother.

Mildred was used to being misunderstood by her mother, who had long since been made hopelessly dull by the suffocating life she led and by pain from her feet, which never left her at ease for a moment except when she had them soaking in cold water. Mrs. Gower had been born with ordinary feet, neither ugly nor pretty and entirely fit for the uses for which nature intended feet. She had spoiled them by wearing shoes to make them look smaller and slimmer than they were. In steady weather she was plaintive; in changeable weather she varied between irritable and violent.

Said Mildred to her brother: "How much—JUST how much is there?"

"I can't say exactly," replied her brother, who had not yet solved to his satisfaction the moral problem of how much of the estate he ought to allow his mother and sister and how much he ought to claim for himself—in such a way that the claim could not be disputed.

Mildred looked fixedly at him. He showed his uneasiness not by glancing away, but by the appearance of a certain hard defiance in his eyes. Said she:

"What is the very most we can hope for?"

A silence. Her mother broke it. "Mildred, how CAN you talk of those things—already?"

"I don't know," replied Mildred. "Perhaps because it's got to be done."

This seemed to them all—and to herself—a lame excuse for such apparent hardness of heart. Her father had always been SENDER-HEARTED—HAD NEVER SPOKEN OF MONEY, OR ENCOURAGED HIS FAMILY IN SPEAKING OF IT.

A LONG AND PAINFUL SILENCE. THEN, THE WIDOW ABRUPTLY:

"YOU'RE SURE, Frank, there's NO insurance?"

"Father always said that you disliked the idea," replied her son; "that you thought insurance looked like your calculating on his death."

Under her husband's adroit prompting Mrs. Gower had discovered such a view of insurance in her brain. She now recalled expressing it—and regretted. But she was silenced. She tried to take her mind of the subject of money. But, like Mildred, she could not. The thought of imminent poverty was nagging at them like toothache. "There'll be enough for a year or so?" she said, timidly interrogative.

"I hope so," said Frank.

Mildred was eying him fixedly again. Said she: "Have you found anything at all?"

"He had about eight thousand dollars in bank," said Frank. "But most of it will go for the pressing debts."

"But how did HE expect to live?" urged Mildred.

"Yes, there must have been SOMETHING," said her mother.

"Of course, there's his share of the unsettled and unfinished business of the firm," admitted Frank.

"How much will that be?" persisted Mildred.

"I can't tell, offhand," said Frank, with virtuous reproach. "My mind's been on—other things."

Henry Gower's widow was not without her share of instinctive shrewdness. Neither had she, unobservant though she was, been within sight of her son's character for twenty-eight years without having unconfessed, unformed misgivings concerning it. "You mustn't bother about these things now, Frank dear," said she. "I'll get my brother to look into it."

"That won't be necessary," hastily said Frank. "I don't want any rival lawyer peeping into our firm's affairs."

"My brother Wharton is the soul of honor," said Mrs. Gower, the elder, with dignity. "You are too young to take all the responsibility of settling the estate. Yes, I'll send for Wharton to-morrow."

"It'll look as though you didn't trust me," said Frank sourly.

"We mustn't do anything to start the gossips in this town," said his wife, assisting.

"Then send for him yourself, Frank," said Mildred, "and give him charge of the whole matter."

Frank eyed her furiously. "How ashamed father would be!" exclaimed he.

But this solemn invoking of the dead man's spirit was uneffectual. The specter of poverty was too insistent, too terrible. Said the widow:

"I'm sure, in the circumstances, my dear dead husband would want me to get help from someone older and more experienced."

And Frank, guilty of conscience and an expert in the ways of conventional and highly moral rascality, ceased to resist. His wife, scenting danger to their getting the share that "rightfully belongs to the son, especially when he has been the brains of the firm for several years," made angry and indiscreet battle for no outside interference. The longer she talked the firmer the widow and the daughter became, not only because she clarified suspicions that had been too hazy to take form, but also because they disliked her intensely. The following day Wharton Conover became unofficial administrator. He had no difficulty in baffling Frank Gower's half-hearted and clumsy efforts to hide two large fees due the dead man's estate. He discovered clear assets amounting in all to sixty-three thousand dollars, most of it available within a few months.

"As you have the good-will of the firm and as your mother and sister have only what can be realized in cash," said he to Frank, "no doubt you won't insist on your third."

"I've got to consider my wife," said Frank. "I can't do as I'd like."

"You are going to insist on your third?" said Conover, with an accent that made Frank quiver.

"I can't do otherwise," said he in a dogged, shamed way.

"Um," said Conover. "Then, on behalf of my sister and her daughter I'll have to insist on a more detailed accounting than you have been willing to give—and on the production of that small book bound in red leather which disappeared from my brother-in-law's desk the afternoon of his death."

A wave of rage and fear surged up within Frank Gower and crashed against the seat of his life. For days thereafter he was from time to time seized with violent spasms of trembling; years afterward he was attributing premature weaknesses of old age to the effects of that moment of horror. His uncle's words came as a sudden, high shot climax to weeks of exasperating peeping and prying and questioning, of sneer and insinuation. Conover had been only moderately successful at the law, had lost clients to Frank's father, had been beaten when they were on opposite sides. He hated the father with the secret, hypocritical hatred of the highly moral and religious man. He despised the son. It is not often that a Christian gentleman has such an opportunity to combine justice and revenge, to feed to bursting an ancient grudge, the while conscious that he is but doing his duty.

Said Frank, when he was able to speak: "You have been listening to the lies of some treacherous clerk here."

"Don't destroy that little book," proceeded Conover tranquilly. "We can prove that you took it."

Young Gower rose. "I must decline to have anything further to say to you, sir," said he. "You will leave this office, and you will not be admitted here again unless you come with proper papers as administrator."

Conover smiled with cold satisfaction and departed. There followed a series of quarrels—between Frank and his sister, between Frank and his mother, between Frank's wife and his mother, between Mildred and her mother, between the mother and Conover. Mrs. Gower was suspicious of her son; but she knew her brother for a pinchpenny, exacting the last drop of what he regarded as his own. And she discovered that, if she authorized him to act as administrator for her, he could—and beyond question would—take a large share of the estate. The upshot was that Frank paid over to his mother and sister forty-seven thousand dollars, and his mother and her brother stopped speaking to each other.

"I see that you have turned over all your money to mother," said Frank to Mildred a few days after the settlement.

"Of course," said Mildred. She was in a mood of high scorn for sordidness—a mood induced by the spectacle of the shameful manners of Conover, Frank, and his wife.

"Do you think that's wise?" suggested Frank.

"I think it's decent," said Mildred.

"Well, I hope you'll not live to regret it," said her brother.

Neither Mrs. Gower nor her daughter had ever had any experience in the care of money. To both forty-seven thousand dollars seemed a fortune—forty-seven thousand dollars in cash in the bank, ready to issue forth and do their bidding at the mere writing of a few figures and a signature on a piece of paper. In a sense they knew that for many years the family's annual expenses had ranged between forty and fifty thousand, but in the sense of actuality they knew nothing about it—a state of affairs common enough in families where the man is in absolute control and spends all he makes. Money always had been forthcoming; therefore money always would be forthcoming.

The mourning and the loss of the person who had filled and employed their lives caused the widow and the daughter to live very quietly during the succeeding year. They spent only half of their capital. For reasons of selfish and far-sighted prudence which need no detailing Frank moved away to New York within six months of his father's death and reduced communication between himself and wife and his mother and sister to a frigid and rapidly congealing minimum. He calculated that by the time their capital was consumed they would have left no feeling of claim upon him or he feeling of duty toward them.

It was not until eighteen months after her father's death, when the total capital was sunk to less than fifteen thousand dollars, that Mildred awakened to the truth of their plight. A few months at most, and they would have to give up that beautiful house which had been her home all her life. She tried to grasp the meaning of the facts as her intelligence presented them to her, but she could not. She had no practical training whatever. She had been brought up as a rich man's child, to be married to a rich man, and never to know anything of the material details of life beyond what was necessary in managing servants after the indifferent fashion of the usual American woman of the comfortable classes. She had always had a maid; she could not even dress herself properly without the maid's assistance. Life without a maid was inconceivable; life without servants was impossible.

She wandered through the house, through the grounds. She said to herself again and again: "We have got to give up all this, and be miserably poor—with not a servant, with less than the tenement people have." But the words conveyed no meaning to her. She said to herself again and again: "I must rouse myself. I must do something. I must—must—must!" But she did not rouse, because there was nothing to rouse. So far as practical life was concerned she was as devoid of ideas as a new-born baby.

There was but the one hope—marriage, a rich marriage. It is the habit of men who can take care of themselves and of women who are securely well taken care of to scorn the woman or the helpless-bred man who marries for money or even entertains that idea. How little imagination these scorners have! To marry for a mere living, hardly better than one could make for oneself, assuredly does show a pitiful lack of self-reliance, a melancholy lack of self-respect. But for men or women all their lives used to luxury and with no ability whatever at earning money—for such persons to marry money in order to save themselves from the misery and shame that poverty means to them is the most natural, the most human action conceivable. The man or the woman who says he or she would not do it, either is a hypocrite or is talking without thinking. You may in honesty criticize and condemn a social system that suffers men and women to be so crudely and criminally miseducated by being given luxury they did not earn. But to condemn the victims of that system for acting as its logic compels is sheer folly or sheer phariseeism.

Would Mildred Gower have married for money? As the weeks fled, as the bank account dwindled, she would have grasped eagerly at any rich man who might have offered himself—no matter how repellent he might have been. She did not want a bare living; she did not want what passes with the mass of middle-class people for comfort. She wanted what she had—the beautiful and spacious house, the costly and fashionable clothing, the servants, the carriages and motors, the thousand and one comforts, luxuries, and vanities to which she had always been used. In the brain of a young woman of poor or only comfortably off family the thoughts that seethed in Mildred Gower's brain would have been so many indications of depravity. In Mildred Gower's brain they were the natural, the inevitable, thoughts. They indicated everything as to her training, nothing as to her character. So, when she, thinking only of a rich marriage with no matter whom, and contrasting herself with the fine women portrayed in the novels and plays, condemned herself as shameless and degraded, she did herself grave injustice.

But no rich man, whether attractive or repulsive, offered. Indeed, no man of any kind offered. Instead, it was her mother who married.

A widower named James Presbury, elderly, with an income of five to six thousand a year from inherited wealth, stumbled into Hanging Rock to live, was impressed by the style the widow Gower maintained, believed the rumor that her husband had left her better off than was generally thought, proposed, and was accepted. And two years and a month after Henry Gower's death his widow became Mrs. James Presbury—and ceased to veil from her new husband the truth as to her affairs.

Mildred had thought that, than the family quarrels incident to settling her father's estate, human nature could no lower descend. She was now to be disillusioned. When a young man or a young woman blunders into a poor marriage in trying to make a rich one, he or she is usually withheld from immediate and frank expression by the timidity of youth. Not so the elderly man or woman. As we grow older, no matter how timidly conventional we are by nature, we become, through selfishness or through indifference to the opinion of others or through impatience of petty restraint, more and more outspoken. Old Presbury discovered how he had tricked himself four days after the wedding. He and his bride were at the Waldorf in New York, a-honeymooning.

The bride had never professed to be rich. She had simply continued in her lifelong way, had simply acted rich. She well knew the gaudy delusions her admirer was entertaining, and she saw to it that nothing was said or done to disturb him. She inquired into his affairs, made sure of the substantiality of the comparatively small income he possessed, decided to accept him as her best available chance to escape becoming a charge upon her anything but eager and generous relatives. She awaited the explosion with serenity. She cared not a flip for Presbury, who was a soft and silly old fool, full of antiquated compliments and so drearily the inferior of Henry Gower, physically and mentally, that even she could appreciate the difference, the descent. She rather enjoyed the prospect of a combat with him, of the end of dissimulating her contempt. She had thought out and had put in arsenal ready for use a variety of sneers, jeers, and insults that suggested themselves to her as she listened and simpered and responded while he was courting.

Had the opportunity offered earlier than the fourth day she would have seized it, but not until that fourth morning was she in just the right mood. She had eaten too much dinner the night before, and had followed it after two hours in a stuffy theater with an indigestible supper. He liked the bedroom windows open at night; she liked them closed. After she fell into a heavy sleep, he slipped out of bed and opened the windows wide—to teach her by the night's happy experience that she was entirely mistaken as to the harmfulness of fresh winter air. The result was that she awakened with a frightful cold and a splitting headache. And as the weather was about to change she had shooting pains like toothache through her toes the instant she thrust them into her shoes. The elderly groom, believing he had a rich bride, was all solicitude and infuriating attention. She waited until he had wrought her to the proper pitch of fury. Then she said—in reply to some remark of his:

"Yes, I shall rely upon you entirely. I want you to take absolute charge of my affairs."

The tears sprang to his eyes. His weak old mouth, rapidly falling to pieces, twisted and twitched with emotion. "I'll try to deserve your confidence, darling," said he. "I've had large business experience—in the way of investing carefully, I mean. I don't think your affairs will suffer in my hands."

"Oh, I'm sure they'll not trouble you," said she in a sweet, sure tone as the pains shot through her feet and her head. "You'll hardly notice my little mite in your property." She pretended to reflect. "Let me see—there's seven thousand left, but of course half of that is Millie's."

"It must be very well invested," said he. "Those seven thousand shares must be of the very best."

"Shares?" said she, with a gentle little laugh. "I mean dollars."

Presbury was about to lift a cup of cafe au lait to his lips. Instead, he turned it over into the platter of eggs and bacon.

"We—Mildred and I," pursued his bride, "were left with only forty-odd thousand between us. Of course, we had to live. So, naturally, there's very little left."

Presbury was shaking so violently that his head and arms waggled like a jumping-jack's. He wrapped his elegant white fingers about the arms of his chair to steady himself. In a suffocated voice he said: "Do you mean to say that you have only seven thousand dollars in the world?"

"Only half that," corrected she. "Oh, dear, how my head aches! Less than half that, for there are some debts."

She was impatient for the explosion; the agony of her feet and head needed outlet and relief. But he disappointed her. That was one of the situations in which one appeals in vain to the resources of language. He shrank and sank back in his chair, his jaw dropped, and he vented a strange, imbecile cackling laugh. It was not an expression of philosophic mirth, of sense of the grotesqueness of an anti-climax. It was not an expression of any emotion whatever. It was simply a signal from a mind temporarily dethroned.

"What are you laughing at?" she said sharply.

His answer was a repetition of the idiotic sound.

"What's the matter with you?" demanded she. "Please close your mouth."

It was a timely piece of advice; for his upper and false teeth had become partially dislodged and threatened to drop upon the shirt-bosom gayly showing between the lapels of his dark-blue silk house-coat. He slowly closed his mouth, moving his teeth back into place with his tongue—a gesture that made her face twitch with rage and disgust.

"Seven thousand dollars," he mumbled dazedly.

"I said less than half that," retorted she sharply.

"And I—thought you were—rich."

A peculiar rolling of the eyes and twisting of the lips gave her the idea that he was about to vent that repulsive sound again. "Don't you laugh!" she cried. "I can't bear your laugh—even at its best."

Suddenly he galvanized into fury. "This is an outrage!" he cried, waving his useless-looking white fists. "You have swindled me—SWINDLED me!"

Her head stopped aching. The pains in her feet either ceased or she forgot them. In a suspiciously calm voice she said: "What do you mean?"

"I mean that you are a swindler!" he shouted, banging one fist on the table and waving the other.

She acted as though his meaning were just dawning upon her. "Do you mean," said she tranquilly, "that you married me for money?"

"I mean that I thought you a substantial woman, and that I find you are an adventuress."

"Did you think," inquired she, "that any woman who had money would marry YOU?" She laughed very quietly. "You ARE a fool!"

He sat back to look at her. This mode of combat in such circumstances puzzled him.

"I knew that you were rich," she went on, "or you would not have dared offer yourself to me. All my friends were amazed at my stooping to accept you. Your father was an Irish Tammany contractor, wasn't he?—a sort of criminal? But I simply had to marry. So I gave you my family and position and name in exchange for your wealth—a good bargain for you, but a poor one for me."

These references to HIS wealth were most disconcerting, especially as they were accompanied by remarks about his origin, of which he was so ashamed that he had changed the spelling of his name in the effort to clear himself of it. However, some retort was imperative. He looked at her and said:

"Swindler and adventuress!"

"Don't repeat that lie," said she. "You are the adventurer—despite the fact that you are very rich."

"Don't say that again," cried he. "I never said or pretended I was rich. I have about five thousand a year—and you'll not get a cent of it, madam!"

She knew his income, but no one would have suspected it from her expression of horror. "What!" she gasped. "You dared to marry ME when you were a—beggar! Me—the widow of Henry Gower! You impudent old wreck! Why, you haven't enough to pay my servants. What are we to live on, pray?"

"I don't know what YOU'LL live on," replied he. "*I* shall live as I always have."

"A beggar!" she exclaimed. "I—married to a beggar." She burst into tears. "How men take advantage of a woman alone! If my son had been near me! But there's surely some law to protect me. Yes, I'm sure there is. Oh, I'll punish you for having deceived me." Her eyes dried as she looked at him. "How dare you sit there? How dare you face me, you miserable fraud!"

Early in her acquaintance with him she had discovered that determining factors in his character were sensitiveness about his origin and sensitiveness about his social position. On this knowledge of his weaknesses was securely based her confidence that she could act as she pleased toward him. To ease her pains she proceeded to pour out her private opinion of him—all the disagreeable things, all the insults she had been storing up.

She watched him as only a woman can watch a man. She saw that his rage was not dangerous, that she was forcing him into a position where fear of her revenging herself by disgracing him would overcome anger at the collapse of his fatuous dreams of wealth. She did not despise him the more deeply for sitting there, for not flying from the room or trying to kill her or somehow compelling her to check that flow of insult. She already despised him utterly; also, she attached small importance to self-respect, having no knowledge of what that quality really is.

When she grew tired, she became quiet. They sat there a long time in silence. At last he ran up the white flag of abject surrender by saying:

"What'll we live on—that's what I'd like to know?"

An eavesdropper upon the preceding violence of upward of an hour would have assumed that at its end this pair must separate, never to see each other again voluntarily. But that idea, even as a possibility, had not entered the mind of either. They had lived a long time; they were practical people. They knew from the outset that somehow they must arrange to go on together. The alternative meant a mere pittance of alimony for her; meant for him social ostracism and the small income cut in half; meant for both scandal and confusion.

Said she fretfully: "Oh, I suppose we'll get along, somehow. I don't know anything about those things. I've always been looked after—kept from contact with the sordid side of life."

"That house you live in," he went on, "does it belong to you?"

She gave him a contemptuous glance. "Of course," said she. "What low people you must have been used to!"

"I thought perhaps you had rented it for your bunco game," retorted he. "The furniture, the horses, the motor—all those things—do they belong to you?"

"I shall leave the room if you insult me," said she.

"Did you include them in the seven thousand dollars?"

"The money is in the bank. It has nothing to do with our house and our property."

He reflected, presently said: "The horses and carriages must be sold at once—and all those servants dismissed except perhaps two. We can live in the house."

She grew purple with rage. "Sell MY carriages! Discharge MY servants! I'd like to see you try!"

"Who's to pay for keeping up that establishment?" demanded he.

She was silent. She saw what he had in mind.

"If you want to keep that house and live comfortably," he went on, "you've got to cut expenses to the bone. You see that, don't you?"

"I can't live any way but the way I've been used to all my life," wailed she.

He eyed her disgustedly. Was there anything equal to a woman for folly?

"We've got to make the most of what little we have," said he.

"I tell you I don't know anything about those things," repeated she. "You'll have to look after them. Mildred and I aren't like the women you've been used to. We are ladies."

Presbury's rage boiled over again at the mention of Mildred. "That daughter of yours!" he cried. "What's to be done about her? I've got no money to waste on her."

"You miserable Tammany THING!" exclaimed she. "Don't you dare SPEAK of my daughter except in the most respectful way."

And once more she opened out upon him, wreaking upon him all her wrath against fate, all the pent-up fury of two years—fury which had been denied such fury's usual and natural expression in denunciations of the dead bread-winner. The generous and ever-kind Henry Gower could not be to blame for her wretched plight; and, of course, she herself could not be to blame for it. So, until now there had been no scapegoat. Presbury therefore received the whole burden. He, alarmed lest a creature apparently so irrational, should in wild rage drive him away, ruin him socially, perhaps induce a sympathetic court to award her a large part of his income as alimony, said not a word in reply. He bade his wrath wait. Later on, when the peril was over, when he had a firm grip upon the situation—then he would take his revenge.

They gave up the expensive suite at the Waldorf that very day and returned to Hanging Rock. They alternated between silence and the coarsest, crudest quarrelings, for neither had the intelligence to quarrel wittily or the refinement to quarrel artistically. As soon as they arrived at the Gower house, Mildred was dragged into the wrangle.

"I married this terrible man for your sake," was the burden of her mother's wail. "And he is a beggar—wants to sell off everything and dismiss the servants."

"You are a pair of paupers," cried the old man. "You are shameless tricksters. Be careful how you goad me!"

Mildred had anticipated an unhappy ending to her mother's marriage, but she had not knowledge enough of life or of human nature to anticipate any such horrors as now began. Every day, all day long the vulgar fight raged. Her mother and her stepfather withdrew from each other's presence only to think up fresh insults to fling at each other. As soon as they were armed they hastened to give battle again. She avoided Presbury. Her mother she could not avoid; and when her mother was not in combat with him, she was weeping or wailing or railing to Mildred.

It was at Mildred's urging that her mother acquiesced in Presbury's plans for reducing expenses within income. At first the girl, even more ignorant than her mother of practical affairs, did not appreciate the wisdom, not to say the necessity, of what he wished to do, but soon she saw that he was right, that the servants must go, that the horses and carriages and the motors must be sold. When she was convinced and had convinced her mother, she still did not realize what the thing really meant. Not until she no longer had a maid did she comprehend. To a woman who has never had a maid, or who has taken on a maid as a luxury, it will seem an exaggeration to say that Mildred felt as helpless as a baby lying alone in a crib before it has learned to crawl. Yet that is rather an understatement of her plight. The maid left in the afternoon. Mildred, not without inconveniences that had in the novelty their amusing side, contrived to dress that evening for dinner and to get to bed; but when she awakened in the morning and was ready to dress, the loss of Therese became a tragedy. It took the girl nearly four hours to get herself together presentably—and then, never had she looked so unkempt. With her hair, thick and soft, she could do nothing.

"What a wonderful person Therese was!" thought she. "And I always regarded her as rather stupid." Her mother, who had not had a maid until she was about thirty and had never become completely dependent, fared somewhat better, though, hearing her moans, you would have thought she was faring worse.

Mildred's unhappiness increased from day to day, as her wardrobe fell into confusion and disrepair. She felt that she must rise to the situation, must teach herself, must save herself from impending dowdiness and slovenliness. But her brain seemed to be paralyzed. She did not know how or where to begin to learn. She often in secret gave way to the futility of tears.

There were now only a cook and one housemaid and a man of all work—all three newcomers, for Presbury insisted—most wisely—that none of the servants of the luxurious, wasteful days would be useful in the new circumstances. He was one of those small, orderly men who have a genius for just such situations as the one he now proceeded to grapple with and solve. In his pleasure at managing everything about that house, in distributing the work among the three servants, in marketing, and, in inspecting purchases and nosing into the garbage-barrel, in looking for dust on picture-frames and table-tops and for neglected weeds in the garden walks—in this multitude of engrossing delights he forgot his anger over the trick that had been played upon him. He still fought with his wife and denounced her and met insult with insult. But that, too, was one of his pleasures. Also, he felt that on the whole he had done well in marrying. He had been lonely as a bachelor, had had no one to talk with, or to quarrel with, nothing to do. The marriage was not so expensive, as his wife had brought him a house—and it such a one as he had always regarded as the apogee of elegance. Living was not dear in Hanging Rock, if one understood managing and gave time to it. And socially he was at last established.

Soon his wife was about as contented as she had ever been in her life. She hated and despised her husband, but quarreling with him and railing against him gave her occupation and aim—two valuable assets toward happiness that she had theretofore lacked. Her living—shelter, food, clothing enough—was now secure. But the most important factor of all in her content was the one apparently too trivial to be worthy of record. From girlhood she could not recall a single day in which she had not suffered from her feet. And she had been ashamed to say anything about it—had never let anyone, even her maid, see her feet, which were about the only unsightly part of her. None had guessed the cause of her chronic ill-temper until Presbury, that genius for the little, said within a week of their marriage:

"You talk and act like a woman with chronic corns."

He did not dream of the effect this chance thrust had upon his wife. For the first time he had really "landed." She concealed her fright and her shame as best she could and went on quarreling more viciously than ever. But he presently returned to the attack. Said he:

"Your feet hurt you. I'm sure they do. Now that I think of it, you walk that way."

"I suppose I deserve my fate," said she. "When a woman marries beneath her she must expect insult and low conversation."

"You must cure your feet," said he. "I'll not live in the house with a person who is made fiendish by corns. I think it's only corns. I see no signs of bunions."

"You brute!" cried his wife, rushing from the room.

But when they met again, he at once resumed the subject, telling her just how she could cure herself—and he kept on telling her, she apparently ignoring but secretly acting on his advice. He knew what he was about, and her feet grew better, grew well—and she was happier than she had been since girlhood when she began ruining her feet with tight shoes.

Six months after the marriage, Presbury and his wife were getting on about as comfortably as it is given to average humanity to get on in this world of incessant struggle between uncomfortable man and his uncomfortable environment. But Mildred had become more and more unhappy. Her mother, sometimes angrily, again reproachfully—and that was far harder to bear—blamed her for "my miserable marriage to this low, quarrelsome brute." Presbury let no day pass without telling her openly that she was a beggar living off him, that she would better marry soon or he would take drastic steps to release himself of the burden. When he attacked her before her mother, there was a violent quarrel from which Mildred fled to hide in her room or in the remotest part of the garden. When he hunted her out to insult her alone, she sat or stood with eyes down and face ghastly pale, mute, quivering. She did not interrupt, did not try to escape. She was like the chained and spiritless dog that crouches and takes the shower of blows from its cruel master.

Where could she go? Nowhere. What could she do? Nothing. In the days of prosperity she had regarded herself as proud and high spirited. She now wondered at herself! What had become of the pride? What of the spirit? She avoided looking at her image in the glass—that thin, pallid face, those circled eyes, the drawn, sick expression about the mouth and nose. "I'm stunned," she said to herself. "I've been stunned ever since father's death. I've never recovered—nor has mother." And she gave way to tears—for her father, she fancied; in fact, from shame at her weakness and helplessness. She thought—hoped—that she would not be thus feeble and cowardly, if she were not living at home, in the house she loved, the house where she had spent her whole life. And such a house! Comfort and luxury and taste; every room, every corner of the grounds, full of the tenderest and most beautiful associations. Also, there was her position in Hanging Rock. Everywhere else she would be a stranger and would have either no position at all or one worse than that of the utter outsider. There, she was of the few looked up to by the whole community. No one knew, or even suspected, how she was degraded by her step-father. Before the world he was courteous and considerate toward her as toward everybody. Indeed, Presbury's natural instincts were gentle and kindly. His hatred of Mildred and his passion for humiliating her were the result of his conviction that he had been tricked into the marriage and his inability to gratify his resentment upon his wife. He could not make the mother suffer; but he could make the daughter suffer—and he did. Besides, she was of no use to him and would presently be an expense.

"Your money will soon be gone," he said to her. "If you paid your just share of the expenses it would be gone now. When it is gone, what will you do?"

She was silent.

"Your mother has written to your brother about you."

Mildred lifted her head, a gleam of her former spirit in her eyes. Then she remembered, and bent her gaze upon the ground.

"But he, like the cur that he is, answered through a secretary that he wished to have nothing to do with either of you."

Mildred guessed that Frank had made the marriage an excuse.

"Surely some of your relatives will do something for you. I have my hands full, supporting your mother. I don't propose to have two strapping, worthless women hanging from my neck."

She bent her head lower, and remained silent.

"I warn you to bestir yourself," he went on. "I give you four months. After the first of the year you can't stay here unless you pay your share— your third."

No answer.

"You hear what I say, miss?" he demanded.

"Yes," replied she.

"If you had any sense you wouldn't wait until your last cent was gone. You'd go to New York now and get something to do."

"What?" she asked—all she could trust herself to speak.

"How should *I* know?" retorted he furiously. "You are a stranger to me. You've been educated, I assume. Surely there's something you can do. You've been out six years now, and have had no success, for you're neither married nor engaged. You can't call it success to be flattered and sought by people who wanted invitations to this house when it was a social center."

He paused for response from her. None came.

"You admit you are a failure?" he said sharply.

"Yes," said she.

"You must have realized it several years ago," he went on. "Instead of allowing your mother to keep on wasting money in entertaining lavishly here to give you a chance to marry, you should have been preparing yourself to earn a living." A pause. "Isn't that true, miss?"

He had a way of pronouncing the word "miss" that made it an epithet, a sneer at her unmarried and unmarriageable state. She colored, paled, murmured:

"Yes."

"Then, better late than never. You'll do well to follow my advice and go to New York and look about you."

"I'll—I'll think of it," stammered she.

And she did think of it. But in all her life she had never considered the idea of money-making. That was something for men, and for the middle and lower classes—while Hanging Rock was regarded as most noisomely middle class by fashionable people, it did not so regard itself. Money-making was not for ladies. Like all her class, she was a constant and a severe critic of the women of the lower orders who worked for her as milliners, dressmakers, shop-attendants, cooks, maids. But, as she now realized, it is one thing to pass upon the work of others; it is another thing to do work oneself. She— There was literally nothing that she could do. Any occupation, even the most menial, was either beyond her skill or beyond her strength, or beyond both.

Suddenly she recalled that she could sing. Her prostrate spirit suddenly leaped erect. Yes, she could sing! Her voice had been praised by experts. Her singing had been in demand at charity entertainments where amateurs had to compete with professionals. Then down she dropped again. She sang well enough to know how badly she sang—the long and toilsome and expensive training that lay between her and operatic or concert or even music-hall stage. Her voice was fine at times. Again—most of the time—it was unreliable. No, she could not hope to get paying employment even as a church choir-singer. Miss Dresser who sang in the choir of the Good Shepherd for ten dollars a Sunday, had not nearly so good a voice as she, but it was reliable.

"There is nothing I can do—nothing!"

All at once, with no apparent bridge across the vast chasm, her heart went out, not in pity but in human understanding and sisterly sympathy, to the women of the pariah class at whom, during her stops in New York, she had sometimes gazed in wonder and horror. "Why, we and they are only a step apart," she said to herself in amazement. "We and they are much nearer than my maid or the cook and they!"

And then her heart skipped a beat and her skin grew cold and a fog swirled over her brain. If she should be cast out—if she could find no work and no one to support her—would she— "O my God!" she moaned. "I must be crazy, to think such thoughts. I never could! I'd die first—DIE!" But if anyone had pictured to her the kind of life she was now leading—the humiliation and degradation she was meekly enduring with no thought of flight, with an ever stronger desire to stay on, regardless of pride and self-respect—if anyone had pictured this to her as what she would endure, what would she have said? She could see herself flashing scornful denial, saying that she would rather kill herself. Yet she was living—and was not even contemplating suicide as a way out!

A few days after Presbury gave her warning, her mother took advantage of his absence for his religiously observed daily constitutional to say to her:

"I hope you didn't think I was behind him in what he said to you about going away?"

Mildred had not thought so, but in her mother's guilty tone and guiltier eyes she now read that her mother wished her to go.

"It'd be awful for me to be left here alone with him," wailed her mother insincerely. "Of course we've got no money, and beggars can't be choosers. But it'd just about kill me to have you go."

Mildred could not speak.

"I don't know a thing about money," Mrs. Presbury went on. "Your father always looked after everything." She had fallen into the way of speaking of her first husband as part of some vague, remote past, which, indeed, he had become for her. "This man"—meaning Presbury—"has only about five thousand a year, as you know. I suppose that's as small as he says it is. I remember our bills for one month used to be as much or more than that." She waved her useless, pretty hands helplessly. "I don't see HOW we are to get on, Mildred!"

Her mother wished her to go! Her mother had fallen under the influence of Presbury—her mother, woman-like, or rather, ladylike, was of kin to the helpless, flabby things that float in the sea and attach themselves to whatever they happen to lodge against. Her mother wished her to go!

"At the same time," Mrs. Presbury went on, "I can't live without somebody here to stand between me and him. I'd kill him or kill myself."

Mildred muttered some excuse and fled from the room, to lock herself in.

But when she came forth again to descend to dinner, she had resolved nothing, because there was nothing to resolve. When she was a child she leaned from the nursery window one day and saw a stable-boy drowning a rat that was in a big, oval, wire cage with a wooden bottom. The boy pressed the cage slowly down in the vat of water. The rat, in the very top of the cage, watched the floor sink, watched the water rise. And as it watched it uttered a strange, shrill, feeble sound which she could still remember distinctly and terribly. It seemed to her now that if she were to utter any sound at all, it would be that one.

II

ON the Monday before Thanksgiving, Presbury went up to New York to look after one of the little speculations in Wall Street at which he was so clever. Throughout the civilized world nowadays, and especially in and near the great capitals of finance, there is a class of men and women of small capital and of a character in which are combined iron self-restraint, rabbit-like timidity, and great shrewdness, who make often a not inconsiderable income by gambling in stocks. They buy only when the market is advancing strongly; they sell as soon as they have gained the scantest margin of profit. They never permit themselves to be tempted by the most absolute certainty of larger gains. They will let weeks, months even, go by without once risking a dollar. They wait until they simply cannot lose. Tens of thousands every year try to join this class. All but the few soon succumb to the hourly dazzling temptations the big gamblers dangle before the eyes of the little gamblers to lure them within reach of the merciless shears.

Presbury had for many years added from one to ten thousand a year to his income by this form of gambling, success at which is in itself sufficient to stamp a man as infinitely little of soul. On that Monday he, venturing for the first time in six months, returned to Hanging Rock on the three-thirty train the richer by two hundred and fifty dollars—as large a "killing" as he had ever made in any single day, one large enough to elevate him to the rank of prince among the "sure-thing snides." He said nothing about his luck to his family, but let them attribute his unprecedented good humor to the news he brought and announced at dinner.

"I met an old friend in the street this afternoon," said he. "He has invited us to take Thanksgiving dinner with him. And I think it will be a dinner worth while—the food, I mean, and the wine. Not the guests; for there won't be any guests but us. General Siddall is a stranger in New York."

"There are Siddalls in New York," said his wife; "very nice, refined people—going in the best society."

Presbury showed his false teeth in a genial smile; for the old-fashioned or plate kind of false teeth they were extraordinarily good—when exactly in place. "But not my old friend Bill Siddall," said he. "He's next door to an outlaw. I'd not have accepted his invitation if he had been asking us to dine in public. But this is to be at his own house—his new house—and a very grand house it is, judging by the photos he showed me. A regular palace!

He'll not be an outlaw long, I guess. But we must wait and see how he comes out socially before we commit ourselves."

"Did you accept for me, too?" asked Mrs. Presbury.

"Certainly," said Presbury. "And for your daughter, too."

"I can't go," said Mildred. "I'm dining with the Fassetts."

The family no longer had a servant in constant attendance in the dining-room. The maid of many functions also acted as butler and as fetch-and-carry between kitchen and butler's pantry. Before speaking, Presbury waited until this maid had withdrawn to bring the roast and the vegetables. Then he said:

"You are going, too, miss." This with the full infusion of insult into the "miss."

Mildred was silent.

"Bill Siddall is looking for a wife," proceeded Presbury. "And he has Heaven knows how many millions."

"Do you think there's a chance for Milly?" cried Mrs. Presbury, who was full of alternating hopes and fears, both wholly irrational.

"She can have him—if she wants him," replied Presbury. "But it's only fair to warn her that he's a stiff dose."

"Is the money—CERTAIN?" inquired Mildred's mother with that shrewdness whose rare occasional displays laid her open to the unjust suspicion of feigning her habitual stupidity.

"Yes," said Presbury amiably. "It's nothing like yours was. He's so rich he doesn't know what to do with his income. He owns mines scattered all over the world. And if they all failed, he's got bundles of railway stocks and bonds, and gilt-edged trust stocks, too. And he's a comparatively young man—hardly fifty, I should say. He pretends to be forty."

"It's strange I never heard of him," said Mrs. Presbury.

"If you went to South America or South Africa or Alaska, you'd hear of him," said Presbury. He laughed. "And I guess you'd hear some pretty dreadful things. When I knew him twenty-five years ago he had just been arrested for forging my father's name to a check. But he got out of that—and it's all past and gone. Probably he hasn't committed any worse crimes than have most of our big rich men. Bill's handicap has been that he hadn't much education or any swell relatives. But he's a genius at money-making." Presbury looked at Mildred with a grin. "And he's just the husband for

Mildred. She can't afford to be too particular. Somebody's got to support her. *I* can't and won't, and she can't support herself."

"You'll go—won't you, Mildred?" said her mother. "He may not be so bad."

"Yes, I'll go," said Mildred. Her gaze was upon the untouched food on her plate.

"Of course she'll go," said Presbury. "And she'll marry him if she can. Won't you, miss?"

He spoke in his amiably insulting way—as distinguished from the way of savagely sneering insult he usually took with her. He expected no reply. She surprised him. She lifted her tragic eyes and looked fixedly at him. She said:

"Yes, I'll go. And I'll marry him if I can."

"I told him he could have you," said Presbury. "I explained to him that you were a rare specimen of the perfect lady—just what he wanted—and that you, and all your family, would be grateful to anybody who would undertake your support."

Mrs. Presbury flushed angrily. "You've made it perfectly useless for her to go!" she cried.

"Calm yourself, my love," said her husband. "I know Bill Siddall thoroughly. I said what would help. I want to get rid of her as much as you do—and that's saying a great deal."

Mrs. Presbury flamed with the wrath of those who are justly accused. "If Mildred left, I should go, too," cried she.

"Go where?" inquired her husband. "To the poorhouse?"

By persistent rubbing in Presbury had succeeded in making the truth about her poverty and dependence clear to his wife. She continued to frown and to look unutterable contempt, but he had silenced her. He noted this with a sort of satisfaction and went on:

"If Bill Siddall takes her, you certainly won't go there. He wouldn't have you. He feels strongly on the subject of mothers-in-law."

"Has he been married before?" asked Mrs. Presbury.

"Twice," replied her husband. "His first wife died. He divorced the second for unfaithfulness."

Mildred saw in this painstaking recital of all the disagreeable and repellent facts about Siddall an effort further to humiliate her by making it apparent how desperately off she was, how she could not refuse any offer, revolting though it might be to her pride and to her womanly instincts. Doubtless this was in part the explanation of Presbury's malicious candor. But an element in that candor was a prudent preparing of the girl's mind for worse than the reality. That he was in earnest in his profession of a desire to bring about the match showed when he proposed that they should take rooms at a hotel in New York, to give her a chance to dress properly for the dinner. True, he hastened to say that the expense must be met altogether out of the remnant of Mildred's share of her father's estate, but the idea would not have occurred to him had he not been really planning a marriage.

Never had Mildred looked more beautiful or more attractive than when the three were ready to sally forth from the Manhattan Hotel on that Thanksgiving evening. At twenty-five, a soundly healthy and vigorous twenty-five, it is impossible for mind and nerves, however wrought upon, to make serious inroads upon surface charms. The hope of emancipation from her hideous slavery had been acting upon the girl like a powerful tonic. She had gained several pounds in the three intervening days; her face had filled out, color had come back in all its former beauty to her lips. Perhaps there was some slight aid from art in the extraordinary brilliancy of her eyes.

Presbury inventoried her with a succession of grunts of satisfaction. "Yes, he'll want you," he said. "You'll strike him as just the show piece he needs. And he's too shrewd not to be aware that his choice is limited."

"You can't frighten me," said Mildred, with a radiant, coquettish smile— for practice. "Nothing could frighten me."

"I'm not trying," replied Presbury. "Nor will Siddall frighten you. A woman who's after a bill-payer can stomach anything."

"Or a man," said Mildred.

"Oh, your mother wasn't as bad as all that," said Presbury, who never lost an opportunity.

Mrs. Presbury, seated beside her daughter in the cab, gave an exclamation of rage. "My own daughter insulting me!" she said.

"Such a thought did not enter my head," protested Mildred. "I wasn't thinking of anyone in particular."

"Let's not quarrel now," said Presbury, with unprecedented amiability. "We must give Bill a spectacle of the happy family."

The cab entered the porte-cochere of a huge palace of white stone just off Fifth Avenue. The house was even grander than they had anticipated.

The wrought-iron fence around it had cost a small fortune; the house itself, without reference to its contents, a large fortune. The massive outer doors were opened by two lackeys in cherry-colored silk and velvet livery; a butler, looking like an English gentleman, was waiting to receive them at the top of a short flight of marble steps between the outer and the inner entrance doors. As Mildred ascended, she happened to note the sculpturing over the inner entrance—a reclining nude figure of a woman, Cupids with garlands and hymeneal torches hovering about her.

Mildred had been in many pretentious houses in and near New York, but this far surpassed the grandest of them. Everything was brand new, seemed to have been only that moment placed, and was of the costliest—statuary, carpets, armor, carved seats of stone and wood, marble staircase rising majestically, tapestries, pictures, drawing-room furniture. The hall was vast, but the drawing-room was vaster. Empty, one would have said that it could not possibly be furnished. Yet it was not only full, but crowded-chairs and sofas, hassocks and tete-a-tetes, cabinets, tables, pictures, statues, busts, palms, flowers, a mighty fireplace in which, behind enormous and costly andirons, crackled enormous and costly logs. There was danger in moving about; one could not be sure of not upsetting something, and one felt that the least damage that could be done there would be an appallingly expensive matter.

Before that cavernous fireplace posed General Siddall. He was a tiny mite of a man with a thin wiry body supporting the head of a professional barber. His black hair was glossy and most romantically arranged. His black mustache and imperial were waxed and brilliantined. There was no mistaking the liberal use of dye, also. From the rather thin, very sharp face looked a pair of small, muddy, brown-green eyes—dull, crafty, cold, cruel. But the little man was so insignificant and so bebarbered and betailored that one could not take him seriously. Never had there been so new, so carefully pressed, so perfectly fitting evening clothes; never a shirt so expensively got together, or jeweled studs, waistcoat buttons and links so high priced. From every part of the room, from every part of the little man's perfumed and groomed person, every individual article seemed to be shrieking, "The best is not too good for Bill Siddall!"

Mildred was agreeably surprised—she was looking with fierce determination for agreeable surprises—when the costly little man spoke, in a quiet, pleasant voice with an elusive, attractive foreign accent.

"My, but this is grand—grand, General Siddall!" said Presbury in the voice of the noisy flatterer. "Princely! Royal!"

Mildred glanced nervously at Siddall. She feared that Presbury had taken the wrong tone. She saw in the unpleasant eyes a glance of gratified vanity. Said he:

"Not so bad, not so bad. I saw the house in Paris, when I was taking a walk one day. I went to the American ambassador and asked for the best architect in Paris. I went to him, told him about the house—and here it is."

"Decorations, furniture, and all!" exclaimed Presbury.

"No, just the house. I picked up the interiors in different parts of Europe—had everything reproduced where I couldn't buy outright. I want to enjoy my money while I'm still young. I didn't care what it cost to get the proper surroundings. As I said to my architect and to my staff of artists, I expected to be cheated, but I wanted the goods. And I got the goods. I'll show you through the house after dinner. It's on this same scale throughout. And they're putting me together a country place—same sort of thing." He threw back his little shoulders and protruded his little chest. "And the joke of it is that the whole business isn't costing me a cent."

"Not a cent less than half a dozen or a dozen millions," said Presbury.

"Not so much as that—not quite," protested the delightedly sparkling little general. "But what I meant was that, as fast as these fellows spend, I go down-town and make. Fact is, I'm a little better off than I was when I started in to build."

"Well, you didn't get any of MY money," laughed Presbury. "But I suppose pretty much everybody else in the country must have contributed."

General Siddall smiled. Mildred wondered whether the points of his mustache and imperial would crack and break of, if he should touch them. She noted that his hair was roached absurdly high above the middle of his forehead and that he was wearing the tallest heels she had ever seen. She calculated that, with his hair flat and his feet on the ground, he would hardly come to her shoulder—and she was barely of woman's medium height. She caught sight of his hands—the square, stubby hands of a working man; the fingers permanently slightly curved as by the handle of shovel and pick; the skin shriveled but white with a ghastly, sickening bleached white, the nails repulsively manicured into long white curves. "If he should touch me, I'd scream," she thought. And then she looked at Presbury—and around her at the evidences of enormous wealth.

The general—she wondered where he had got that title—led her mother in to dinner, Presbury gave her his arm. On the way he found opportunity to mutter:

"Lay it on thick! Flatter the fool. You can't offend him. Tell him he's divinely handsome—a Louis Fourteen, a Napoleon. Praise everything— napkins, tablecloth, dishes, food. Rave over the wine."

But Mildred could not adopt this obviously excellent advice. She sat silent and cold, while Presbury and her mother raved and drew out the general to talk of himself—the only subject in the whole world that seemed to him thoroughly worth while. As Mildred listened and furtively observed, it seemed to her that this tiny fool, so obviously pleased by these coarse and insulting flatteries, could not possibly have had the brains to amass the vast fortune he apparently possessed. But presently she noted that behind the personality that was pleased by this gross fawning and bootlicking there lay—lay in wait and on guard—another personality, one that despised these guests of his, estimating them at their true value and using them contemptuously for the gratification of his coarse appetites. In the glimpse she caught of that deeper and real personality, she liked it even less than she liked the one upon the surface.

It was evidence of superior acumen that she saw even vaguely the real Bill Siddall, the money-maker, beneath the General William Siddall, raw and ignorant and vulgar—more vulgar in his refinement than the most shocking bum at home and at ease in foul-smelling stew. Every man of achievement hides beneath his surface—personality this second and real man, who makes the fortune, discovers the secret of chemistry, fights the battle, carries the election, paints the picture, commits the frightful murder, evolves the divine sermon or poem or symphony. Thus, when we meet a man of achievement, we invariably have a sense of disappointment. "Why, that's not the man!" we exclaim. "There must be some mistake." And it is, indeed, not the man. Him we are incapable of seeing. We have only eyes for surfaces; and, not being doers of extraordinary deeds, but mere plodders in the routines of existence, we cannot believe that there is any more to another than there is to ourselves. The pleasant or unpleasant surface for the conventional relations of life is about all there is to us; therefore it is all there is to human nature. Well, there's no help for it. In measuring our fellow beings we can use only the measurements of our own selves; we have no others, and if others are given to us we are as foozled as one knowing only feet and inches who has a tape marked off in meters and centimeters.

It so happened that in her social excursions Mildred had never been in any of the numerous homes of the suddenly and vastly rich of humble origin. She was used to—and regarded as proper and elegant—the ordinary ostentations and crudities of the rich of conventional society. No more than you or I was she moved to ridicule or disdain by the silliness and the tawdry vulgarity of the life of palace and liveried lackey and empty ceremonial, by the tedious entertainments, by the displays of costly and poisonous food. But General Siddall's establishment presented a new phase to her—and she thought it unique in dreadfulness and absurdity.

The general had had a home life in his youth—in a coal-miner's cabin near Wilkes-Barre. Ever since, he had lived in boarding-houses or hotels. As his shrewd and rapacious mind had gathered in more and more wealth, he had lived more and more luxuriously—but always at hotels. He had seen little of the private life of the rich. Thus he had been compelled to get his ideas of luxury and of ceremonial altogether from the hotel-keepers and caterers who give the rich what the more intelligent and informed of the rich are usually shamed by people of taste from giving themselves at home.

She thought the tablecloth, napkins, and gaudy gold and flowery cut glass a little overdone, but on the whole not so bad. She had seen such almost as grand at a few New York houses. The lace in the cloth and in the napkins was merely a little too magnificent. It made the table lumpy, it made the napkins unfit for use. But the way the dinner was served! You would have said you were in a glorified palace-hotel restaurant. You looked about for the cashier's desk; you were certain a bill would be presented after the last course.

The general, tinier and more grotesque than ever in the great high-backed, richly carved armchair, surveyed the progress of the banquet with the air of a god performing miracles of creation and passing them in review and giving them his divine endorsement. He was well pleased with the enthusiastic praises Presbury and his wife lavished upon the food and drink. He would have been better pleased had they preceded and followed every mouthful with a eulogy. He supplemented their compliments with even more fulsome compliments, adding details as to the origin and the cost.

"Darcy"—this to the butler—"tell the chef that this fish is the best yet—really exquisite." To Presbury: "I had it brought over from France—alive, of course. We have many excellent fish, but I like a change now and then. So I have a standing order with Prunier—he's the big oyster- and fish-man of Paris—to send me over some things every two weeks by special express. That way, an oyster costs about fifty cents and a fish about five or six dollars."

To Mrs. Presbury: "I'll have Darcy make you and Miss Presbury—excuse me, Miss Gower—bouquets of the flowers afterward. Most of them come from New York—and very high really first-class flowers are. I pay two dollars apiece for my roses even at this season. And orchids—well, I feel really extravagant when I indulge in orchids as I have this evening. Ten dollars apiece for those. But they're worth it."

The dinner was interminably long—upward of twenty kinds of food, no less than five kinds of wine; enough served and spoiled to have fed and intoxicated a dozen people at least. And upon every item of food and drink the general had some remarks to make. He impressed it upon his guests that this dinner was very little better than the one served to him every night, that the increase in expense and luxury was not in their honor, but in his own—to show them what he could do when he wished to make a holiday. Finally the grand course was reached. Into the dining-room, to the amazement of the guests, were rolled two great restaurant joint wagons. Instead of being made of silver-plated nickel or plain nickel they were of silver embossed with gold, and the large carvers and serving-spoons and forks had gold-mounted silver handles. When the lackeys turned back the covers there were disclosed several truly wonderful young turkeys, fattened as if by painstaking and skillful hand and superbly browned.

Up to that time the rich and costly food had been sadly medium—like the wines. But these turkeys were a genuine triumph. Even Mildred gave them a look of interest and admiration. In a voice that made General Siddall ecstatic Presbury cried:

"GOD bless my soul! WHERE did you get those beauties, old man!"

"Paris," said Siddall in a voice tremulous with pride and self-admiration. You would have thought that he had created not merely the turkeys, but Paris, also. "Potin sends them over to me. Potin, you know, is the finest dealer in groceries, fruit, game, and so on in the world. I have a standing order with him for the best of—everything that comes in. I'd hate to tell you what my bill with Potin is every month—he only sends it to me once a year. Really, I think I ought to be ashamed of myself, but I reason that, if a man can afford it, he's a fool to put anything but the best into his stomach."

"You're right there!" mumbled Presbury. His mouth was full of turkey. "You HAVE got a chef, General!"

"He ought to cook well. I pay him more than most bank-presidents get. What do you think of those joint wagons, Mrs. Presbury?"

"They're very—interesting," replied she, a little nervous because she suspected they were some sort of vulgar joke.

"I knew you'd like them," said the general. "My own idea entirely. I saw them in several restaurants abroad—only of course those they had were just ordinary affairs, not fit to be introduced into a gentleman's dining-room. But I took the idea and adapted it to my purposes—and there you are!"

"Very original, old man," said Presbury, who had been drinking too much. "I've never seen it before, and I don't think I ever shall again. Got the idea patented?"

But Siddall in his soberest moment would have been slow to admit a suspicion that any of the human race, which he regarded as on its knees before him, was venturing to poke fun at him. Drunk as he now was, the openest sarcasm would have been accepted as a compliment. After a gorgeous dessert which nobody more than touched—a molded mousse of whipped and frozen cream and strawberries—"specially sent on to me from Florida and costing me a dollar apiece, I guess"—after this costly wonder had disappeared fruit was served. General Siddall had ready a long oration upon this course. He delivered it in a disgustingly thick tone. The pineapple was an English hothouse product, the grapes were grown by a costly process under glass in Belgium. As for the peaches, Potin had sent those delicately blushing marvels, and the charge for this would be "not less than a louis apiece, sir—a louis d'or—which, as you no doubt know, is about four dollars of Uncle Sam's money."

The coffee—"the Queen of Holland may have it on her PRIVATE table—MAY, I say—but I doubt if anyone else in the world gets a smell of it except me"—the coffee and the brandy came not a moment too soon. Presbury was becoming stupefied with indigestion; his wife was nodding and was wearing that vague, forced, pleasant smile which stands propriety-guard over a mind asleep; Mildred Gower felt that her nerves would endure no more; and the general was falling into a besotted state, spilling his wine, mumbling his words. The coffee and the brandy revived them all somewhat. Mildred, lifting her eyes, saw by way of a mirrored section of the enormous sideboard the English butler surveying master and guests with slowly moving, sneering glance of ineffable contempt.

In the drawing-room again Mildred, requested by Siddall and ordered by Presbury, sang a little French song and then—at the urging of Siddall—"Annie Laurie." Siddall was wiping his eyes when she turned around. He said to Presbury:

"Take your wife into the conservatory to look at my orchids. I want to say a word to your stepdaughter."

Mildred started up nervously. She saw how drunk the general was, saw the expression of his face that a woman has to be innocent indeed not to understand. She was afraid to be left alone with him. Presbury came up to her, said rapidly, in a low tone:

"It's all right. He's got a high sense of what's due a respectable woman of our class. He isn't as drunk as he looks and acts."

Having said which, he took his wife by the arm and pushed her into the adjoining conservatory. Mildred reseated herself upon the inlaid piano-bench. The little man, his face now shiny with the sweat of drink and emotion, drew up a chair in front of her. He sat—and he was almost as tall sitting as standing. He said graciously:

"Don't be afraid, my dear girl. I'm not that dangerous."

She lifted her eyes and looked at him. She tried to conceal her aversion; she feared she was not succeeding. But she need not have concerned herself about that. General Siddall, after the manner of very rich men, could not conceive of anyone being less impressed with his superiority in any way than he himself was. For years he had heard only flatteries of himself—his own voice singing his praises, the fawning voices of those he hired and of those hoping to get some financial advantage. He could not have imagined a mere woman not being overwhelmed by the prospect of his courting her. Nor would it have entered his head that his money would be the chief, much less the only, consideration with her. He had long since lost all point of view, and believed that the adulation paid his wealth was evoked by his charms of person, mind, and manner. Those who imagine this was evidence of folly and weak-mindedness and extraordinary vanity show how little they know human nature. The strongest head could not remain steady, the most accurate eyes could not retain their measuring skill, in such an environment as always completely envelops wealth and power. And the much-talked-of difference between those born to wealth and power and those who rise to it from obscurity resolves itself to little more than the difference between those born mad and those who go insane.

Looking at the little man with the disagreeable eyes, so dull yet so shrewd, Mildred saw that within the drunkard who could scarcely sit straight upon the richly upholstered and carved gilt chair there was another person, coldly sober, calmly calculating. And she realized that it was this person with whom she was about to have the most serious conversation of her life thus far.

The drunkard smiled with a repulsive wiping and smacking of the thin, sensual lips. "I suppose you know why I had you brought here this evening?" said he.

Mildred looked and waited.

"I didn't intend to say anything to-night. In fact, I didn't expect to find in you what I've been looking for. I thought that old fool of a stepfather of yours was cracking up his goods beyond their merits. But he wasn't. My dear, you suit me from the ground up. I've been looking you over carefully. You were made for the place I want to fill."

Mildred had lowered her eyes. Her face had become deathly pale. "I feel faint," she murmured. "It is very warm here."

"You're not sickly?" inquired the general sharply. "You look like a good solid woman—thin but wiry. Ever been sick? I must look into your health. That's a point on which I must be satisfied."

A wave of anger swept through her, restoring her strength. She was about to speak—a rebuke to his colossal impudence that he would not soon forget. Then she remembered, and bit her lips.

"I don't ask you to decide to-night," pursued he, hastening to explain this concession by adding: "I don't intend to decide, myself. All I say is that I am willing—if the goods are up to the sample."

Mildred saw her stepfather and her mother watching from just within the conservatory door. A movement of the portiere at the door into the hall let her know that Darcy, the butler, was peeping and listening there. She stood up, clenched her hands, struck them together, struck them against her temples, crossed the room swiftly, flung herself down upon a sofa, and burst into tears. Presbury and his wife entered. Siddall was standing, looking after Mildred with a grin. He winked at Presbury and said:

"I guess we gave her too much of that wine. It's all old and stronger than you'd think."

"My daughter hardly touched her glasses," cried Mrs. Presbury.

"I know that, ma'am," replied Siddall. "I watched her. If she'd done much drinking, I'd have been done, then and there."

"I suspect she's upset by what you've been saying, General," said Presbury. "Wasn't it enough to upset a girl? You don't realize how magnificent you are—how magnificent everything is here."

"I'm sorry if I upset her," said the general, swelling and loftily contrite. "I don t know why it is that people never seem to be able to act natural with me." He hated those who did, regarding them as sodden, unappreciative fools.

Mrs. Presbury was quieting her daughter. Presbury and Siddall lighted cigars and went into the smoking—and billiard-room across the hall. Said Presbury:

"I didn't deceive you, did I, General?"

"She's entirely satisfactory," replied Siddall. "I'm going to make careful inquiries about her character and her health. If those things prove to be all right I'm ready to go ahead."

"Then the thing's settled," said Presbury. "She's all that a lady should be. And except a cold now and then she never has anything the matter with her. She comes of good healthy stock."

"I can't stand a sickly, ailing woman," said Siddall. "I wouldn't marry one, and if one I married turned out to be that kind, I'd make short work of her. When you get right down to facts, what is a woman? Why, a body. If she ain't pretty and well, she ain't nothing. While I'm looking up her pedigree, so to speak, I want you to get her mother to explain to her just what kind of a man I am."

"Certainly, certainly," said Presbury.

"Have her told that I don't put up with foolishness. If she wants to look at a man, let her look at me."

"You'll have no trouble in that way," said Presbury.

"I DID have trouble in that way," replied the general sourly. "Women are fools—ALL women. But the principal trouble with the second Mrs. Siddall was that she wasn't a lady born."

"That's why I say you'll have no trouble," said Presbury.

"Well, I want her mother to talk to her plainer than a gentleman can talk to a young lady. I want her to understand that I am marrying so that I can have a WIFE—cheerful, ready, and healthy. I'll not put up with foolishness of any kind."

"I understand," said Presbury. "You'll find that she'll meet all your conditions."

"Explain to her that, while I'm the easiest, most liberal-spending man in the world when I'm getting what I want, I am just the opposite when I'm not getting what I pay for. If I take her and if she acts right, she'll have more of everything that women want than any woman in the world. I'd take a pride in my wife. There isn't anything I wouldn't spend in showing her off to advantage. And I'm willing to be liberal with her mother, too."

Presbury had been hoping for this. His eyes sparkled. "You're a prince, General," he said. "A genuine prince. You know how to do things right."

"I flatter myself I do," said the general. "I've been up and down the world, and I tell you most of the kings live cheap beside me. And when I get a wife worth showing of, I'll do still better. I've got wonderful creative ability. There isn't anything I can't and won't buy."

Presbury noted uneasily how cold and straight, how obviously repelled and repelling the girl was as she yielded her fingers to Siddall at the leave-taking. He and her mother covered the silence and ice with hot and voluble sycophantry. They might have spared themselves the exertion. To Siddall Mildred was at her most fascinating when she was thus "the lady and the queen." The final impression she made upon him was the most favorable of all.

In the cab Mrs. Presbury talked out of the fullness of an overflowing heart. "What a remarkable man the general is!" said she. "You've only to look at him to realize that you're in the presence of a really superior person. And what tact he has!—and how generous he is!—and how beautifully he entertains! So much dignity—so much simplicity—so much—"

"Fiddlesticks!" interrupted Presbury. "Your daughter isn't a damn fool, Mrs. Presbury."

Mildred gave a short, dry laugh.

Up flared her mother. "I mean every word I said!" cried she. "If I hadn't admired and appreciated him, I'd certainly not have acted as I did. *I* couldn't stoop to such hypocrisy."

"Fiddlesticks!" sneered Presbury. "Bill Siddall is a horror. His house is a horror. His dinner was a horror. These loathsome rich people! They're ruining the world—as they always have. They're making it impossible for anyone to get good service or good food or good furniture or good clothing or good anything. They don't know good things, and they pay exorbitant prices for showy trash, for crude vulgar luxury. They corrupt taste. They make everyone round them or near them sycophants and cheats. They substitute money for intelligence and discrimination. They degrade every fine thing in life. Civilization is built up by brains and hard work, and along come the rich and rot and ruin it!"

Mildred and her mother were listening in astonishment. Said the mother:

"I'd be ashamed to confess myself such a hypocrite."

"And I, madam, would be ashamed to be such a hypocrite without taking a bath of confession afterward," retorted Presbury.

"At least you might have waited until Mildred wasn't in hearing," snapped she.

"I shall marry him if I can," said Mildred.

"And blissfully happy you'll be," said Presbury. "Women, ladies—true ladies, like you and your mother—have no sensibilities. All you ask is luxury. If Bill Siddall were a thousand times worse than he is, his money would buy him almost any refined, delicate lady anywhere in Christendom."

Mrs. Presbury laughed angrily. "YOU, talking like this—you of all men. Is there anything YOU wouldn't stoop to for money?"

"Do you think I laid myself open to that charge by marrying you?" said Presbury, made cheerful despite his savage indigestion by the opportunity for effective insult she had given him and he had promptly seized. "I am far too gallant to agree with you. But I'm also too gallant to contradict a lady. By the way, you must be careful in dealing with Siddall. Rich people like to be fawned on, but not to be slobbered on. You went entirely too far."

Mrs. Presbury, whom indigestion had rendered stupid, could think of no reply. So she burst into tears. "And my own daughter sitting silent while that man insults her mother!" she sobbed.

Mildred sat stiff and cold.

"It'll be a week before I recover from that dinner," Presbury went on sourly. "What a dinner! What a villainous mess! These vulgar, showy rich! That champagne! He said it cost him six dollars a bottle, and no doubt it did. I doubt if it ever saw France. The dealers rarely waste genuine wine on such cattle. The wine-cellars of fine houses the world through are the laughing-stock of connoisseurs—like their picture-galleries and their other attempts to make money do the work of taste. I forgot to put my pills in my bag. I'll have to hunt up an all-night drug-store. I'd not dare go to bed without taking an antidote for that poison."

But Presbury had not been altogether improvident. He had hoped great things of Bill Siddall's wine-cellar—this despite an almost unbroken series of bitter disillusionments and disappointments in experience with those who had the wealth to buy, if they had had the taste to select, the fine wines he loved. So, resolving to indulge himself, he had put into his bag his pair of gout-boots.

This was a device of his own inventing, on which he prided himself. It consisted of a pair of roomy doe-skin slippers reenforced with heavy soles and provided with a set of three thin insoles to be used according as the state of his toes made advisable. The cost of the Presbury gout-boot had been, thanks to patient search for a cheap cobbler, something under four dollars—this, when men paid shoe specialists twenty, thirty, and even forty dollars a pair for gout-boots that gave less comfort. The morning after the dinner at which he had drunk to drown his chagrin and to give him courage and tongue for sycophantry, he put on the boots. Without them it would have been necessary to carry him from his room to a cab and from cab to train. With them he was able to hobble to a street-car. He tried to distract his mind from his sufferings by lashing away without ceasing at his wife and his step-daughter.

When they were once more at home, and the mother and daughter escaped from him, the mother said:

"I was glad to see that you put up with that wretch, and didn't answer him back."

"Of course," said Mildred. "He's mad to be rid of me, but if I offended him he might snatch away this chance."

"He would," said Mrs. Presbury. "I'm sure he would. But—" she laughed viciously—"once you're married you can revenge yourself—and me!"

"I wonder," said Mildred thoughtfully.

"Why not?" exclaimed her mother, irritated.

"I can't make Mr. Presbury out," replied the girl. "I understand why he's helping me to this chance, but I don't understand why he isn't making friends with me, in the hope of getting something after I'm married."

Her mother saw the point, and was instantly agitated. "Perhaps he's simply leading you on, intending to upset it all at the last minute." She gritted her teeth. "Oh, what a wretch!"

Mildred was not heeding. "I must have General Siddall looked up carefully," she went on. "It may be that he isn't rich, or that he has another wife somewhere, or that there's some other awful reason why marrying him would be even worse than it seems."

"Worse than it seems!" cried her mother. "How CAN you talk so, Milly! The general seems to be an ideal husband—simply ideal! I wish _I_ had your chance. Any sensible woman could love him."

A strange look came into the girl's face, and her mother could not withstand her eyes. "Don't, mother," she said quietly. "Either you take me for a fool or you are trying to show me that you have no self-respect. I am not deceiving myself about what I'm doing."

Mrs. Presbury opened her lips to remonstrate, changed her mind, drew a deep sigh. "It's frightful to be a woman," she said.

"To be a lady, Mr. Presbury would say," suggested Mildred.

After some discussion, they fixed upon Joseph Tilker as the best available investigator of General Siddall. Tilker had been head clerk for Henry Gower. He was now in for himself and had offered to look after any legal business Mrs. Presbury might have without charging her. He presently reported that there was not a doubt as to the wealth of the little general. "There are all sorts of ugly stories about how he made his money," said

Tilker; "but all the great fortunes have a scandalous history, and I doubt if Siddall's is any worse than the others. I don't see how it well could be. Siddall has the reputation of being a mean and cruel little tyrant. He is said to be pompous, vain, ignorant—"

"Indeed he's not," cried Mrs. Presbury. "He's a rough diamond, but a natural gentleman. I've met him."

"Well, he's rich enough, and that was all you asked me to find out," said Tilker. "But I must warn you, Mrs. Presbury, not to have any business or intimate personal relations with him."

Mrs. Presbury congratulated herself on her wisdom in having come alone to hear Tilker's report. She did not repeat any part of it to Mildred except what he had said about the wealth. That she enlarged upon until Mildred's patience gave out. She interrupted with a shrewd:

"Anything else, mamma? Anything about him personally?"

"We've got to judge him in that way for ourselves," replied Mrs. Presbury. "You know how wickedly they lie about anyone who has anything."

"I should like to read a full account of General Siddall," said Mildred reflectively; "just to satisfy my curiosity."

Mrs. Presbury made no reply.

Presbury had decided that it was best to make no advance, but to wait until they heard from Siddall. He let a week, ten days, go by; then his impatience got the better of his shrewdness. He sought admittance to the great man at the offices of the International Metals and Minerals Company in Cedar Street. After being subjected to varied indignities by sundry under-strappers, he received a message from the general through a secretary: "The general says he'll let you know when he's ready to take up that matter. He says he hasn't got round to it yet." Presbury apologized courteously for his intrusion and went away, cursing under his breath. You may be sure that he made his wife and his stepdaughter suffer for what he had been through. Two weeks more passed—three—a month. One morning in the mail there arrived this note—type-written upon business paper:

JAMES   PRESBURY,   Esqr.:

DEAR SIR:

General Siddall asks me to present his compliments and to say that he will be pleased if you and your wife and the young lady will dine with him at his house next Thursday the seventeenth at half-past seven sharp.

ROBERT CHANDLESS, Secretary.

The only words in longhand were the two forming the name of the secretary. Presbury laughed and tossed the note across the breakfast table to his wife. "You see what an ignorant creature he is," said he. "He imagines he has done the thing up in grand style. He's the sort of man that can't be taught manners because he thinks manners, the ordinary civilities, are for the lower orders of people. Oh, he's a joke, is Bill Siddall—a horrible joke."

Mrs. Presbury read and passed the letter to Mildred. She simply glanced at it and returned it to her step-father.

"I'm just about over that last dinner," pursued Presbury. "I'll eat little Thursday and drink less. And I'd advise you to do the same, Mrs. Presbury."

He always addressed her as "Mrs. Presbury" because he had discovered that when so addressed she always winced, and, if he put a certain tone into his voice, she quivered.

"That dinner aged you five years," he went on. "Besides, you drank so much that it went to your head and made you slather him with flatteries that irritated him. He thought you were a fool, and no one is stupid enough to like to be flattered by a fool."

Mrs. Presbury bridled, swallowed hard, said mildly: "We'll have to spend the night in town again, I suppose."

"You and your daughter may do as you like," said Presbury. "I shall return here that night. I always catch cold in strange beds."

"We might as well all return here," said Mildred. "I shall not wear evening dress; that is, I'll wear a high-neck dress and a hat."

She had just got a new hat that was peculiarly becoming to her. She had shown Siddall herself at the best in evening attire; another sort of costume would give him a different view of her looks, one which she flattered herself was not less attractive. But Presbury interposed an emphatic veto.

"You'll wear full evening dress," said he. "Bare neck and arms for men like Bill Siddall. They want to see what they're getting."

Mildred flushed scarlet and her lips trembled as though she were about to cry. In fact, her emotion was altogether shame—a shame so poignant that even Presbury was abashed, and mumbled something apologetic. Nevertheless she wore a low-neck dress on Thursday evening, one as daring as the extremely daring fashions of that year permitted an unmarried woman to wear. It seemed to her that Siddall was still more costly and elegant-looking than before, though this may have been due to the fact that he always created an impression that in the retrospect of memory seemed exaggerated. It seemed impossible that anyone could be so clean, so polished and scoured, so groomed and tailored, so bedecked, so high-heeled and loftily coiffed. His mean little countenance with its grotesquely waxed mustache and imperial wore an expression of gracious benignity that assured his guests they need anticipate no disagreeable news.

"I owe you an apology for keeping you in suspense so long," said he. "I'm a very busy man, with interests in all parts of the world. I keep house—some of 'em bigger than this—open and going in six different places. I always like to be at home wherever my business takes me."

Mrs. Presbury rolled her eyes. "Isn't that WONDERFUL!" she exclaimed. "What an interesting life you must lead!"

"Oh, so—so," replied the general. "But I get awful lonesome. I'm naturally a domestic man. I don't care for friends. They're expensive and dangerous. A man in my position is like a king. He can't have friends. So, if he hasn't got a family, he hasn't got noth—anything."

"Nothing like home life," said Presbury.

"Yes, indeed," cried Mrs. Presbury.

The little general smiled upon Mildred, sitting pale and silent, with eyes downcast. "Well, I don't intend to be alone much longer, if I can help it," said he. "And I may say that I can make a woman happy if she's the right sort—if she has sense enough to appreciate a good husband." This last he said sternly, with more than a hint of his past matrimonial misfortunes in his frown and in his voice. "The trouble with a great many women is that they're fools—flighty, ungrateful fools. If I married a woman like that, I'd make short work of her."

"And she'd deserve it, General," said Mildred's mother earnestly. "But you'll have no trouble if you select a lady—a girl who's been well brought up and has respect for herself."

"That's my opinion, ma'am," said the general. "I'm convinced that while a man can become a gentleman, a woman's got to be born a lady or she never is one."

"Very true, General," cried Mrs. Presbury. "I never thought of it before, but it's the truest thing I ever heard."

Presbury grinned at his plate. He stole a glance at Mildred. Their eyes met. She flushed faintly.

"I've had a great deal of experience of women," pursued the general. "In my boyhood days I was a ladies' man. And of course since I've had money they've swarmed round me like bees in a clover-patch."

"Oh, General, you're far too modest," cried Mrs. Presbury. "A man like you wouldn't need to be afraid, if he hadn't a cent."

"But not the kind of women I want," replied he, firmly if complacently. "A lady needs money to keep up her position. She has to have it. On the other hand, a man of wealth and station needs a lady to assist him in the proper kind of life for men of his sort. So they need each other. They've got to have each other. That's the practical, sensible way to look at it."

"Exactly," said Presbury.

"And I've made up my mind to marry, and marry right away. But we'll come back to this later on. Presbury, you're neglecting that wine."

"I'm drinking it slowly to enjoy it better," said Presbury.

The dinner was the same unending and expensive function that had wearied them and upset their digestions on Thanksgiving Day. There was too much of everything, and it was all just wrong. The general was not quite so voluble as he had been before; his gaze was fixed most of the time on Mildred—roving from her lovely face to her smooth, slender shoulders and back again. As he drank and ate his gesture of slightly smacking his thin lips seemed to include an enjoyment of the girl's charms. And a sensitive observer might have suspected that she was not unconscious of this and was suffering some such pain as if abhorrent and cruel lips and teeth were actually mouthing and mumbling her. She said not a word from sitting down at table until they rose to go into the library for coffee.

"Do tell me about your early life, General," Mrs. Presbury said. "Only the other day Millie was saying she wished she could read a biography of your romantic career."

"Yes, it has been rather—unusual," conceded the general with swelling chest and gently waving dollar-and-a-half-apiece cigar.

"I do so ADMIRE a man who carves out his own fortune," Mrs. Presbury went on—she had not obeyed her husband's injunction as to the champagne. "It seems so wonderful to me that a man could with his own hands just dig a fortune out of the ground."

"He couldn't, ma'am," said the general, with gracious tolerance. "It wasn't till I stopped the fool digging and hunting around for gold that I began to get ahead. I threw away the pick and shovel and opened a hotel." (There were two or three sleeping-rooms of a kind in that "hotel," but it was rather a saloon of the species known as "doggery.") "Yes, it was in the hotel that I got my start. The fellows that make the money in mining countries ain't the prospectors and diggers, ma'am."

"Really!" cried Mrs. Presbury breathlessly. "How interesting!"

"They're fools, they are," proceeded the general. "No, the money's made by the fellows that grub-stake the fools—give 'em supplies and send 'em out to nose around in the mountains. Then them that find anything have to give half to the fellow that did the grub-staking. And he looks into the claim, and if there's anything in it, why, he buys the fool out. In mines, like everywhere else, ma'am, it ain't work, it's brains that makes the money. No miner ever made a mining fortune—not one. It's the brainy, foxy fellows that stay back in the camps. I used to send out fifty and a hundred men a year. Maybe only two or three'd turn up anything worth while. No, ma'am, I never got a dollar ahead on my digging. All the gold I ever dug went right off for grub—or a good time."

"Wonderful!" exclaimed Mrs. Presbury. "I never heard of such a thing."

"But we're not here to talk about mines," said the general, his eyes upon Mildred. "I've been looking into matters—to get down to business—and I've asked you here to let you know that I'm willing to go ahead."

Profound silence. Mildred suddenly drew in her breath with a sound so sharp that the three others started and glanced hastily at her. But she made no further sign. She sat still and cold and pale.

The general, perfectly at ease, broke the silence. "I think Miss Gower and I would get on faster alone."

Presbury at once stood up; his wife hesitated, her eyes uneasily upon her daughter. Presbury said: "Come on, Alice." She rose and preceded him into the adjoining conservatory. The little general posed himself before the huge open fire, one hand behind him, the other at the level of his waistcoat, the big cigar between his first and second fingers. "Well, my dear?" said he.

Mildred somewhat hesitatingly lifted her eyes; but, once she had them up, their gaze held steadily enough upon his—too steadily for his comfort. He addressed himself to his cigar:

"I'm not quite ready to say I'm willing to go the limit," said he. "We don't exactly know each other sufficiently well as yet, do we?"

"No," said Mildred.

"I've been making inquiries," he went on; "that is, I had my chief secretary make them—and he's a very thorough man, thanks to my training. He reports everything entirely all right. I admire dignity and reserve in a woman, and you have been very particular. Were you engaged to Stanley Baird?"

Mildred flushed, veiled her eyes to hide their resentful flash at this impertinence. She debated with herself, decided that any rebuke short of one that would anger him would be wasted upon him. "No," said she.

"That agrees with Harding's report," said the general. "It was a mere girlish flirtation—very dignified and proper," he hastened to add. "I don't mean to suggest that you were at all flighty."

"Thank you," said Mildred sweetly.

"Are there any questions you would like to ask about me?" inquired he.

"No," said Mildred.

"As I understand it—from my talk with Presbury—you are willing to go on?"

"Yes," said Mildred.

The general smiled genially. "I think I may say without conceit that you will like me as you know me better. I have no bad habits—I've too much regard for my health to over-indulge or run loose. In my boyhood days I may have put in rather a heavy sowing of wild oats"—the general laughed; Mildred conjured up the wintriest and faintest of echoing smiles—"but that's all past," he went on, "and there's nothing that could rise up to interfere with our happiness. You are fond of children?"

A pause, then Mildred said quite evenly, "Yes."

"Excellent," said the general. "I'll expect you and your mother and father to dinner Sunday night. Is that satisfactory?"

"Yes," said Mildred.

A longish pause. Then the general: "You seem to be a little—afraid of me. I don't know why it is that people are always that way with me." A halt, to give her the opportunity to say the obvious flattering thing. Mildred said nothing, gave no sign. He went on: "It will wear away as we know each other better. I am a simple, plain man—kind and generous in my instincts. Of course I am dignified, and I do not like familiarity. But I do not mean to inspire fear and awe."

A still longer pause. "Well, everything is settled," said the general. "We understand each other clearly?—not an engagement, nothing binding on either side—simply a—a—an option without forfeit." And he laughed—his laugh was a ghoulish sound, not loud but explosive and an instant check upon demonstration of mirth from anyone else.

"I understand," said Mildred with a glance toward the door through which Presbury and his wife had disappeared.

"Now, we'll join the others, and I'll show you the house"—again the laugh—"what may be your future home—one of them."

The four were soon started upon what was for three of them a weariful journey despite the elevator that spared them the ascents of the stairways. The house was an exaggerated reproduction of all the establishments of the rich who confuse expenditure with luxury and comfort. Bill Siddall had bought "the best of everything"; that is, the things into which the purveyors of costly furnishings have put the most excuses for charging. Of taste, of comfort, of discrimination, there were few traces and these obviously accidental. "I picked out the men acknowledged to be the best in their different lines," said the general, "and I gave them carte blanche."

"I see that at a glance," said Presbury. "You've done the grand thing on the grandest possible scale."

"I've looked into the finest of the famous places on the other side," said the general. "All I can say is, I've had no regrets."

"I should say not," cried Mrs. Presbury.

With an affectation of modest hesitation—to show that he was a gentleman with a gentleman's fine appreciation of the due of maiden modesty—Siddall paused at the outer door of his own apartments. But at one sentence of urging from Mrs. Presbury he opened the door and ushered them in. And soon he was showing them everything—his Carrara marble bathroom and bathing-pool, his bed that had been used by several French kings, his dressing-room with its appliances of gold and platinum and precious stones, his clothing. They had to inspect a room full of suits, huge chiffoniers crowded with shirts and ties and underclothes. He exhibited silk dressing-robes and pajamas, pointed out the marks of the fashionable London and Paris makers, the monograms, the linings of ermine and sable. "I'm very particular about everything that touches me," explained he. "It seems to me a gentleman can't be too particular." With a meaning glance at Mildred, "And I'd feel the same way about my wife."

"You hear that, Mildred?" said Presbury, with a nasty little laugh. He had been relieving the tedium of this sight-seeing tour by observing—and from time to time aggravating—Mildred's sufferings.

The general released his mirth-strangling goat laugh; Mrs. Presbury echoed it with a gale of rather wild hysterics. So well pleased was the general with the excursion and so far did he feel advanced toward intimacy that on the way down the majestic marble stairway he ventured to give Mildred's arm a gentle, playful squeeze. And at the parting he kissed her hand. Presbury had changed his mind about returning to the country. On the way to the hotel he girded at Mildred, reviewing all that the little general had said and done, and sneering, jeering at it. Mildred made not a single retort until they were upstairs in the hotel. At the door to her room she said to Presbury—said it in a quiet, cold, terrible way:

"If you really want me to go through with this thing, you will stop insulting him and me. If you do it again, I'll give up—and go on the streets before I'll marry him."

Presbury shrugged his shoulders and went on to the other room. But he did not begin again the next day, and from that time forth avoided reference to the general. In fact, there was an astonishing change in his whole demeanor. He ceased to bait his wife, became polite, even affable. If he had conducted himself thus from the outset, he would have got far less credit, would have made far less progress toward winning the liking of his wife, and of her daughter, than he did in a brief two weeks of change from petty and malignant tyrant to good-natured, interestingly talkative old gentleman. After the manner of human nature, Mildred and her mother, in their relief, in their pleasure through this amazing sudden and wholly unexpected geniality, not merely forgave but forgot all they had suffered at his hands. Mildred was not without a suspicion of the truth that this change, inaugurated in his own good time, was fresh evidence of his contempt for both of them—of his feeling that he could easily make reparation with a little kindness and decency and put himself in the way of getting any possible benefits from the rich alliance. But though she practically knew what was going on in his mind, she could not prevent herself from softening toward him.

Now followed a succession of dinners, of theater- and opera-goings, of week-ends at the general's new country palace in the fashionable region of Long Island. All these festivities were of the same formal and tedious character. At all the general was the central sun with the others dim and draggled satellites, hardly more important than the outer rim of satellite servants. He did most of the talking; he was the sole topic of conversation; for when he was not talking about himself he wished to be hearing about himself. If Mildred had not been seeing more and more plainly that other and real personality of his, her contempt for him and for herself would have grown beyond control. But, with him or away from him, at every instant there was the sense of that other real William Siddall—a shadowy menace full of terror. She dreamed of it—was startled from sleep by visions of a monstrous and mighty distortion of the little general's grotesque exterior. "I shall marry him if I can," she said to her self. "But—can I?" And she feared and hoped that she could not, that courage would fail her, or would come to her rescue, whichever it was, and that she would refuse him. Aside from the sense of her body that cannot but be with any woman who is beautiful, she had never theretofore been especially physical in thought. That side of life had remained vague, as she had never indulged in or even been strongly tempted with the things that rouse it from its virginal sleep. But now she thought only of her body, because that it was, and that alone, that had drawn this prospective purchaser, and his eyes never let her forget it. She fell into the habit of looking at herself in the glass—at her face, at her shoulders, at her whole person, not in vanity but in a kind of wonder or aversion. And in the visions, both the waking and the sleeping, she reached the climax of horror when the monster touched her—with clammy, creepy fingers, with munching lips, with the sharp ends of the mustache or imperial.

Said Mrs. Presbury to her husband, "I'm afraid the general will be irritated by Mildred's unresponsiveness."

"Don't worry," replied Presbury. "He's so crazy about himself that he imagines the whole world is in the same state."

"Isn't it strange that he doesn't give her presents? Never anything but candy and flowers."

"And he never will," said Presbury.

"Not until they're married, I suppose."

Presbury was silent.

"I can't help thinking that if Milly were to rouse herself and show some—some liking—or at least interest, it'd be wiser."

"She's taking the best possible course," said Presbury. "Unconsciously to both of them, she's leading him on. He thinks that's the way a lady should act—restrained, refined."

Mildred's attitude was simple inertia. The most positive effort she made was avoiding saying or doing anything to displease him—no difficult matter, as she was silent and almost lifeless when he was near. Without any encouragement from her he gradually got a deep respect for her—which meant that he became convinced of her coldness and exclusiveness, of her absolute trustworthiness. Presbury was more profoundly right than he knew. The girl pursued the only course that made possible the success she longed for, yet dreaded and loathed. For at the outset Siddall had not been nearly so strongly in earnest in his matrimonial project as he had professed and had believed himself. He wished to marry, wished to add to his possessions the admirable show-piece and exhibition opportunity afforded by the right sort of wife; but in the bottom of his heart he felt that such a woman as he dreamed of did not exist in all the foolish, fickle, and shallow female sex. This girl—so cold, so proud, beautiful yet not eager to display her charms or to have them praised—she was the rare bird he sought.

In a month he asked her to marry him; that is, he said: "My dear, I find that I am ready to go the limit—if you are." And she assented. He put his arm around her and kissed her cheek—and was delighted to discover that the alluring embrace made no impression upon the ice of her "purity and ladylike dignity." Up to the very last moment of the formal courtship he held himself ready to withdraw should she reveal to his watchfulness the slightest sign of having any "unladylike" tendencies or feelings. She revealed no such sign, but remained "ladylike"; and certainly, so the general reasoned, a woman who could thus resist him, even in the license of the formal engagement, would resist anybody.

As soon as the engagement was formally concluded, the general hurried on the preparations for the wedding. He opened accounts at half a dozen shops in New York—dressmakers, milliners, dealers in fine and fashionable clothing of every kind—and gave them orders to execute whatever commands Miss Gower or her mother—for HER—might give them. When he told her of this munificence and magnificence and paused for the outburst of gratitude, he listened in vain. Mildred colored to the roots of her hair and was silent, was seeking the courage to refuse.

"I know that you and your people can't afford to do the thing as things related to me must be done," he went on to say. "So I decided to just start in a little early at what I've got to do anyhow. Not that I blame you for your not having money, my dear. On the contrary, that's one of your merits with me. I wouldn't marry a woman with money. It puts the family life on a wrong basis."

"I had planned a quiet wedding," said Mildred. "I'd much prefer it."

"Now you can be frank with me, my dear," said the general. "I know you ladies—how cheated you feel if you aren't married with all the frills and fixings. So that's the way it shall be done."

"Really," protested Mildred, "I'm absolutely frank. I wish it to be quite quiet—in our drawing-room, with no guests."

Siddall smiled, genial and tolerant. "Don't argue with me, my dear. I know what you want, and I'll see that you get it. Go ahead with these shop-people I've put at your disposal—and go as far as you like. There isn't anything—ANYTHING—in the way of clothes that you can't have—that you mustn't have. Mrs. General Siddall is going to be the best-dressed woman in the world—as she is the prettiest. I haven't opened an account for you with Tiffany's or any of those people. I'll look out for that part of the business, myself."

"I don't care for jewelry," said Mildred.

"Naturally not for the kind that's been within your means heretofore," replied he; "but you'll open your eyes when you see MY jewelry for MY wife. All in good time, my dear. You and your mother must start right in with the shopping; and, a week or so before the wedding, I'll send my people down to transform the house. I may be wrong, but I rather think that the Siddall wedding will cause some talk."

He was not wrong. Through his confidential secretary, Harding the thorough, the newspaper press was induced to take an interest in the incredible extravagance Siddall was perpetrating in arranging for a fitting wedding for General William Siddall. For many days before the ceremony there were daily columns about him and his romantic career and his romantic wooing of the New Jersey girl of excellent family and social position but of comparatively modest means. The shopkeepers gave interviews on the trousseau. The decorators and caterers detailed the splendors and the costliness of the preparations of which they had charge. From morning until dark a crowd hung round the house at Hanging Rock, and on the wedding day the streets leading to it were blocked—chiefly with people come from a distance, many of them from New York.

At the outset all this noise was deeply distasteful to Mildred, but after a few days she recovered her normal point of view, forgot the kind of man she was marrying in the excitement and exultation over her sudden splendor and fame. So strongly did the delusion presently become, that she was looking at the little general with anything but unfavorable eyes. He seemed to her a quaint, fascinating, benevolent necromancer, having miraculous powers which he was exercising in her behalf. She even reproached herself with ingratitude in not being wildly in love with him. Would not any other girl, in her place, have fallen over ears in love with this marvelous man?

However, while she could not quite convince herself that she loved, she became convinced without effort that she was happy, that she was going to be still happier. The excitement wrought her into a state of exaltation and swept her through the wedding ceremony and the going away as radiant a bride as a man would care to have.

There is much to be said against the noisy, showy wedding. Certainly love has rarely been known to degrade himself to the point of attending any such. But there is something to be said for that sort of married start—for instance, where love is neither invited nor desired, an effort must be made to cover the painful vacancy his absence always causes.

The little general's insistence on a "real wedding" was most happy for him. It probably got him his bride.

III

THE intoxication of that wedding held on long enough and strongly enough to soften and blunt the disillusionments of the first few days of the honeymoon. In the prospect that period had seemed, even to Mildred's rather unsophisticated imagination, appalling beyond her power to endure. In the fact—thanks in large part to that intoxication—it was certainly not unendurable. A human being, even an innocent young girl, can usually bear up under any experience to which a human being can be subjected. The general in pajamas—of the finest silk and of pigeon's-egg blue with a vast gorgeous monogram on the pocket—was more grotesque, rather than more repellent, than the general in morning or evening attire. Also he—that is, his expert staff of providers of luxury—had arranged for the bride a series of the most ravishing sensations in whisking her, like the heroine of an Arabian Night's tale, from straitened circumstances to the very paradise of luxury.

The general's ideas on the subject of woman were old fashioned, of the hard-shell variety. Woman was made for luxury, and luxury was made for woman. His woman must be the most divinely easeful of the luxurious. At all times she must be fit and ready for any and every sybaritic idea that might enter her husband's head—and other purpose she had none. When she was not directly engaged in ministering to his joy she must be busy preparing herself for his next call upon her. A woman was a luxury, was the luxury of luxuries, must have and must use to their uttermost all capacities for gratifying his senses and his vanity. Alone with him, she must make him constantly feel how rich and rare and expensive a prize he had captured. When others were about, she must be constantly making them envy and admire him for having exclusive rights in such wonderful preserves. All this with an inflexible devotion to the loftiest ideals of chastity.

But the first realizations of her husband's notions as to women were altogether pleasant. As she entered the automobile in which they went to the private car in the special train that took them to New York and the steamer—as she entered that new and prodigally luxurious automobile, she had a first, keen sense of her changed position. Then there was the superb private car—her car, since she was his wife—and there was the beautiful suite in the magnificent steamer. And at every instant menials thrusting attentions upon her, addressing her as if she were a queen, revealing in their nervous tones and anxious eyes their eagerness to please, their fear of displeasing. And on the steamer, from New York to Cherbourg, she was never permitted to lose sight of the material splendors that were now hers.

All the servants, all the passengers, reminded her by their looks, their tones. At Paris, in the hotel, in the restaurants, in the shops—especially in the shops—those snobbish instincts that are latent in the sanest and the wisest of us were fed and fattened and pampered until her head was quite turned. And the general began to buy jewels for her. Such jewels—ropes of diamonds and pearls and emeralds, rings such as she had never dreamed existed! Those shopping excursions of theirs in the Rue de la Paix would make such a tale as your ordinary simple citizen, ignorant of the world's resources in luxury and therefore incredulous about them, would read with a laugh at the extravagance of the teller.

Before the intoxication of the wedding had worn away it was re-enforced by the intoxication of the honeymoon—not an intoxication of love's providing, but one exceeding potent in its influence upon our weak human brains and hearts, one from which the strongest of us, instead of sneering at poor Mildred, would better be praying to be delivered.

At her marriage she had a few hundred dollars left of her patrimony—three hundred and fifty and odd, to be more exact. She spent a little money of her own here and there—in tips, in buying presents for her mother, in picking up trifles for her own toilet. The day came when she looked in her purse and found two one-franc pieces, a fifty-franc note, and a few coppers. And suddenly she sat back and stared, her mouth open like her almost empty gold bag, which the general had bought her on their first day in the Rue de la Paix. About ten dollars in all the world, and the general had forgotten to speak—or to make any arrangement, at least any arrangement of which she was aware—about a further supply of money.

They had been married nearly a month. He knew that she was poor. Why hadn't he said something or, better still, DONE something? Doubtless he had simply forgotten. But since he had forgotten for a month, might he not continue to forget? True, he had himself been poor at one time in his life, very poor, and that for a long time. But it had been so many years ago that he had probably lost all sense of the meaning of poverty. She frowned at this evidence of his lack of the finer sensibilities—by no means the first time that lack had been disagreeably thrust upon her. Soon she would be without money—and she must have money—not much, as all the serious expenses were looked after by the general, but still a little money. How could she get it? How could she remind him of his neglect without seeming to be indelicate? It was a difficult problem. She worked at it more and more continuously, and irritably, and nervously, as the days went by and her fifty-two francs dwindled to five.

She lay awake, planning long and elaborate conversations that would imperceptibly lead him up to where he must see what she needed without seeing that he had been led. She carried out these ingenious conversations. She led him along, he docilely and unsuspectingly following. She brought him up to where it seemed to her impossible for any human being endowed with the ordinary faculties to fail to see what was so plainly in view. All in vain. General William Siddall gazed placidly—and saw nothing.

Several days of these failures, and with her funds reduced to a fifty-centime piece and a two-sous copper she made a frontal attack. When they went forth for the day's shopping she left her gold bag behind. After an hour or so she said:

"I've got to go to the Galleries Lafayette for some little things. I shan't ask you to sacrifice yourself. I know you hate those stuffy, smelly big shops."

"Very well," said he. "I'll use the time in a call on my bankers."

As they were about to separate, she taking the motor and he walking, she made a face of charming dismay and said: "How provoking! I've left my bag at the hotel."

Instead of the expected prompt offer of money he said, "It'll only take you a minute or so to drive there."

"But it's out of the way," she replied. "I'll need only a hundred francs or so."

Said he: "I've an account at the Bon Marche. Go there and have the things charged. It's much the best big shop in Paris."

"Very well," was all she could trust herself to say. She concealed her anger beneath a careless smile and drove away. How dense he was! Could anything be more exasperating—or more disagreeable? What SHOULD she do? The situation was intolerable; yet how could it be ended, except by a humiliating direct request for money? She wondered how young wives habitually dealt with this problem, when they happened to marry husbands so negligent, not to say underbred, as to cause them the awkwardness and the shame. There followed several days during which the money idea was an obsession, nagging and grinning at her every instant. The sight of money gave her a peculiar itching sensation. When the little general paid for anything—always drawing out a great sheaf of bank notes in doing it—she flushed hot and cold, her glance fell guiltily and sought the money furtively. At last her desperation gave birth to an inspiration.

About her and the general, or, rather, about the general, revolved the usual rich man's small army of satellites of various degrees—secretaries, butlers, footmen, valets, other servants male and female, some of them supposed to be devoted entirely to her service, but all in fact looking ever to the little general. The members of this company, regardless of differences of rank and pay, were banded together in a sort of democratic fellowship, talking freely with one another, on terms of perfect equality. She herself had, curiously, gotten on excellent terms with this motley fraternity and found no small relief from the strain of the general's formal dignity in talking with them with a freedom and ease she had never before felt in the society of underlings. The most conspicuous and most agreeable figure in this company was Harding, the general's factotum. Why not lay the case before Harding? He was notably sensible, and sympathetic—and discreet.

The following day she did so. Said she, blushing furiously: "Mr. Harding, I find myself in a very embarrassing position. I wonder if you can help me?"

Harding, a young man and of one of the best blond types, said: "No doubt I can—and I'll be glad to."

"The fact is"— Her voice was trembling with nervousness. She opened the gold bag, took out the little silver pieces and the big copper piece, extended her pink palm with them upon it—"there's all I've got left of the money I brought with me."

Harding gazed at the exhibit tranquilly. He was chiefly remarkable for his perfect self-possession. Said he: "Do you wish me to cash a check for you?"

The stupidity of men! Tears of vexation gathered in her eyes. When she could speak she faltered:

"No."

He was looking at her now—a grave, kind glance.

She somehow felt encouraged and heartened. She went on: "I was hoping—that—that the gen—that my husband had said something to you and that you perhaps had not thought to say anything to me."

Their glances met, his movingly sympathetic and understanding, hers piteously forlorn—the look of a lovely girl, stranded and friendless in a far strange land. Presently he said gently:

"Yes, he told me to say something to you—if you should speak to me about this matter." His tone caused in her heart a horrible stillness of suspense. He went on: "He said—I give you his exact words: 'If my wife should ask you for money, tell her my ideas on the subject.'"

A pause. She started up, crimson, her glance darting nervously this way and that to avoid his. "Never mind. Really, it's of no importance. Thank you—I'll get on very well—I'm sorry to have troubled you—"

"Pardon me, Mrs. Siddall," he interposed, "but I think you'd best let me finish."

She started to protest, she tried to move toward the door. Her strength failed her, she sat down, waited, nervously clasping and unclasping the costly, jewel-embroidered bag.

"He has explained to me, many times," continued Harding, "that he believes women do not understand the value of money and ought not to be trusted with it. He proposes to provide everything for you, every comfort and luxury—I am using his own language, Mrs. Siddall—and he has open accounts at the principal shops in every city where you will go—New York, Washington, Chicago, Denver, Paris, London, Rome. He says you are at liberty to get practically anything you please at these shops, and he will pay the bills. He thus entirely spares you the necessity of ever spending any money. Should you see anything you wish at some shop where he has no account, you can have it sent collect, and I or my assistant, Mr. Drawl, will settle for it. All he asks is that you use discretion in this freedom. He says it would be extremely painful to him to have to withdraw it."

Harding had pronounced this long speech in a dry monotonous voice, like one reading mechanically from a dull book. As Mildred listened, her thoughts began to whirl about the central idea until she fell into a kind of stupor. When he finished she was staring vacantly at the bag in her lap—the bag she was holding open wide.

Harding continued: "He also instructed me to say something about his former—his experiences. The first Mrs. Siddall he married when he was very young and poor. As he grew rich, she became madly extravagant. And as they had started on a basis on which she had free access to his money he could not check her. The result, finally, was a succession of bitter quarrels, and they were about to divorce when she died. He made the second Mrs. Siddall an allowance, a liberal allowance. Her follies compelled him to withdraw it. She resorted to underhanded means to get money from him without his knowing it. He detected the fraud. After a series of disagreeable incidents she committed the indiscretion which caused him to divorce her. He says that these experiences have convinced him that—"

"The second Mrs. Siddall," interrupted Mildred, "is she still alive?"

Harding hesitated. "Yes," he said reluctantly.

"Is she—poor?" asked Mildred.

"I should prefer not to—"

"Did the general forbid you to tell me?"

"On the contrary, he instructed me— But I'd rather not talk about it, Mrs. Siddall."

"Is she poor?" repeated Mildred.

"Yes."

"What became of her?"

A long pause. Then Harding said: "She was a poor girl when the general married her. After the divorce she lived for a while with the man. But he had nothing. They separated. She tried various kinds of work—and other things. Since she lost her looks— She writes from time to time, asking for money."

"Which she never gets?" said Mildred.

"Which she never gets," said Harding. "Lately she was cashier or head waitress in a cheap restaurant in St. Louis."

After a long silence Mildred said: "I understand. I understand." She drew a long breath. "I shall understand better as time goes on, but I understand fairly well now."

"I need not tell you, Mrs. Siddall," said Harding in his gentle, tranquil way, "that the general is the kindest and most generous of men, but he has his own methods—as who has not?"

Mildred had forgotten that he was there—not a difficult matter, when he had in its perfection the secretarial manner of complete self-effacement. Said she reflectively, like one puzzling out a difficult problem:

"He buys a woman, as he buys a dog or a horse. He does not give his dog, his horse, pocket-money. Why should he give his woman pocket-money?"

"Will it help matters, Mrs. Siddall, to go to the other extreme and do him a grave injustice?"

She did not hear. At the picture presented to her mind by her own thoughts she gave a short satirical laugh. "How stupid of me not to have understood from the outset," said she. "Why, I've often heard of this very thing."

"It is more and more the custom among men of large property, I believe," said Harding. "Perhaps, Mrs. Siddall, you would not blame them if you were in their position. The rich men who are careless—they ruin everybody about them, I assure you. I've seen it again and again."

But the young wife was absorbed in her own thoughts. Harding, feeling her mood, did not interrupt. After a while she said:

"I must ask you some questions. These jewels the general has been buying—"

Harding made a movement of embarrassment and protest. She smiled ironically and went on:

"One moment, please. Every time I wish to wear any of them I have to go to him to get them. He asks me to return them when I am undressing. He says it is safer to keep everything in his strong box. I have been assuming that that was the only reason. I begin to suspect— Am I right, Mr. Harding?"

"Really I can't say, Mrs. Siddall," said Harding. "These are not matters to discuss with me, if you will permit me to say so."

"Oh, yes, they are," replied she laughingly. "Aren't we all in the same boat?—all employes of the general?"

Harding made no reply.

Mildred was beside herself with a kind of rage that, because outlet was necessary and because raving against the little general would be absolutely futile, found outlet in self-mockery and reckless sarcasm.

"I understand about the jewels, too," she went on. "They are not mine. Nothing is mine. Everything, including myself, belongs to him. If I give satisfaction in the position for which I've been hired for my board and clothes, I may continue to eat the general's food and sleep in the general's house and wear the general's jewels and dresses and ride in the general's traps and be waited on by the general's servants. If I don't like my place or he doesn't like my way of filling it"—she laughed merrily, mockingly—"out I go—into the streets—after the second Mrs. Siddall. And the general will hire a new—" She paused, cast about for a word in vain, appealed to the secretary, "What would you call it, Mr. Harding?"

Harding rose, looking at her with a very soothing tranquillity. "If I were you, Mrs. Siddall," said he, "I should get into the auto and go for a long drive—out to the Bois—out to Versailles—a long, long drive. I should be gone four or five hours at least, and I should look at the thing from all sides. Especially, I'd look at it from HIS standpoint."

Mildred, somewhat quieter, but still mocking, said: "If I should decide to quit, would my expenses be paid back to where I was engaged? I fancy not."

Harding looked grave. "If you had had money enough to pay your own expenses about, would you have married him?" said he. "Isn't he paying—paying liberally, Mrs. Siddall—for ALL he gets?"

Mildred, stung, drew herself up haughtily, gave him a look that reminded him who she was and who he was. But Harding was not impressed.

"You said a moment ago—truly—that we are all in the same boat," observed he. "I put those questions to you because I honestly wish to help you—because I wish you not to act foolishly, hastily."

"Thank you, Mr. Harding," said Mildred coldly. And with a slight nod she went, angry and ashamed that she had so unaccountably opened up her secret soul, bared its ugly wounds, before a man she knew so slightly, a man in a position but one remove from menial. However, she took his advice—not as to trying to view the matter from all sides, for she was convinced that there was only the one side, but as to calming herself by a long drive alone in the woods and along quiet roads. When she returned she was under control once more.

She found the general impatiently awaiting her. Many packages had come—from the jewelers, from the furriers, from a shop whose specialty was the thinnest and most delicate of hand-made underwear. The general loved to open and inspect finery for her—loved it more than he loved inspecting finery for himself, because feminine finery was far more attractive than masculine. To whet his pleasure to the keenest she must be there to admire with him, to try on, to exhibit. As she entered the salon where the little man was fussing about among the packages, their glances met. She saw that Harding had told him—at least in discreet outline—of their conversation. She also saw that if she reopened the subject she would find herself straightway whirled out upon a stormy sea of danger that might easily overwhelm her flimsy boat. She silently and sullenly dropped into her place; she ministered to the general's pleasure in packages of finery. But she did not exclaim, or admire, or respond in any way. The honeymoon was over. Her dream of wifehood was dissipated.

She understood now the look she so often had seen on the faces of rich men's poor wives driving in state in Fifth Avenue. That night, as she inspected herself in the glass while the general's maid for her brushed her long thick hair, she saw the beginnings of that look in her own face. "I don't know just what I am," she said to herself. "But I do know what I am not. I am not a wife."

She sent away the maid, and sat there in the dressing-room before the mirror, waiting, her glance traveling about and noting the profuse and prodigal luxury. In the corner stood a circular rack loaded with dressing-gowns—more than a score of exquisite combinations of silk and lace or silk and chiffon. It so happened that there was nowhere in sight a single article of her apparel or for her toilet that was not bought with the general's money. No, there were some hairpins that she had paid for herself, and a comb with widely separated teeth that she had chanced to see in a window when she was alone one day. Anything else? Yes, a two-franc box of pins. And that was all. Everything else belonged to the general. In the closets, in the trunks—all the general's, part of the trousseau he had paid for. Not an undergarment; not an outer garment; not a hat or a pair of shoes, not a wrap, not a pair of gloves. All, the general's.

He was in the door of the dressing-room—the small wiry figure in rose-silk pajamas. The mustache and imperial were carefully waxed as always, day and night. On the little feet were high-heeled slippers. On the head was a rose-silk Neapolitan nightcap with gay tassel. The nightcap hid the bald spot from which the lofty toupee had been removed. A grotesque little figure, but not grotesque to her. Through the mask of the vain, boastful little face she saw the general watching her, as she had seen him that afternoon when she came in—the mysterious and terrible personality that had made the vast fortune, that had ridden ruthlessly over friend and foe, over man and woman and child—to the goal of its desires.

"It's late, my dear?" said the little man. "Come to bed."

She rose to obey—she in the general's purchases of filmy nightgown under a pale-pink silk dressing-gown.

He smiled with that curious noiseless mumbling and smacking of the thin lips. She sat down again.

"Don't keep me waiting. It's chilly," he said, advancing toward her.

"I shall sleep in here to-night—on the couch," said she. She was trembling with fright at her own audacity. She could see a fifty-centime piece and a copper dancing before her eyes. She felt horribly alone and weak, but she had no desire to retract the words with which she had thrown down the gauntlet.

The little general halted. The mask dropped; the man, the monster, looked at her. "What's the matter?" said he in an ominously quiet voice.

"Mr. Harding delivered your message to-day," said she, and her steady voice astonished her. "So I am going back home."

He waited, looking steadily at her.

"After he told me and I thought about it, I decided to submit, but just now I saw that I couldn't. I don't know what possesses me. I don't know what I'm going to do, or how I'm going to do it. But it's all over between us." She said this rapidly, fluently, in a decisive way, quite foreign to her character as she had thought it.

"You are coming to bed, where you belong," said he quietly.

"No," replied she, pressing herself against her chair as if force were being used to drag her from it. She cast about for something that would make yielding impossible. "You are—repulsive to me."

He looked at her without change of countenance. Said he: "Come to bed. I ask you for the last time."

There was no anger in his voice, no menace either open or covert; simply finality—the last word of the man who had made himself feared and secure in the mining-camps where the equation of personal courage is straightway applied to every situation. Mildred shivered. She longed to yield, to stammer out some excuse and obey him. But she could not; nor was she able to rise from her chair. She saw in his hard eyes a look of astonishment, of curiosity as to this unaccountable defiance in one who had seemed docile, who had apparently no alternative but obedience. He was not so astonished at her as she was at herself. "What is to become of me?" her terror-stricken soul was crying. "I must do as he says—I must—yet I cannot!" And she looked at him and sat motionless.

He turned away, moved slowly toward the door, halted at the threshold to give her time, was gone. A fit of trembling seized her; she leaned forward and rested her arms upon the dressing-table or she would have fallen from the chair to the floor. Yet, even as her fear made her sick and weak, she knew that she would not yield.

The cold drove her to the couch, to lie under half a dozen of the dressing-gowns and presently to fall into a sleep of exhaustion. When she awoke after what she thought was a few minutes of unconsciousness, the clamor of traffic in the Rue de Rivoli startled her. She started up, glanced at the clock on the chimneypiece. It was ten minutes past nine! When, by all the rules governing the action of the nerves, she ought to have passed a wakeful night she had overslept more than an hour. Indeed, she had had the first sound and prolonged sleep that had come to her since the honeymoon began; for until then she had slept alone all her life and the new order had almost given her chronic insomnia. She rang for her maid and began to dress. The maid did not come. She rang again and again; apparently the bell was broken. She finished dressing and went out into the huge, grandly and gaudily furnished salon. Harding was at a carved old-gold and lacquer desk, writing. As she entered he rose and bowed.

"Won't you please call one of the servants?" said she. "I want my coffee. I guess the bell in my room is broken. My maid doesn't answer."

"No, the bell is not broken," said Harding.

She looked at him questioningly.

"The general has issued an order that nothing is to be done in this apartment, and nothing served, unless he personally authorizes it."

Mildred paled, drew herself up in what seemed a gesture of haughtiness but was an effort to muster her strength. To save herself from the humiliation of a breakdown before him, she hastily retreated by the way she had come. After perhaps a quarter of an hour she reappeared in the salon; she was now dressed for the street. Harding looked up from his writing, rose and bowed gravely. Said she:

"I am going out for a walk. I'll be back in an hour or so."

"One moment," said Harding, halting her as she was opening the door into the public hall. "The general has issued an order that if you go out, you are not to be allowed to return."

Her hand fell from the knob. With flashing eyes she cried, "But that is impossible!"

"It is his orders," said Harding, in his usual quiet manner. "And as he pays the bills he will be obeyed."

She debated. Against her will, her trembling hand sought the knob again. Against her will, her weak arm began to draw the door open. Harding came toward her, stood before her and looked directly into her eyes. His eyes had dread and entreaty in them, but his voice was as always when he said:

"You know him, Mrs. Siddall."

"Yes," she said.

"The reason he has got ALL he wanted—whatever he wanted—is that he will go to any length. Every other human being, almost, has a limit, beyond which they will not go—a physical fear or a moral fear or a fear of public opinion. But the general—he has no limit."

"Yes," she said. And deathly pale and almost staggering she drew open the door and went out into the public hall.

"For God's sake, Mrs. Siddall!" cried Harding, in great agitation. "Come in quickly. They are watching—they will tell him! Are you mad?"

"I think I must be," said she. "I am sick with fear. I can hardly keep from dropping down here in a faint. Yet—" a strange look, a mingling of abject terror and passionate defiance, gave her an aspect quite insane—"I am going. Perhaps I, too, have no limit."

And she went along the corridor, past a group of gaping and frightened servants, down the stairway and out by the private entrance for the grand apartments of the hotel in the Rue Raymond de l'Isle. She crossed the Rue de Rivoli and entered the Tuileries Gardens. It was only bracingly cool in the sunshine of that winter day. She seated herself on a chair on the terrace to regain her ebbed strength. Hardly had she sat down when the woman collector came and stood waiting for the two sous for the chair. Mildred opened her bag, found two coins. She gave the coppers to the woman. The other—all the money she had—was the fifty-centime piece.

"But the bag—I can get a good deal for that," she said aloud.

"I beg your pardon—I didn't catch that."

She came back to a sense of her surroundings. Stanley Baird was standing a few feet away, smiling down at her. He was, if possible, even more attractively dressed than in the days when he hovered about her, hoping vague things of which he was ashamed and trying to get the courage to put down his snobbishness and marry her because she so exactly suited him. He was wearing a new kind of collar and tie, striking yet in excellent quiet taste. Also, his face and figure had filled out just enough—he had been too thin in the former days. But he was now entered upon that period of the fearsome forties when, unless a man amounts to something, he begins to look insignificant. He did not amount to anything; he was therefore paling and waning as a personality.

"Was I thinking aloud?" said Mildred, as she gave him her hand.

"You said something about 'getting a good deal.'" He inspected her with the freedom of an old friend and with the thoroughness of a connoisseur. Women who took pains with themselves and were satisfied with the results liked Stanley Baird's knowing and appreciative way of noting the best points in their toilets. "You're looking fine," declared he. "It must be a pleasure to them up in the Rue de la Paix to dress you. That's more than can be said for nine out of ten of the women who go there. Yes, you're looking fine—and in grand health, too. Why, you look younger than I ever saw you. Nothing like marriage to freshen a girl up. Well, I suppose waiting round for a husband who may or may not turn up does wear a woman down."

"It almost killed me," laughed Mildred. "And you were largely responsible."

"I?" said Baird. "You didn't want me. I was too old for you."

"No, I didn't want you," said Mildred. "But you spoiled me. I couldn't endure the boys of my own age."

Stanley was remembering that Mildred had married a man much older than he. With some notion of a careless sort of tact in mind he said, "I was betwixt and between—neither young enough nor old enough."

"You've married, too, since we met. By the way, thank you again for that charming remembrance. You always did have such good taste. But why didn't you come to the wedding—you and your wife?"

He laughed. "We were busy busting up," said he. "You hadn't heard? It's been in the papers. She's gone back to her people. Oh, nothing disgraceful on either side. Simply that we bored each other to death. She was crazy about horses and dogs, and that set. I think the stable's the place for horses—don't care to have 'em parading through the house all the time, every room, every meal, sleeping and waking. And dogs—the infernal brutes always have fleas. Fleas only tickled her, but they bite me—raise welts and hills. There's your husband now, isn't it?"

Baird was looking up at the windows of the Continental, across the street. Mildred's glance slowly and carelessly followed his. At one window stood the little general, gazing abstractedly out over the gardens. At another window Mildred saw Harding; at a third, her maid; at a fourth, Harding's assistant, Drawl; at a fifth, three servants of the retinue. Except the general, all were looking at her.

"You've married a very extraordinary man," said Baird, in a correct tone of admiration. "One of the ablest and most interesting men we've got, *I* think."

"So you are free again?" said Mildred, looking at him with a queer, cold smile.

"Yes, and no," replied Stanley. "I hope to be entirely free. It's her move next. I'm expecting it every day. But I'm thoroughly respectable. Won't you and the general dine with me?"

"Thanks, but I'm sailing for home to-morrow or next day."

"That's interesting," said Baird, with enthusiasm. "So am I. What ship do you go on?"

"I don't know yet. I'm to decide this afternoon, after lunch." She laughed. "I'm sitting here waiting for someone to ask me to lunch. I've not had even coffee yet."

"Lunch with me!" cried Baird. "I'll go get the general—I know him slightly."

"I didn't say anything about the general," said Mildred.

Stanley smiled apologetically. "It wouldn't do for you to go about with me—not when my missus is looking for grounds for divorce."

"Why not?" said Mildred. "So's my husband."

"You busted up, too? Now, that's what *I* call jolly." And he cast a puzzled glance up at the abstracted general. "I say, Mildred, this is no place for either of us, is it?"

"I'd rather be where there's food," confessed she.

"You think it's a joke, but I assure you— Oh, you WERE joking— about YOUR bust-up?"

"No, indeed," she assured him. "I walked out a while ago, and I couldn't go back if I would—and I don't think I would if I could."

"That's foolish. Better go back," advised he. He was preparing hastily to decamp from so perilous a neighborhood. "One marriage is about like another, once you get through the surface. I'm sure you'll be better off than—back with your stepfather."

"I've no intention of going to his house," she declared. "Oh, there's your brother. I forgot."

"So had I forgotten him. I'll not go there, either. In fact, I've not thought where I'll go."

"You seem to have done mighty little thinking before you took a very serious step for a woman." He was uneasily eying the rigid, abstracted little figure a story up across the way.

"Those things aren't a question of thinking," said she absently. "I never thought in my life—don't think I could if I tried. But when the time came I—I walked out." She came back to herself, laughed. "I don't understand why I'm telling you all this, especially as you're mad with fright and wild to get away. Well, good-by, Stanley."

He lifted his hat. "Good-by. We'll meet when we can do so without my getting a scandal on you." He walked a few paces, turned, and came back.

"By the way, I'm sailing on the Deutschland. I thought you'd like to know—so that you and I wouldn't by any chance cross on the same boat."

"Thanks," said she dryly.

"What's the matter?" asked he, arrested, despite his anxiety to be gone, by the sad, scornful look in her eyes.

"Nothing. Why?"

"You had such a—such a queer look."

"Really? Good-by."

In fact, she had thought—had hoped for the sake of her liking for him—that he had come back to make the glaringly omitted offer of help that should have come from any human being learning that a fellow being was in the precarious position in which she had told him she was. Not that she would have accepted any such offer. Still, she would have liked to have heard the kindly words. She sat watching his handsome, graceful figure, draped in the most artistically cut of long dark overcoats, until he disappeared in the crowd in the Rue de Castiglione. Then, without a glance up at the interested, not to say excited windows of the general's splendid and spreading apartments, she strolled down the gardens toward the Place Concorde. In Paris the beautiful, on a bright and brisk day it is all but impossible to despair when one still has left youth and health. Mildred was not happy—far from it. The future, the immediate future, pressed its terrors upon her. But in mitigation there was, perhaps born of youth and inexperience, a giddy sense of relief. She had not realized how abhorrent the general was—married life with the general. She had been resigning herself to it, accepting it as the only thing possible, keeping it heavily draped with her vanities of wealth and luxury—until she discovered that the wealth and the luxury were in reality no more hers than they were her maid's. And now she was free!

That word free did not have its full meaning for her. She had never known what real freedom was; women of the comfortable class—and men, too, for that matter—usually are born into the petty slavery of conventions at least, and know nothing else their whole lives through—never know the joy of the thought and the act of a free mind and a free heart. Still, she was released from a bondage that seemed slavish even to her, and the release gave her a sensation akin to the joy of freedom. A heavy hand that was crushing her very soul had been lifted off—no, FLUNG off, and by herself. That thought, terrifying though it was, also gave her a certain new and exalting self-respect. After all, she was not a worm. She must have somewhere in her the germs of something less contemptible than the essential character of so many of the eminently respectable women she knew. She could picture them in the situation in which she had found herself. What would they have done? Why, what every instinct of her education impelled her to do; what some latent love of freedom, some unsuspected courage of self-respect had forbidden her to do, had withheld her from doing.

Her thoughts and the gorgeous sunshine and her youth and health put her in a steadily less cheerless mood as by a roundabout way she sought the shop of the jeweler who sold the general the gold bag she had selected. The proprietor himself was in the front part of the shop and received "Madame la Generale" with all the honors of her husband's wealth. She brought no experience and no natural trading talent to the enterprise she was about to undertake; so she went directly to the main point.

"This bag," said she, laying it upon the glass between them, "I bought it here a short time ago."

"I remember perfectly, madame. It is the handsomest, the most artistic, we have sold this year."

"I wish to sell it back to you," said she.

"You wish to get something else and include it as part payment, madame?"

"No, I wish to get the money for it."

"Ah, but that is difficult. We do not often make those arrangements. Second-hand articles—"

"But the bag is quite new. Anyhow, it must have some value. Of course I'd not expect the full price."

The jeweler smiled. "The full price? Ah, madame, we should not think of offering it again as it is. We should—"

"No matter," interrupted Mildred. The man's expression—the normally pleasant and agreeable countenance turned to repulsive by craft and lying—made her eager to be gone. "What is the most you will give me?"

"I shall have to consider—"

"I've only a few minutes. Please do not irritate me."

The man was studying her countenance with a desperate look. Why was she, the bride of the monstrously rich American, why was she trying to sell the bag? Did it mean the end of her resources? Or, were there still huge orders to be got from her? His shrewdness, trained by thirty years of dealing with all kinds of luxurious human beings, went exploring in vain. He was alarmed by her frown. He began hesitatingly:

"The jewels and the gold are only a small part of the value. The chief value is the unique design, so elegant yet so simple. For the jewels and the gold, perhaps two thousand francs—"

"The purse was twelve thousand francs," interrupted she.

"Perfectly, madame. But—" "I am in great haste. How much will you give me?"

"The most would be four thousand, I fear. I shall count up more carefully, if madame will—"

"No, four thousand will do."

"I will send the money to madame at her hotel. The Continental, is it not?"

"No, I must have it at once."

The jeweler hesitated. Mildred, flushing scarlet with shame—but he luckily thought it anger—took up the bag and moved toward the door.

"Pardon, madame, but certainly. Do you wish some gold or all notes?"

"Notes," answered she. "Fifty and hundred-franc notes."

A moment later she was in the street with the notes in a small bundle in the bosom of her wrap. She went hurriedly up the street. As she was about to turn the corner into the boulevard she on impulse glanced back. An automobile had just drawn up at the jeweler's door and General Siddall— top-hat, sable-lined overcoat, waxed mustache and imperial, high-heeled boots, gold-mounted cane—was descending. And she knew that he had awakened to his one oversight, and was on his way to repair it. But she did not know that the jeweler—old and wise in human ways—would hastily vanish with the bag and that an assistant would come forward with assurances that madame had not been in the shop and that, if she should come in, no business would be negotiated without the general's express consent. She all but fainted at the narrowness of her escape and fled round into the boulevard. She entered a taxi and told the man to drive to Foyot's restaurant on the left bank—where the general would never think of looking for her.

When she had breakfasted she strolled in the Luxembourg Gardens, in even better humor with herself and with the world. There was still that horrid-faced future, but it was not leering into her very face. It was nearly four thousand francs away—"and if I hadn't been so stupid, I'd have got eight thousand, I'm sure," she said. But she was rather proud of a stupidity about money matters. And four thousand francs, eight hundred dollars— that was quite a good sum.

She had an instinct that the general would do something disagreeable about the French and English ports of departure for America. But perhaps he would not think of the Italian ports. That night she set out for Genoa, and three days later, in a different dress and with her hair done as she never wore it, sailed as Miss Mary Stevens for America on a German Mediterranean boat.

She had taken the whole of a cabin on the quieter deck below the promenade, paying for it nearly half of what was left of the four thousand francs. The first three days she kept to her cabin except at the dinner-hour, when she ventured to the deck just outside and walked up and down for exercise. Then followed four days of nasty weather during which she did not leave her bed. As the sea calmed, she, wretched and reckless, had a chair put for herself under her window and sat there, veiled and swathed and turning her face away whenever a rare wandering passenger happened to pass along. Toward noon a man paused before her to light a cigarette. She, forgetting for the moment her precautions, looked at him. It chanced that he looked at her at exactly the same instant. Their glances met. He started nervously, moved on a few steps, returned. Said she mockingly:

"You know you needn't speak if you don't want to, Stanley."

"There isn't a soul on board that anybody ever knew or that ever knew anybody," said he. "So why not?"

"And you look horribly bored."

"Unspeakably," replied Baird. "I've spoken to no one since I left Paris."

"What are you doing on this ship?" inquired she.

"To be perfectly honest," said he, "I came this way to avoid you. I was afraid you'd take passage on my steamer just to amuse yourself with my nervousness. And—here you are!"

"Amusing myself with your nervousness."

"But I'm not nervous. There's no danger. Will you let me have a chair put beside yours?"

"It will be a charity on your part," said she.

When he was comfortably settled, he explained his uneasiness. "I see I've got to tell you," said he, "for I don't want you to think me a shouting ass. The fact is my wife wants to get a divorce from me and to soak me for big alimony. She's a woman who'll do anything to gain her end, and—well, for some reason she's always been jealous of you. I didn't care to get into trouble, or to get you into trouble."

"I'm traveling as Mary Stevens," said Mildred. "No one knows I'm aboard."

"Oh, I'm sure we're quite safe. We can enjoy the rest of this voyage."

A sea voyage not merely induces but compels a feeling of absolute detachment from the world. To both Stanley and Mildred their affairs—the difficulties in which they were involved on terra firma—ceased for the time to have any reality. The universe was nothing but a vast stretch of water under a vast stretch of sky; the earth and the things thereof were a retrospect and a foreboding. Without analyzing it, both he and she felt that they were free—free from cares, from responsibilities—free to amuse themselves. And they proceeded to enjoy themselves in the necessarily quiet and limited way imposed by the littleness of their present world and the meagerness of the resources.

As neither had the kind of mind that expands in abstractions, they were soon talking in the most intimate and personal way about themselves—were confessing things which neither would have breathed to anyone on land. It was the man who set the example of breaking through the barriers of conventional restraint—perhaps of delicacy, though it must be said that human beings are rarely so fine in their reticences as the theory of refinement would have us believe. Said Stanley, after the preliminaries of partial confidence and halting avowal that could not be omitted, even at sea, by a man of "gentlemanly instinct":

"I don't know why I shouldn't own up. I know you'll never tell anybody. Fact is, I and my wife were never in love with each other for a second. We married because we were in the same set and because our incomes together gave us enough to do the thing rather well." After a solemn pause. "I was in love with another woman—one I couldn't marry. But I'll not go into that. As for my wife, I don't think she was in love with anyone. She's as cold as a stone."

Mildred smiled ironically.

Baird saw and flushed. "At least, she was to me. I was ready to make a sort of bluff. You see, a man feels guilty in those circumstances and doesn't want to humiliate a woman. But she—" he laughed unpleasantly—"she wasn't bothering about MY feelings. That's a nice, selfish little way you ladies have."

"She probably saw through you and hated you for playing the hypocrite to her," said Mildred.

"You may be right, I never thought of that," confessed he. "She certainly had a vicious way of hammering the other woman indirectly. Not that she ever admitted being jealous. I guess she knew. Everybody usually knows everything."

"And there was a great deal of talk about you and me," said Mildred placidly.

"I didn't say it was you," protested Stanley, reddening.

"No matter," said Mildred. "Don't bother about that. It's all past and gone."

"Well, at any rate, my marriage was the mistake of my life. I'm determined that she shan't trip me up and trim me for any alimony. And as matters stand, she can't. She left me of her own accord."

"Then," said Mildred thoughtfully, "if the wife leaves of her own accord, she can't get alimony?"

"Certainly not—not a cent."

"I supposed so," said she. "I'm not sure I'd take it if I could get it. Still, I suppose I would." She laughed. "What's the use of being a hypocrite with oneself? I know I would. All I could get."

"Then you had no LEGAL excuse for leaving?"

"No," said she. "I—just bolted. I don't know what's to become of me. I seem not to care, at present, but no doubt I shall as soon as we see land again."

"You'll go back to him," said Stanley.

"No," replied she, without emphasis or any accent whatever.

"Sure you will," rejoined he. "It's your living. What else can you do?"

"That's what I must find out. Surely there's something else for a woman besides such a married life as mine. I can't and won't go back to my husband. And I can't and won't go to the house at Hanging Rock. Those two things are settled."

"You mean that?"

"Absolutely. And I've got—less than three hundred and fifty dollars in the whole world."

Baird was silent. He was roused from his abstraction by gradual consciousness of an ironical smile on the face of the girl, for she did not look like a married woman. "You are laughing at me. Why?" inquired he.

"I was reading your thoughts."

"You think you've frightened me?"

"Naturally. Isn't a confession such as I made enough to frighten a man? It sounded as though I were getting ready to ask alms."

"So it did," said he. "But I wasn't thinking of it in that way. You WILL be in a frightful fix pretty soon, won't you?"

"It looks that way. But you need not be uneasy."

"Oh, I want to help you. I'll do everything I can. I was trying to think of something you could make money at. I was thinking of the stage, but I suppose you'd balk at that. I'll admit it isn't the life for a lady. But the same thing's true of whatever money can be made at. If I were you, I'd go back."

"If I were myself, I'd go back," said Mildred. "But I'm not myself."

"You will be again, as soon as you face the situation."

"No," said she slowly, "no, I shall never be myself again."

"But you could have everything a woman wants. Except, of course— perhaps— But you never struck me as being especially sentimental."

"Sentiment has nothing to do with it," rejoined she. "Do you think I could get a place on the stage?"

"Oh, you'd have to study a while, I suppose."

"But I can't afford that. If I could afford to study, I'd have my voice trained."

Baird's face lighted up with enthusiasm. "The very thing!" he cried. "You've got a voice, a grand-opera voice. I've heard lots of people say so, and it sounded that way to me. You must cultivate your voice."

Mildred laughed. "Don't talk nonsense. Even I know that's nonsense. The lessons alone would cost thousands of dollars. And how could I live for the four or five years?"

"You didn't let me finish," said Baird. "I was going to say that when you get to New York you must go and have your voice passed on—by some impartial person. If that person says it's worth cultivating, why, I'm willing to back you—as a business proposition. I can afford to take the risk. So, you see, it's all perfectly simple."

He had spoken rapidly, with a covert suggestion of fear lest she would rebuke him sharply for what she might regard as an impertinent offer. She surprised him by looking at him calmly, reflectively, and saying:

"Yes, you could afford it, couldn't you?"

"I'm sure I could. And it's the sort of thing that's done every day. Of course, no one'd know that we had made this little business arrangement. But that's easily managed. I'd be glad if you'd let me do it, Mildred. I'd like to feel that I was of some use in the world. And I'd like to do something for YOU."

By way of exceedingly cautious experiment he ventured to put ever so slight an accent of tenderness upon the "you." He observed her furtively but nervously. He could not get a hint of what was in her mind. She gazed out toward the rising and falling horizon line. Presently she said:

"I'll think about it."

"You must let me do it, Mildred. It's the sensible thing—and you know me well enough to know that my friendship can be counted on."

"I'll think about it," was all she would concede.

They discussed the singing career all that and the succeeding days—the possibilities, the hopes, the dangers—but the hopes a great deal more than the dangers. He became more and more interested in her and in the project, as her beauty shone out with the tranquillizing sea and as her old charm of cleverness at saying things that amused him reasserted itself. She, dubious and lukewarm at first, soon was trying to curb her own excited optimism; but long before they sighted Sandy Hook she was merely pretending to hang back. He felt discouraged by her parting! "If I decide to go on, I'll write you in a few days." But he need not have felt so. She had made up her mind to accept his offer. As for the complications involved in such curiously intimate relations with a man of his temperament, habits, and inclinations, she saw them very vaguely indeed—refused to permit herself to see them any less vaguely. Time enough to deal with complications when and as they arose; why needlessly and foolishly annoy herself and hamper herself? Said she to herself, "I must begin to be practical."

IV

AT the pier Mildred sent her mother a telegram, giving the train by which she would arrive—that and nothing more. As she descended from the parlor-car there stood Mrs. Presbury upon the platform, face wreathed in the most joyous of welcoming smiles, not a surface trace of the curiosity and alarm storming within. After they had kissed and embraced with a genuine emotion which they did not try to hide, because both suddenly became unconscious of that world whereof ordinarily they were constantly mindful—after caresses and tears Mrs. Presbury said:

"It's all very well to dress plain, when everyone knows you can afford the best. But don't you think you're overdoing it a little?"

Mildred laughed somewhat nervously. "Wait till we're safe at home," said she.

On the way up from the station in the carriage they chattered away in the liveliest fashion, to make the proper impression upon any observing Hanging-Rockers. "Luckily, Presbury's gone to town to-day," said his wife. "But really he's quite livable—hasn't gone back to his old ways. He doesn't know it, but he's rapidly growing deaf. He imagines that everyone is speaking more and more indistinctly, and he has lost interest in conversation. Then, too, he has done well in Wall Street, and that has put him in a good humor."

"He'll not be surprised to see me—alone," said Mildred.

"Wait till we're home," said her mother nervously.

At the house Mrs. Presbury carried on a foolish, false-sounding conversation for the benefit of the servants, and finally conducted Mildred to her bedroom and shut doors and drew portieres and glanced into closets before saying: "Now, what IS the matter, Millie? WHERE is your husband?"

"In Paris, I suppose," replied Mildred. "I have left him, and I shall never go back."

"Presbury said you would!" cried her mother. "But I didn't believe it. I don't believe it. I brought you up to do your duty, and I know you will."

This was Mildred's first opportunity for frank and plain speaking; and that is highly conducive to frank and plain thinking. She now began to see clearly why she had quit the general. Said she: "Mamma, to be honest and not mince words, I've left him because there's nothing in it."

"Isn't he rich?" inquired her mother. "I've always had a kind of present—"

"Oh, he's rich, all right," interrupted the girl. "But he saw to it that I got no benefit from that."

"But you wrote me how he was buying you everything!"

"So I thought. In fact he was buying ME nothing." And she went on to explain the general's system.

Her mother listened impatiently. She would have interrupted the long and angry recital many times had not Mildred insisted on a full hearing of her grievances, of the outrages that had been heaped upon her. "And," she ended, "I suppose he's got it so arranged that he could have me arrested as a thief for taking the gold bag."

"Yes, it's terrible and all that," said her mother. "But I should have thought living with me here when Presbury was carrying on so dreadfully would have taught you something. Your case isn't an exception, any more than mine is. That's the sort of thing we women have to put up with from men, when we're in their power."

"Not I," said Mildred loftily.

"Yes, you," retorted her mother. "ANY woman. EVERY woman. Unless we have money of our own, we all have trouble with the men about money, sooner or later, in one way or another. And rich men!—why, it's notorious that they're always more or less mean about money. A wife has got to use tact. Why, I even had to use some tact with your father, and he was as generous a man as ever lived. Tact—that's a woman's whole life. You ought to have used tact. You'll go back to him and use tact."

"You don't know him, mamma!" cried Mildred. "He's a monster. He isn't human."

Mrs. Presbury drew a long face and said in a sad, soothing voice: "Yes, I know, dear. Men are very, very awful, in some ways, to a nice woman— with refined, ladylike instincts. It's a great shock to a pure—"

"Oh, gammon!" interrupted Mildred. "Don't be silly, mother. It isn't worth while for one woman to talk that kind of thing to another. I didn't fully know what I was doing when I married a man I didn't love—a man who was almost repulsive to me. But I knew enough. And I was getting along well enough, as any woman does, no matter what she may say—yes, you needn't look shocked, for that's hypocrisy, and I know it now— But, as I was saying, I didn't begin to HATE him until he tried to make a slave of me. A slave!" she shuddered. "He's a monster!"

"A little tact, and you can get everything you want," insisted her mother.

"I tell you, you don't know the man," cried Mildred. "By tact I suppose you mean I could have sold things behind his back—and all that." She laughed. "He hasn't got any back. He had it so arranged that those cold, wicked eyes of his were always watching me. His second wife tried 'tact.' He caught her and drove her into the streets. I'd have had no chance to get a cent, and if I had gotten it I'd not have dared spend it. Do you imagine I ran away from him without having THOUGHT? If there'd been any way of staying on, any way of making things even endurable, I'd have stayed."

"But you've got to go back, Milly," cried her mother, in tears.

"You mean that you can't support me?"

"And your brother Frank—" Mrs. Presbury's eyes flashed and her rather stout cheeks quivered. "I never thought I'd tell anybody, but I'll tell you. I never liked your brother Frank, and he never liked me. That sounds dreadful, doesn't it?"

"No, mother dear," said Mildred gently. "I've learned that life isn't at all as—as everybody pretends."

"Indeed it isn't," said her mother. "Mothers always have favorites among their children, and very often a mother dislikes one of her children. Of course she hides her feeling and does her duty. But all the same she can't help the feeling that is down in her heart. I had a presentiment before he was born that I wouldn't like him, and sure enough, I didn't. And he didn't like me, or his father, or any of us."

"It would never occur to me to turn to him," said Mildred.

"Then you see that you've got to go back to the general. You can't get a divorce and alimony, for it was you that left him—and for no cause. He was within his rights."

Mildred hesitated, confessed: "I had thought of going back to him and acting in such a way that he'd be glad to give me a divorce and an allowance."

"Yes, you might do that," said her mother. "A great many women do. And, after all, haven't they a right to? A lady has got to have proper support, and is it just to ask her to live with a man she loathes?"

"I haven't thought of the right or wrong of it," said Mildred. "It looks to me as though right and wrong have very little to do with life as it's lived. They're for hypocrites—and fools."

"Mildred!" exclaimed her mother, deeply shocked.

Mildred was not a little shocked at her own thoughts as she inspected them in the full light into which speech had dragged them. "Anyhow," she went on, "I soon saw that such a plan was hopeless. He's not the man to be trifled with. Long before I could drive him to give me a living and let me go he would have driven me to flight or suicide."

Her mother had now had time to reflect upon Mildred's revelations. Aided by the impressions she herself had gotten of the little general, she began to understand why her daughter had fled and why she would not return. She felt that the situation was one which time alone could solve. Said she: "Well, the best thing is for you to stay on here and wait until he makes some move."

"He'll have me watched—that's all he'll do," said Mildred. "When he gets ready he'll divorce me for deserting him."

Mrs. Presbury felt that she was right. But, concealing her despondency, she said: "All we can do is to wait and see. You must send for your luggage."

"I've nothing but a large bag," said Mildred. "I checked it in the parcel-room of the New York station."

Mrs. Presbury was overwhelmed. How account to Hanging Rock for the reappearance of a baggageless and husbandless bride? But she held up bravely. With a cheerfulness that did credit to her heart and showed how well she loved her daughter she said: "We must do the best we can. We'll get up some story."

"No," said Mildred. "I'm going back to New York. You can tell people here what you please—that I've gone to rejoin him or to wait for him—any old thing."

"At least you'll wait and talk with Presbury," pleaded her mother. "He is VERY sensible."

"If he has anything to suggest," said Mildred, "he can write it. I'll send you my address."

"Milly," cried her mother, agitated to the depths, "where ARE you going? WHAT are you going to do? You look so strange—not at all like yourself."

"I'm going to a hotel to-night—probably to a boarding-house to-morrow," said Mildred. "In a few days I shall begin to—" she hesitated, decided against confidence—"begin to support myself at something or other."

"You must be crazy!" cried her mother. "You wouldn't do anything—and you couldn't."

"Let's not discuss it, mamma," said the girl tranquilly.

The mother looked at her with eyes full of the suspicion one lady cannot but have as to the projects of another lady in such circumstances.

"Mildred," she said pleadingly, "you must be careful. You'll find yourself involved in a dreadful scandal. I know you wouldn't DO anything WRONG no matter how you were driven. But—"

"I'll not do anything FOOLISH, mamma," interrupted the girl. "You are thinking about men, aren't you?"

"Men are always ready to destroy a woman," said her mother. "You must be careful—"

Mildred was laughing. "Oh, mamma," she cried, "do be sensible and do give me credit for a little sense. I've got a very clear idea of what a woman ought to do about men, and I assure you I'm not going to be FOOLISH. And you know a woman who isn't foolish can be trusted where a woman who's only protected by her principles would yield to the first temptation—or hunt round for a temptation."

"But you simply can't go to New York and live there all alone—and with nothing!"

"Can I stay here—for more than a few days?"

"But maybe, after a few days—" stammered her mother.

"You see, I've got to begin," said Mildred. "So why delay? I'd gain nothing. I'd simply start Hanging Rock to gossiping—and start Mr. Presbury to acting like a fiend again."

Her mother refused to be convinced—was the firmer, perhaps, because she saw that Mildred was unshakable in her resolve to leave forthwith—the obviously sensible and less troublesome course. They employed the rest of Mildred's three hours' stop in arguing—when Mildred was not raging against the little general. Her mother was more than willing to assist her in this denunciation, but Mildred preferred to do it all herself. She had—perhaps by unconsciously absorbed training from her lawyer father—an unusual degree of ability to see both sides of a question. When she assailed her husband, she saw only her own side; but somehow when her mother railed and raved, she began to see another side—and the sight was not agreeable. She wished to feel that her husband was altogether in the wrong; she did not wish to have intruded upon her such facts as that she had sold herself to him—quite in the customary way of ladies, but nevertheless quite shamelessly—or that in strict justice she had done nothing for him to entitle her to a liberal money allowance or any allowance at all.

On the train, going back to New York, she admitted to herself that the repulsive little general had held strictly to the terms of the bargain—"but only a devil and one with not a single gentlemanly instinct would insist on such a bargain." It took away much of the shame, and all of the sting, of despising herself to feel that she was looking still lower when she turned to despising him.

To edge out the little general she began to think of her mother, but as she passed in review what her mother had said and how she had said it she saw that for all the protests and arguings her mother was more than resigned to her departure. Mildred felt no bitterness; ever since she could remember her mother had been a shifter of responsibility. Still, to stare into the face of so disagreeable a fact as that one had no place on earth to go to, no one on earth to turn to, not even one's own mother—to stare on at that grimacing ugliness did not tend to cheerfulness. Mildred tried to think of the future—but how could she think of something that was nothing? She knew that she would go on, somehow, in some direction, but by no effort of her imagination could she picture it. She was so impressed by the necessity of considering the future that, to rouse herself, she tried to frighten herself with pictures of poverty and misery, of herself a derelict in the vast and cold desert of New York—perhaps in rags, hungry, ill, but all in vain. She did not believe it. Always she had had plenty to wear and to eat, and comfortable surroundings. She could no more think of herself as without those things than a living person can imagine himself dead.

"I'm a fool," she said to herself. "I'm certain to get into all sorts of trouble. How can it be otherwise, when I've no money, no friends, no experience, no way of making a living—no honest way—perhaps no way of the other kind, either?" There are many women who ecstasize their easily tickled vanities by fancying that if they were so disposed they need only flutter an eyelid to have men by the legion striving for their favors, each man with a bag of gold. Mildred, inexperienced as she was, had no such delusions. Her mind happened not to be of that chastely licentious caste which continually revolves and fantastically exaggerates the things of the body.

She could not understand her own indifference about the future. She did not realize that it was wholly due to Stanley Baird's offer. She was imagining she was regarding that offer as something she might possibly consider, but probably would not. She did not know that her soul had seized upon it, had enfolded it and would on no account let it go. It is the habit of our secret selves thus to make decisions and await their own good time for making us acquainted with them.

With her bag on the seat beside her she set out to find a temporary lodging. Not until several hotels had refused her admittance on the pretext that they were "full up" did she realize that a young woman alone is an object of suspicion in New York. When a fourth room-clerk expressed his polite regrets she looked him straight in the eye and said:

"I understand. But I can't sleep in the street. You must tell me where I can go."

"Well, there's the Ripon over in Seventh Avenue," said he.

"Is it respectable?" said she.

"Oh, it's very clean and comfortable there," said he. "They'll treat you right."

"Is it respectable?" said she.

"Well, now, it doesn't LOOK queer, if that's what you mean," replied he. "You'll do very nicely there. You can be just as quiet as you want."

She saw that hotel New York would not believe her respectable. So to the Ripon she went, and was admitted without discussion. As the last respectable clerk had said, it did not LOOK queer. But it FELT queer; she resolved that she would go into a boarding-house the very next day.

Here again what seemed simple proved difficult. No respectable boarding-house would have Miss Mary Stevens. She was confident that nothing in her dress or manner hinted mystery. Yet those sharp-eyed landladies seemed to know at once that there was something peculiar about her. Most of them became rude the instant they set eyes upon her. A few— of the obviously less prosperous class—talked with her, seemed to be listening for something which her failing to say decided them upon all but ordering her out of the house. She, hindered by her innocence, was slow in realizing that she could not hope for admission to any select respectable circle, even of high-class salesladies and clerks, unless she gave a free and clear account of herself—whence she had come, what she was doing, how she got her money.

Toward the end of the second day's wearisome and humiliating search she found a house that would admit her. It was a pretentious, well-furnished big house in Madison Avenue. The price—thirty-five dollars a week for board, a bedroom with a folding bed in an alcove, and a bath, was more than double what she had counted on paying, but she discovered that decent and clean lodgings and food fit to eat were not to be had for less.

"And I simply can't live pig-fashion," said she. "I'd be so depressed that I could do nothing. I can't live like a wild animal, and I won't." She had some vague notion—foreboding—that this was not the proper spirit with which to face life. "I suppose I'm horribly foolish," reflected she, "but if I must go down, I'll go down with my colors flying." She did not know precisely what that phrase meant, but it sounded fine and brave and heartened her to take the expensive lodgings.

The landlady was a Mrs. Belloc. Mildred had not talked with her twenty minutes before she had a feeling that this name was assumed. The evening of her first day in the house she learned that her guess was correct—learned it from the landlady herself. After dinner Mrs. Belloc came into her room to cheer her up, to find out about her and to tell her about herself.

"Now that you've come," said she, "the house is full up—except some little rooms at the top that I'd as lief not fill. The probabilities are that any ladies who would take them wouldn't be refined enough to suit those I have. There are six, not counting me, every one with a bath and two with private parlors. And as they're all handsome, sensible women, ladylike and steady, I think the prospects are that they'll pay promptly and that I won't have any trouble."

Mildred reflected upon this curious statement. It sounded innocent enough, yet what a peculiar way to put a simple fact.

"Of course it's none of my business how people live as long as they keep up the respectabilities," pursued Mrs. Belloc. "It don't do to inquire into people in New York. Most of 'em come here because they want to live as they please."

"No doubt," said Mildred a little nervously, for she suspected her landlady of hitting at her, and wondered if she had come to cross-examine her and, if the results were not satisfactory, to put her into the street.

"I know *I* came for that reason," pursued Mrs. Belloc. "I was a school-teacher up in New England until about two years ago. Did you ever teach school?"

"Not yet," said Mildred. "And I don't think I ever shall. I don't know enough."

"Oh, yes, you do. A teacher doesn't need to know much. The wages are so poor—at least up in New England—that they don't expect you to know anything. It's all in the books. I left because I couldn't endure the life. Lord! how dull those little towns are! Ever live in a little town?"

"All my life," said Mildred.

"Well, you'll never go back."

"I hope not."

"You won't. Why should you? A sensible woman with looks—especially if she knows how to carry her clothes—can stay in New York as long as she pleases, and live off the fat of the land."

"That's good news," said Mildred. She began to like the landlady—not for what she said, but for the free and frank and friendly way of the saying—a human way, a comradely way, a live-and-let-live way.

"I didn't escape from New England without a struggle," continued Mrs. Belloc, who was plainly showing that she had taken a great fancy to "Mary Stevens."

"I suppose it was hard to save the money out of your salary," said Mildred.

Mrs. Belloc laughed. She was about thirty-five years old, though her eyes and her figure were younger than that. Her mouth was pleasant enough, but had lost some of its freshness. "Save money!" cried she. "I'd never have succeeded that way. I'd be there yet. I had never married—had two or three chances, but all from poor sticks looking for someone to support them. I saw myself getting old. I was looking years older than I do now. Talk about sea air for freshening a woman up—it isn't in it with the air of New York. Here's the town where women stay young. If I had come here five years ago I could almost try for the squab class."

"Squab class?" queried Mildred.

"Yes, squabs. Don't you see them around everywhere?—the women dressed like girls of sixteen to eighteen—and some of them are that, and younger. They go hopping and laughing about—and they seem to please the men and to have no end of a good time. Especially the oldish men. Oh, yes, you know a squab on sight—tight skirt, low shoes and silk stockings, cute pretty face, always laughing, hat set on rakishly and hair done to match, and always a big purse or bag—with a yellow-back or so in it—as a kind of a hint, I guess."

Mildred had seen squabs. "I've envied them—in a way," said she. "Their parents seem to let them do about as they please."

"Their parents don't know—or don't care. Sometimes it's one, sometimes the other. They travel in two sets. One is where they meet young fellows of their own class—the kind they'll probably marry, unless they happen to draw the capital prize. The other set they travel in—well, it's the older men they meet round the swell hotels and so on—the yellow-back men."

"How queer!" exclaimed Mildred, before whose eyes a new world was opening. "But how do they—these—squabs—account for the money?"

"How do a thousand and one women in this funny town account at home for money and things?" retorted Mrs. Belloc. "Nothing's easier. For instance, often these squabs do—or pretend to do—a little something in the way of work—a little canvassing or artists' model or anything you please. That helps them to explain at home—and also to make each of the yellow-back men think he's the only one and that he's being almost loved for himself alone."

Mrs. Belloc laughed. Mildred was too astonished to laugh, and too interested—and too startled or shocked.

"But I was telling you how *I* got down here," continued the landlady. "Up in my town there was an old man—about seventy-five—close as the bark on a tree, and ugly and mean." She paused to draw a long breath and to shake her head angrily yet triumphantly at some figure her fancy conjured up. "Oh, he WAS a pup!—and is! Well, anyhow, I decided that I'd marry him. So I wrote home for fifty dollars. I borrowed another fifty here and there. I had seventy-five saved up against sickness. I went up to Boston and laid it all out in underclothes and house things—not showy but fine and good to look at. Then one day, when the weather was fine and I knew the old man would be out in his buggy driving round—I dressed myself up to beat the band. I took hours to it—scrubbing, powdering, sacheting, perfuming, fixing the hair, fixing my finger-nails, fixing up my feet, polishing every nail and making them look better than most hands."

Mildred was so interested that she was excited. What strange freak was coming?

"You never could guess," pursued Mrs. Belloc, complacently. "I took my sunshade and went out, all got up to kill. And I walked along the road until I saw the old man's buggy coming with him in it. Then I gave my ankle a frightful wrench. My! How it hurt!"

"What a pity!" said Mildred sympathetically. "What a shame!"

"A pity? A shame?" cried Mrs. Belloc, laughing. "Why, my dear, I did it a-purpose."

"On purpose!" exclaimed Mildred.

"Certainly. That was my game. I screamed out with pain—and the scream was no fake, I can tell you. And I fell down by the roadside on a nice grassy spot where no dust would get on me. Well, up comes the old skinflint in his buggy. He climbed down and helped me get off my slipper and stocking. I knew I had him the minute I saw his old face looking at that foot I had fixed up so beautifully."

"How DID you ever think of it?" exclaimed Mildred.

"Go and teach school for ten years in a dull little town, my dear—and look in the glass every day and see your youth fading away—and you'll think of most anything. Well, to make a long story short, the old man took me in the buggy to his house where he lived with his deaf, half-blind old widowed daughter. I had to stay there three weeks. I married him the fourth week. And just two months to a day from the afternoon I sprained my ankle, he gave me fifty dollars a week—all signed and sealed by a lawyer—to go away and leave him alone. I might have stood out for more, but I was too anxious to get to New York. And here I am!" She gazed about the well-furnished room, typical of that almost luxurious house, with an air of triumphant satisfaction. Said she: "I've no patience with a woman who says she can't get on. Where's her brains?"

Mildred was silent. Perhaps it was a feeling of what was hazily in the younger woman's mind and a desire to answer it that led Mrs. Belloc to say further: "I suppose there's some that would criticize my way of getting there. But I want to know, don't all women get there by working men? Only most of them are so stupid that they have to go on living with the man. I think it's low to live with a man you hate."

"Oh, I'm not criticizing anybody," said Mildred.

"I didn't think you were," said Mrs. Belloc. "If I hadn't seen you weren't that kind, I'd not have been so confidential. Not that I'm secretive with anybody. I say and do what I please. Anyone who doesn't like my way or me can take the other side of the street. I didn't come to New York to go in society. I came here to LIVE."

Mildred looked at her admiringly. There were things about Mrs. Belloc that she did not admire; other things—suspected rather than known things—that she knew she would shrink from, but she heartily admired and profoundly envied her utter indifference to the opinion of others, her fine independent way of walking her own path at her own gait.

"I took this boarding-house," Mrs. Belloc went on, "because I didn't want to be lonesome. I don't like all—or even most of—the ladies that live here. But they're all amusing to talk with—and don't put on airs except with their men friends. And one or two are the real thing—good-hearted, fond of a joke, without any meanness. I tell you, New York is a mighty fine place if you get 'in right.' Of course, if you don't, it's h-e-l-l." (Mrs. Belloc took off its unrefined edge by spelling it.) "But what place isn't?" she added.

"And your husband never bothers you?" inquired Mildred.

"And never will," replied Mrs. Belloc. "When he dies I'll come into a little more—about a hundred and fifty a week in all. Not a fortune, but enough with what the boarding-house brings in. I'm a pretty fair business woman."

"I should say so!" exclaimed Mildred.

"You said you were Miss Stevens, didn't you?" said Mrs. Belloc—and Mildred knew that her turn had come.

"Yes," replied she. "But I am also a married woman." She hesitated, reddened. "I didn't give you my married name."

"That's your own business," said Mrs. Belloc in her easiest manner. "My right name isn't Belloc, either. But I've dropped that other life. You needn't feel a bit embarrassed in this house. Some of my boarders SEEM to be married. All that have regular-appearing husbands SAY they are. What do I care, so long as everything goes along smoothly? I don't get excited about trifles."

"Some day perhaps I'll tell you about myself," said Mildred. "Just at present I—well, I seem not to be able to talk about things."

"It's not a bad idea to keep your mouth shut, as long as your affairs are unsettled," advised Mrs. Belloc. "I can see you've had little experience. But you'll come out all right. Just keep cool, and don't fret about trifles. And don't let any man make a fool of you. That's where we women get left. We're afraid of men. We needn't be. We can mighty easily make them afraid of us. Use the soft hand till you get him well in your grip. Then the firm hand. Nothing coarse or cruel or mean. But firm and self-respecting."

Mildred was tempted to take Mrs. Belloc fully into her confidence and get the benefit of the advice of shrewdness and experience. So strong was the temptation, she would have yielded to it had Mrs. Belloc asked a few tactful, penetrating questions. But Mrs. Belloc refrained, and Mildred's timidity or delicacy induced her to postpone. The next day she wrote Stanley Baird, giving her address and her name and asking him to call "any afternoon at four or five." She assumed that he would come on the following day, but the letter happened to reach him within an hour of her mailing it, and he came that very afternoon.

When she went down to the drawing-room to receive him, she found him standing in the middle of the room gazing about with a quizzical expression. As soon as the greetings were over he said:

"You must get out of here, Mildred. This won't do."

"Indeed I shan't," said she. "I've looked everywhere, and this is the only comfortable place I could find—where the rates were reasonable and where the landlady didn't have her nose in everybody's business."

"You don't understand," said he. "This is a bird-cage. Highly gilded, but a bird-cage."

She had never heard the phrase, but she understood—and instantly she knew that he was right. She colored violently, sat down abruptly. But in a moment she recovered herself, and with fine defiance said:

"I don't care. Mrs. Belloc is a kind-hearted woman, and it's as easy to be respectable here as anywhere."

"Sure," assented he. "But you've got to consider appearances to a certain extent. You won't be able to find the right sort of a boarding-house—one you'd be comfortable in. You've got to have a flat of your own."

"I can't afford it," said Mildred. "I can't afford this, even. But I simply will not live in a shabby, mussy way."

"That's right!" cried Stanley. "You can't do proper work in poor surroundings. Some women could, but not your sort. But don't worry. I'm going to see you through. I'll find a place—right away. You want to start in at once, don't you?"

"I've got to," said Mildred.

"Then leave it all to me."

"But WHAT am I to do?"

"Sing, if you can. If not, then act. We'll have you on the stage within a year or so. I'm sure of it. And I'll get my money back, with interest."

"I don't see how I can accept it," said Mildred very feebly.

"You've got to," said Stanley. "What alternative is there? None. So let's bother no more about it. I'll consult with those who know, find out what the thing costs, and arrange everything. You're as helpless as a baby, and you know it."

Yes, Mildred knew it.

He looked at her with an amused smile. "Come, out with it!" he cried. "You've got something on your mind. Let's get everything straight—and keep it that way."

Mildred hung her head.

"You're uneasy because I, a man, am doing this for you, a young woman? Is that it?"

"Yes," she confessed.

He leaned back in his chair, crossed his legs, and spoke in a brisk, businesslike way. "In the first place, it's got to be done, hasn't it? And someone has got to do it? And there is no one offering but me? Am I right?"

She nodded.

"Then *I*'ve got to do it, and you've GOT to let me. There's logic, if ever there was logic. A Philadelphia lawyer couldn't knock a hole in it. You trust me, don't you?"

She was silent.

"You don't trust me, then," said he cheerfully. "Well, perhaps you're right. But you trust yourself, don't you?"

She moved restlessly, but remained silent.

"You are afraid I might put you in a difficult position?"

"Something like that," she admitted, in a low, embarrassed voice.

"You fear that I expect some return which you do not intend to give?"

She was silent.

"Well, I don't," said he bluntly. "So put your mind at rest. Some day I'll tell you why I am doing this, but I want you to feel that I ask nothing of you but my money back with interest, when you can afford to pay."

"I can't feel that," said she. "You're putting me in your debt—so heavily that I'd feel I ought to pay anything you asked. But I couldn't and wouldn't pay."

"Unless you felt like it?" suggested he.

"It's honest for me to warn you that I'm not likely to feel that way."

"There is such a thing as winning a woman's love, isn't there?" said he jestingly. It was difficult to tell when Stanley Baird was jesting and when he was in earnest.

"Is that what you expect?" said she gravely.

"If I say yes?"

She lowered her eyes and laughed in an embarrassed way.

He was frankly amused. "You see, you feel that you're in my power. And you are. So why not make the best of it?" A pause, then he said abruptly and with a convincing manliness, "I think, Mildred, you can trust me not to be a beast."

She colored and looked at him with quick contrition. "I'm ashamed of myself," said she. "Please forget that I said anything. I'll take what I must, and I'll pay it back as soon as I can. And—thank you, Stanley." The tears were in her eyes. "If I had anything worth your taking I'd be glad to give it to you. What vain fools we women are!"

"Aren't you, though!" laughed he. "And now it's all settled—until you're on the stage, and free, and the money's paid back—WITH interest. I shall charge you six per cent."

When she first knew him she had not been in the least impressed by what now seemed to her his finest and rarest trait, for, in those days she had been as ignorant of the realities of human nature as one who has never adventured his boat beyond the mouth of the peaceful land-locked harbor is ignorant of the open sea. But in the hard years she had been learning— not only from Presbury and General Siddall, but from the cook and the housemaid, from every creditor, every tradesman, everyone whose attitude socially toward her had been modified by her changed fortunes—and whose attitude had not been changed? Thus, she was now able to appreciate—at least in some measure—Stanley Baird's delicacy and tact. No, not delicacy and tact, for that implied effort. His ability to put this offer in such a way that she could accept without serious embarrassment arose from a genuine indifference to money as money, a habit of looking upon it simply as a means to an end. He offered her the money precisely as he would have offered her his superior strength if it had been necessary to cross a too deep and swift creek. She had the sense that he felt he was doing something even less notable than he admitted, and that he talked of it as a valuable and rather unusual service simply because it was the habit thus to regard such matters.

As they talked on of "the great career" her spirits went up and up. It was evident that he now had a new and keen interest in life, that she was doing him a greater favor than he was doing her. He had always had money, plenty of it, more than he could use. He now had more than ever—for, several rich relatives had died and, after the habit of the rich, had left everything to him, the one of all the connections who needed it least. He had a very human aversion to spending money upon people or things he did not like. He would have fought to the last court an attempt by his wife to get alimony. He had a reputation with the "charity gang" of being stingy because he would not give them so much as the price of a bazaar ticket. Also, the impecunious spongers at his clubs spread his fame as a "tight-wad" because he refused to let them "stick him up" for even a round of drinks. Where many a really stingy man yielded through weakness or fear of public opinion, he stood firm. His one notable surrender of any kind had been his marriage; that bitter experience had cured him of the surrendering habit for all time. Thenceforth he did absolutely and in everything as he pleased.

Mildred had heard that he was close about money. She had all but forgotten it, because her own experience with him had made such a charge seem ridiculous. She now assumed—so far as she thought about it at all—that he was extremely generous. She did not realize what a fine discriminating generosity his was, or how striking an evidence of his belief in her as well as of his liking for her.

As he rose to go he said: "You mustn't forget that our arrangement is a secret between us. Neither of us can afford to have anyone know it."

"There isn't anyone in the world who wouldn't misunderstand it," said she, without the least feeling of embarrassment.

"Just so," said he. "And I want you to live in such a way that I can come to call. We must arrange things so that you will take your own name—"

"I intend to use the name Mary Stevens in my work," she interrupted.

"But there mustn't be any concealment, any mystery to excite curiosity and scandal—"

This time the interruption was her expression. He turned to see what had startled her, and saw in the doorway of the drawing-room the grotesquely neat and stylish figure of the little general. Before either could speak he said:

"How d'you do, Mr. Baird? You'll pardon me if I ask you to leave me alone with my WIFE."

Stanley met the situation with perfect coolness. "How are you, General?" said he. "Certainly, I was just going." He extended his hand to Mildred, said in a correct tone of conventional friendliness, "Then you'll let me know when you're settled?" He bowed, moved toward the door, shook hands with the general, and passed out, giving from start to finish a model example of a man of the world extricating himself from an impossible situation and leaving it the better for his having been entangled. To a man of Siddall's incessant and clumsy self-consciousness such unaffected ease could not but be proof positive of Mildred's innocence—unless he had overheard. And his first words convinced her that he had not. Said he:

"So you sent for your old admirer?"

"I ran across him accidentally," replied Mildred.

"I know," said the little general. "My men picked you up at the pier and haven't lost sight of you since. It's fortunate that I've kept myself informed, or I might have misunderstood that chap's being here." A queer, cloudy look came into his eyes. "I must give him a warning for safety's sake." He waved his hand in dismissal of such an unimportant trifle as the accidental Baird. He went on, his wicked eyes bent coldly and dully upon her: "Do you know what kind of a house this is?"

"Stanley Baird urged me to leave," replied she. "But I shall stay until I find a better—and that's not easy."

"Yes, my men have reported to me on the difficulties you've had. It was certainly fortunate for you that I had them look after you. Otherwise I'd never have understood your landing in this sort of a house. You are ready to come with me?"

"Your secretary explained that if I left the hotel it was the end."

"He told you that by my orders."

"So he explained," said Mildred. She seated herself, overcome by a sudden lassitude that was accompanied not by fear, but by indifference. "Won't you sit down? I am willing to hear what you have to say."

The little general, about to sit, was so astonished that he straightened and stiffened himself. "In consenting to overlook your conduct and take you back I have gone farther than I ever intended. I have taken into consideration your youth and inexperience."

"But I am not going back," said Mildred.

The little general slowly seated himself. "You have less than two hundred and fifty dollars left," said he.

"Really? Your spies know better than I."

"I have seen Presbury. He assures me that in no circumstances will he and your mother take you back."

"They will not have the chance to refuse," said Mildred.

"As for your brother—"

"I have no brother," said she coldly.

"Then you are coming back with me."

"No," said Mildred. "I should"—she cast about for an impressive alternative—"I should stay on here, rather."

The little general—his neat varnished leather and be-spatted shoes just touched the floor—examined his highly polished top-hat at several angles. Finally he said: "You need not fear that your misconduct will be remembered against you. I shall treat you in every way as my wife. I shall assume that your—your flight was an impulse that you regret."

"I shan't go back," said Mildred. "Nothing you could offer would change me."

"I cannot make any immediate concession on the—the matter that caused you to go," pursued he, as if she had not spoken, "but if I see that you have reliability and good sense, I'll agree to give you an allowance later."

Mildred eyed him curiously. "Why are you making these offers, these concessions?" she said. "You think everyone in the world is a fool except yourself. You're greatly deceived. I know that you don't mean what you've been saying. I know that if you got me in your power again, you would do something frightful. I've seen through that mask you wear. I know the kind of man you are."

"If you know that," said the general in his even slow way, monotonous, almost lifeless, "you know you'd better come with me than stand out against me."

She did not let him see how this struck terror into her. She said: "No matter what you might do to me, when I'm away from you, it would be less than you'd do with me under your roof. At any rate, it'd seem less."

The general reflected, decided to change to another point: "You made a bargain with me. You've broken it. I never let anyone break a bargain with me without making them regret it. I'm giving you a chance to keep your bargain."

She was tempted to discuss, but she could not find the words, or the strength. Besides, how futile to discuss with such a man. She sank back in her chair wearily. "I shall never go back," she said.

He looked at her, his face devoid of expression, but she had a sense of malignance unutterable eying her from behind a screen. He said: "I see you've misunderstood my generosity. You think I'm weak where you are concerned because I've come to you instead of doing as I said and making you come to me." He rose. "Well, my offer to you is closed. And once more I say, you will come to me and ask to be taken back. I may or may not take you back. It depends on how I'll feel at that time."

Slowly, with his ludicrously pompous strut, he marched to the drawing-room door. She had not felt like smiling, but if there had been any such inclination it would have fled before the countenance that turned upon her at the threshold. It was the lean, little face with the funny toupee and needle-like mustache and imperial, but behind it lay a personality like the dull, cold, yellow eyes of the devil-fish ambushed in the hazy mass of dun-colored formlessness of collapsed body and tentacles. He said:

"You'd best be careful how you conduct yourself. You'll be under constant observation. And any friends you make—they'd do well to avoid you."

He was gone. She sat without the power of motion, without the power of thought. After a time—perhaps long, perhaps short, she did not know—Mrs. Belloc came in and entered upon a voluble apology for the maid's having shown "the little gentleman" into the drawing-room when another was already there. "That maid's as green as spring corn," said she. "Such a thing never happened in my house before. And it'll never happen again. I do hope it didn't cause trouble."

"It was my husband," said Mildred. "I had to see him some time."

"He's certainly a very elegant little gentleman," said Mrs. Belloc. "I rather like small men, myself."

Mildred gazed at her vaguely and said, "Tell me—a rich man, a very rich man—if he hates anyone, can he make trouble?"

"Money can do anything in this town," replied Mrs. Belloc. "But usually rich men are timid and stingy. If they weren't, they'd make us all cringe. As it is, I've heard some awful stories of how men and women who've got some powerful person down on them have been hounded."

Mildred turned deathly sick. "I think I'll go to my room," she said, rising uncertainly and forcing herself toward the door.

Mrs. Belloc's curiosity could not restrain itself. "You're leaving?" she asked. "You're going back to your husband?"

She was startled when the girl abruptly turned on her and cried with flashing eyes and voice strong and vibrant with passion: "Never! Never! No matter what comes—NEVER!"

The rest of the day and that night she hid in her room and made no effort to resist the terror that preyed upon her. Just as our strength is often the source of weakness, so our weaknesses often give birth to strength. Her terror of the little general, given full swing, shrieked and grimaced itself into absurdity. She was ashamed of her orgy, was laughing at it as the sun and intoxicating air of a typical New York morning poured in upon her. She accepted Mrs. Belloc's invitation to take a turn through the park and up Riverside Drive in a taxicab, came back restored to her normal state of blind confidence in the future. About noon Stanley Baird telephoned.

"We must not see each other again for some time," said he. "I rather suspect that you—know—who may be having you watched."

"I'm sure of it," said she. "He warned me."

"Don't let that disturb you," pursued Stanley. "A man—a singing teacher—his name's Eugene Jennings—will call on you this afternoon at three. Do exactly as he suggests. Let him do all the talking."

She had intended to tell Baird frankly that she thought, indeed knew, that it was highly dangerous for him to enter into her affairs in any way, and to urge him to draw off. She felt that it was only fair to act so toward one who had been unselfishly generous to her. But now that the time for speaking had come, she found herself unable to speak. Only by flatly refusing to have anything to do with his project could she prevail upon him. To say less than that she had completely and finally changed her mind would sound, and would be, insincere. And that she could not say. She felt how noble it would be to say this, how selfish, and weak, too, it was to cling to him, possibly to involve him in disagreeable and even dangerous complications, but she had no strength to do what she would have denounced another as base for not doing. Instead of the lofty words that flow so freely from the lips of stage and fiction heroines, instead of the words that any and every reader of this history would doubtless have pronounced in the same circumstances, she said:

"You're quite sure you want to go on?"

"Why not?" came instantly back over the wire.

"He is a very, very relentless man," replied she.

"Did he try to frighten you?"

"I'm afraid he succeeded."

"You're not going back on the career!" exclaimed he excitedly. "I'll come down there and—"

"No, no," cried she. "I was simply giving you a chance to free yourself." She felt sure of him now. She scrambled toward the heights of moral grandeur. "I want you to stop. I've no right to ask you to involve yourself in my misfortunes. Stanley, you mustn't. I can't allow it."

"Oh, fudge!" laughed he. "Don't give me these scares. Don't forget— Jennings at three. Good-by and good luck."

And he rang off that she might have no chance on impulse to do herself mischief with her generous thoughtfulness for him. She felt rather mean, but not nearly so mean as she would have felt had she let the opportunity go by with no generous word said. "And no doubt my aversion for that little wretch," thought she, "makes me think him more terrible than he is. After all, what can he do? Watch me—and discover nothing, because there'll be nothing to discover."

Jennings came exactly at three—came with the air of a man who wastes no one's time and lets no one waste his time. He was a youngish man of forty or thereabouts, with a long sharp nose, a large tight mouth, and eyes that seemed to be looking restlessly about for money. That they had not looked in vain seemed to be indicated by such facts as that he came in a private brougham and that he was most carefully dressed, apparently with the aid of a valet.

"Miss Stevens," he said with an abrupt bow, before Mildred had a chance to speak, "you have come to New York to take singing lessons—to prepare yourself for the stage. And you wish a comfortable place to live and to work." He extended his gloved hand, shook hers frigidly, dropped it. "We shall get on—IF you work, but only if you work. I do not waste myself upon triflers." He drew a card from his pocket. "If you will go to see the lady whose name and address are written on this card, I think you will find the quarters you are looking for."

"Thank you," said Mildred.

"Come to me—my address is on the card, also—at half-past ten on Saturday. We will then lay out your work."

"If you find I have a voice worth while," Mildred ventured.

"That, of course," said Mr. Jennings curtly. "Until half-past ten on Saturday, good day."

Again he gave the abrupt foreign bow and, while Mildred was still struggling with her surprise and confusion, she saw him, through the window, driving rapidly away. Mrs. Belloc came drifting through the room; she had the habit of looking about whenever there were new visitors, and in her it was not irritating because her interest was innocent and sympathetic. Said Mildred:

"Did you see that man, Mrs. Belloc?"

"What an extraordinary nose he had," replied she.

"Yes, I noticed that," said Mildred. "But it was the only thing I did notice. He is a singing teacher—Mr. Jennings."

"Eugene Jennings?"

"Yes, Eugene."

"He's the best known singing teacher in New York. He gets fifteen dollars a half-hour."

"Then I simply can't take from him!" exclaimed Mildred, before she thought. "That's frightful!"

"Isn't it, though?" echoed Mrs. Belloc. "I've heard his income is fifty thousand a year, what with lessons and coaching and odds and ends. There's a lot of them that do well, because so many fool women with nothing to do cultivate their voices—when they can't sing a little bit. But he tops them all. I don't see how ANY teacher can put fifteen dollars of value into half an hour. But I suppose he does, or he wouldn't get it. Still, his may be just another case of New York nerve. This is the biggest bluff town in the world, I do believe. Here, you can get away with anything, I don't care what it is, if only you bluff hard enough."

As there was no reason for delay and many reasons against it, Mildred went at once to the address on the card Jennings had left. She found Mrs. Howell Brindley installed in a plain comfortable apartment in Fifty-ninth Street, overlooking the park and high enough to make the noise of the traffic endurable. A Swedish maid, prepossessingly white and clean, ushered her into the little drawing-room, which was furnished with more simplicity and individual taste than is usual anywhere in New York, cursed of the mania for useless and tasteless showiness. There were no messy draperies, no fussy statuettes, vases, gilt boxes, and the like. Mildred awaited the entrance of Mrs. Brindley hopefully.

She was not disappointed. Presently in came a quietly-dressed, frank-looking woman of a young forty—a woman who had by no means lost her physical freshness, but had gained charm of another and more enduring kind. As she came forward with extended but not overeager hand, she said:

"I was expecting you, Mrs. Siddall—that is, Miss Stevens."

"Mr. Jennings did not say when I was to come. If I am disturbing you—"

Mrs. Brindley hastened to assure her that her visit was quite convenient. "I must have someone to share the expense of this apartment with me, and I want the matter settled. Mr. Jennings has explained about you to me, and now that I've seen you—" here she smiled charmingly—"I am ready to say that it is for you to say."

Mildred did not know how to begin. She looked at Mrs. Brindley with appeal in her troubled young eyes.

"You no doubt wish to know something about me," said Mrs. Brindley. "My husband was a composer—a friend of Mr. Jennings. He died two years ago. I am here in New York to teach the piano. What the lessons will bring, with my small income, will enable me to live—if I can find someone to help out at the expenses here. As I understand it, you are willing to pay forty dollars a week, I to run the house, pay all the bills, and so on—all, of course, if you wish to come here."

Mildred made a not very successful attempt to conceal her embarrassment.

"Perhaps you would like to look at the apartment?" suggested Mrs. Brindley.

"Thank you, yes," said Mildred.

The tour of the apartment—two bedrooms, dining-room, kitchen, sitting-room, large bath-room, drawing-room—took only a few minutes, but Mildred and Mrs. Brindley contrived to become much better acquainted. Said Mildred, when they were in the drawing-room again:

"It's most attractive—just what I should like. What—how much did Mr. Jennings say?"

"Forty dollars a week." She colored slightly and spoke with the nervousness of one not in the habit of discussing money matters. "I do not see how I could make it less. That is the fair share of the—"

"Oh, I think that is most reasonable," interrupted Mildred. "And I wish to come."

Mrs. Brindley gave an almost childlike sigh of relief and smiled radiantly. "Then it's settled," said she. "I've been so nervous about it." She looked at Mildred with friendly understanding. "I think you and I are somewhat alike about practical things. You've not had much experience, either, have you? I judge so from the fact that Mr. Jennings is looking after everything for you."

"I've had no experience at all," said Mildred. "That is why I'm hesitating. I'm wondering if I can afford to pay so much."

Mrs. Brindley laughed. "Mr. Jennings wished to fix it at sixty a week, but I insisted that forty was enough," said she.

Mildred colored high with embarrassment. How much did Mrs. Brindley know?—or how little? She stammered: "Well, if Mr. Jennings says it is all right, I'll come."

"You'll let me know to-morrow? You can telephone Mr. Jennings."

"Yes, I'll let you know to-morrow. I'm almost sure I'll come. In fact, I'm quite sure. And—I think we shall get on well together."

"We can help each other," said Mrs. Brindley. "I don't care for anything in the world but music."

"I want to be that way," said Mildred. "I shall be that way."

"It's the only sure happiness—to care for something, for some THING," said Mrs. Brindley. "People die, or disappoint one, or become estranged. But when one centers on some kind of work, it gives pleasure always—more and more pleasure."

"I am so afraid I haven't voice enough, or of the right kind," said Mildred. "Mr. Jennings is going to try me on Saturday. Really I've no right to settle anything until he has given his opinion."

Mrs. Brindley smiled with her eyes only, and Mildred wondered.

"If he should say that I wouldn't do," she went on, "I'd not know which way to turn."

"But he'll not say that," said Mrs. Brindley. "You can sing, can't you? You have sung?"

"Oh, yes."

"Then you'll be accepted by him. And it will take him a long time to find out whether you'll do for a professional."

"I'm afraid I sing very badly."

"That will not matter. You'll sing better than at least half of Jennings's pupils."

"Then he doesn't take only those worth while?"

Mrs. Brindley looked amused. "How would he live if he did that? It's a teacher's business to teach. Learning—that's the pupil's lookout. If teachers taught only those who could and would learn, how would they live?"

"Then I'll not know whether I'll do!" exclaimed Mildred.

"You'll have to find out for yourself," said Mrs. Brindley. "No one can tell you. Anyone's opinion might be wrong. For example, I've known Jennings, who is a very good judge, to be wrong—both ways." Hesitatingly: "Why not sing for me? I'd like to hear."

"Would you tell me what you honestly thought?" said Mildred.

Mrs. Brindley laughingly shook her head. Mildred liked her honesty. "Then it'd be useless to sing for you," said she. "I'm not vain about my voice. I'd simply like to make a living by it, if I could. I'll even confess that there are many things I care for more than for music. Does that prove that I can never sing professionally?"

"No, indeed," Mrs. Brindley assured her. "It'd be strange if a girl of your age cared exclusively for music. The passion comes with the work, with progress, success. And some of the greatest—that is, the most famous and best paid—singers never care much about music, except as a vanity, and never understand it. A singer means a person born with a certain shape of mouth and throat, a certain kind of vocal chords. The rest may be natural or acquired. It's the instrument that makes the singer, not brains or temperament."

"Do let me sing for you," said Mildred. "I think it will help me."

Between them they chose a little French song—"Chanson d'Antonine"—and Mrs. Brindley insisted on her playing her own accompaniment. "I wish to listen," said she, "and I can't if I play."

Mildred was surprised at her own freedom from nervousness. She sang neither better nor worse than usual—sang in the clear and pleasant soprano which she flattered herself was not unmusical. When she finished she said:

"That's about as I usually sing. What do you think?"

Mrs. Brindley reflected before she replied: "I BELIEVE it's worth trying. If I were you, I should keep on trying, no matter what anyone said."

Mildred was instantly depressed. "You think Mr. Jennings may reject me?" she asked.

"I KNOW he will not," replied Mrs. Brindley. "Not as long as you can pay for the lessons. But I was thinking of the real thing—of whether you could win out as a singer."

"And you don't think I can?" said Mildred.

"On the contrary, I believe you can," replied Mrs. Brindley. "A singer means so much besides singing. The singing is the smallest part of it. You'll understand when you get to work. I couldn't explain now. But I can say that you ought to go ahead."

Mildred, who had her share of vanity, had hoped for some enthusiasm. Mrs. Brindley's judicial tone was a severe blow. She felt a little resentful, began to cast about for vanity-consoling reasons for Mrs. Brindley's restraint. "She means well," she said to herself, "but she's probably just a tiny bit jealous. She's not so young as she once was, and she hasn't the faintest hope of ever being anything more than a piano-teacher."

Mrs. Brindley showed that she had more than an inkling of Mildred's frame of mind by going on to say in a gentle, candid way: "I want to help you. So I shall be careful not to encourage you to believe too much in what you have. That would prevent you from getting what you need. You must remember, you are no longer a drawing-room singer, but a candidate for the profession. That's a very different thing."

Mildred saw that she was mistaken, that Mrs. Brindley was honest and frank and had doubtless told her the exact truth. But her vanity remained sore. Never before had anyone said any less of her singing than that it was wonderful, marvelous, equal to a great deal that passed for fine in grand opera. She had known that this was exaggeration, but she had not known how grossly exaggerated. Thus, this her first experience of the professional attitude was galling. Only her unusual good sense saved her from being angry with Mrs. Brindley. And it was that same good sense that moved her presently to try to laugh at herself. With a brave attempt to smile gayly she said:

"You don't realize how you've taken me down. I had no idea I was so conceited about my singing. I can't truthfully say I like your frankness, but there's a part of me that's grateful to you for it, and when I get over feeling hurt, I'll be grateful through and through."

Mrs. Brindley's face lighted up beautifully. "You'll DO!" she cried. "I'm sure you'll do. I've been waiting and watching to see how you would take my criticism. That's the test—how they take criticism. If they don't take it at all, they'll not go very far, no matter how talented they are. If they take it as you've taken it, there's hope—great hope. Now, I'm not afraid to tell you that you sang splendidly for an amateur—that you surprised me."

"Don't spoil it all," said Mildred. "You were right; I can't sing."

"Not for grand opera, not for comic opera even," replied Mrs. Brindley. "But you will sing, and sing well, in one or the other, if you work."

"You really mean that?" said Mildred.

"If you work intelligently and persistently," said Mrs. Brindley. "That's a big if—as you'll discover in a year or so."

"You'll see," said Mildred confidently. "Why, I've nothing else to do, and no other hope."

Mrs. Brindley's smile had a certain sadness in it. She said:

"It's the biggest if in all this world."

V

AT Mrs. Belloc's a telephone message from Jennings was awaiting her; he would call at a quarter-past eight and would detain Miss Stevens only a moment. And at eight fifteen exactly he rang the bell. This time Mildred was prepared; she refused to be disconcerted by his abrupt manner and by his long sharp nose that seemed to warn away, to threaten away, even to thrust away any glance seeking to investigate the rest of his face or his personality. She looked at him candidly, calmly, and seeingly. Seeingly. With eyes that saw as they had never seen before. Perhaps from the death of her father, certainly from the beginning of Siddall's courtship, Mildred had been waking up. There is a part of our nature—the active and aggressive part—that sleeps all our lives long or becomes atrophied if we lead lives of ease and secure dependence. It is the important part of us, too—the part that determines character. The thing that completed the awakening of Mildred was her acquaintance with Mrs. Belloc. That positive and finely-poised lady fascinated her, influenced her powerfully—gave her just what she needed at the particular moment. The vital moments in life are not the crises over which shallow people linger, but are the moments where we met and absorbed the ideas that enabled us to weather these crises. The acquaintance with Mrs. Belloc was one of those vital moments; for, Mrs. Belloc's personality—her look and manner, what she said and the way she said it—was a proffer to Mildred of invaluable lessons which her awakening character eagerly absorbed. She saw Jennings as he was. She decided that he was of common origin, that his vanity was colossal and aquiver throughout with sensitiveness; that he belonged to the familiar type of New-Yorker who succeeds by bluffing. Also, she saw or felt a certain sexlessness or indifference to sex—and this she later understood. Men whose occupation compels them constantly to deal with women go to one extreme or the other—either become acutely sensitive to women as women or become utterly indifferent, unless their highly discriminated taste is appealed to—which cannot happen often. Jennings, teaching only women because only women spending money they had not earned and could not earn would tolerate his terms and his methods, had, as much through necessity as through inclination, gone to the extreme of lack of interest in all matters of sex. One look at him and the woman who had come with the idea of offering herself in full or part payment for lessons drooped in instinctive discouragement.

Jennings hastened to explain to Mildred that she need not hesitate about closing with Mrs. Brindley. "Your lessons are arranged for," said he. "There has been put in the Plaza Trust Company to your credit the sum of five thousand dollars. This gives you about a hundred dollars a week for your board and other personal expenses. If that is not enough, you will let me know. But I estimated that it would be enough. I do not think it wise for young women entering upon the preparation for a serious career to have too much money."

"It is more than enough," murmured the girl. "I know nothing about those things, but it seems to me—"

"You can use as little of it as you like," interrupted Jennings, rising.

Mildred felt as though she had been caught and exposed in a hypocritical protest. Jennings was holding out something toward her. She took it, and he went on:

"That's your check-book. The bank will send you statements of your account, and will notify you when any further sums are added. Now, I have nothing more to do with your affairs—except, of course, the artistic side— your development as a singer. You've not forgotten your appointment?"

"No," said Mildred, like a primary school-child before a formidable teacher.

"Be prompt, please. I make no reduction for lessons wholly or partly missed. The half-hour I shall assign to you belongs to you. If you do not use it, that is your affair. At first you will probably be like all women— careless about your appointments, coming with lessons unprepared, telephoning excuses. But if you are serious you will soon fall into the routine." "I shall try to be regular," murmured Mildred.

Jennings apparently did not hear. "I'm on my way to the opera-house," said he. "One of my old pupils is appearing in a new role, and she is nervous. Good night."

Once more that swift, quiet exit, followed almost instantaneously by the sound of wheels rolling away. Never had she seen such rapidity of motion without loss of dignity. "Yes, he's a fraud," she said to herself, "but he's a good one."

The idea of a career had now become less indefinite. It was still without any attraction—not because of the toil it involved, for that made small impression upon her who had never worked and had never seen anyone work, but because a career meant cutting herself off from everything she had been brought up to regard as fit and proper for a lady. She was ashamed of this; she did not admit its existence even to herself, and in her talks with Baird about the career she had professed exactly the opposite view. Yet there it was—nor need she have been ashamed of a feeling that is instilled into women of her class from babyhood as part of their ladylike education. The career had not become definite. She could not imagine herself out on a stage in some sort of a costume, with a painted face, singing before an audience. Still, the career was less indefinite than when it had no existence beyond Stanley Baird's enthusiasm and her own whipped-up pretense of enthusiasm.

She shrank from the actual start, but at the same time was eager for it. Inaction began to fret her nerves, and she wished to be doing something to show her appreciation of Stanley Baird's generosity. She telephoned Mrs. Brindley that she would come in the morning, and then she told her landlady.

Mrs. Belloc was more than regretful; she was distressed. Said she: "I've taken a tremendous fancy to you, and I hate to give you up. I'd do most anything to keep you."

Mildred explained that her work compelled her to go.

"That's very interesting," said Mrs. Belloc. "If I were a few years younger, and hadn't spent all my energy in teaching school and putting through that marriage, I'd try to get on the stage, myself. I don't want to lose sight of you."

"Oh, I'll come to see you from time to time."

"No, you won't," said Mrs. Belloc practically. "No more than I'd come to see you. Our lives lie in different directions, and in New York that means we'll never have time to meet. But we may be thrown together again, some time. As I've got a twenty years' lease on this house, I guess you'll have no trouble in finding me. I suppose I could look you up through Professor Jennings?"

"Yes," said Mildred. Then impulsively, "Mrs. Belloc, there's a reason why I'd like to change without anyone's knowing what has become of me— I mean, anyone that might be—watching me."

"I understand perfectly," said Mrs. Belloc with a ready sympathy that made Mildred appreciate the advantages of the friendship of unconventional, knock-about people. "Nothing could be easier. You've got no luggage but that bag. I'll take it up to the Grand Central Station and check it, and bring the check back here. You can send for it when you please."

"But what about me?" said Mildred.

"I was coming to that. You walk out of here, say, about half an hour after I go in the taxi. You walk through to the corner of Lexington Avenue and Thirty-seventh Street—there aren't any cabs to be had there. I'll be waiting in the taxi, and we'll make a dash up the East Side and I can drop you at some quiet place in the park and go on—and you can walk to your new address. How does that strike you?"

Mildred expressed her admiration. The plan was carried out, as Mrs. Belloc—a born genius at all forms of intrigue—had evolved it in perfection on the spur of the moment. As they went up the far East Side, Mrs. Belloc, looking back through the little rear window, saw a taxi a few blocks behind them. "We haven't given them the slip yet," said she, "but we will in the park." They entered the park at East Ninetieth Street, crossed to the West Drive. Acting on Mrs. Belloc's instructions, the motorman put on full speed—with due regard to the occasional policeman. At a sharp turning near the Mall, when the taxi could be seen from neither direction, he abruptly stopped. Out sprang Mildred and disappeared behind the bushes completely screening the walk from the drive. At once the taxi was under-way again. She, waiting where the screen of bushes was securely thick, saw the taxi that had followed them in the East Side flash by—in pursuit of Mrs. Belloc alone.

She was free—at least until some mischance uncovered her to the little general. At Mrs. Brindley's she found a note awaiting her—a note from Stanley Baird:

DEAR MILDRED:

I'm of for the Far West, and probably shall not be in town again until the early summer. The club forwards my mail and repeats telegrams as marked. Go in and win, and don't hesitate to call on me if you need me. No false pride, PLEASE! I'm getting out of the way because it's obviously best for the present.

STANLEY.

As she finished, her sense of freedom was complete. She had not realized how uneasy she was feeling about Stanley. She did not doubt his generosity, did not doubt that he genuinely intended to leave her free, and she believed that his delicacy was worthy of his generosity. Still, she was constantly fearing lest circumstances should thrust them both—as much against his will as hers—into a position in which she would have to choose between seeming, not to say being, ungrateful, and playing the hypocrite, perhaps basely, with him. The little general eluded, Stanley voluntarily removed; she was indeed free. Now she could work with an untroubled mind, could show Mrs. Brindley that intelligent and persistent work—her "biggest if in all the world"—was in fact a very simple matter.

She had not been settled at Mrs. Brindley's many hours before she discovered that not only was she free from all hindrances, but was to have a positive and great help. Mrs. Brindley's talent for putting people at their ease was no mere drawing-room trick.

She made Mildred feel immediately at home, as she had not felt at home since her mother introduced James Presbury into their house at Hanging Rock. Mrs. Brindley was absolutely devoid of pretenses. When Mildred spoke to her of this quality in her she said:

"I owe that to my husband. I was brought up like everybody else—to be more or less of a poser and a hypocrite. In fact, I think there was almost nothing genuine about me. My husband taught me to be myself, to be afraid of nobody's opinion, to show myself just as I was and to let people seek or avoid me as they saw fit. He was that sort of man himself."

"He must have been a remarkable man," said Mildred.

"He was," replied Mrs. Brindley. "But not attractive—at least not to me. Our marriage was a mistake. We quarreled whenever we were not at work with the music. If he had not died, we should have been divorced." She smiled merrily. "Then he would have hired me as his musical secretary, and we'd have got on beautifully."

Mildred was still thinking of Mrs. Brindley's freedom from pretense. "I've never dared be myself," confessed she. "I don't know what myself really is like. I was thinking the other day how for one reason and another I've been a hypocrite all my life. You see, I've always been a dependent— have always had to please someone in order to get what I wanted."

"You can never be yourself until you have an independent income, however small," said Mrs. Brindley. "I've had that joy only since my husband died. It's as well that I didn't have it sooner. One is the better for having served an apprenticeship at self-repression and at pretending to virtues one has not. Only those who earn their freedom know how to use it. If I had had it ten or fifteen years ago I'd have been an intolerable tyrant, making everyone around me unhappy and therefore myself. The ideal world would be one where everyone was born free and never knew anything else. Then, no one being afraid or having to serve, everyone would have to be considerate in order to get himself tolerated."

"I wonder if I really ever shall be able to earn a living?" sighed Mildred.

"You must decide that whatever you can make shall be for you a living," said the older woman. "I have lived on my fixed income, which is under two thousand a year. And I am ready to do it again rather than tolerate anything or anybody that does not suit me."

"I shall have to be extremely careful," laughed Mildred. "I shall be a dreadful hypocrite with you."

Mrs. Brindley smiled; but underneath, Mildred saw—or perhaps felt—that her new friend was indeed not one to be trifled with. She said:

"You and I will get on. We'll let each other alone. We have to be more or less intimate, but we'll never be familiar."

After a time she discovered that Mrs. Brindley's first name was Cyrilla, but Mrs. Brindley and Miss Stevens they remained to each other for a long time—until circumstances changed their accidental intimacy into enduring friendship. Not to anticipate, in the course of that same conversation Mildred said:

"If there is anything about me—about my life—that you wish me to explain, I shall be glad to do so."

"I know all I wish to know," replied Cyrilla Brindley. "Your face and your manner and your way of speaking tell me all the essentials."

"Then you must not think it strange when I say I wish no one to know anything about me."

"It will be impossible for you entirely to avoid meeting people," said Cyrilla. "You must have some simple explanation about yourself, or you will attract attention and defeat your object."

"Lead people to believe that I'm an orphan—perhaps of some obscure family—who is trying to get up in the world. That is practically the truth."

Mrs. Brindley laughed. "Quite enough for New York," said she. "It is not interested in facts. All the New-Yorker asks of you is, 'Can you pay your bills and help me pay mine?'"

Competent men are rare; but, thanks to the advantage of the male sex in having to make the struggle for a living, they are not so rare as competent women. Mrs. Brindley was the first competent woman Mildred had ever known. She had spent but a few hours with her before she began to appreciate what a bad atmosphere she had always breathed—bad for a woman who has her way to make in the world, or indeed for any woman not willing to be content as mere more or less shiftless, more or less hypocritical and pretentious, dependent and parasite. Mrs. Brindley—well bred and well educated—knew all the little matters which Mildred had been taught to regard as the whole of a lady's education. But Mildred saw that these trifles were but a trifling incident in Mrs. Brindley's knowledge. She knew real things, this woman who was a thorough-going housekeeper and who trebled her income by giving music lessons a few hours a day to such pupils as she thought worth the teaching. When she spoke, she always said something one of the first things noticed by Mildred, who, being too lazy to think except as her naturally good mind insisted on exercising itself, usually talked simply to kill time and without any idea of getting anywhere. But while Cyrilla—without in the least intending it—roused her to a painful sense of her own limitations, she did not discourage her. Mildred also began to feel that in this new atmosphere of ideas, of work, of accomplishment, she would rapidly develop into a different sort of person. It was extremely fortunate for her, thought she, that she was living with such a person as Cyrilla Brindley. In the old atmosphere, or with any taint of it, she would have been unable to become a serious person. She would simply have dawdled along, twaddling about "art" and seriousness and careers and sacrifice, content with the amateur's methods and the amateur's results—and deluding herself that she was making progress. Now—It was as different as public school from private school—public school where the mind is rudely stimulated, private school where it is sedulously mollycoddled. She had come out of the hothouse into the open.

At first she thought that Jennings was to be as great a help to her as Cyrilla Brindley. Certainly if ever there was a man with the air of a worker and a place with the air of a workshop, that man and that place were Eugene Jennings and his studio in Carnegie Hall. When Mildred entered, on that Saturday morning, at exactly half-past ten, Jennings—in a plain if elegant house-suit—looked at her, looked at the clock, stopped a girl in the midst of a burst of tremulous noisy melody.

"That will do, Miss Bristow," said he. "You have never sung it worse. You do not improve. Another lesson like this, and we shall go back and begin all over again."

The girl, a fattish, "temperamental" blonde, burst into tears.

"Kindly take that out into the hall," said Jennings coldly. "Your time is up. We cannot waste Miss Stevens's time with your hysterics."

Miss Bristow switched from tears to fury. "You brute! You beast!" she shrieked, and flung herself out of the room, slamming the door after her. Jennings took a book from a pile upon a table, opened it, and set it on a music-stand. Evidently Miss Bristow was forgotten—indeed, had passed out of his mind at half-past ten exactly, not to enter it again until she should appear at ten on Monday morning. He said to Mildred:

"Now, we'll see what you can do. Begin."

"I'm a little nervous," said Mildred with a shy laugh. "If you don't mind, I'd like to wait till I've got used to my surroundings."

Jennings looked at her. The long sharp nose seemed to be rapping her on the forehead like a woodpecker's beak on the bark of the tree. "Begin," he said, pointing to the book.

Mildred flushed angrily. "I shall not begin until I CAN begin," said she. The time to show this man that he could not treat her brutally was at the outset.

Jennings opened the door into the hall. "Good day, Miss Stevens," he said with his abrupt bow.

Mildred looked at him; he looked at her. Her lip trembled, the hot tears flooded and blinded her eyes. She went unsteadily to the music-stand and tried to see the notes of the exercises. Jennings closed the door and seated himself at the far end of the room. She began—a ridiculous attempt. She stopped, gritted her teeth, began again. Once more the result was absurd; but this time she was able to keep on, not improving, but maintaining her initial off-key quavering. She stopped.

"You see," said she. "Shall I go on?"

"Don't stop again until I tell you to, please," said he.

She staggered and stumbled and somersaulted through two pages of DO-RE-ME-FA-SOL-LA-SI. Then he held up his finger.

"Enough," said he.

Silence, an awful silence. She recalled what Mrs. Belloc had told her about him, what Mrs. Brindley had implied. But she got no consolation. She said timidly:

"Really, Mr. Jennings, I can do better than that. Won't you let me try a song?"

"God forbid!" said he. "You can't stand. You can't breathe. You can't open your mouth. Naturally, you can't sing."

She dropped to a chair.

"Take the book, and go over the same thing, sitting," said he.

She began to remove her wraps.

"Just as you are," he commanded. "Try to forget yourself. Try to forget me. Try to forget what a brute I am, and what a wonderful singer you are. Just open your mouth and throw the notes out."

She was rosy with rage. She was reckless. She sang. At the end of three pages he stopped her with an enthusiastic hand-clapping. "Good! Good!" he cried. "I'll take you. I'll make a singer of you. Yes, yes, there's something to work on."

The door opened. A tall, thin woman with many jewels and a superb fur wrap came gliding in. Jennings looked at the clock. The hands pointed to eleven. Said he to Mildred:

"Take that book with you. Practice what you've done to-day. Learn to keep your mouth open. We'll go into that further next time." He was holding the door open for her. As she passed out, she heard him say:

"Ah, Mrs. Roswell. We'll go at that third song first."

The door closed. Reviewing all that had occurred, Mildred decided that she must revise her opinion of Jennings. A money-maker he no doubt was. And why not? Did he not have to live? But a teacher also, and a great teacher. Had he not destroyed her vanity at one blow, demolished it?—yet without discouraging her. And he went straight to the bottom of things— very different from any of the teachers she used to have when she was posing in drawing-rooms as a person with a voice equal to the most difficult opera, if only she weren't a lady and therefore not forced to be a professional singing person. Yes, a great teacher—and in deadly earnest. He would permit no trifling! How she would have to work!

And she went to work with an energy she would not have believed she possessed. He instructed her minutely in how to stand, in how to breathe, in how to open her mouth and keep it open, in how to relax her throat and leave it relaxed. He filled every second of her half-hour; she had never before realized how much time half an hour was, how use could be made of every one of its eighteen hundred seconds. She went to hear other teachers give lessons, and she understood why Jennings could get such prices, could treat his pupils as he saw fit. She became an extravagant admirer of him as a teacher, thought him a genius, felt confident that he would make a great singer of her. With the second lesson she began to progress rapidly. In a few weeks she amazed herself. At last she was really singing. Not in a great way, but in the beginnings of a great way. Her voice had many times the power of her drawing-room days. Her notes were full and round, and came without an effort. Her former ideas of what constituted facial and vocal expression now seemed ridiculous to her. She was now singing without making those dreadful faces which she had once thought charming and necessary. Her lower register, always her best, was almost perfect. Her middle register—the test part of a voice—was showing signs of strength and steadiness and evenness. And she was fast getting a real upper register, as distinguished from the forced and shrieky high notes that pass as an upper register with most singers, even opera singers. After a month of this marvelous forward march, she sang for Mrs. Brindley—sang the same song she had essayed at their first meeting. When she finished, Mrs. Brindley said:

"Yes, you've done wonders. I've been noticing your improvement as you practiced. You certainly have a very different voice and method from those you had a month ago," and so on through about five minutes of critical and discriminating praise.

Mildred listened, wondering why her dissatisfaction, her irritation, increased as Mrs. Brindley praised on and on. Beyond question Cyrilla was sincere, and was saying even more than Mildred had hoped she would say. Yet— Mildred sat moodily measuring off octaves on the keyboard of the piano. If she had been looking at her friend's face she would have flared out in anger; for Cyrilla Brindley was taking advantage of her abstraction to observe her with friendly sympathy and sadness. Presently she concealed this candid expression and said:

"You are satisfied with your progress, aren't you, Miss Stevens?"

Mildred flared up angrily. "Certainly!" replied she. "How could I fail to be?"

Mrs. Brindley did not answer—perhaps because she thought no answer was needed or expected. But to Mildred her silence somehow seemed a denial.

"If you can only keep what you've got—and go on," said Mrs. Brindley.

"Oh, I shall, never fear," retorted Mildred.

"But I do fear," said Mrs. Brindley. "I think it's always well to fear until success is actually won. And then there's the awful fear of not being able to hold it."

After a moment's silence Mildred, who could not hide away resentment against one she liked, said: "Why aren't YOU satisfied, Mrs. Brindley?"

"But I am satisfied," protested Cyrilla. "Only it makes me afraid to see YOU so well satisfied. I've seen that often in people first starting, and it's always dangerous. You see, my dear, you've got a straight-away hundred miles to walk. Can't you see that it would be possible for you to become too much elated by the way you walked the first part of the first mile?"

"Why do you try to discourage me?" said Mildred.

Mrs. Brindley colored. "I do it because I want to save you from despair a little later," said she. "But that is foolish of me. I shall only irritate you against me. I'll not do it again. And please don't ask my opinion. If you do, I can't help showing exactly what I think."

"Then you don't think I've done well?" cried Mildred.

"Indeed you have," replied Cyrilla warmly.

"Then I don't understand. What DO you mean?"

"I'll tell you, and then I'll stop and you must not ask my opinion again. We live too close together to be able to afford to criticize each other. What I meant was this: You have done well the first part of the great task that's before you. If you had done it any less well, it would have been folly for you to go on."

"That is, what I've done doesn't amount to anything? Mr. Jennings doesn't agree with you."

"Doubtless he's right," said Mrs. Brindley. "At any rate, we all agree that you have shown that you have a voice."

She said this so simply and heartily that Mildred could not but be mollified. Mrs. Brindley changed the subject to the song Mildred had sung, and Mildred stopped puzzling over the mystery of what she had meant by her apparently enthusiastic words, which had yet diffused a chill atmosphere of doubt.

She was doing her scales so well that she became impatient of such "tiresome child's play." And presently Jennings gave her songs, and did not discourage her when she talked of roles, of getting seriously at what, after all, she intended to do. Then there came a week of vile weather, and Mildred caught a cold. She neglected it. Her voice left her. Her tonsils swelled. She had a bad attack of ulcerated sore throat. For nearly three weeks she could not take a single one of the lessons, which were, nevertheless, paid for. Jennings rebuked her sharply.

"A singer has no right to be sick," said he.

"You have a cold yourself," retorted she.

"But I am not a singer. I've nothing that interferes with my work."

"It's impossible not to take cold," said Mildred. "You are unreasonable with me."

He shrugged his shoulders. "Go get well," he said.

The sore throat finally yielded to the treatment of Dr. Hicks, the throat-specialist. His bill was seventy-five dollars. But while the swelling in the tonsils subsided it did not depart. She could take lessons again. Some days she sang as well as ever, and on those days Jennings was charming. Other days she sang atrociously, and Jennings treated her as if she were doing it deliberately. A third and worse state was that of the days when she in the same half-hour alternately sang well and badly. On those days Jennings acted like a lunatic. He raved up and down the studio, all but swearing at her. At first she was afraid of him—withered under his scorn, feared he would throw open his door and order her out and forbid her ever to enter again. But gradually she came to understand him—not enough to lose her fear of him altogether, but enough to lose the fear of his giving up so profitable a pupil.

The truth was that Jennings, like every man who succeeds at anything in this world, operated upon a system to which he rigidly adhered. He was a man of small talent and knowledge, but of great, persistence and not a little common sense. He had tried to be a singer, had failed because his voice was small and unreliable. He had adopted teaching singing as a means of getting a living. He had learned just enough about it to enable him to teach the technical elements—what is set down in the books. By observing other and older teachers he had got together a teaching system that was as good—and as bad—as any, and this he dubbed the Jennings Method and proceeded to exploit as the only one worth while. When that method was worked out and perfected, he ceased learning, ceased to give a thought to the professional side of his profession, just as most professional men do. He would have resented a suggestion or a new idea as an attack upon the Jennings Method. The overwhelming majority of the human race—indeed, all but a small handful—have this passion for stagnation, this ferocity against change. It is in large part due to laziness; for a new idea means work in learning it and in unlearning the old ideas that have been true until the unwelcome advent of the new. In part also this resistance to the new idea arises from a fear that the new idea, if tolerated, will put one out of business, will set him adrift without any means of support. The coachman hates the automobile, the hand-worker hates the machine, the orthodox preacher hates the heretic, the politician hates the reformer, the doctor hates the bacteriologist and the chemist, the old woman hates the new—all these in varying proportions according to the degree in which the iconoclast attacks laziness or livelihood. Finally we all hate any and all new ideas because they seem to imply that we, who have held the old ideas, have been ignorant and stupid in so doing. A new idea is an attack upon the vanity of everyone who has been a partisan of the old ideas and their established order.

Jennings, thoroughly human in thus closing his mind to all ideas about his profession, was equally human in that he had his mind and his senses opened full width to ideas on how to make more money. If there had been money in new ideas about teaching singing Jennings would not have closed to them. But the money was all in studying and learning how better to handle the women—they were all women who came to him for instruction. His common sense warned him at the outset that the obviously easygoing teacher would not long retain his pupils. On the other hand, he saw that the really severe teacher would not retain his pupils, either.

Who were these pupils? In the first place, they were all ignorant, for people who already know do not go to school to learn. They had the universal delusion that a teacher can teach. The fact is that a teacher is a well. Some wells are full, others almost dry. Some are so arranged that water cannot be got from them, others have attachments of various kinds, making the drawing of water more or less easy. But not from the best well with the latest pump attachment can one get a drink unless one does the drinking oneself. A teacher is rarely a well. The pupil must not only draw the water, but also drink it, must not only teach himself, but also learn what he teaches. Now we are all of us born thirsty for knowledge, and nearly all of us are born both capable of teaching ourselves and capable of learning what we teach, that is, of retaining and assimilating it. There is such a thing as artificially feeding the mind, just as there is such a thing as artificially feeding the body; but while everyone knows that artificial feeding of the body is a success only to a limited extent and for a brief period, everyone believes that the artificial feeding of the mind is not only the best method, but the only method. Nor does the discovery that the mind is simply the brain, is simply a part of the body, subject to the body's laws, seem materially to have lessened this fatuous delusion.

Some of Jennings's pupils—not more than two of the forty-odd were in genuine earnest; that is, those two were educating themselves to be professional singers, were determined so to be, had limited time and means and endless capacity for work. Others of the forty—about half-thought they were serious, though in fact the idea of a career was more or less hazy. They were simply taking lessons and toiling aimlessly along, not less aimlessly because they indulged in vague talk and vaguer thought about a career. The rest—the other half of the forty—were amusing themselves by taking singing lessons. It killed time, it gave them a feeling of doing something, it gave them a reputation of being serious people and not mere idlers, it gave them an excuse for neglecting the domestic duties which they regarded as degrading—probably because to do them well requires study and earnest, hard work. The Jennings singing lesson, at fifteen dollars a half-hour, was rather an expensive hypocrisy; but the women who used it as a cloak for idleness as utter as the mere yawners and bridgers and shoppers had rich husbands or fathers.

Thus it appears that the Jennings School was a perfect microcosm, as the scientists would say, of the human race—the serious very few, toiling more or less successfully toward a definite goal; the many, compelled to do something, and imagining themselves serious and purposeful as they toiled along toward nothing in particular but the next lesson—that is, the next day's appointed task; the utterly idle, fancying themselves busy and important when in truth they were simply a fraud and an expense.

Jennings got very little from the deeply and genuinely serious. One of them he taught free, taking promissory notes for the lessons. But he held on to them because when they finally did teach themselves to sing and arrived at fame, his would be part of the glory—and glory meant more and more pupils of the paying kinds. His large income came from the other two kinds of pupils, the larger part of it from the kind that had no seriousness in them. His problem was how to keep all these paying pupils and also keep his reputation as a teacher. In solving that problem he evolved a method that was the true Jennings's method. Not in all New York, filled as it is with people living and living well upon the manipulation of the weaknesses of their fellow beings—not in all New York was there an adroiter manipulator than Eugene Jennings. He was harsh to brutality when he saw fit to be so— or, rather, when he deemed it wise to be so. Yet never had he lost a paying pupil through his harshness. These were fashionable women—most delicate, sensitive ladies—at whom he swore. They wept, stayed on, advertised him as a "wonderful serious teacher who won't stand any nonsense and doesn't care a hang whether you stay or go—and he can teach absolutely anybody to sing!" He knew how to be gentle without seeming to be so; he knew how to flatter without uttering a single word that did not seem to be reluctant praise or savage criticism; he knew how to make a lady with a little voice work enough to make a showing that would spur her to keep on and on with him; he knew how to encourage a rich woman with no more song than a peacock until she would come to him three times a week for many years—and how he did make her pay for what he suffered in listening to the hideous squawkings and yelpings she inflicted upon him!

Did Jennings think himself a fraud? No more than the next human being who lives by fraud. Is there any trade or profession whose practitioners, in the bottom of their hearts, do not think they are living excusably and perhaps creditably? The Jennings theory was that he was a great teacher; that there were only a very few serious and worth-while seekers of the singing art; that in order to live and to teach these few, he had to receive the others; that, anyhow, singing was a fine art for anyone to have and taking singing lessons made the worst voice a little less bad—or, at the least, singing was splendid for the health. One of his favorite dicta was, "Every child should be taught singing—for its health, if for nothing else." And perhaps he was right! At any rate, he made his forty to fifty thousand a year—and on days when he had a succession of the noisy, tuneless squawkers, he felt that he more than earned every cent of it.

Mildred did not penetrate far into the secret of the money-making branch of the Jennings method. It was crude enough, too. But are not all the frauds that fool the human race crude? Human beings both cannot and will not look beneath surfaces. All Mildred learned was that Jennings did not give up paying pupils. She had not confidence enough in this discovery to put it to the test. She did not dare disobey him or shirk—even when she was most disposed to do so. But gradually she ceased from that intense application she had at first brought to her work. She kept up the forms. She learned her lessons. She did all that was asked. She seemed to be toiling as in the beginning. In reality, she became by the middle of spring a mere lesson-taker. Her interest in clothes and in going about revived. She saw in the newspapers that General Siddall had taken a party of friends on a yachting trip around the world, so she felt that she was no longer being searched for, at least not vigorously. She became acquainted with smart, rich West Side women, taking lessons at Jennings's. She amused herself going about with them and with the "musical" men they attracted—amateur and semi-professional singers and players upon instruments. She drew Mrs. Brindley into their society. They had little parties at the flat in Fifty-ninth Street—the most delightful little parties imaginable—dinners and suppers, music, clever conversations, flirtations of a harmless but fascinating kind. If anyone had accused Mildred of neglecting her work, of forgetting her career, she would have grown indignant, and if Mrs. Brindley had overheard, she would have been indignant for her. Mildred worked as much as ever. She was making excellent progress. She was doing all that could be done. It takes time to develop a voice, to make an opera-singer. Forcing is dangerous, when it is not downright useless.

In May—toward the end of the month—Stanley Baird returned. Mildred, who happened to be in unusually good voice that day, sang for him at the Jennings studio, and he was enchanted. As the last note died away he cried out to Jennings:

"She's a wonder, isn't she?"

Jennings nodded. "She's got a voice," said he.

"She ought to go on next year."

"Not quite that," said Jennings. "We want to get that upper register right first. And it's a young voice—she's very young for her age. We must be careful not to strain it."

"Why, what's a voice for if not to sing with?" said Stanley.

"A fine voice is a very delicate instrument," replied the teacher. He added coldly, "You must let me judge as to what shall be done."

"Certainly, certainly," said Stanley in haste.

"She's had several colds this winter and spring," pursued Jennings. "Those things are dangerous until the voice has its full growth. She should have two months' complete rest."

Jennings was going away for a two months' vacation. He was giving this advice to all his pupils.

"You're right," said Baird. "Did you hear, Mildred?"

"But I hate to stop work," objected Mildred. "I want to be doing something. I'm very impatient of this long wait."

And honest she was in this protest. She had no idea of the state of her own mind. She fancied she was still as eager as ever for the career, as intensely interested as ever in her work. She did not dream of the real meaning of her content with her voice as it was, of her lack of uneasiness over the appalling fact that such voice as she had was unreliable, came and went for no apparent reason.

"Absolute rest for two months," declared Jennings grimly. "Not a note until I return in August."

Mildred gave a resigned sigh.

There is much inveighing against hypocrisy, a vice unsightly rather than desperately wicked. And in the excitement about it its dangerous, even deadly near kinsman, self-deception, escapes unassailed. Seven cardinal sins; but what of the eighth?—the parent of all the others, the one beside which the children seem almost white?

During the first few weeks Mildred had been careful about spending money. Economy she did not understand; how could she, when she had never had a lesson in it or a valuable hint about it? So economy was impossible. The only way in which such people can keep order in their finances is by not spending any money at all. Mildred drew nothing, spent nothing. This, so long as she gave her whole mind to her work. But after the first great cold, so depressing, so subtly undermining, she began to go about, to think of, to need and to buy clothes, to spend money in a dozen necessary ways. After all, she was simply borrowing the money. Presently, she would be making a career, would be earning large sums. She would pay back everything, with interest. Stanley meant for her to use the money. Really, she ought to use it. How would her career be helped by her going about looking a dowd and a frump? She had always been used to the comforts of life. If she deprived herself of them, she would surely get into a frame of mind where her work would suffer. No, she must lead the normal life of a woman of her class. To work all the time—why, as Jennings said, that took away all the freshness, made one stale and unfit. A little distraction—always, of course, with musical people, people who talked and thought and did music—that sort of distraction was quite as much a part of her education as the singing lessons. Mrs. Brindley, certainly a sensible and serious woman if ever there was one—Mrs. Brindley believed so, and it must be so.

After that illness and before she began to go about, she had fallen into several fits of hideous blues, had been in despair as to the future. As soon as she saw something of people—always the valuable, musical sort of people—her spirits improved. And when she got a few new dresses—very simple and inexpensive, but stylish and charming—and the hats, too, were successful—as soon as she was freshly arrayed she was singing better and was talking hopefully of the career again. Yes, it was really necessary that she live as she had always been used to living.

When Stanley came back her account was drawn up to the last cent of the proportionate amount. In fact, it might have been a few dollars—a hundred or so—overdrawn. She was not sure. Still, that was a small matter. During the summer she would spend less, and by fall she would be far ahead again—and ready to buy fall clothes. One day he said:

"You must be needing more money."

"No indeed," cried she. "I've been living within the hundred a week—or nearly. I'm afraid I'm frightfully extravagant, and—"

"Extravagant?" laughed he. "You are afraid to borrow! Why, three or four nights of singing will pay back all you've borrowed."

"I suppose I WILL make a lot of money," said she. "They all tell me so. But it doesn't seem real to me." She hastily added: "I don't mean the career. That seems real enough. I can hardly wait to begin at the roles. I mean the money part. You see, I never earned any money and never really had any money of my own."

"Well, you'll have plenty of it in two or three years," said Stanley, confidently. "And you mustn't try to live like girls who've been brought up to hardship. It isn't necessary, and it would only unfit you for your work."

"I think that's true," said she. "But I've enough—more than enough." She gave him a nervous, shy, almost agonized look. "Please don't try to put me under any heavier obligations than I have to be."

"Please don't talk nonsense about obligation," retorted he. "Let's get away from this subject. You don't seem to realize that you're doing me a favor, that it's a privilege to be allowed to help develop such a marvelous voice as yours. Scores of people would jump at the chance."

"That doesn't lessen my obligation," said she. And she thought she meant it, though, in fact, his generous and plausible statement of the case had immediately lessened not a little her sense of obligation.

On the whole, however, she was not sorry she had this chance to talk of obligation. Slowly, as they saw each other from time to time, often alone, Stanley had begun—perhaps in spite of himself and unconsciously—to show his feeling for her. Sometimes his hand accidentally touched hers, and he did not draw it away as quickly as he might. And she—it was impossible for her to make any gesture, much less say anything, that suggested sensitiveness on her part. It would put him in an awkward position, would humiliate him most unjustly. He fell into the habit of holding her hand longer than was necessary at greeting or parting, of touching her caressingly, of looking at her with the eyes of a lover instead of a friend. She did not like these things. For some mysterious reason—from sheer perversity, she thought—she had taken a strong physical dislike to him. Perfectly absurd, for there was nothing intrinsically repellent about this handsome, clean, most attractively dressed man, of the best type of American and New-Yorker. No, only perversity could explain such a silly notion. She was always afraid he would try to take advantage of her delicate position—always afraid she would have to yield something, some trifle; yet the idea of giving anything from a sense of obligation was galling to her. His very refraining made her more nervous, the more shrinking. If he would only commit some overt act—seize her, kiss her, make outrageous demands—but this refraining, these touches that might be accidental and again might be stealthy approach— She hated to have him shake hands with her, would have liked to draw away when his clothing chanced to brush against hers.

So she was glad of the talk about obligation. It set him at a distance, immediately. He ceased to look lovingly, to indulge in the nerve-rasping little caresses. He became carefully formal. He was evidently eager to prove the sincerity of his protestations—too eager perhaps, her perverse mind suggested. Still, sincere or not, he held to all the forms of sincerity.

Some friends of Mrs. Brindley's who were going abroad offered her their cottage on the New Jersey coast near Seabright, and a big new touring-car and chauffeur. She and Mildred at once gave up the plan for a summer in the Adirondacks, the more readily as several of the men and women they saw the most of lived within easy distance of them at Deal Beach and Elberon. When Mildred went shopping she was lured into buying a lot of summer things she would not have needed in the Adirondacks—a mere matter of two hundred and fifty dollars or thereabouts. A little additional economy in the fall would soon make up for such a trifle, and if there is one time more than another when a woman wishes to look well and must look well, that time is summer—especially by the sea.

When her monthly statement from the bank came on the first of July she found that five thousand dollars had been deposited to her credit. She was moved by this discovery to devote several hours—very depressed hours they were—to her finances. She had spent a great deal more money than she had thought; indeed, since March she had been living at the rate of fifteen thousand a year. She tried to account for this amazing extravagance. But she could recall no expenditure that was not really almost, if not quite, necessary. It took a frightful lot of money to live in New York. How DID people with small incomes manage to get along? Whatever would have become of her if she had not had the good luck to be able to borrow from Stanley? What would become of her if, before she was succeeding on the stage, Stanley should die or lose faith in her or interest in her? What would become of her! She had been living these last few months among people who had wide-open eyes and knew everything that was going on—and did some "going-on" themselves, as she was now more than suspecting. There were many women, thousands of them—among the attractive, costily dressed throngs she saw in the carriages and autos and cabs—who would not like to have it published how they contrived to live so luxuriously. No, they would not like to have it published, though they cared not a fig for its being whispered; New York too thoroughly understood how necessary luxurious living was, and was too completely divested of the follies of the old-fashioned, straight-laced morality, to mind little shabby details of queer conduct in striving to keep up with the procession. Even the married women, using their husbands—and letting their husbands use them—did not frown on the irregularities of their sisters less fortunately married or not able to find a permanent "leg to pull." As for the girls—Mildred had observed strange things in the lives of the girls she knew more or less well nowadays. In fact, all the women, of all classes and conditions, were engaged in the same mad struggle to get hold of money to spend upon fun and finery—a struggle matching in recklessness and resoluteness the struggle of the men down-town for money for the same purposes. It was curious, this double mania of the men and the women—the mania to get money, no matter how; the instantly succeeding mania to get rid of it, no matter how. Looking about her, Mildred felt that she was peculiar and apart from nearly all the women she knew. SHE got her money honorably. SHE did not degrade herself, did not sell herself, did not wheedle or cajole or pretend in the least degree. She had grown more liberal as her outlook on life had widened with contact with the New York mind—no, with the mind of the whole easy-going, luxury-mad, morality-scorning modern world. She still kept her standard for herself high, and believed in a purity for herself which she did not exact or expect in her friends. In this respect she and Cyrilla Brindley were sympathetically alike. No, Mildred was confident that in no circumstances, in NO circumstances, would she relax her ideas of what she personally could do and could not do. Not that she blamed, or judged at all, women who did as she would not; but she could not, simply could not, however hard she might be driven, do those things—though she could easily understand how other women did them in preference to sinking down into the working class or eking out a frowsy existence in some poor boarding-house. The temptation would be great. Thank Heaven, it was not teasing her. She would resist it, of course. But—

What if Stanley Baird should lose interest? What if, after he lost interest, she should find herself without money, worse of than she had been when she sold herself into slavery—highly moral and conventionally correct slavery, but still slavery—to the little general with the peaked pink-silk nightcap hiding the absence of the removed toupee—and with the wonderful pink-silk pajamas, gorgeously monogramed in violet—and the tiny feet and ugly hands—and those loathsome needle-pointed mustaches and the hideous habit of mumbling his tongue and smacking his lips? What if, moneyless, she should not be able to find another Stanley or a man of the class gentleman willing to help her generously even on ANY terms? What then?

She was looking out over the sea, her bank-book and statements and canceled checks in her lap. Their cottage was at the very edge of the strand; its veranda was often damp from spray after a storm. It was not storming as she sat there, "taking stock"; under a blue sky an almost tranquil sea was crooning softly in the sunlight, innocent and happy and playful as a child. She, dressed in a charming negligee and looking forward to a merry day in the auto, with lunch and dinner at attractive, luxurious places farther down the coast—she was stricken with a horrible sadness, with a terror that made her heart beat wildly.

"I must be crazy!" she said, half aloud. "I've never earned a dollar with my voice. And for two months it has been unreliable. I'm acting like a crazy person. What WILL become of me?"

Just then Stanley Baird came through the pretty little house, seeking her. "There you are!" he cried. "Do go get dressed."

Hastily she flung a scarf over the book and papers in her lap. She had intended to speak to him about that fresh deposit of five thousand dollars—to refuse it, to rebuke him. Now she did not dare.

"What's the matter?" he went on. "Headache?"

"It was the wine at dinner last night," explained she. "I ought never to touch red wine. It disagrees with me horribly."

"That was filthy stuff," said he. "You must take some champagne at lunch. That'll set you right."

She stealthily wound the scarf about the papers. When she felt that all were secure she rose. She was looking sweet and sad and peculiarly beautiful. There was an exquisite sheen on her skin. She had washed her hair that morning, and it was straying fascinatingly about her brow and ears and neck. Baird looked at her, lowered his eyes and colored.

"I'll not be long," she said hurriedly.

She had to pass him in the rather narrow doorway. From her garments shook a delicious perfume. He caught her in his arms. The blood had flushed into his face in a torrent, swelling out the veins, giving him a distorted and wild expression.

"Mildred!" he cried. "Say that you love me a little! I'm so lonely for you—so hungry for you!"

She grew cold with fear and with repulsion. She neither yielded to his embrace nor shook it off. She simply stood, her round smooth body hard though corsetless. He kissed her on the throat, kissed the lace over her bosom, crying out inarticulately. In the frenzy of his passion he did not for a while realize her lack of response. As he felt it, his arms relaxed, dropped away from her, fell at his side. He hung his head. He was breathing so heavily that she glanced into the house apprehensively, fearing someone else might hear.

"I beg pardon," he muttered. "You were too much for me this morning. It was your fault. You are maddening!"

She moved on into the house.

"Wait a minute!" he called after her.

She halted, hesitating.

"Come back," he said. "I've got something to say to you."

She turned and went back to the veranda, he retreating before her and his eyes sinking before the cold, clear blue of hers.

"You're going up, not to come down again," he said. "You think I've insulted you—think I've acted outrageously."

How glad she was that he had so misread her thoughts—had not discovered the fear, the weakness, the sudden collapse of all her boasted confidence in her strength of character.

"You'll never feel the same toward me again," he went fatuously on. "You think I'm a fraud. Well, I'll admit that I am in love with you—have been ever since the steamer—always was crazy about that mouth of yours—and your figure, and the sound of your voice. I'll admit I'm an utter fool about you—respect you and trust you as I never used to think any woman deserved to be respected and trusted. I'll even admit that I've been hoping—all sorts of things. I knew a woman like you wouldn't let a man help her unless she loved him."

At this her heart beat wildly and a blush of shame poured over her face and neck. He did not see. He had not the courage to look at her—to face that expression of the violated goddess he felt confident her face was wearing. In love, he reasoned and felt about her like an inexperienced boy, all his experience going for nothing. He went on:

"I understand we can never be anything to each other until you're on the stage and arrived. I'd not have it otherwise, if I could. For I want YOU, and I'd never believe I had you unless you were free."

The color was fading from her cheeks. At this it flushed deeper than before. She must speak. Not to speak was to lie, was to play the hypocrite. Yet speak she dared not. At least Stanley Baird was better than Siddall. Anyhow, who was she, that had been the wife of Siddall, to be so finicky?

"You don't believe me?" he said miserably. "You think I'll forget myself sometime again?"

"I hope not," she said gently. "I believe not. I trust you, Stanley."

And she went into the house. He looked after her, in admiration of the sweet and pure calm of this quiet rebuke. She tried to take the same exalted view of it herself, but she could not fool herself just then with the familiar "good woman" fake. She knew that she had struck the flag of self-respect. She knew what she would really have done had he been less delicate, less in love, and more "practical." And she found a small and poor consolation in reflecting, "I wonder how many women there are who take high ground because it costs nothing." We are prone to suspect everybody of any weakness we find in ourselves—and perhaps we are not so far wrong as are those who accept without question the noisy protestations of a world of self-deceivers.

Thenceforth she and Stanley got on better than ever—apparently. But though she ignored it, she knew the truth—knew her new and deep content was due to her not having challenged his assertion that she loved him. He, believing her honest and high minded, assumed that the failure to challenge was a good woman's way of admitting. But with the day of reckoning—not only with him but also with her own self-respect—put off until that vague and remote time when she should be a successful prima donna, she gave herself up to enjoyment. That was a summer of rarely fine weather, particularly fine along the Jersey coast. They—always in gay parties— motored up and down the coast and inland. Several of the "musical" men—notably Richardson of Elberon—had plenty of money; Stanley, stopping with his cousins, the Frasers, on the Rumson Road, brought several of his friends, all rich and more or less free. As every moment of Mildred's day was full and as it was impossible not to sleep and sleep well in that ocean air, with the surf soothing the nerves as the lullaby of a nurse soothes a baby, she was able to put everything unpleasant out of mind. She was resting her voice, was building up her health; therefore the career was being steadily advanced and no time was being wasted. She felt sorry for those who had to do unpleasant or disagreeable things in making their careers. She told herself that she did not deserve her good fortune in being able to advance to a brilliant career not through hardship but over the most delightful road imaginable—amusing herself, wearing charming and satisfactory clothes, swimming and dancing, motoring and feasting. Without realizing it, she was strongly under the delusion that she was herself already rich—the inevitable delusion with a woman when she moves easily and freely and luxuriously about, never bothered for money, always in the company of rich people. The rich are fated to demoralize those around them. The stingy rich fill their satellites with envy and hatred. The generous rich fill them with the feeling that the light by which they shine and the heat with which they are warm are not reflected light and heat but their own.

Never had she been so happy. She even did not especially mind Donald Keith, a friend of Stanley's and of Mrs. Brindley's, who, much too often to suit her, made one of the party. She had tried in vain to discover what there was in Keith that inspired such intense liking in two people so widely different as expansive and emotional Stanley Baird and reserved and distinctly cold Cyrilla Brindley. Keith talked little, not only seemed not to listen well, but showed plainly, even in tete-a-tete conversations, that his thoughts had been elsewhere. He made no pretense of being other than he was—an indifferent man who came because it did not especially matter to him where he was. Sometimes his silence and his indifference annoyed Mildred; again—thanks to her profound and reckless contentment—she was able to forget that he was along. He seemed to be and probably was about forty years old. His head was beautifully shaped, the line of its profile—front, top, and back—being perfect in intellectuality, strength and symmetry. He was rather under the medium height, about the same height as Mildred herself. He was extremely thin and loosely built, and his clothes seemed to hang awry, giving him an air of slovenliness which became surprising when one noted how scrupulously neat and clean he was. His brown hair, considerably tinged with rusty gray, grew thinly upon that beautiful head. His skin was dry and smooth and dead white. This, taken with the classic regularity of his features, gave him an air of lifelessness, of one burnt out by the fire of too much living; but whether the living had been done by Keith himself or by his immediate ancestors appearances did not disclose. This look of passionless, motionless repose, like classic sculpture, was sharply and startlingly belied by a pair of really wonderful eyes—deeply and intensely blue, brilliant, all seeing, all comprehending, eyes that seemed never to sleep, seemed the ceaselessly industrious servants of a brain that busied itself without pause. The contrast between the dead white calm of his face, the listlessness of his relaxed figure, and these vivid eyes, so intensely alive, gave to Donald Keith's personality an uncanniness that was most disagreeable to Mildred.

"That's what fascinates me," said Cyrilla, when they were discussing him one day.

"Fascinates!" exclaimed Mildred. "He's tiresome—when he isn't rude."

"Rude?"

"Not actively rude but, worse still, passively rude."

"He is the only man I've ever seen with whom I could imagine myself falling in love," said Mrs. Brindley.

Mildred laughed in derision. "Why, he's a dead man!" cried she.

"You don't understand," said Cyrilla. "You've never lived with a man." She forgot completely, as did Mildred herself, so completely had Mrs. Siddall returned to the modes and thoughts of a girl. "At home—to live with—you want only reposeful things. That is why the Greeks, whose instincts were unerring, had so much reposeful statuary. One grows weary of agitating objects. They soon seem hysterical and shallow. The same thing's true of persons. For permanent love and friendship you want reposeful men—calm, strong, silent. The other kind either wear you out or wear themselves out with you."

"You forget his eyes," put in Stanley. "Did you ever see such eyes!"

"Yes, those eyes of his!" cried Mildred. "You certainly can't call them reposeful, Mrs. Brindley."

Mrs. Brindley did not seize the opportunity to convict her of inconsistency. Said she:

"I admit the eyes. They're the eyes of the kind of man a woman wants, or another man wants in his friend. When Keith looks at you, you feel that you are seeing the rarest being in the world—an absolutely reliable person. When I think of him I think of reliable, just as when you think of the sun you think of brightness."

"I had no idea it was so serious as this," teased Stanley.

"Nor had I," returned Cyrilla easily, "until I began to talk about him. Don't tell him, Mr. Baird, or he might take advantage of me."

The idea amused Stanley. "He doesn't care a rap about women," said he. "I hear he has let a few care about him from time to time, but he soon ceased to be good-natured. He hates to be bored."

As he came just then, they had to find another subject. Mildred observed him with more interest. She had learned to have respect for Mrs. Brindley's judgments. But she soon gave over watching him. That profound calm, those eyes concentrating all the life of the man like a burning glass— She had a disagreeable sense of being seen through, even to her secretest thought, of being understood and measured and weighed—and found wanting. It occurred to her for the first time that part of the reason for her not liking him was the best of reasons—that he did not like her.

The first time she was left alone with him, after this discovery, she happened to be in an audacious and talkative mood, and his lack of response finally goaded her into saying: "WHY don't you like me?" She cared nothing about it; she simply wished to hear what he would say—if he could be roused into saying anything. He was sitting on the steps leading from the veranda to the sea—was smoking a cigarette and gazing out over the waves like a graven image, as if he had always been posed there and always would be there, the embodiment of repose gazing in ineffable indifference upon the embodiment of its opposite. He made no answer.

"I asked you why you do not like me," said she. "Did you hear?"

"Yes," replied he.

She waited; nothing further from him. Said she:

"Well, give me one of your cigarettes."

He rose, extended his case, then a light. He was never remiss in those kinds of politeness. When she was smoking, he seated himself again and dropped into the former attitude. She eyed him, wondering how it could be possible that he had endured the incredible fatigues and hardships Stanley Baird had related of him—hunting and exploring expeditions into tropics and into frozen regions, mountain climbs, wild sea voyages in small boats, all with no sign of being able to stand anything, yet also with no sign of being any more disturbed than now in this seaside laziness. Stanley had showed them a picture of him taken twenty years and more ago when he was in college; he had looked almost the same then—perhaps a little older.

"Well, I am waiting," persisted she.

She thought he was about to look at her—a thing he had never done, to her knowledge, since they had known each other. She nerved herself to receive the shock, with a certain flutter of expectancy, of excitement even. But instead of looking, he settled himself in a slightly different position and fixed his gaze upon another point in the horizon. She noted that he had splendid hands—ideal hands for a man, with the same suggestion of intense vitality and aliveness that flashed from his eyes. She had not noted this before. Next she saw that he had good feet, and that his boots were his only article of apparel that fitted him, or rather, that looked as if made for him.

She tossed her cigarette over the rail to the sand. He startled her by speaking, in his unemotional way. He said:

"Now, I like you better."

"I don't understand," said she.

No answer from him. The cigarette depending listlessly from his lips seemed—as usual—uncertain whether it would stay or fall. She watched this uncertainty with a curious, nervous interest. She was always thinking that cigarette would fall, but it never did. Said she:

"Why did you say you liked me less?"

"Better," corrected he.

"We used to have a pump in our back yard at home," laughed she. "One toiled away at the handle, but nothing ever came. And it was a promising-looking pump, too."

He smiled—a slow, reluctant smile, but undeniably attractive. Said he:

"Because you threw away your cigarette."

"You object to women smoking?"

"No," said he. His tone made her feel how absurd it was to suspect him of such provincialism.

"You object to MY smoking?" suggested she; laughing, "Pump! Pump!"

"No," said he.

"Then your remark meant nothing at all?"

He was silent.

"You are rude," said she coldly, rising to go into the house.

He said something, what she did not hear, in her agitation. She paused and inquired:

"What did you say?"

"I said, I am not rude but kind," replied he.

"That is detestable!" cried she. "I have not liked you, but I have been polite to you because of Stanley and Mrs. Brindley. Why should you be insulting to me?"

"What have I done?" inquired he, unmoved. He had risen as she rose, but instead of facing her he was leaning against the post of the veranda, bent upon his seaward vigil.

"You have insinuated that your reasons for not liking me were a reflection on me."

"You insisted," said he.

"You mean that they are?" demanded she furiously. She was amazed at her wild, unaccountable rage.

He slowly turned his head and looked at her—a glance without any emotion whatever, simply a look that, like the beam of a powerful searchlight, seemed to thrust through fog and darkness and to light up everything in its path. Said he:

"Do you wish me to tell you why I don't like you?"

"No!" she cried hysterically. "Never mind—I don't know what I'm saying." And she went hastily into the house. A moment later, in her own room upstairs, she was wondering at herself. Why had she become confused? What did he mean? What had she seen—or half seen—in the darkness and fog within herself when he looked at her? In a passion she cried:

"If he would only stay away!"

VI

BUT he did not stay away. He owned and lived in a small house up on the Rumson Road. While the house was little more than a bungalow and had a simplicity that completely hid its rare good taste from the average observer, its grounds were the most spacious in that neighborhood of costly, showy houses set in grounds not much more extensive than a city building lot. The grounds had been cleared and drained to drive out and to keep out the obnoxious insect life, but had been left a forest, concealing the house from the roads. Stanley Baird was now stopping with Keith, and brought him along to the cottage by the sea every day.

The parties narrowed to the same four persons. Mrs. Brindley seemed never to tire of talking to Keith—or to tire of talking about him when the two men had left, late each night. As for Stanley, he referred everything to Keith—the weather prospects, where they should go for the day, what should be eaten and drunk, any point about politics or fashion, life or literature or what not, that happened to be discussed. And he looked upon Donald's monosyllabic reply to his inquiry as a final judgment, ending all possibility of argument. Mildred held out long. Then, in spite of herself, she began to yield, ceased to dislike him, found a kind of pleasure—or, perhaps, fascinated interest—in the nervousness his silent and indifferent presence caused her. She liked to watch that immobile, perfect profile, neither young nor old, indeed not suggesting age in any degree, but only experience and knowledge—and an infinite capacity for emotion, for passion even. The dead-white color declared it had already been lived; the brilliant, usually averted or veiled eyes asserted present vitality, pulsing under a calm surface.

One day when Stanley, in the manner of one who wishes a thing settled and settled right, said he would ask Donald Keith about it, Mildred, a little piqued, a little amused, retorted:

"And what will he answer? Why, simply yes or no."

"That's all," assented Stanley. "And that's quite enough, isn't it?"

"But how do you know he's as wise as he pretends?"

"He doesn't pretend to be anything or to know anything. That's precisely it."

Mildred suddenly began to like Keith. She had never thought of this before. Yes, it was true, he did not pretend. Not in the least, not about anything. When you saw him, you saw at once the worst there was to see. It was afterward that you discovered he was not slovenly, but clean and neat, not badly but well dressed, not homely but handsome, not sickly but soundly well, not physically weak but strong, not dull but vividly alive, not a tiresome void but an unfathomable mystery.

"What does he do?" she asked Mrs. Brindley.

Cyrilla's usually positive gray eyes looked vague. She smiled. "I never asked," said she. "I've known him nearly three years, and it never occurred to me to ask, or to wonder. Isn't that strange? Usually about the first inquiry we make is what a man does."

"I'll ask Stanley," said Mildred. And she did about an hour later, when they were in the surf together, with the other two out of earshot. Said Stanley:

"He's a lawyer, of course. Also, he's written a novel or two and a book of poems. I've never read them. Somehow, I never get around to reading."

"Oh, he's a lawyer? That's the way he makes his living."

"A queer kind of lawyer. He never goes to court, and his clients are almost all other lawyers. They go to him to get him to tell them what to do, and what not to do. He's got a big reputation among lawyers, Fred Norman tells me, but makes comparatively little, as he either can't or won't charge what he ought. I told him what Norman said, and he only smiled in that queer way he has. I said: 'You make twenty or thirty thousand a year. You ought to make ten times that.'"

"And what did he answer?" asked Mildred. "Nothing?"

"He said: 'I make all I want. If I took in more, I'd be bothered getting rid of it or investing it. I can always make all I'll want—unless I go crazy. And what could a crazy man do with money? It doesn't cost anything to live in a lunatic asylum.'"

Several items of interest to add to those she had collected. He could talk brilliantly, but he preferred silence. He could make himself attractive to women and to men, but he preferred to be detached. He could be a great lawyer, but he preferred the quiet of obscurity. He could be a rich man, but he preferred to be comparatively poor.

Said Mildred: "I suppose some woman—some disappointment in love—has killed ambition, and everything like that."

"I don't think so," replied Baird. "The men who knew him as a boy say he was always as he is now. He lived in the Arabian desert for two years."

"Why didn't he stay?" laughed Mildred. "That life would exactly suit him."

"It did," said Stanley. "But his father died, and he had to come home and support his mother—until she died. That's the way his whole life has been. He drifts in the current of circumstances. He might let himself be blown away to-morrow to the other end of the earth and stay away years—or never come back."

"But how would he live?"

"On his wits. And as well or as poorly as he cared. He's the sort of man everyone instinctively asks advice of—me, you, his valet, the farmer who meets him at a boundary fence, the fellow who sits nest him in a train—anyone."

Mildred did not merely cease to dislike him; she went farther, and rapidly. She began to like him, to circle round that tantalizing, indolent mystery as a deer about a queer bit of brush in the undergrowth. She liked to watch him. She was alternately afraid to talk before him and recklessly confidential—all with no response or sign of interest from him. If she was silent, when they were alone together, he was silent, too. If she talked, still he was silent. What WAS he thinking about? What did he think of her?—that especially.

"What ARE you thinking?" she interrupted herself to say one afternoon as they sat together on the strand under a big sunshade. She had been talking on and on about her career—talking conceitedly, as her subject intoxicated her—telling him what triumphs awaited her as soon as she should be ready to debut. As he did not answer, she repeated her question, adding:

"I knew you weren't listening to me, or I shouldn't have had the courage to say the foolish things I did."

"No, I wasn't," admitted he.

"Why not?"

"For the reason you gave."

"That what I said was—just talk?"

"Yes."

"You don't believe I'll do those things?"

"Do you?"

"I've GOT to believe it," said she. "If I didn't—" She came to a full stop.

"If you didn't, then what?" It was the first time he had ever flattered her with interest enough to ask her a question about herself.

"If I didn't believe I was going to succeed—and succeed big—" she began. After a pause, she added, "I'd not dare say it."

"Or think it," said he.

She colored. "What do you mean?" she asked.

He did not reply.

"What do you mean, Mr. Keith?" she urged.

"You are always asking me questions to which you already know the answer," said he.

"You're referring to a week or so ago, when I asked you why you disliked me?"

No answer. No sign of having heard. No outward sign of interest in anything, even in the cigarette drooping from the corner of his mouth.

"Wasn't that it?" she insisted.

"You are always asking me questions to which you already know the answer," repeated he.

"I am annoying you?"

No answer.

She laughed. "Do you want me to go away and leave you in peace with that—law case—or whatever it is?"

"I don't like to be alone."

"But anyone would do?—a dog?"

No reply.

"You mean, a dog would be better because it doesn't ask questions to which it knows the answer."

No reply.

"Well, I have a pleasant-sounding voice. As I'm saying nothing, it may be soothing—like the sound of the waves. I've learned to take you as you are. I rather like your pose."

No reply. No sign that he was even tempted to rise to this bait and protest.

"But you don't like mine," she went on. "Yes, it is a pose. But I've got to keep it up, and to pretend to myself that it isn't. And it isn't altogether. I shall be a successful singer."

"When?" said he. Actually he was listening!

She answered: "In—about two years, I think."

No comment.

"You don't believe it?"

"Do you?" A pause. "Why ask these questions you've already answered yourself?"

"I'll tell you why," replied she, her face suddenly flushed with earnestness. "Because I want you to help me. You help everyone else. Why not me?"

"You never asked me," said he.

"I didn't know I wanted it until just now—as I said it. But YOU must have known, because you are so much more experienced than I—and understand people—what's going on in their minds, deeper than they can see." Her tone became indignant, reproachful. "Yes, you must have known I needed your help. And you ought to have helped me, even if you did dislike me. You've no right to dislike anyone as young as I."

He was looking at her now, the intensely alive blue eyes sympathetic, penetrating, understanding. It was frightful to be so thoroughly understood—all one's weaknesses laid bare—yet it was a relief and a joy, too—like the cruel healing knife of the surgeon. Said he:

"I do not like kept women."

She gasped, grew ghastly. It was a frightful insult, one for which she was wholly unprepared. "You—believe—that?" she said slowly.

"Another of those questions," he said. And he looked calmly away, out over the sea, as if his interest in the conversation were at an end.

What should she say? How deny—how convince him? For convince him she must, and then go away and never permit him to speak to her again until he had apologized. She said quietly: "Mr. Keith, you have insulted me."

"I do not like kept women, either with or without a license," said he in the same even, indifferent way. "When you ceased to be a kept woman, I would help you, if I could. But no one can help a kept woman."

There was nothing to do but to rise and go away. She rose and went toward the house. At the veranda she paused. He had not moved. She returned. He was still inspecting the horizon, the cigarette depending from his lips—how DID he keep it alight? She said:

"Mr. Keith, I am sure you did not mean to insult me. What did you mean?"

"Another of those questions," said he.

"Honestly, I do not understand."

"Then think. And when you have thought, you will understand."

"But I have thought. I do not understand."

"Then it would be useless to explain," said he. "That is one of those vital things which, if one cannot understand them for oneself, one is hopeless—is beyond helping."

"You mean I am not in earnest about my career?"

"Another of those questions. If you had not seen clearly what I meant, you would have been really offended. You'd have gone away and not come back."

She saw that this was true. And, seeing, she wondered how she could have been so stupid as not to have seen it at once. She had yet to learn that overlooking the obvious is a universal human failing and that seeing the obvious is the talent and the use of the superior of earth—the few who dominate and determine the race.

"You reproach me for not having helped you," he went on. "How does it happen that you are uneasy in mind—so uneasy that you are quarreling at me?"

A light broke upon her. "You have been drawing me on, from the beginning," she cried. "You have been helping me—making me see that I needed help."

"No," said he. "I've been waiting to see whether you would rouse from your dream of grandeur."

"YOU have been rousing me."

"No," he said. "You've roused yourself. So you may be worth helping or, rather, worth encouraging, for no one can HELP you but yourself."

She looked at him pathetically. "But what shall I do?" she asked. "I've got no money, no experience, no sense. I'm a vain, luxury-loving fool, cursed with a—with a—is it a conscience?"

"I hope it's something more substantial. I hope it's common sense."

"But I have been working—honestly I have."

"Don't begin lying to yourself again."

"Don't be harsh with me."

He drew in his legs, in preparation for rising—no doubt to go away.

"I don't mean that," she cried testily. "You are not harsh with me. It's the truth that's harsh—the truth I'm beginning to see—and feel. I am afraid—afraid. I haven't the courage to face it."

"Why whine?" said he. "There's nothing in that."

"Do you think there's any hope for me?"

"That depends," said he.

"On what?"

"On what you want."

"I want to be a singer, a great singer."

"No, there's no hope."

She grew cold with despair. He had a way of saying a thing that gave it the full weight of a verdict from which there was no appeal.

"Now, if you wanted to make a living," he went on, "and if you were determined to learn to sing as well as you could, with the idea that you might be able to make a living—why, then there might be hope."

"You think I can sing?"

"I never heard you. Can you?"

"They say I can."

"What do YOU say?"

"I don't know," she confessed. "I've never been able to judge. Sometimes I think I'm singing well, and I find out afterward that I've sung badly. Again, it's the other way."

"Then, obviously, what's the first thing to do?"

"To learn to judge myself," said she. "I never thought of it before—how important that is. Do you know Jennings—Eugene Jennings?"

"The singing teacher? No."

"Is he a good teacher?"

"No."

"Why not?"

"Because he has not taught you that you will never sing until you are your own teacher. Because he has not taught you that singing is a small and minor part of a career as a singer."

"But it isn't," protested she.

A long silence. Looking at him, she felt that he had dismissed her and her affairs from his mind.

"Is it?" she said, to bring him back.

"What?" asked he vaguely.

"You said that a singer didn't have to be able to sing."

"Did I?" He glanced down the shore toward the house. "It feels like lunch-time." He rose.

"What did you mean by what you said?"

"When you have thought about your case a while longer, we'll talk of it again—if you wish. But until you've thought, talking is a waste of time."

She rose, stood staring out to sea. He was observing her, a faint smile about his lips. He said:

"Why bother about a career? After all, kept woman is a thoroughly respectable occupation—or can be made so by any preacher or justice of the peace. It's followed by many of our best women—those who pride themselves on their high characters—and on their pride."

"I could not belong to a man unless I cared for him," said she. "I tried it once. I shall never do it again."

"That sounds fine," said he. "Let's go to lunch."

"You don't believe me?"

"Do you?"

She sank down upon the sand and burst into a wild passion of sobs and tears. When her fight for self-control was over and she looked up to apologize for her pitiful exhibition of weakness—and to note whether she had made an impression upon his sympathies—she saw him just entering the house, a quarter of a mile away. To anger succeeded a mood of desperate forlornness. She fell upon herself with gloomy ferocity. She could not sing. She had no brains. She was taking money—a disgracefully large amount of money—from Stanley Baird under false pretenses. How could she hope to sing when her voice could not be relied upon? Was not her throat at that very moment slightly sore? Was it not always going queer? She—sing! Absurd. Did Stanley Baird suspect? Was he waiting for the time when she would gladly accept what she must have from him, on his own terms? No, not on his terms, but on the terms she herself would arrange— the only terms she could make. No, Stanley believed in her absolutely— believed in her career. When he discovered the truth, he would lose interest in her, would regard her as a poor, worthless creature, would be eager to rid himself of her. Instead of returning to the house, she went in the opposite direction, made a circuit and buried herself in the woods beyond the Shrewsbury. She was mad to get away from her own company; but the only company she could fly to was more depressing than the solitude and the taunt and sneer and lash of her own thoughts. It was late in the afternoon before she nerved herself to go home. She hoped the others would have gone off somewhere; but they were waiting for her, Stanley anxious and Cyrilla Brindley irritated. Her eyes sought Keith. He was, as usual, the indifferent spectator.

"Where have you been?" cried Stanley.

"Making up my mind," said she in the tone that forewarns of a storm.

A brief pause. She struggled in vain against an impulse to look at Keith. When her eyes turned in his direction he, not looking at her, moved in his listless way toward the door. Said he:

"The auto's waiting. Come on."

She vacillated, yielded, began to put on the wraps Stanley was collecting for her. It was a big touring-car, and they sat two and two, with the chauffeur alone. Keith was beside Mildred. When they were under way, she said:

"Why did you stop me? Perhaps I'll never have the courage again."

"Courage for what?" asked he.

"To take your advice, and break off."

"MY advice?"

"Yes, your advice."

"You have to clutch at and cling to somebody, don't you? You can't bear the idea of standing up by your own strength."

"You think I'm trying to fasten to you?" she said, with an angry laugh.

"I know it. You admitted it. You are not satisfied with the way things are going. You have doubts about your career. You shrink from your only comfortable alternative, if the career winks out. You ask me my opinion about yourself and about careers. I give it. Now, I find you asked only that you might have someone to lean on, to accuse of having got you into a mess, if doing what you think you ought to do turns out as badly as you fear."

It was the longest speech she had heard him make. She had no inclination to dispute his analysis of her motives. "I did not realize it," said she, "but that is probably so. But—remember how I was brought up."

"There's only one thing for you to do."

"Go back to my husband? You know—about me—don't you?"

"Yes"

"I can't go back to him."

"No."

"Then—what?" she asked.

"Go on, as now," replied he.

"You despise me, don't you?"

"No."

"But you said you did."

"Dislike and despise are not at all the same."

"You admit that you dislike me," cried she triumphantly. He did not answer.

"You think me a weak, clinging creature, not able to do anything but make pretenses."

No answer.

"Don't you?" she persisted.

"Probably I have about the same opinion of you that you have of yourself."

"What WILL become of me?" she said. Her face lighted up with an expression of reckless beauty. "If I could only get started I'd go to the devil, laughing and dancing—and taking a train with me."

"You ARE started," said he, with an amiable smile. "Keep on. But I doubt if you'll be so well amused as you may imagine. Going to the devil isn't as it's painted in novels by homely old maids and by men too timid to go out of nights. A few steps farther, and your disillusionment will begin. But there'll be no turning back. Already, you are almost too old to make a career."

"I'm only twenty-four. I flattered myself I looked still younger."

"It's worse than I thought," said he. "Most of the singers, even the second-rate ones, began at fifteen—began seriously. And you haven't begun yet."

"That's unjust," she protested. "I've done a little. Many great people would think it a great deal."

"You haven't begun yet," repeated he calmly. "You have spent a lot of money, and have done a lot of dreaming and talking and listening to compliments, and have taken a lot of lessons of an expensive charlatan. But what have those things to do with a career?"

"You've never heard me sing."

"I do not care for singing."

"Oh!" said she in a tone of relief. "Then you know nothing about all this."

"On the contrary, I know everything about a career. And we were talking of careers, not of singing."

"You mean that my voice is worthless because I haven't the other elements?"

"What else could I have meant?" said he. "You haven't the strength. You haven't the health."

She laughed as she straightened herself. "Do I look weak and sickly?" cried she.

"For the purposes of a career as a female you are strong and well," said he. "For the purpose of a career as a singer—" He smiled and shook his head. "A singer must have muscles like wire ropes, like a blacksmith or a washerwoman. The other day we were climbing a hill—a not very steep hill. You stopped five times for breath, and twice you sat down to rest."

She was literally hanging her head with shame. "I wasn't very well that day," she murmured.

"Don't deceive yourself," said he. "Don't indulge in the fatal folly of self-excuse."

"Go on," she said humbly. "I want to hear it all."

"Is your throat sore to-day?" pursued he.

She colored. "It's better," she murmured.

"A singer with sore throat!" mocked he. "You've had a slight fogginess of the voice all summer."

"It's this sea air," she eagerly protested. "It affects everyone."

"No self-excuse, please," interrupted he. "Cigarettes, champagne, all kinds of foolish food, an impaired digestion—that's the truth, and you know it."

"I've got splendid digestion! I can eat anything!" she cried. "Oh, you don't know the first thing about singing. You don't know about temperament, about art, about all the things that singing really means."

"We were talking of careers," said he. "A career means a person who can be relied upon to do what is demanded of him. A singer's career means a powerful body, perfect health, a sound digestion. Without them, the voice will not be reliable. What you need is not singing teachers, but teachers of athletics and of hygiene. To hear you talk about a career is like listening to a child. You think you can become a professional singer by paying money to a teacher. There are lawyers and doctors and business men in all lines who think that way about their professions—that learning a little routine of technical knowledge makes a lawyer or a doctor or a merchant or a financier."

"Tell me—WHAT ought I to learn?"

"Learn to think—and to persist. Learn to concentrate. Learn to make sacrifices. Learn to handle yourself as a great painter handles his brush and colors. Then perhaps you'll make a career as a singer. If not, it'll be a career as something or other."

She was watching him with a wistful, puzzled expression. "Could I ever do all that?"

"Anyone could, by working away at it every day. If you gain only one inch a day, in a year you'll have gained three hundred and sixty-five inches. And if you gain an inch a day for a while and hold it, you soon begin to gain a foot a day. But there's no need to worry about that." He was gazing at her now with an expression of animation that showed how feverishly alive he was behind that mask of calmness. "The day's work—that's the story of success. Do the day's work persistently, thoroughly, intelligently. Never mind about to-morrow. Thinking of it means dreaming or despairing—both futilities. Just the day's work."

"I begin to understand," she said thoughtfully. "You are right. I've done nothing. Oh, I've been a fool—more foolish even than I thought."

A long silence, then she said, somewhat embarrassed and in a low voice, though there was no danger of those in front of them hearing:

"I want you to know that there has been nothing wrong—between Stanley and me."

"Do you wish me to put that to your credit or to your discredit?" inquired he.

"What do you mean?"

"Why, you've just told me that you haven't given Stanley anything at all for his money—that you've cheated him outright. The thing itself is discreditable, but your tone suggests that you think I'll admire you for it."

"Do you mean to say that you'd think more highly of me if I were—what most women would be in the same circumstances?"

"I mean to say that I think the whole business is discreditable to both of you—to his intelligence, to your character."

"You are frank," said she, trying to hide her anger.

"I am frank," replied he, undisturbed. He looked at her. "Why should I not be?"

"You know that I need you, that I don't dare resent," said she. "So isn't it—a little cowardly?"

"Why do you need me? Not for money, for you know you'll not get that."

"I don't want it," cried she, agitated. "I never thought of it."

"Yes, you've probably thought of it," replied he coolly. "But you will not get it."

"Well, that's settled—I'll not get it."

"Then why do you need me? Of what use can I be to you? Only one use in the world. To tell you the truth—the exact truth. Is not that so?"

"Yes," she said. "That is what I want from you—what I can't get from anyone else. No one else knows the truth—not even Mrs. Brindley, though she's intelligent. I take back what I said about your being cowardly. Oh, you do stab my vanity so! You mustn't mind my crying out. I can't help it—at least, not till I get used to you."

"Cry out," said he. "It does no harm."

"How wonderfully you understand me!" exclaimed she. "That's why I let you say to me anything you please."

He was smiling peculiarly—a smile that somehow made her feel uncomfortable. She nerved herself for some still deeper stab into her vanity. He said, his gaze upon her and ironical:

"I'm sorry I can't return the compliment."

"What compliment?" asked she.

"Can't say that you understand me. Why do you think I am doing this?"

She colored. "Oh, no indeed, Mr. Keith," she protested, "I don't think you are in love with me—or anything of that sort. Indeed, I do not. I know you better than that."

"Really?" said he, amused. "Then you are not human."

"How can you think me so vain?" she protested.

"Because you are so," replied he. "You are as vain—no more so, but just as much so—as the average pretty and attractive woman brought up as you have been. You are not obsessed by the notion that your physical charms are all-powerful, and in that fact there is hope for you. But you attach entirely too much importance to them. You will find them a hindrance for a long time before they begin to be a help to you in your career. And they will always be a temptation to you to take the easy, stupid way of making a living—the only way open to most women that is not positively repulsive."

"I think it is the most repulsive," said Mildred.

"Don't cant," replied he, unimpressed. "It's not so repulsive to your sort of woman as manual labor—or as any kind of work that means no leisure, no luxury and small pay."

"I wonder," said Mildred. "I—I'm afraid you're right. But I WON'T admit it. I don't dare."

"That's the finest, truest thing I've ever heard you say," said Keith.

Mildred was pleased out of all proportion to the compliment. Said she with frank eagerness, "Then I'm not altogether hopeless?"

"As a character, no indeed," replied he. "But as a career— I was about to say, you may set your mind at rest. I shall never try to collect for my services. I am doing all this solely out of obstinacy."

"Obstinacy?" asked the puzzled girl.

"The impossible attracts me. That's why I've never been interested to make a career in law or politics or those things. I care only for the thing that can't be done. When I saw you and studied you, as I study every new thing, I decided that you could not possibly make a career."

"Why have you changed your mind?" she interrupted eagerly.

"I haven't," replied he. "If I had, I should have lost interest in you. Just as soon as you show signs of making a career, I shall lose interest in you. I have a friend, a doctor, who will take only cases where cure is impossible. Looking at you, it occurred to me that here was a chance to make an experiment more interesting than any of his. And as I have no other impossible task inviting me at present, I decided to undertake you—if you were willing."

"Why do you tell me this?" she asked. "To discourage me?"

"No. Your vanity will prevent that."

"Then why?"

"To clear myself of all responsibility for you. You understand—I bind myself to nothing. I am free to stop or to go on at any time."

"And I?" said Mildred.

"You must do exactly as I tell you."

"But that is not fair," cried she.

"Why not?" inquired he. "Without me you have no hope—none whatever."

"I don't believe that," declared she. "It is not true."

"Very well. Then we'll drop the business," said he tranquilly. "If the time comes when you see that I'm your only hope, and if then I'm in my present humor, we will go on."

And he lapsed into silence from which she soon gave over trying to rouse him. She thought of what he had said, studied him, but could make nothing of it. She let four days go by, days of increasing unrest and unhappiness. She could not account for herself. Donald Keith seemed to have cast a spell over her—an evil spell. Her throat gave her more and more trouble. She tried her voice, found that it had vanished. She examined herself in the glass, and saw or fancied that her looks were going—not so that others would note it, but in the subtle ways that give the first alarm to a woman who has beauty worth taking care of and thinks about it intelligently. She thought Mrs. Brindley was beginning to doubt her, suspected a covert uneasiness in Stanley. Her foundations, such as they were, seemed tottering and ready to disintegrate. She saw her own past with clear vision for the first time—saw how futile she had been, and why Keith believed there was no hope for her. She made desperate efforts to stop thinking about past and future, to absorb herself in present comfort and luxury and opportunities for enjoyment. But Keith was always there—and to see him was to lose all capacity for enjoyment. She was curt, almost rude to him—had some vague idea of forcing him to stay away. Yet every time she lost sight of him, she was in terror until she saw him again.

She was alone on the small veranda facing the high-road. She happened to glance toward the station; her gaze became fixed, her body rigid, for, coming leisurely and pompously toward the house, was General Siddall, in the full panoply of his wonderful tailoring and haberdashery. She thought of flight, but instantly knew that flight was useless; the little general was not there by accident. She waited, her rigidity giving her a deceptive seeming of calm and even ease. He entered the little yard, taking off his glossy hat and exposing the rampant toupee. He smiled at her so slightly that the angle of the needle-pointed mustaches and imperial was not changed. The cold, expressionless, fishy eyes simply looked at her.

"A delightful little house," said he, with a patronizing glance around. "May I sit down?"

She inclined her head.

"And you are looking well, charming," he went on, and he seated himself and carefully planted his neat boots side by side. "For the summer there's nothing equal to the seashore. You are surprised to see me?"

"I thought you were abroad," said Mildred.

"So I was—until yesterday. I came back because my men had found you. And I'm here because I venture to hope that you have had enough of this foolish escapade. I hope we can come to an understanding. I've lost my taste for wandering about. I wish to settle down—to have a home and to stay in it. By that I mean, of course, two or three—or possibly four— houses, according to the season." Mildred sent her glance darting about. The little general saw and began to talk more rapidly. "I've given considerable thought to our—our misunderstanding. I feel that I gave too much importance to your—your— I did not take your youth and inexperience of the world and of married life sufficiently into account. Also the first Mrs. Siddall was not a lady—nor the second. A lady, a young lady, was a new experience to me. I am a generous man. So I say frankly that I ought to have been more patient."

"You said you would never see me again until I came to you," said Mildred. As he was not looking at her, she watched his face. She now saw a change—behind the mask. But he went on in an unchanged voice:

"Were you aware that Mrs. Baird is about to sue her husband for a separation—not for a divorce but for a separation—and name you?"

Mildred dropped limply back in her chair.

"That means scandal," continued Siddall, "scandal touching my name—my honor. I may say, I do not believe what Mrs. Baird charges. My men have had you under observation for several weeks. Also, Mrs. Brindley is, I learn, a woman of the highest character. But the thing looks bad—you hiding from your husband, living under an assumed name, receiving the visits of a former admirer."

"You are mistaken," said Mildred. "Mrs. Baird would not bring such a false, wicked charge."

"You are innocent, my dear," said the general.

"You don't realize how your conduct looks. She intends to charge that her husband has been supporting you."

Mildred, quivering, started up, sank weakly back again.

"But," he went on, "you will easily prove that your money is your inheritance from your father. I assured myself of that before I consented to come here."

"Consented?" said Mildred. "At whose request?"

"That of my own generosity," replied he. "But my honor had to be reassured. When I was satisfied that you were innocent, and simply flighty and foolish, I came. If there had been any taint upon you, of course I could not have taken you back. As it is, I am willing—I may say, more than willing. Mrs. Baird can be bought off and frightened off. When she finds you have me to protect you, she will move very cautiously, you may be sure."

As the little man talked, Mildred saw and felt behind the mask the thoughts, the longings of his physical infatuation for her coiling and uncoiling and reaching tremulously out toward her like unclean, horrible tentacles. She was drawn as far as could be back into her chair, and her soul was shrinking within her body.

"I am willing to make you a proper allowance, and to give you all proper freedom," he went on. He showed his sharp white teeth in a gracious smile. "I realize I must concede something of my old-fashioned ideas to the modern spirit. I never thought I would, but I didn't appreciate how fond I was of you, my dear." He mumbled his tongue and noiselessly smacked his thin lips. "Yes, you are worth concessions and sacrifices."

"I am not going back," said Mildred. "Nothing you could offer me would make any difference." She felt suddenly calm and strong. She stood. "Please consider this final."

"But, my dear," said the general softly, though there was a wicked gleam behind the mask, "you forget the scandal—"

"I forget nothing," interrupted she. "I shall not go back."

Before he could attempt further to detain her she opened the screen door and entered. It closed on the spring and on the spring lock.

Donald Keith, coming in from the sea-front veranda, was just in time to save her from falling. She pushed him fiercely away and sank down on the sofa just within the pretty little drawing-room. She said:

"Thank you. I didn't mean to be rude. I was only angry with myself. I'm getting to be one of those absurd females who blubber and keel over."

"You're white and limp," said he. "What's the matter?"

"General Siddall is out there."

"Um—he's come back, has he?" said Keith.

"And I am afraid of him—horribly afraid of him."

"In some places and circumstances he would be a dangerous proposition," said Keith. "But not here in the East—and not to you."

"He would do ANYTHING. I don't know what he can do, but I am sure it will be frightful—will destroy me."

"You are going with him?"

She laughed. "I loathe him. I thought I left him through fear and anger. I was mistaken. It was loathing. And my fear of him—it's loathing, too."

"You mean that?" said Keith, observing her intently. "You wish to be rid of him?"

"What a poor opinion you have of me," said she. "Really, I don't deserve quite that."

"Then come with me."

The look of terror and shrinking returned. "Where? To see him?"

"For the last time," said Keith. "There'll be no scene."

It was the supreme test of her confidence in him. Without hesitation, she rose, preceded him into the hall, and advanced firmly toward the screen door through which the little general could be seen. He was standing at the top step, his back to them. At the sound of the opening door he turned.

"This is Mr. Donald Keith," said Mildred. "He wishes to speak to you."

The general bowed; Keith bent his head. They eyed each other with the measuring glance. Keith said in his dry, terse way: "I asked Miss Gower to come with me because I wish her to hear what I have to say to you."

"You mean my wife," said the general with a gracious smile.

"I mean Miss Gower," returned Keith. "As you know, she is not your wife."

Mildred uttered a cry; but the two men continued to look each at the other, with impassive countenances.

"Your only wife is the woman who has been in the private insane asylum of Doctor Rivers at Pueblo, Colorado, for the past eleven years. For about twenty years before that she was in the Delavan private asylum near Denver. You could not divorce her under the laws of Colorado. The divorce you got in Nevada was fraudulent."

"That's a lie," said the general coldly.

Keith went on, as if he had not heard: "You will not annoy this lady again. And you will stop bribing Stanley Baird's wife to make a fool of herself. And you will stop buying houses in the blocks where Baird owns real estate, and moving colored families into them."

"I tell you that about my divorce is a lie," replied Siddall.

"I can prove it," said Keith. "And I can prove that you knew it before you married your second wife."

For the first time Siddall betrayed at the surface a hint of how hard he was hit. His skin grew bright yellow; wrinkles round his eyes and round the base of his nose sprang into sudden prominence.

"I see you know what I mean—that attempt to falsify the record at Carson City," said Keith. He opened the screen door for Mildred to pass in. He followed her, and the door closed behind them. They went into the drawing-room. He dropped into an easy chair, crossed his legs, leaned his head back indolently—a favorite attitude of his.

"How long have you known?" said she. Her cheeks were flushed with excitement.

"Oh, a good many years," replied he. "It was one of those accidental bits of information a man runs across in knocking about. As soon as Baird told me about you, I had the thing looked up, quietly. I was going up to see him to-morrow—about the negroes and Mrs. Baird's suit."

"Does Stanley know?" inquired she.

"No," said Keith. "Not necessary. Never will be. If you like, you can have the marriage annulled without notoriety. But that's not necessary, either."

After a long silence, she said: "What does this make out of me?"

"You mean, what would be thought of you, if it were known?" inquired he. "Well, it probably wouldn't improve your social position."

"I am disgraced," said she, curiously rather than emotionally.

"Would be, if it were known," corrected he, "and if you are nothing but a woman without money looking for a husband. If you happened to be a singer or an actress, it would add to your reputation—make you more talked about."

"But I am not an actress or a singer."

"On the other hand, I should say you didn't amount to much socially. Except in Hanging Rock, of course—if there is still a Hanging Rock. Don't worry about your reputation. Fussing and fretting about your social position doesn't help toward a career."

"Naturally, you take it coolly. But you can hardly expect me to," cried she.

"You are taking it coolly," said he. "Then why try to work yourself up into a fit of hysterics? The thing is of no importance—except that you're free now—will never be bothered by Siddall again. You ought to thank me, and forget it. Don't be one of the little people who are forever agitating about trifles."

Trifles! To speak of such things as trifles! And yet— Well, what did they actually amount to in her life? "Yes, I AM free," she said thoughtfully. "I've got what I wanted—got it in the easiest way possible."

"That's better," said he approvingly.

"And I've burnt my bridges behind me," pursued she. "There's nothing for me now but to go ahead."

"Which road?" inquired he carelessly.

"The career," cried she. "There's no other for me. Of course I COULD marry Stanley, when he's free, as he would be before very long, if I suggested it. Yes, I could marry him."

"Could you?" observed he.

"Doesn't he love me?"

"Undoubtedly."

"Then why do you say he would not marry me?" demanded she.

"Did I say that?"

"You insinuated it. You suggested that there was a doubt."

"Then, there is no doubt?"

"Yes, there is," she cried angrily. "You won't let me enjoy the least bit of a delusion. He might marry me if I were famous. But as I am now— He's an inbred snob. He can't help it. He simply couldn't marry a woman in my position. But you're overlooking one thing—that *I* would not marry HIM."

"That's unimportant, if true," said Keith.

"You don't believe it?"

"I don't care anything about it, my dear lady," said Keith. "Have you got time to waste in thinking about how much I am in love with you? What a womanly woman you are, to be sure. Your true woman, you know, never thinks of anything but love—not how much she loves, but how much she is loved."

"Be careful!" she warned. "Some day you'll go too far in saying outrageous things to me."

"And then?" said he smilingly.

"You care nothing for our friendship?"

"The experiment is the only interest I have in you," replied he.

"That is not true," said she. "You have always liked me. That's why you looked up my hus— General Siddall and got ready for him. That's why you saved me to-day. You are a very tender-hearted and generous man—and you hide it as you do everything else about yourself."

He was looking off into space from the depths of the easy chair, a mocking smile on his classical, impassive face.

"What puzzles me," she went on, "is why you interest yourself in as vain and shallow and vacillating a woman as I am. You don't care for my looks—and that's all there is to me."

"Don't pause to be contradicted," said he.

She was in a fine humor now. "You might at least have said I was up to the female average, for I am. What have they got to offer a man but their looks? Do you know why I despise men?"

"Do you?"

"I do. And it's because they put up with women as much as they do—spend so much money on them, listen to their chatter, admire their ridiculous clothes. Oh, I understand why. I've learned that. And I can imagine myself putting up with anything in some one man I happened to fancy strongly. But men are foolish about the whole sex—or all of them that have a shadow of a claim to good looks."

"Yes, the men make fools of themselves," admitted he. "But I notice that the men manage somehow to make the careers, and hold on to the money and the power, while the women have to wheedle and fawn and submit in order to get what they want from the men. There's nothing to be said for your sex. It's been hopelessly corrupted by mine. For all the talk about the influence of woman, what impression has your sex made upon mine? And your sex—it has been made by mine into exactly what we wished it to be. Take my advice, get out of your sex. Abandon it, and make a career."

After a while she recalled with a start the events of less than an hour ago—events that ought to have seemed wildly exciting, arousing the deepest and strongest emotions. Yet they had made no impression upon her. Absolutely none. She had no horror in the thought that she had been the victim of a bigamist; she had no elation over her release into freedom and safety. She wondered whether this arose from utter frivolousness or from indifference to the trifles of conventional joys, sorrows, agitations, excitements which are the whole life of most people—that indifference which is the cause of the general opinion that men and women who make careers are usually hardened in the process.

As she lay awake that night—she had got a very bad habit of lying awake hour after hour—she suddenly came to a decision. But she did not tell Keith for several days. She did it in this way:

"Don't you think I'm looking better?" she asked.

"You're sleeping again," said he.

"Do you know why? Because my mind's at rest. I've decided to accept your offer."

"And my terms?" said he, apparently not interested by her announcement.

"And your terms," assented she. "You are free to stop whenever the whim strikes you; I must do exactly as you bid. What do you wish me to do?"

"Nothing at present," replied he. "I will let you know."

She was disappointed. She had assumed that something—something new and interesting, probably irritating, perhaps enraging, would occur at once. His indifference, his putting off to a future time, which his manner made seem most hazily indefinite, gave her the foolish and collapsing sense of having broken through an open door.

VII

THE first of September they went up to town. Stanley left at once for his annual shooting trip; Donald Keith disappeared, saying—as was his habit—neither what he was about nor when he would be seen again. Mrs. Brindley summoned her pupils and her musical friends. Mildred resumed the lessons with Jennings. There was no doubt about it, she had astonishingly improved during the summer. There had come—or, rather, had come back—into her voice the birdlike quality, free, joyous, spontaneous, that had not been there since her father's death and the family's downfall. She was glad that her arrangement with Donald Keith was of such a nature that she was really not bound to go on with it—if he should ever come back and remind her of what she had said. Now that Jennings was enthusiastic—giving just and deserved praise, as her own ear and Mrs. Brindley assured her, she was angry at herself for having tolerated Keith's frankness, his insolence, his insulting and contemptuous denials of her ability. She was impatient to see him, that she might put him down. She said to Jennings:

"You think I can make a career?"

"There isn't a doubt in my mind now," replied he. "You ought to be one of the few great lyric sopranos within five years."

"A man, this summer—a really unusual man in some ways—told me there was no hope for me."

"A singing teacher?"

"No, a lawyer. A Mr. Keith—Donald Keith."

"I've heard of him," said Jennings. "His mother was Rivi, the famous coloratura of twenty years ago."

Mildred was astounded. "He must know something about music."

"Probably," replied Jennings. "He lived with her in Italy, I believe, until he was almost grown. Then she died. You sang for him?"

"No," Mildred said it hesitatingly.

"Oh!" said Jennings, and his expression—interested, disturbed, puzzled—made Mildred understand why she had been so reluctant to confess. Jennings did not pursue the subject, but abruptly began the lesson. That day and several days thereafter he put her to tests he had never used before. She saw that he was searching for something—for the flaw implied in the adverse verdict of the son of Lucia Rivi. She was enormously relieved when he gave over the search without having found the flaw. She felt that Donald Keith's verdict had been proved false or at least faulty. Yet she was not wholly reassured, and from time to time she suspected that Jennings had not been, either.

Soon the gayety of the preceding winter and spring was in full swing again. Keith did not return, did not write, and Cyrilla Brindley inquired and telephoned in vain. Mildred worked with enthusiasm, with hope, presently with confidence. She hoped every day that Keith would come; she would make him listen to her, force him to admit. She caught a slight cold, neglected it, tried to sing it away. Her voice left her abruptly. She went to Jennings as usual the day she found herself able to do nothing more musical than squeak. She told him her plight. Said he:

"Begin! Let's hear."

She made a few dismal attempts, stopped short, and, half laughing, half ashamed, faced him for the lecture she knew would be forthcoming. Now, it so happened that Jennings was in a frightful humor that day—one of those humors in which the most prudent lose their self-control. He had been listening to a succession of new pupils—women with money and no voice, women who screeched and screamed and thoroughly enjoyed themselves and angled confidently for compliments. As Jennings had an acute musical ear, his sufferings had been frightful. He was used to these torments, had the habit of turning the fury into which they put him into excellent financial or disciplinary account. But on this particular day his nerves went to pieces, and it was with Mildred that the explosion came. When she looked at him, she was horrified to see a face distorted and discolored by sheer rage.

"You fool!" he shouted, storming up and down. "You fool! You can't sing! Keith was right. You wouldn't do even for a church choir. You can't be relied on. There's nothing behind your voice—no strength, no endurance, no brains. No brains! Do you hear?—no brains, I say!"

Mildred was terrified. She had seen him in tantrums before, but always there had been a judicious reserving of part of the truth. Instead of resenting, instead of flashing eye or quivering lips, Mildred sat down and with white face and dazed eyes stared straight before her. Jennings raved and roared himself out. As he came to his senses from this debauch of truth-telling his first thought was how expensive it might be. Thus, long before there was any outward sign that the storm had passed, the ravings, the insults were shrewdly tempered with qualifyings. If she kept on catching these colds, if she did not obey his instructions, she might put off her debut for years—for three years, for two years at least. And she would always be rowing with managers and irritating the public—and so on and on. But the mischief had been done. The girl did not rouse.

"No use to go on to-day," he said gruffly—the pretense at last rumblings of an expiring storm.

"Nor any other day," said Mildred.

She stood and straightened herself. Her face was beautiful rather than lovely. Its pallor, its strong lines, the melancholy intensity of the eyes, made her seem more the woman fully developed, less, far less, the maturing girl.

"Nonsense!" scolded Jennings. "But no more colds like that. They impair the quality of the voice."

"I have no voice," said the girl. "I see the truth."

Jennings was inwardly cursing his insane temper. In about the kindliest tone he had ever used with her, he said: "My dear Miss Stevens, you are in no condition to judge to-day. Come back to-morrow. Do something for that cold to-night. Clear out the throat—and come back to-morrow. You will see."

"Yes, I know those tricks," said she, with a sad little smile. "You can make a crow seem to sing. But you told me the truth."

"To-morrow," he cried pleasantly, giving her an encouraging pat on the shoulder. He knew the folly of talking too much, the danger of confirming her fears by pretending to make light of them. "A good sleep, and to-morrow things will look brighter."

He did not like her expression. It was not the one he was used to seeing in those vain, "temperamental" pupils of his—the downcast vanity that will be up again in a few hours. It was rather the expression of one who has been finally and forever disillusioned.

On her way home she stopped to send Keith a telegram: "I must see you at once."

There were several at the apartment for tea, among them Cullan, an amateur violinist and critic on music whom she especially liked. For, instead of the dreamy, romantic character his large brown eyes and sensitive features suggested, he revealed in talk and actions a boyish gayety—free, be it said, from boyish silliness—that was most infectious. His was one of those souls that put us in the mood to laugh at all seriousness, to forget all else in the supreme fact of the reality of existence. He made her forget that day—forget until Keith's answering telegram interrupted: "Next Monday afternoon."

A week less a day away! She shrank and trembled at the prospect of relying upon herself alone for six long days. Every prop had been taken away from her. Even the dubious prop of the strange, unsatisfactory Keith. For had he not failed her? She had said, "must" and "at once"; and he had responded with three words of curt refusal.

After dinner Stanley unexpectedly appeared. He hardly waited for the necessary formalities of the greeting before he said to Mrs. Brindley: "I want to see Mildred alone. I know you won't mind, Mrs. Brindley. It's very important." He laughed nervously but cheerfully. "And in a few minutes I'll call you in. I think I'll have something interesting to tell you."

Mrs. Brindley laughed. With her cigarette in one hand and her cup of after-dinner coffee in the other, she moved toward the door, saying gayly to Mildred:

"I'll be in the next room. If you scream I shall hear. So don't be alarmed."

Stanley closed the door, turned beaming upon Mildred. Said he: "Here's my news. My missus has got her divorce."

Mildred started up.

"Yes, the real thing," he assured her. "Of course I knew what was doing. But I kept mum—didn't want to say anything to you till I could say everything. Mildred, I'm free. We can be married to-morrow, if you will."

"Then you know about me?" said she, confused.

"On the way I stopped in to see Keith. He told me about that skunk—told me you were free, too."

Mildred slowly sat down. Her elbows rested upon the table. There was her bare forearm, slender and round, and her long, graceful fingers lay against her cheek. The light from above reflected charmingly from the soft waves and curves of her hair. "You're lovely—simply lovely!" cried Stanley. "Mildred—darling—you WILL marry me, won't you? You can go right on with the career, if you like. In fact, I'd rather you would, for I'm frightfully proud of your voice. And I've changed a lot since I became sincerely interested in you. The other sort of life and people don't amuse me any more. Mildred, say you'll marry me. I'll make you as happy as the days are long."

She moved slightly. Her hand dropped to the table.

"I guess I came down on you too suddenly," said he. "You look a bit dazed."

"No, I'm not dazed," replied she.

"I'll call Mrs. Brindley in, and we'll all three talk it over."

"Please don't," said she. "I've got to think it out for myself."

"I know there isn't anyone else," he went on. "So, I'm sure—dead sure, Mildred, that I can teach you to love me."

She looked at him pleadingly. "I don't have to answer right away?"

"Certainly not," laughed he. "But why shouldn't you? What is there against our getting married? Nothing. And everything for it. Our marriage will straighten out all the—the little difficulties, and you can go ahead with the singing and not bother about money, or what people might say, or any of those things."

"I—I've got to think about it, Stanley," she said gently. "I want to do the decent thing by you and by myself."

"You're afraid I'll interfere in the career—won't want you to go on? Mildred, I swear I'm—"

"It isn't that," she interrupted, her color high. "The truth is—" she faltered, came to a full stop—cried, "Oh, I can't talk about it to-night."

"To-morrow?" he suggested.

"I—don't know," she stammered. "Perhaps to-morrow. But it may be two or three days."

Stanley looked crestfallen. "That hurts, Mildred," he said. "I was SO full of it, so anxious to be entirely happy, and I thought you'd fall right in with it. Something to do with money? You're horribly sensitive about money, dear. I like that in you, of course. Not many women would have been as square, would have taken as little—and worked hard—and thought and cared about nothing but making good— By Jove, it's no wonder I'm stark crazy about YOU!"

She was flushed and trembling. "Don't," she pleaded. "You're beating me down into the dust. I—I'm—" She started up. "I can't talk to-night. I might say things I'd be— I can't talk about it. I must—"

She pressed her lips together and fled through the hall to her own room, to shut and lock herself in. He stared in amazement. When he heard the distant sound of the turning key he dropped to a chair again and laughed. Certainly women were queer creatures—always doing what one didn't expect. Still, in the end—well, a sensible woman knew a good chance to marry and took it. There was no doubt a good deal of pretense in Mildred's delicacy as to money matters—but a devilish creditable sort of pretense. He liked the ladylike, "nice" pretenses, of women of the right sort—liked them when they fooled him, liked them when they only half fooled him.

Presently he knocked on the door of the little library, opened it when permission came in Cyrilla's voice. She was reading the evening paper—he did not see the glasses she hastily thrust into a drawer. In that soft light she looked a scant thirty, handsome, but for his taste too intellectual of type to be attractive—except as a friend.

"Well," said he, as he lit a cigarette and dropped the match into the big copper ash-bowl, "I'll bet you can't guess what I've been up to."

"Making love to Miss Stevens," replied she. "And very foolish it is of you. She's got a steady head in that way."

"You're mighty right," said he heartily. "And I admire her for that more than for anything else. I'd trust her anywhere."

"You're paying yourself a high compliment," laughed Cyrilla.

"How's that?" inquired he. "You're too subtle for me. I'm a bit slow."

Mrs. Brindley decided against explaining. It was not wise to risk raising an unjust doubt in the mind of a man who fancied that a woman who resisted him would be adamant to every other man. "Then I've got to guess again?" said she.

"I've been asking her to marry me," said Stanley, who could contain it no longer. "Mrs. B. was released from me to-day by the court in Providence."

"But SHE'S not free," said Cyrilla, a little severely.

Stanley looked confused, finally said: "Yes, she is. It's a queer story. Don't say anything. I can't explain. I know I can trust you to keep a close mouth."

"Minding my own business is my one supreme talent," said Cyrilla.

"She hasn't accepted me—in so many words," pursued Baird, "but I've hopes that it'll come out all right."

"Naturally," commented Cyrilla dryly.

"I know I'm not—not objectionable to her. And how I do love her!" He settled himself at his ease. "I can't believe it's really me. I never thought I'd marry—just for love. Did you?"

"You're very self-indulgent," said Cyrilla.

"You mean I'm marrying her because I can't get her any other way. There's where you're wrong, Mrs. Brindley. I'm marrying her because I don't want her any other way. That's why I know it's love. I didn't think I was capable of it. Of course, I've been rather strong after the ladies all my life. You know how it is with men."

"I do," said Mrs. Brindley.

"No, you don't either," retorted he. "You're one of those cold, stand-me-off women who can't comprehend the nature of man."

"As you please," said she. In her eyes there was a gleam that more than suggested a possibility of some man—some man she might fancy—seeing an amazingly different Cyrilla Brindley.

"I may say I was daft about pretty women," continued Baird. "I never read an item about a pretty woman in the papers, or saw a picture of a pretty woman that I didn't wish I knew her—well. Can you imagine that?" laughed he.

"Commonplace," said Cyrilla. "All men are so. That's why the papers always describe the woman as pretty and why the pictures are published."

"Really? Yes, I suppose so." Baird looked chagrined. "Anyhow, here I am, all for one woman. And why? I can't explain it to myself. She's pretty, lovely, entrancing sometimes. She has charm, grace, sweetness. She dresses well and carries herself with a kind of sweet haughtiness. She looks as if she knew a lot—and nothing bad. Do you know, I can't imagine her having been married to that beast! I've tried to imagine it. I simply can't."

"I shouldn't try if I were you," said Mrs. Brindley.

"But I was talking about why I love her. Does this bore you?"

"A little," laughed Cyrilla. "I'd rather hear some man talking about MY charms. But go on. You are amusing, in a way."

"I'll wager I am. You never thought I'd be caught? I believed I was immune—vaccinated against it. I thought I knew all the tricks and turns of the sex. Yet here I am!"

"What do you think caught you?"

"That's the mystery. It's simply that I can't do without her. Everything she looks and says and does interests me more than anything else in the world. And when I'm not with her I'm wishing I were and wondering how she's looking or what she's saying or doing. You don't think she'll refuse me?" This last with real anxiety.

"I haven't an idea," replied Mrs. Brindley. "She's—peculiar. In some moods she would. In others, she couldn't. And I've never been able to settle to my satisfaction which kind of mood was the real Mary Stevens."

"She IS queer, isn't she?" said Stanley thoughtfully. "But I've told her she'd be free to go on with the career. Fact is, I want her to do it."

Mrs. Brindley's eyes twinkled. "You think it would justify you to your set in marrying her, if she made a great hit?"

Stanley blushed ingenuously. "I'll not deny that has something to do with it," he admitted. "And why not?"

"Why not, indeed?" said she. "But, after she had made the hit, you'd want her to quit the stage and take her place in society. Isn't that so?"

"You ARE a keen one," exclaimed he admiringly. "But I didn't say that to her. And you won't, will you?"

"It's hardly necessary to ask that," said Mrs. Brindley. "Now, suppose— You don't mind my talking about this?"

"What I want," replied he. "I can't talk or think anything but her."

"Now, suppose she shouldn't make a hit. Suppose she should fail— should not develop reliable voice enough?"

Stanley looked frightened. "But she can't fail," he cried with over-energy. "There's no question about her voice."

"I understand," Mrs. Brindley hastened to say. "I was simply making conversation with her as the subject."

"Oh, I see." Stanley settled back.

"Suppose she should prove not to be a great artist—what then?" persisted Cyrilla, who was deeply interested in the intricate obscure problem of what people really thought as distinguished from what they professed and also from what they imagined they thought.

"The fact that she's a great artist—that's part of her," said Baird. "If she weren't a great singer, she wouldn't be she—don't you see?"

"Yes, I see," said Mrs. Brindley with an ironic sadness which she indulged openly because there was no danger of his understanding.

"I don't exactly love her because she amounts to a lot—or is sure to," pursued he, vaguely dissatisfied with himself. "It's just as she doesn't care for me because I've got the means to take care of her right, yet that's part of me—and she'd not be able to marry me if I hadn't. Don't you see?"

"Yes, I see," said Mrs. Brindley with more irony and less sadness. "There's always SOME reason beside love."

"I'd say there's always some reason FOR love," said Baird, and he felt that he had said something brilliant—as is the habit of people of sluggish mentality when they say a thing they do not themselves understand. "You don't doubt that I love her?" he went on. "Why should I ask her to marry me if I didn't?"

"I suppose that settles it," said Cyrilla.

"Of course it does," declared he.

For an hour he sat there, talking on, most of it a pretty dull kind of drivel. Mrs. Brindley listened patiently, because she liked him and because she had nothing else to do until bedtime. At last he rose with a long sigh and said:

"I guess I might as well be going."

"She'll not come in to-night again," said Cyrilla slyly.

He laughed. "You are a good one. I'll own up, I've been staying on partly in the hope that she'd come back. But it's been a great joy to talk to you about her. I know you love her, too."

"Yes, I'm extremely fond of her," said she. "I've not known many women—many people without petty mean tricks. She's one."

"Isn't she, though?" exclaimed he.

"I don't mean she's perfect," said Mrs. Brindley. "I don't even mean that she's as angelic as you think her. I'd not like her, if she were. But she's a superior kind of human."

She was tired of him now, and got him out speedily. As she closed the front door upon him, Mildred's door, down the hall, opened. Her head appeared, an inquiring look upon her face. Mrs. Brindley nodded. Mildred, her hair done close to her head, a dressing-robe over her nightgown and her bare feet in little slippers, came down the hall. She coiled herself up in a big chair in the library and lit a cigarette. She looked like a handsome young boy.

"He told you?" she said to Mrs. Brindley.

"Yes," replied Cyrilla.

Silence. In all their intimate acquaintance there had never been an approach to the confidential on either side. It was Cyrilla's notion that confidences were a mistake, and that the more closely people were thrown together the more resolutely they ought to keep certain barriers between them. She and Mildred got on too admirably, liked each other too well, for there to be any trifling with their relations—and over-intimacy inevitably led to trifling. Mildred had restrained herself because Mrs. Brindley had compelled it by rigid example. Often she had longed to talk things over, to ask advice; but she had never ventured further than generalities, and Mrs. Brindley had never proffered advice, had never accepted opportunities to give it except in the vaguest way. She had taught Mildred a great deal, but always by example, by doing, never by saying what ought or ought not to be done. Thus, such development of Mildred's character as there had been was natural and permanent.

"He has put me in a peculiar position," said Mildred. "Or, rather, I have let myself drift into a peculiar position. For I think you're right in saying that oneself is always to blame. Won't you let me talk about it to you, please? I know you hate confidences. But I've got to—to talk. I'd like you to advise me, if you can. But even if you don't, it'll do me good to say things aloud."

"Often one sees more clearly," was Cyrilla's reply—noncommittal, yet not discouraging.

"I'm free to marry him," Mildred went on. "That is, I'm not married. I'd rather not explain—"

"Don't," said Mrs. Brindley. "It's unnecessary."

"You know that it's Stanley who has been lending me the money to live on while I study. Well, from the beginning I've been afraid I'd find myself in a difficult position."

"Naturally," said Mrs. Brindley, as she paused.

"But I've always expected it to come in another way—not about marriage, but—"

"I understand," said Mrs. Brindley. "You feared you'd be called on to pay in the way women usually pay debts to men."

Mildred nodded. "But this is worse than I expected—much worse."

"I hadn't thought of that," said Cyrilla. "Yes, you're right. If he had hinted the other thing, you could have pretended not to understand. If he had suggested it, you could have made him feel cheap and mean."

"I did," said Mildred. "He has been—really wonderful—better than almost any man would have been—more considerate than I deserved. And I took advantage of it."

"A woman has to," said Cyrilla. "The fight between men and women is so unequal."

"I took advantage of him," repeated Mildred. "And he apologized, and I—I went on taking the money. I didn't know what else to do. Isn't that dreadful?"

"Nothing to be proud of," said Cyrilla. "But a very usual transaction."

"And then," pursued Mildred, "I discovered that I—that I'd not be able to make a career. But still I kept on, though I've been trying to force myself to—to show some pride and self-respect. I discovered it only a short time ago, and it wasn't really until to-day that I was absolutely sure."

"You ARE sure?"

"There's hardly a doubt," replied Mildred. "But never mind that now. I've got to make a living at something, and while I'm learning whatever it is, I've got to have money to live on. And I can get it only from him. Now, he asks me to marry him. He wouldn't ask me if he didn't think I was going to be a great singer. He doesn't know it, but I do."

Mrs. Brindley smiled sweetly.

"And he thinks that I love him, also. If I accept him, it will be under doubly false pretenses. If I refuse him I've got to stop taking the money."

A long silence; then Mrs. Brindley said: "Women—the good ones, too—often feel that they've a right to treat men as men treat them. I think almost any woman would feel justified in putting off the crisis."

"You mean, I might tell him I'd give him my answer when I was independent and had paid back."

Cyrilla nodded. Mildred relit her cigarette, which she had let go out. "I had thought of that," said she. "But—I doubt if he'd tolerate it. Also"—she laughed with the peculiar intonation that accompanies the lifting of the veil over a deeply and carefully hidden corner of one's secret self—"I am afraid. If I don't marry him, in a few weeks, or months at most, he'll probably find out that I shall never be a great singer, and then I'd not be able to marry him if I wished to."

"He IS a temptation," said Cyrilla. "That is, his money is—and he personally is very nice."

"I married a man I didn't care for," pursued Mildred. "I don't want ever to do that again. It is—even in the best circumstances—not agreeable, not as simple as it looks to the inexperienced girls who are always doing it."

"Still, a woman can endure that sort of thing," said Mrs. Brindley, "unless she happens to be in love with another man." She was observing the unconscious Mildred narrowly, a state of inward tension and excitement hinted in her face, but not in her voice.

"That's just it?" said Mildred, her face carefully averted. "I—I happen to be in love with another man."

A spasm of pain crossed Cyrilla's face.

"A man who cares nothing about me—and never will. He's just a friend—so much the friend that he couldn't possibly think of me as—as a woman, needing him and wanting him"—her eyes were on fire now, and a soft glow had come into her cheeks—"and never daring to show it because if I did he would fly and never let me see him again."

Cyrilla Brindley's face was tragic as she looked at the beautiful girl, so gracefully adjusted to the big chair. She sighed covertly. "You are lovely," she said, "and young—above all, young."

"This man is peculiar," replied Mildred forlornly. "Anyhow, he doesn't want ME. He knows me for the futile, weak, worthless creature I am. He saw through my bluff, even before I saw through it myself. If it weren't for him, I could go ahead—do the sensible thing—do as women usually do. But—" She came to a full stop.

"Love is a woman's sense of honor," said Cyrilla softly. "We're merciless and unscrupulous—anything—everything—where we don't love. But where we do love, we'll go farther for honor than the most honorable man. That's why we're both worse and better than men—and seem to be so contradictory and puzzling."

"I'd do anything for him," said Mildred. She smiled drearily. "And he wants nothing."

She had nothing more to say. She had talked herself out about Stanley, and her mind was now filled with thoughts that could not be spoken. As she rose to go to bed, she looked appealingly at Cyrilla. Then, with a sudden and shy rush she flung her arms round her and kissed her. "Thank you—so much," she said. "You've done me a world of good. Saying it all out loud before YOU has made me see. I know my own mind, now."

She did not note the pathetic tenderness of Cyrilla's face as she said, "Good night, Mildred." But she did note the use of her first name—and her own right first name—for the first time since they had known each other. She embraced and kissed her again. "Good night, Cyrilla," she said gratefully.

As she entered Jennings's studio the next day he looked at her; and when Jennings looked, he saw—as must anyone who lives well by playing upon human nature. He did not like her expression. She did not habitually smile; her light-heartedness, her optimism, did not show themselves in that inane way. But this seriousness of hers was of a new kind, of the kind that bespeaks sobriety and saneness of soul. And that kind of seriousness—the deep, inward gravity of a person whose days of trifling with themselves and with the facts of life, and of being trifled with, are over—would have impressed Jennings equally had she come in laughing, had her every word been a jest.

"No, I didn't come for a lesson—at least not the usual kind," said she.

He was not one to yield without a struggle. Also he wished to feel his way to the meaning of this new mood. He put her music on the rack. "We'll begin where we—"

"This half-hour of your time is mine, is it not?" said she quietly. "Let's not waste any of it. Yesterday you told me that I could not hope to make a career because my voice is unreliable. Why is it unreliable?"

"Because you have a delicate throat," replied he, yielding at once where he instinctively knew he could not win.

"Then why can I sing so well sometimes?"

"Because your throat is in good condition some days—in perfect condition."

"It's the colds then—and the slight attacks of colds?"

"Certainly."

"If I did not catch colds—if I kept perfectly well—could I rely on my voice?"

"But that's impossible," said he.

"Why?"

"You're not strong enough."

"Then I haven't the physical strength for a career?"

"That—and also you are lacking in muscular development. But after several years of lessons—"

"If I developed my muscles—if I became strong—"

"Most of the great singers come from the lower classes—from people who do manual labor. They did manual labor in their youth. You girls of the better class have to overcome that handicap."

"But so many of the great singers are fat."

"Yes, and under that fat you'll find great ropes of muscle—like a blacksmith."

"What Keith meant," she said. "I wonder— Why do I catch cold so easily? Why do I almost always have a slight catch in the throat? Have you noticed that I nearly always have to clear my throat just a little?"

Her expression held him. He hesitated, tried to evade, gave it up. "Until that passes, you can never hope to be a thoroughly reliable singer," said he.

"That is, I can't hope to make a career?"

His silence was assent.

"But I have the voice?"

"You have the voice."

"An unusual voice?"

"Yes, but not so unusual as might be thought. As a matter of fact, there are thousands of fine voices. The trouble is in reliability. Only a few are reliable."

She nodded slowly and thoughtfully. "I begin to understand what Mr. Keith meant," she said. "I begin to see what I have to do, and how—how impossible it is."

"By no means," declared Jennings. "If I did not think otherwise, I'd not be giving my time to you."

She looked at him gravely. His eyes shifted, then returned defiantly, aggressively. She said:

"You can't help me to what I want. So this is my last lesson—for the present. I may come back some day—when I am ready for what you have to give."

"You are going to give up?"

"Oh, no—oh, dear me, no," replied she. "I realize that you're laughing in your sleeve as I say so, because you think I'll never get anywhere. But you—and Mr. Keith—may be mistaken." She drew from her muff a piece of music—the "Batti Batti," from "Don Giovanni." "If you please," said she, "we'll spend the rest of my time in going over this. I want to be able to sing it as well as possible."

He looked searchingly at her. "If you wish," said he. "But I doubt if you'll be able to sing at all."

"On the contrary, my cold's entirely gone," replied she. "I had an exciting evening, I doctored myself before I went to bed, and three or four times in the night. I found, this morning, that I could sing."

And it was so. Never had she sung better. "Like a true artist!" he declared with an enthusiasm that had a foundation of sincerity. "You know, Miss Stevens, you came very near to having that rarest of all gifts—a naturally placed voice. If you hadn't had singing teachers as a girl to make you self-conscious and to teach you wrong, you'd have been a wonder."

"I may get it back," said Mildred.

"That never happens," replied he. "But I can almost do it."

He coached her for half an hour straight ahead, sending the next pupil into the adjoining room—an unprecedented transgression of routine. He showed her for the first time what a teacher he could be, when he wished. There was an astonishing difference between her first singing of the song and her sixth and last—for they went through it carefully five times. She thanked him and then put out her hand, saying:

"This is a long good-by."

"To-morrow," replied he, ignoring her hand.

"No. My money is all gone. Besides, I have no time for amateur trifling."

"Your lessons are paid for until the end of the month. This is only the nineteenth."

"Then you are so much in." Again she put out her hand.

He took it. "You owe me an explanation."

She smiled mockingly. "As a friend of mine says, don't ask questions to which you already know the answer."

And she departed, the smile still on her charming face, but the new seriousness beneath it. As she had anticipated, she found Stanley Baird waiting for her in the drawing-room of the apartment. Being by habit much interested in his own emotions and not at all in the emotions of others, he saw only the healthful radiance the sharp October air had put into her cheeks and eyes. Certainly, to look at Mildred Gower was to get no impression of lack of health and strength. Her glance wavered a little at sight of him, then the expression of firmness came back.

"You look like that picture you gave me a long time ago," said he. "Do you remember it?"

She did not.

"It has a—different expression," he went on. "I don't think I'd have noticed it but for Keith. I happened to show it to him one day, and he stared at it in that way he has—you know?"

"Yes, I know," said Mildred. She was seeing those uncanny, brilliant, penetrating eyes, in such startling contrast to the calm, lifeless coloring and classic chiseling of features.

"And after a while he said, 'So, THAT'S Miss Stevens!' And I asked him what he meant, and he took one of your later photos and put the two side by side. To my notion the later was a lot the more attractive, for the face was rounder and softer and didn't have a certain kind of—well, hardness, as if you had a will and could ride rough shod. Not that you look so frightfully unattractive."

"I remember the picture," interrupted Mildred. "It was taken when I was twenty—just after an illness."

"The face WAS thin," said Stanley. "Keith called it a 'give away.'"

"I'd like to see it," said Mildred.

"I'll try to find it. But I'm afraid I can't. I haven't seen it since I showed it to Keith, and when I hunted for it the other day, it didn't turn up. I've changed valets several times in the last six months—"

But Mildred had ceased listening. Keith had seen the picture, had called it a "give away," had been interested in it—and the picture had disappeared. She laughed at her own folly, yet she was glad Stanley had given her this chance to make up a silly day-dream. She waited until he had exhausted himself on the subject of valets, their drunkenness, their thievish habits, their incompetence, then she said:

"I took my last lesson from Jennings to-day."

"What's the matter? Do you want to change? You didn't say anything about it? Isn't he good?"

"Good enough. But I've discovered that my voice isn't reliable, and unless one has a reliable voice there's no chance for a grand-opera career— . or for comic opera, either."

Stanley was straightway all agitation and protest. "Who put that notion in your head? There's nothing in it, Mildred. Jennings is crazy about your voice, and he knows."

"Jennings is after the money," replied Mildred. "What I'm saying is the truth. Stanley, our beautiful dream of a career has winked out."

His expression was most revealing.

"And," she went on, "I'm not going to take any more of your money—and, of course, I'll pay back what I've borrowed when I can"—she smiled—"which may not be very soon."

"What's all this about, anyhow?" demanded he. "I don't see any sign of it in your face. You wouldn't take it so coolly if it were so."

"I don't understand why I'm not wringing my hands and weeping," replied she. "Every few minutes I tell myself that I ought to be. But I stay quite calm. I suppose I'm—sort of stupefied."

"Do you really mean that you've given up?" cried he.

"It's no use to waste the money, Stanley. I've got the voice, and that's what deceived us all. But there's nothing BEHIND the voice. With a great singer the greatness is in what's behind the voice, not in the voice itself."

"I don't believe a word of it," cried he violently. "You've been discouraged by a little cold. Everybody has colds. Why, in this climate the colds are always getting the Metropolitan singers down."

"But they've got strong throats, and my throat's delicate."

"You must go to a better climate. You ought to be abroad, anyhow. That was part of my plan—for us to go abroad—" He stopped in confusion, reddened, went bravely on—"and you to study there and make your debut."

Mildred shook her head. "That's all over," said she. "I've got to change my plans entirely."

"You're a little depressed, that's all. For a minute you almost convinced me. What a turn you did give me! I forgot how your voice sounded the last time I heard it. No, you'd not be so calm, if you didn't know everything was all right."

Her eyes lit up with sly humor. "Perhaps I'm calm because I feel that my future's secure as your wife. What more could a woman ask?"

He forced an uncomfortable laugh. "Of course—of course," he said with a painful effort to be easy and jocose.

"I knew you'd marry me, even if I couldn't sing a note. I knew your belief in my career had nothing to do with it."

He hesitated, blurted out the truth. "Speaking seriously, that isn't quite so," said he. "I've got my heart set on your making a great tear—and I know you'll do it."

"And if you knew I wouldn't, you'd not want to marry me?"

"I don't say that," protested he. "How can I say how I'd feel if you were different?"

She nodded. "That's sensible, and it's candid," she said. She laid her hand impulsively on his arm. "I DO like you, Stanley. You have got such a lot of good qualities. Don't worry. I'm not going to insist on your marrying me."

"You don't have to do that, Mildred," said he. "I'm staring, raving crazy about you, though I'm a damn fool to let you know it."

"Yes, it is foolish," said she. "If you'd kept me worrying— Still, I guess not. But it doesn't matter. You can protest and urge all you please, quite safely. I'm not going to marry you. Now let's talk business."

"Let's talk marriage," said he. "I want this thing settled. You know you intend to marry me, Mildred. Why not say so? Why keep me gasping on the hook?"

They heard the front door open, and the rustling of skirts down the hall. Mildred called:

"Mrs. Brindley! Cyrilla!"

An instant and Cyrilla appeared in the doorway. When she and Baird had shaken hands, Mildred said:

"Cyrilla, I want you to tell the exact, honest truth. Is there any hope for a woman with a delicate throat to make a grand-opera career?"

Cyrilla paled, looked pleadingly at Mildred.

"Tell him," commanded Mildred.

"Very little," said Mrs. Brindley. "But—"

"Don't try to soften it," interrupted Mildred. "The truth, the plain truth."

"You've no right to draw me into this," cried Cyrilla indignantly, and she started to leave the room.

"I want him to know," said Mildred. "And he wants to know."

"I refuse to be drawn into it," Cyrilla said, and disappeared.

But Mildred saw that Stanley had been shaken. She proceeded to explain to him at length what a singer's career meant—the hardships, the drafts on health and strength, the absolute necessity of being reliable, of singing true, of not disappointing audiences—what a delicate throat meant—how delicate her throat was—how deficient she was in the kind of physical strength needed—muscular power with endurance back of it. When she finished he understood.

"I'd always thought of it as an art," he said ruefully. "Why, it's mostly health and muscles and things that have nothing to do with music." He was dazed and offended by this uncovering of the mechanism of the art—by the discovery of the coarse and painful toil, the grossly physical basis, of what had seemed to him all idealism. He had been full of the delusions of spontaneity and inspiration, like all laymen, and all artists, too, except those of the higher ranks—those who have fought their way up to the heights and, so, have learned that one does not achieve them by being caught up to them gloriously in a fiery cloud, but by doggedly and dirtily and sweatily toiling over every inch of the cruel climb.

He sat silent when she had finished. She waited, then said:

"Now, you see. I release you, and I'll take no more money to waste."

He looked at her with dumb misery that smote her heart. Then his expression changed—to the shining, hungry eyes, the swollen veins, the reddened countenance, the watering lips of desire. He seized her in his arms, and in a voice trembling with passion, he cried: "You must marry me, anyhow! I've GOT to have you, Mildred."

If she had loved him, his expression, his impassioned voice would have thrilled her. But she did not love him. It took all her liking for him, and the memory of all she owed him—that unpaid debt!—to enable her to push him away gently and to say without any show of the repulsion she felt:

"Stanley, you mustn't do that. And it's useless to talk of marriage. You're generous, so you are taking pity on me. But believe me, I'll get along somehow."

"Pity? I tell you I love you," he cried, catching desperately at her hands and holding them in a grip she could not break. "You've no right to treat me like this."

It was one of those veiled and stealthy reminders of obligation habitually indulged in by delicate people seeking repayment of the debt, but shunning the coarseness of direct demand. Mildred saw her opportunity. Said she quietly:

"You mean you want me to give myself to you in payment, or part payment, for the money you've loaned me?"

He released her hands and sprang up. He had meant just that, but he had not had the courage, or the meanness, or both, to admit boldly his own secret wish. She had calculated on this—had calculated well. "Mildred!" he cried in a shocked voice. "YOU so lacking in delicacy as to say such a thing!"

"If you didn't mean that, Stanley, what DID you mean?"

"I was appealing to our friendship—our—our love for each other."

"Then you should have waited until I was free."

"Good God!" he cried, "don't you see that's hopeless? Mildred, be sensible—be merciful."

"I shall never marry a man when he could justly suspect I did it to live off him."

"What an idea! It's a man's place to support a woman!"

"I was speaking only of myself. I can't do it. And it's absurd for you and me to be talking about love and marriage when anyone can see I'd be marrying you only because I was afraid to face poverty and a struggle."

Her manner calmed him somewhat. "Of course it's obvious that you've got to have money," said he, "and that the only way you can get it is by marriage. But there's something else, too, and in my opinion it's the principal thing—we care for each other. Why not be sensible, Mildred? Why not thank God that as long as you have to marry, you can marry someone you care for."

"Could you feel that I cared for you, if I married you now?" inquired she.

"Why not? I'm not so entirely lacking in self-esteem. I feel that I must count for something."

Mildred sat silently wondering at this phenomenon so astounding, yet a commonplace of masculine egotism. She had no conception of this vanity which causes the man, at whom the street woman smiles, to feel flattered, though he knows full well what she is and her dire necessity. She could not doubt that he was speaking the truth, yet she could not believe that conceit could so befog common sense in a man who, for all his slowness and shallowness, was more than ordinarily shrewd.

"Even if I thought I loved you," said she, "I couldn't be sure in these circumstances that I wasn't after your money."

"Don't worry about that," replied he. "I understand you better than you understand yourself."

"Let's stop talking about it," said she impatiently. "I want to explain to you the business side of this." She took her purse from the table. "Here are the papers." She handed him a check and a note. "I made them out at the bank this morning. The note is for what I owe you—and draws interest at four per cent. The check is for all the money I have left except about four hundred dollars. I've some bills I must pay, and also I didn't dare quite strip myself. The note may not be worth the paper it's written on, but I hope—"

Before she could prevent him he took the two papers, and, holding them out of her reach, tore them to bits.

Her eyes gleamed angrily. "I see you despise me—as much as I've invited. But, I'll make them out again and mail them to you."

"You're a silly child," said he gruffly. "We're going to be married."

She eyed him with amused exasperation. "It's too absurd!" she cried. "And if I yielded, you'd be trying to get out of it." She hesitated whether to tell him frankly just how she felt toward him. She decided against it, not through consideration—for a woman feels no consideration for a man she does not love, if he has irritated her—but through being ashamed to say harsh things to one whom she owed so much. "It's useless for you to pretend and to plead," she went on. "I shall not yield. You'll have to wait until I'm free and independent."

"You'll marry me then?"

"No," replied she, laughing. "But I'll be able to refuse you in such a way that you'll believe."

"But you've got to marry, Mildred, and right away." A suspicion entered his mind and instantly gleamed in his eyes. "Are you in love with someone else?"

She smiled mockingly.

"It looks as if you were," he went on, arguing with himself aloud. "For if you weren't you'd marry me, even though you didn't like me. A woman in your fix simply couldn't keep herself from it. Is THAT why you're so calm?"

"I'm not marrying anybody," said she.

"Then what are you going to do?"

"You'll see."

Once more the passionate side of his nature showed—not merely grotesque, unattractive, repellent, as in the mood of longing, but hideous. Among men Stanley Baird passed for a man of rather arrogant and violent temper, but that man who had seen him at his most violent would have been amazed. The temper men show toward men bears small resemblance either in kind or in degree to the temper of jealous passion they show toward the woman who baffles them or arouses their suspicions; and no man would recognize his most intimate man friend—or himself—when in that paroxysm. Mildred had seen this mood, gleaming at her through a mask, in General Siddall. It had made her sick with fear and repulsion. In Stanley Baird it first astounded her, then filled her with hate.

"Stanley!" she gasped.

"WHO is it?" he ground out between his teeth. And he seized her savagely.

"If you don't release me at once," said she calmly, "I shall call Mrs. Brindley, and have you put out of the house. No matter if I do owe you all that money."

"Stop!" he cried, releasing her. "You're very clever, aren't you?—turning that against me and making me powerless."

"But for that, would you dare presume to touch me, to question me?" said she.

He lowered his gaze, stood panting with the effort to subdue his fury.

She went back to her own room. A few hours later came a letter of apology from him. She answered it friendlily, said she would let him know when she could see him again, and enclosed a note and a check.

VIII

MILDRED went to bed that night proud of her strength of character. Were there many women—was there any other woman she knew or knew about—who in her desperate circumstances would have done what she had done? She could have married a man who would have given her wealth and the very best social position. She had refused him. She could have continued to "borrow" from him the wherewithal to keep her in luxurious comfort while she looked about at her ease for a position that meant independence. She had thrust the temptation from her. All this from purely high-minded motives; for other motive there could be none. She went to sleep, confident that on the morrow she would continue to tread the path of self-respect with unfaltering feet. But when morning came her throat was once more slightly off—enough to make it wise to postpone the excursion in search of a trial for musical comedy. The excitement or the reaction from excitement—it must be the one or the other—had resulted in weakness showing itself, naturally, at her weakest point—that delicate throat. When life was calm and orderly, and her mind was at peace, the trouble would pass, and she could get a position of some kind. Not the career she had dreamed; that was impossible. But she had voice enough for a little part, where a living could be made; and perhaps she would presently fathom the secret of the cause of her delicate throat and would be able to go far—possibly as far as she had dreamed.

The delay of a few days was irritating. She would have preferred to push straight on, while her courage was taut. Still, the delay had one advantage—she could prepare the details of her plan. So, instead of going to the office of the theatrical manager—Crossley, the most successful producer of light, musical pieces of all kinds—she went to call on several of the girls she knew who were more or less in touch with matters theatrical. And she found out just how to proceed toward accomplishing a purpose which ought not to be difficult for one with such a voice as hers and with physical charms peculiarly fitted for stage exhibition.

Not until Saturday was her voice at its best again. She, naturally, decided not to go to the theatrical office on Monday, but to wait until she had seen and talked with Keith. One more day did not matter, and Keith might be stimulating, might even have some useful suggestions to offer. She received him with a manner that was a version, and a most charming version, of his own tranquil indifference. But his first remark threw her into a panic. Said he:

"I've only a few minutes. No, thanks, I'll not sit."

"You needn't have bothered to come," said she coldly.

"I always keep my engagements. Baird tells me you have given up the arrangement you had with him. You'll probably be moving from here, as you'll not have the money to stay on. Send me your new address, please." He took a paper from his pocket and gave it to her. "You will find this useful—if you are in earnest," said he. "Good-by, and good luck. I'll hope to see you in a few weeks."

Before she had recovered herself in the least, she was standing there alone, the paper in her hand, her stupefied gaze upon the door through which he had disappeared. All his movements and his speech had been of his customary, his invariable, deliberateness; but she had the impression of whirling and rushing haste. With a long gasping sigh she fell to trembling all over. She sped to her room, got its door safely closed just in time. Down she sank upon the bed, to give way to an attack of hysterics.

We are constantly finding ourselves putting forth the lovely flowers and fruit of the virtues whereof the heroes and heroines of romance are so prolific. Usually nothing occurs to disillusion us about ourselves. But now and then fate, in unusually brutal ironic mood, forces us to see the real reason why we did this or that virtuous, self-sacrificing action, or blossomed forth in this or that nobility of character. Mildred was destined now to suffer one of these savage blows of disillusionment about self that thrust us down from the exalted moral heights where we have been preening into humble kinship with the weak and frail human race. She saw why she had refused Stanley, why she had stopped "borrowing," why she had put off going to the theatrical managers, why she had delayed moving into quarters within her diminished and rapidly diminishing means. She had been counting on Donald Keith. She had convinced herself that he loved her even as she loved him. He would fling away his cold reserve, would burst into raptures over her virtue and her courage, would ask her to marry him. Or, if he should put off that, he would at least undertake the responsibility of getting her started in her career. Well! He had come; he had shown that Stanley had told him all or practically all; and he had gone, without asking a sympathetic question or making an encouraging remark. As indifferent as he seemed. Burnt out, cold, heartless. She had leaned upon him; he had slipped away, leaving her to fall painfully, and ludicrously, to the ground. She had been boasting to herself that she was strong, that she would of her own strength establish herself in independence. She had not dreamed that she would be called upon to "make good." She raved against Keith, against herself, against fate. And above the chaos and the wreck within her, round and round, hither and yon, flapped and shied the black thought, "What SHALL I do?"

When she sat up and dried her eyes, she chanced to see the paper Keith had left; with wonder at her having forgotten it and with a throb of hope she opened and began to read his small, difficult writing:

A career means self-denial. Not occasional, intermittent, but steady, constant, daily, hourly—a purpose that never relaxes.

A career as a singer means not only the routine, the patient tedious work, the cutting out of time-wasting people and time-wasting pleasures that are necessary to any and all careers. It means in addition—for such a person—sacrifices far beyond a character so undisciplined and so corrupted by conventional life as is yours. The basis of a singing career is health and strength. You must have great physical strength to be able to sing operas. You must have perfect health.

Diet and exercise. A routine life, its routine rigidly adhered to, day in and day out, month after month, year after year. Small and uninteresting and monotonous food, nothing to drink, and, of course, no cigarettes. Such is the secret of a reliable voice for you who have a "delicate throat"—which is the silly, shallow, and misleading way of saying a delicate digestion, for sore throat always means indigestion, never means anything else. To sing, the instrument, the absolutely material machine, must be in perfect order. The rest is easy.

Some singers can commit indiscretions of diet and of lack of exercise. But not you, because you lack this natural strength. Do not be deceived and misled by their example.

Exercise. You must make your body strong, powerful. You have not the muscles by nature. You must acquire them.

The following routine of diet and exercise made one of the great singers, and kept her great for a quarter of a century. If you adopt it, without variation, you can make a career. If you do not, you need not hope for anything but failure and humiliation. Within my knowledge sixty-eight young men and young women have started in on this system. Not one had the character to persist to success. This may suggest why, except two who are at the very top, all of the great singers are men and women whom nature has made powerful of body and of digestion—so powerful that their indiscretions only occasionally make them unreliable.

There Mildred stopped and flung the paper aside. She did not care even to glance at the exercises prescribed or at the diet and the routine of daily work. How dull and uninspired! How grossly material! Stomach! Chewing! Exercising machines! Plodding dreary miles daily, rain or shine! What could such things have to do with the free and glorious career of an inspired singer? Keith was laughing at her as he hastened away, abandoning her to her fate.

She examined herself in the glass to make sure that the ravages of her attack of rage and grief and despair could be effaced within a few hours, then she wrote a note—formal yet friendly—to Stanley Baird, informing him that she would receive him that evening. He came while Cyrilla and Mildred were having their after, dinner coffee and cigarettes. He was a man who took great pains with his clothes, and got them where pains was not in vain. That evening he had arrayed himself with unusual care, and the result was a fine, manly figure of the well-bred New-Yorker type. Certainly Stanley had ground for his feeling that he deserved and got liking for himself. The three sat in the library for perhaps half an hour, then Mrs. Brindley rose to leave the other two alone. Mildred urged her to stay— Mildred who had been impatient of her presence when Stanley was announced. Urged her to stay in such a tone that Cyrilla could not persist, but had to sit down again. As the three talked on and on, Mildred continued to picture life with Stanley—continued the vivid picturing she had begun within ten minutes of Stanley's entering, the picturing that had caused her to insist on Cyrilla's remaining as chaperon. A young girl can do no such picturing as Mildred could not avoid doing. To the young girl married life, its tete-a-tetes, its intimacies, its routine, are all a blank. Any attempt she makes to fill in details goes far astray. But Mildred, with Stanley there before her, could see her life as it would be.

Toward half-past ten, Stanley said, shame-faced and pleading, "Mildred, I should like to see you alone for just a minute before I go."

Mildred said to Cyrilla: "No, don't move. We'll go into the drawing-room."

He followed her there, and when the sound of Mrs. Brindley's step in the hall had died away, he began: "I think I understand you a little now. I shan't insult you by returning or destroying that note or the check. I accept your decision—unless you wish to change it." He looked at her with eager appeal. His heart was trembling, was sick with apprehension, with the sense of weakness, of danger and gloom ahead. "Why shouldn't I help you, at least, Mildred?" he urged.

Whence the courage came she knew not, but through her choking throat she forced a positive, "No."

"And," he went on, "I meant what I said. I love you. I'm wretched without you. I want you to marry me, career or no career."

Her fears were clamorous, but she forced herself to say, "I can't change."

"I hoped—a little—that you sent me the note to-day because you— You didn't?"

"No," said Mildred. "I want us to be friends. But you must keep away."

He bent his head. "Then I'll go 'way off somewhere. I can't bear being here in New York and not seeing you. And when I've been away a year or so, perhaps I'll get control of myself again."

Going away!—to try to forget!—no doubt, to succeed in forgetting! Then this was her last chance.

"Must I go, Mildred? Won't you relent?"

"I don't love you—and I never can." She was deathly white and trembling. She lifted her eyes to begin a retreat, for her courage had quite oozed away. He was looking at her, his face distorted with a mingling of the passion of desire and the passion of jealousy. She shrank, caught at the back of a chair for support, felt suddenly strong and defiant. To be this man's plaything, to submit to his moods, to his jealousies, to his caprices—to be his to fumble and caress, his to have the fury of his passion wreak itself upon her with no response from her but only repulsion and loathing—and the long dreary hours and days and years alone with him, listening to his commonplaces, often so tedious, forced to try to amuse him and to keep him in a good humor because he held the purse-strings—

"Please go," she said.

She was still very young, still had years and years of youth unspent. Surely she could find something better than this. Surely life must mean something more than this. At least it was worth a trial.

He held out his hand. She gave him her reluctant and cold fingers. He said something, what she did not hear, for the blood was roaring in her ears as the room swam round. He was gone, and the next thing she definitely knew she was at the threshold of Cyrilla's room. Cyrilla gave her a tenderly sympathetic glance. She saw herself in a mirror and knew why; her face was gray and drawn, and her eyes lay dully deep within dark circles.

"I couldn't do it," she said. "I sent for him to marry him. But I couldn't."

"I'm glad," said Cyrilla. "Marriage without love is a last resort. And you're a long way from last resorts."

"You don't think I'm crazy?"

"I think you've won a great victory."

"Victory!" And Mildred laughed dolefully. "If this is victory, I hope I'll never know defeat."

Why did Mildred refuse Stanley Baird and cut herself off from him, even after her hopes of Donald Keith died through lack of food, real or imaginary? It would be gratifying to offer this as a case of pure courage and high principle, untainted of the motives which govern ordinary human actions. But unluckily this is a biography, not a romance, a history and not a eulogy. And Mildred Gower is a human being, even as you and I, not a galvanized embodiment of superhuman virtues such as you and I are pretending to be, perhaps even to ourselves. The explanation of her strange aberration, which will be doubted or secretly condemned by every woman of the sheltered classes who loves her dependence and seeks to disguise it as something sweet and fine and "womanly"—the explanation of her almost insane act of renunciation of all that a lady holds most dear is simple enough, puzzling though she found it. Ignorance, which accounts for so much of the squalid failure in human life, accounts also for much if not all the most splendid audacious achievement. Very often—very, very often— the impossibilities are achieved by those who in their ignorance advance not boldly but unconcernedly where a wiser man or woman would shrink and retreat. Fortunate indeed is he or she who in a crisis is by chance equipped with neither too little nor too much knowledge—who knows enough to enable him to advance, but does not know enough to appreciate how perilous, how foolhardy, how harsh and cruel, advance will be. Mildred was in this instance thus fortunate—unfortunate, she was presently to think it. She knew enough about loveless marriage to shrink from it. She did not know enough about what poverty, moneylessness, and friendlessness mean in the actuality to a woman bred as she had been. She imagined she knew—and sick at heart her notion of poverty made her. But imagination was only faintest foreshadowing of actuality. If she had known, she would have yielded to the temptation that was almost too strong for her. And if she had yielded—what then? Not such a repulsive lot, as our comfortable classes look at it. Plenty to eat and drink and to wear, servants and equipages and fine houses and fine society, the envy of her gaping kind—a comfortable life for the body, a comfortable death for mind and heart, slowly and softly suffocated in luxury. Partly through knowledge that strongly affected her character, which was on the whole aspiring and sensitive beyond the average to the true and the beautiful, partly through ignorance that veiled the future from her none too valorous and hardy heart, she did not yield to the temptation. And thus, instead of dying, she began to live, for what is life but growth in experience, in strength and knowledge and capability?

A baby enters the world screaming with pain. The first sensations of living are agonizing. It is the same with the birth of souls, for a soul is not really born until that day when it is offered choice between life and death and chooses life. In Mildred Gower's case this birth was an agony. She awoke the following morning with a dull headache, a fainting heart, and a throat so sore that she felt a painful catch whenever she tried to swallow. She used the spray; she massaged her throat and neck vigorously. In vain; it was folly to think of going where she might have to risk a trial of her voice that day. The sun was brilliant and the air sharp without being humid or too cold. She dressed, breakfasted, went out for a walk. The throat grew worse, then better. She returned for luncheon, and afterward began to think of packing, not that she had chosen a new place, but because she wished to have some sort of a sense of action. But her unhappiness drove her out again—to the park where the air was fine and she could walk in comparative solitude.

"What a silly fool I am!" thought she. "Why did I do this in the worst, the hardest possible way? I should have held on to Stanley until I had a position. No, I'm such a poor creature that I could never have done it in that way. I'd simply have kept on bluffing, fooling myself, putting off and putting of. I had to jump into the water with nobody near to help me, or I'd never have begun to learn to swim. I haven't begun yet. I may never learn to swim. I may drown. Yes, I probably shall drown."

She wandered aimlessly on—around the upper reservoir where the strong breeze freshened her through and through and made her feel less forlorn in spite of her chicken heart. She crossed the bridge at the lower end and came down toward the East Drive. A taxicab rushed by, not so fast, however, that she failed to recognize Donald Keith and Cyrilla Brindley. They were talking so earnestly—Keith was talking, for a wonder, and Mrs. Brindley listening—that they did not see her. She went straight home. But as she was afoot, the journey took about half an hour. Cyrilla was already there, in a negligee, looking as if she had not been out of the little library for hours. She was writing a letter. Mildred strolled in and seated herself. Cyrilla went on writing. Mildred watched her impatiently. She wished to talk, to be talked to, to be consoled and cheered, to hear about Donald Keith. Would that letter never be finished? At last it was, and Cyrilla took a book and settled herself to reading. There was a vague something in her manner—a change, an attitude toward Mildred—that disturbed Mildred. Or, was that notion of a change merely the offspring of her own somber mood? Seeing that Mrs. Brindley would not begin, she broke the silence herself. Said she awkwardly:

"I've decided to move. In fact, I've got to move."

Cyrilla laid down the book and regarded her tranquilly. "Of course," said she. "I've already begun to arrange for someone else."

Mildred choked, and the tears welled into her eyes. She had not been mistaken; Cyrilla had changed toward her. Now that she had no prospects for a brilliant career, now that her money was gone, Cyrilla had begun to— to be human. No doubt, in the course of that drive, Cyrilla had discovered that Keith had no interest in her either. Mildred beat down her emotion and was soon able to say in a voice as unconcerned as Cyrilla's:

"I'll find a place to-morrow or next day, and go at once."

"I'll be sorry to lose you," said Mrs. Brindley, "but I agree with you that you can't get settled any too soon."

"You don't happen to know of any cheap, good place?" said Mildred.

"If it's cheap, I don't think it's likely to be good—in New York," replied Cyrilla. "You'll have to put up with inconveniences—and worse. I'd offer to help you find a place, but I think everything self-reliant one does helps one to learn. Don't you?"

"Yes, indeed," assented Mildred. The thing was self-evidently true; still she began to hate Cyrilla. This cold-hearted New York! How she would grind down her heel when she got it on the neck of New York! Friendship, love, helpfulness—what did New York and New-Yorkers know of these things? "Or Hanging Rock, either," reflected she. What a cold and lonely world!

"Have you been to see about a position?" inquired Cyrilla.

Mildred was thrown into confusion. "I can't go—for a—day or so," she stammered. "The changeable weather has rather upset my throat. Nothing serious, but I want to be at my best."

"Certainly," said Mrs. Brindley. Her direct gaze made Mildred uncomfortable. She went on: "You're sure it's the weather?"

"What else could it be?" demanded Mildred with a latent resentment whose interesting origin she did not pause to inquire into.

"Well, salad, or sauces, or desserts, or cafe au lait in the morning, or candy, or tea," said Cyrilla. "Or it might be cigarettes, or all those things— and thin stockings and low shoes—mightn't it?"

Never before had she known Cyrilla to say anything meddlesome or cattish. Said Mildred with a faint sneer, "That sounds like Mr. Keith's crankiness."

"It is," replied Cyrilla. "I used to think he was a crank on the subject of singing and stomachs, and singing and ankles. But I've been convinced, partly by him, mostly by what I've observed."

Mildred maintained an icy silence.

"I see you are resenting what I said," observed Cyrilla.

"Not at all," said Mildred. "No doubt you meant well."

"You will please remember that you asked me a question."

So she had. But the discovery that she was clearly in the wrong, that she had invited the disguised lecture, only aggravated her sense of resentment against Mrs. Brindley. She spent the rest of the afternoon in sorting and packing her belongings—and in crying. She came upon the paper Donald Keith had left. She read it through carefully, thoughtfully, read it to the last direction as to exercise with the machine, the last arrangement for a daily routine of life, the last suggestion as to diet.

"Fortunately all that isn't necessary," said she to herself, when she finished. "If it were, I could never make a career. I'm not stupid enough to be able to lead that kind of life. Why, I'd not care to make a career, at that price. Slavery—plain slavery."

When she went in to dinner, she saw instantly that Cyrilla too had been crying. Cyrilla did not look old, anything but that, indeed was not old and would not begin to be for many a year. Still, after thirty-five or forty a woman cannot indulge a good cry without its leaving serious traces that will show hours afterward. At sight of the evidences of Cyrilla's grief Mildred straightway forgot her resentment. There must have been some other cause for Cyrilla's peculiar conduct. No matter what, since it was not hardness of heart.

It was a sad, even a gloomy dinner. But the two women were once more in perfect sympathy. And afterward Mildred brought the Keith paper and asked Cyrilla's opinion. Cyrilla read slowly and without comment. At last she said:

"He got this from his mother, Lucia Rivi. Have you read her life?"

"No. I've heard almost nothing about her, except that she was famous."

"She was more than that," said Mrs. Brindley. "She was great, a great personality. She was an almost sickly child and girl. Her first attempts on the stage were humiliating failures. She had no health, no endurance, nothing but a small voice of rare quality." Cyrilla held up the paper. "This tells how she became one of the surest and most powerful dramatic sopranos that ever lived."

"She must have been a dull person to have been able to lead the kind of life that's described there," said Mildred.

"Only two kinds of persons could do it," replied Cyrilla—"a dull person—a plodder—and a genius. Middling people—they're the kind that fill the world, they're you and I, my dear—middling people have to fuss with the trifles that must be sacrificed if one is to do anything big. You call those trifles your freedom, but they're your slavery. And by sacrificing them the Lucia Rivis buy their freedom." Cyrilla looked at the paper with a heavy sigh. "Ah, I wish I had seen this when I was your age. Now, it's too late."

Said Mildred: "Would you seriously advise me to try that?"

Cyrilla came and sat beside her and put an arm around her. "Mildred," she said, "I've never thrust advice on you. I only dare do it now because you ask me, and because I love you. You must try it. It's your one chance. If you do not, you will fail. You don't believe me?"

In a tone that was admission, Mildred said: "I don't know."

"Keith has given you there the secret of a successful career. You'll never read it in any book, or get it from any teacher, or from any singer or manager or doctor. You must live like that, you must do those things or you will fail even in musical comedy. You would fail even as an actress, if you tried that, when you found out that the singing was out of the question."

Mildred was impressed. Perhaps she would have been more impressed had she not seen Keith and Mrs. Brindley in the taxi, Keith talking earnestly and Mrs. Brindley listening as if to an oracle. Said she: "Perhaps I'll adopt some of the suggestions."

Cyrilla shook her head. "It's a route to success. You must go the whole route or not at all."

"Don't forget that there have been other singers besides Rivi."

"Not any that I recall who weren't naturally powerful in every way. And how many of them break down? Mildred, please do put the silly nonsense about nerves and temperament and inspiration and overwork and weather and climate—put all that out of your head. Build your temple of a career as high and graceful and delicate as you like, but build it on the coarse, hard, solid rock, dear!"

Mildred tried to laugh lightly. "How Mr. Keith does hypnotize people!" cried she.

Mrs. Brindley's cheeks burned, and her eyes lowered in acute embarrassment. "He has a way of being splendidly and sensibly right," said she. "And the truth is wonderfully convincing—once one sees it." She changed the subject, and it did not come up—or, perhaps, come OUT again—before they went to bed. The next day Mildred began the depressing, hopeless search for a place to live that would be clean, comfortable, and cheap. Those three adjectives describe the ideal lodging; but it will be noted that all these are relative. In fact, none of the three means exactly the same thing to any two members of the human family. Mildred's notion of clean—like her notion of comfortable—on account of her bringing up implied a large element of luxury. As for the word "cheap," it really meant nothing at all to her. From one standpoint everything seemed cheap; from another, everything seemed dear; that is, too dear for a young woman with less than five hundred dollars in the world and no substantial prospect of getting a single dollar more—unless by hook and crook, both of which means she was resolved not to employ.

Never having earned so much as a single penny, the idea of anyone's giving her anything for what she might be able to do was disturbingly vague and unreal. On the other hand, looking about her, she saw scores of men and women, personally known to her to be dull of conversation, and not well mannered or well dressed or well anything, who were making livings without overwhelming difficulty. Why not Mildred Gower? In this view the outlook was not discouraging. "I'll no doubt go through some discomfort, getting myself placed. But somewhere and somehow I shall be placed—and how I shall revenge myself on Donald Keith!" His fascination for her had not been destroyed by his humiliating lack of belief in her, nor by his cold-hearted desertion at just the critical moment. But his conduct had given her the incentive of rage, of stung vanity—or wounded pride, if you prefer. She would get him back; she would force him to admit; she would win him, if she could—and that ought not to be difficult when she should be successful. Having won him, then— What then? Something superb in the way of revenge; she would decide what, when the hour of triumph came. Meanwhile she must search for lodgings.

In her journeyings under the guidance of attractive advertisements and "carefully selected" agents' lists, she found herself in front of her first lodgings in New York—the house of Mrs. Belloc. She had often thought of the New England school-teacher, arrived by such strange paths at such a strange position in New York. She had started to call on her many times, but each time had been turned aside; New York makes it more than difficult to find time to do anything that does not have to be done at a definite time and for a definite reason. She was worn out with her futile trampings up and down streets, up and down stairs. Up the stone steps she went and rang the bell.

Yes, Mrs. Belloc was in, and would be glad to see her, if Miss Stevens would wait in the drawing-room a few minutes. She had not seated herself when down the stairs came the fresh, pleasantly countrified voice of Mrs. Belloc, inviting her to ascend. As Mildred started up, she saw at the head of the stairs the frank and cheerful face of the lady herself. She was holding together at the neck a thin silk wrapper whose lines strongly suggested that it was the only garment she had on.

"Why should old friends stand on ceremony?" said Mrs. Belloc. "Come right up. I've been taking a bath. My masseuse has just gone." Mrs. Belloc enclosed her in a delightfully perfumed embrace, and they kissed with enthusiasm.

"I AM glad to see you," said Mildred, feeling all at once a thrilling sense of at-homeness. "I didn't realize how glad I'd be till I saw you."

"It'd be a pretty stiff sort that wouldn't feel at home with me," observed Mrs. Belloc. "New York usually stiffens people up. It's had the opposite effect on me. Though I must say, I have learned to stiffen with people I don't like—and I'll have to admit that I like fewer and fewer. People don't wear well, do they? What IS the matter with them? Why can't they be natural and not make themselves into rubbishy, old scrap-bags full of fakes and pretenses? You're looking at my hair."

They were in Mrs. Belloc's comfortable sitting-room now, and she was smoking a cigarette and regarding Mildred with an expression of delight that was most flattering. Said Mildred:

"Your hair does look well. It's thicker—isn't it?"

"Think so?" said Mrs. Belloc. "It ought to be, with all the time and money I've spent on it. My, how New York does set a woman to repairing and fixing up. Nothing artificial goes here. It mustn't be paint and plumpers and pads, but the real teeth. Why, I've had four real teeth set in as if they were rooted—and my hips toned down. You may remember what heavy legs I had—piano-legs. Look at 'em now." Mrs. Belloc drew the wrapper to her knee and exposed in a pale-blue silk stocking a thin and comely calf.

"You HAVE been busy!" said Mildred.

"That's only a little part. I started to tell you about the hair. It was getting gray—not in a nice, pretty way, all over, but in spots and streaks. Nothing else makes a woman look so ragged and dingy and old as spotted, streaky gray hair. So I had the hair-woman touch it up. She vows it won't make my face hard. That's the trouble with dyed or touched hair, you know. But this is a new process."

"It's certainly a success," said Mildred. And in fact it was, and thanks to it and the other improvements Mrs. Belloc was an attractive and even a pretty woman, years younger than when Mildred saw her.

"Yes, I think I've improved," said Mrs. Belloc. "Nothing to scream about—but worth while. That's what we're alive for—to improve—isn't it? I've no patience with people who slide back, or don't get on—people who get less and less as they grow older. The trouble with them is they're vain, satisfied with themselves as they are, and lazy. Most women are too lazy to live. They'll only fix up to catch a man."

Mildred had grown sober and thoughtful.

"To catch a man," continued Mrs. Belloc. "And not much even for that. I'll warrant YOU'RE getting on. Tell me about it."

"Tell me about yourself, first," said Mildred.

"WHY all this excitement about improving?" And she smiled significantly.

"No, you'll have to guess again," said Mrs. Belloc. "Not a man. You remember, I used to be crazy about gay life in New York—going out, and men, theaters, and lobster-palaces—everything I didn't get in my home town, everything the city means to the jays. Well, I've gotten over all that. I'm improving, mind and body, just to keep myself interested in life, to keep myself young and cheerful. I'm interested in myself, in my house and in woman's suffrage. Not that the women are fit to vote. They aren't, any more than the men. But what MAKES people? Why, responsibility. That old scamp I married—he's dead. And I've got the money, and everything's very comfortable with me. Just think, I didn't have any luck till I was an old maid far gone. I'm not telling my age. All my life it had rained bad luck— pitchforks, tines down. And why?"

"Yes, why?" said Mildred. She did not understand how it was, but Mrs. Belloc seemed to be saying the exact things she needed to hear.

"I'll tell you why. Because I didn't work. Drudging along isn't work any more than dawdling along. Work means purpose, means head. And my luck began just as anybody's does—when I rose up and got busy. You may say it wasn't very creditable, the way I began; but it was the best *I* could do. I know it isn't good morals, but I'm willing to bet that many a man has laid the foundations of a big fine career by doing something that wasn't at all nice or right. He had to do it, to 'get through.' If he hadn't done it, he'd never have 'got through.' Anyhow, whether that's so or not, everyone's got to make a fight to break into the part of the world where living's really worth living. But I needn't tell YOU that. You're doing it."

"No, I'm not," replied Mildred. "I'm ashamed to say so, but I'm not. I've been bluffing—and wasting time."

"That's bad, that's bad," said Mrs. Belloc. "Especially, as you've got it in you to get there. What's been the trouble? The wrong kind of associations?"

"Partly," said Mildred.

Mrs. Belloc, watching her interestedly, suddenly lighted up. "Why not come back here to live?" said she. "Now, please don't refuse till I explain. You remember what kind of people I had here?"

Mildred smiled. "Rather—unconventional?"

"That's polite. Well, I've cleared 'em out. Not that I minded their unconventionality; I liked it. It was so different from the straight-jackets and the hypocrisy I'd been living among and hating. But I soon found out that—well, Miss Stevens, the average human being ought to be pretty conventional in his morals of a certain kind. If he—or SHE—isn't, they begin to get unconventional in every way—about paying their bills, for instance, and about drinking. I got sick and tired of those people. So, I put 'em all out—made a sweep. And now I've become quite as respectable as I care to be—or as is necessary. The couples in the house are married, and they're nice people of good families. It was Mrs. Dyckman—she's got the whole second floor front, she and her husband and the daughter—it was

Mrs. Dyckman who interested me in the suffrage movement. You must hear her speak. And the daughter does well at it, too—and keeps a fashionable millinery-shop—and she's only twenty-four. Then there's Nora Blond."

"The actress?"

"The actress. She's the quietest, hardest-working person here. She's got the whole first floor front. Nobody ever comes to see her, except on Sunday afternoon. She leads the queerest life."

"Tell me about that," said Mildred.

"I don't know much about it," confessed Mrs. Belloc. "She's regular as a clock—does everything on time, and at the same time. Two meals a day—one of them a dry little breakfast she gets herself. Walks, fencing, athletics, study."

"What slavery!"

"She's the happiest person I ever saw," retorted Mrs. Belloc. "Why, she's got her work, her career. You don't look at it right, Miss Stevens. You don't look happy. What's the matter? Isn't it because you haven't been working right—because you've been doing these alleged pleasant things that leave a bad taste in your mouth and weaken you? I'll bet, if you had been working hard, you'd not be unhappy now. Better come here to live."

"Will you let me tell you about myself?"

"Go right ahead. May I ask questions, where I want to know more? I do hate to get things halfway."

Mildred freely gave her leave, then proceeded to tell her whole story, omitting nothing that was essential to an understanding. In conclusion she said: "I'd like to come. You see, I've very little money. When it's gone, I'll go, unless I make some more."

"Yes, you must come. That Mrs. Brindley seems to be a nice woman, a mighty nice woman. But her house, and the people that come there—they aren't the right sort for a girl that's making a start. I can give you a room on the top floor—in front. The young lady next to you is a clerk in an architect's office, and a fine girl she is."

"How much does she pay?" said Mildred.

"Your room won't be quite as nice as hers. I put you at the top because you can sing up there, part of the mornings and part of the afternoons, without disturbing anybody. I don't have a general table any more. You can take your meals in your room or at the restaurant in the apartment-house next door. It's good and quite reasonable."

"How much for the room?" persisted Mildred, laughing.

"Seven dollars a week, and the use of the bath."

Mildred finally wrung from her that the right price was twelve dollars a week, and insisted on paying that—"until my money gets low."

"Don't worry about that," said Mrs. Belloc.

"You mustn't weaken me," cried Mildred. "You mustn't encourage me to be a coward and to shirk. That's why I'm coming here."

"I understand," said Mrs. Belloc. "I've got the New England streak of hardness in me, though I believe that masseuse has almost ironed it out of my face. Do I look like a New England schoolmarm?"

Mildred could truthfully answer that there wasn't a trace of it.

When she returned to Mrs. Brindley's—already she had ceased to think of it as home—she announced her new plans. Mrs. Brindley said nothing, but Mildred understood the quick tightening of the lines round her mouth and the shifting of the eyes. She hastened to explain that Mrs. Belloc was no longer the sort of woman or the sort of landlady she had been a few months before. Mrs. Brindley of the older New York, could neither understand nor believe in the people of the new and real New York whom it molds for better or for worse so rapidly—and even remolds again and again. But Mildred was able to satisfy her that the house was at least not suspicious.

"It doesn't matter where you're going," said Mrs. Brindley. "It's that you are going. I can't bear giving you up. I had hoped that our lives would flow on and on together." She was with difficulty controlling her emotions. "It's these separations that age one, that take one's life. I almost wish I hadn't met you."

Mildred was moved, herself. Not so much as Mrs. Brindley because she had the necessities of her career gripping her and claiming the strongest feelings there were in her. Also, she was much the younger, not merely in years but in experience. And separations have no real poignancy in them for youth.

"Yes, I know you love me," said Cyrilla, "but love doesn't mean to you what it means to me. I'm in that middle period of life where everything has its fullest meaning. In youth we're easily consoled and distracted because life seems so full of possibilities, and we can't believe friendship and love are rare, and still more rarely worth while. In old age, when the arteries harden and the blood flows slow and cold, we become indifferent. But between thirty-five and fifty-five how the heart can ache!" She smiled, with trembling lips. "And how it can rejoice!" she cried bravely. "I must not forget to mention that. Ah, my dear, you must learn to live intensely. If I had had your chance!"

"Ridiculous!" laughed Mildred. "You talk like an old woman. And I never think of you as older than myself."

"I AM an old woman," said Cyrilla. And, with a tightening at the heart Mildred saw, deep in the depths of her eyes, the look of old age. "I've found that I'm too old for love—for man-and-woman love—and that means I'm an old woman."

Mildred felt that there was only a thin barrier of reserve between her and some sad secret of this strange, shy, loving woman's—a barrier so thin that she could almost hear the stifled moan of a broken heart. But the barrier remained; it would have been impossible for Cyrilla Brindley to talk frankly about herself.

When Mildred came out of her room the next morning, Cyrilla had gone, leaving a note:

> I can't bear good-bys. Besides, we'll see each other very soon. Forgive me for shrinking, but really I can't.

Before night Mildred was settled in the new place and the new room, with no sense of strangeness. She was reproaching herself for hardness, for not caring about Cyrilla, the best and truest friend she had ever had. But the truth lay in quite a different direction. The house, the surroundings, where she had lived luxuriously, dreaming her foolish and fatuous dreams, was not the place for such a struggle as was now upon her. And for that struggle she preferred, to sensitive, sober, refined, impractical Cyrilla Brindley, the companionship and the sympathy, the practical sympathy, of Agnes Belloc. No one need be ashamed or nervous before Agnes Belloc about being poor or unsuccessful or having to resort to shabby makeshifts or having to endure coarse contacts. Cyrilla represented refinement, appreciation of the finished work—luxurious and sterile appreciation and enjoyment. Agnes represented the workshop—where all the doers of all that is done live and work. Mildred was descending from the heights where live those who have graduated from the lot of the human race and have lost all that superficial or casual resemblance to that race. She was going down to live with the race, to share in its lot. She was glad Agnes Belloc was to be there.

Generalizing about such a haphazard conglomerate as human nature is highly unsatisfactory, but it may be cautiously ventured that in New England, as in old England, there is a curiously contradictory way of dealing with conventionality. Nowhere is conventionality more in reverence; yet when a New-Englander, man or woman, happens to elect to break with it, nowhere is the break so utter and so defiant. If Agnes Belloc, cut loose from the conventions that had bound her from childhood to well into middle life, had remained at home, no doubt she would have spent a large part of her nights in thinking out ways of employing her days in outraging the conventionalities before her horrified and infuriated neighbors. But of what use in New York to cuff and spit upon deities revered by only an insignificant class—and only officially revered by that class? Agnes had soon seen that there was no amusement or interest whatever in an enterprise which in her New England home would have filled her life to the brim with excitement. Also, she saw that she was well into that time of life where the absence of reputation in a woman endangers her comfort, makes her liable to be left alone—not despised and denounced, but simply avoided and ignored. So she was telling Mildred the exact truth. She had laid down the arms she had taken up against the social system, and had come in—and was fighting it from the safer and wiser inside. She still insisted that a woman had the same rights as a man; but she took care to make it clear that she claimed those rights only for others, that she neither exercised them nor cared for them for herself. And to make her propaganda the more effective, she was not only circumspect herself, but was exceedingly careful to be surrounded by circumspect people. No one could cite her case as proof that woman would expand liberty into license. In theory there was nothing lively that she did not look upon at least with tolerance; in practice, more and more she disliked seeing one of her sex do anything that might cause the world to say "woman would abuse liberty if she had it." "Sensible people," she now said, "do as they like. But they don't give fools a chance to titter and chatter."

Agnes Belloc was typical—certainly of a large and growing class in this day—of the decay of ancient temples and the decline of the old-fashioned idealism that made men fancy they lived nobly because they professed and believed nobly. She had no ethical standards. She simply met each situation as it arose and dealt with it as common sense seemed in that particular instance to dictate. For a thousand years genius has been striving with the human race to induce it to abandon its superstitions and hypocrisies and to defy common sense, so adaptable, so tolerant, so conducive to long and healthy and happy life. Grossly materialistic, but alluringly comfortable.

Whether for good or for evil or for both good and evil, the geniuses seem in a fair way at last to prevail over the idealists, religious and political. And Mrs. Belloc, without in the least realizing it, was a most significant sign of the times.

"Your throat seems to be better to-day," said she to Mildred at breakfast. "Those simple house-remedies I tried on you last night seem to have done some good. Nothing like heat—hot water—and no eating. The main thing was doing without dinner last night."

"My nerves are quieter," advanced Mildred as the likelier explanation of the return of the soul of music to its seat. "And my mind's at rest."

"Yes, that's good," said plain Agnes Belloc. "But getting the stomach straight and keeping it straight's the main thing. My old grandmother could eat anything and do anything. I've seen her put in a glass of milk or a saucer of ice-cream on top of a tomato-salad. The way she kept well was, whenever she began to feel the least bit off, she stopped eating. Not a bite would she touch till she felt well again."

Mildred, moved by an impulse stronger than her inclination, produced the Keith paper. "I wish you'd read this, and tell me what you think of it. You've got so much common sense."

Agnes read it through to the end, began at the beginning and read it through again. "That sounds good to me," said she. "I want to think it over. If you don't mind I'd like to show it to Miss Blond. She knows a lot about those things. I suppose you're going to see Mr. Crossley to-day?—that's the musical manager's name, isn't it?"

"I'm going at eleven. That isn't too early, is it?"

"If I were you, I'd go as soon as I was dressed for the street. And if you don't get to see him, wait till you do. Don't talk to under-staffers. Always go straight for the head man. You've got something that's worth his while. How did he get to be head man? Because he knows a good thing the minute he sees it. The under fellows are usually under because they are so taken up with themselves and with impressing people how grand they are that they don't see anything else. So, when you talk to them, you wear yourself out and waste your time."

"There's only one thing that makes me nervous," said Mildred. "Everyone I've ever talked with about going on the stage—everyone who has talked candidly—has said—"

"Yes, I know," said Mrs. Belloc, as Mildred paused to search for smooth-sounding words in which to dress, without disguising, a distinctly ugly idea. "I've heard that, too. I don't know whether there's anything in it or not." She looked admiringly at Mildred, who that morning was certainly lovely enough to tempt any man. "If there is anything in it, why, I reckon YOU'D be up against it. That's the worst of having men at the top in any trade and profession. A woman's got to get her chance through some man, and if he don't choose to let her have it, she's likely to fail."

Mildred showed how this depressed her.

"But don't you fret about that till you have to," advised Mrs. Belloc. "I've a notion that, even if it's true, it may not apply to you. Where a woman offers for a place that she can fill about as well as a hundred other women, she's at the man's mercy; but if she knows that she's far and away the best for the place, I don't think a man's going to stand in his own light. Let him see that he can make money through YOU, money he won't make if he don't get you. Then, I don't think you'll have any trouble."

But Mildred's depression did not decrease. "If my voice could only be relied on!" she exclaimed. "Isn't it exasperating that I've got a delicate throat!"

"It's always something," said Mrs. Belloc. "One thing's about as bad as another, and anything can be overcome."

"No, not in my case," said Mildred. "The peculiar quality of my voice— what makes it unusual—is due to the delicateness of my throat."

"Maybe so," said Mrs. Belloc.

"Of course, I can always sing—after a fashion," continued Mildred. "But to be really valuable on the stage you've got to be able always to sing at your best. So I'm afraid I'm in the class of those who'll suit, one about as well as another."

"You've got to get out of that class," said Mrs. Belloc. "The men in that class, and the women, have to do any dirty work the boss sees fit to give 'em—and not much pay, either. Let me tell you one thing, Miss Stevens. If you can't get among the few at the top in the singing game, you must look round for some game where you can hope to be among the few. No matter WHAT it is. By using your brains and working hard, there's something you can do better than pretty nearly anybody else can or will do it. You find that."

The words sank in, sank deep. Mildred, sense of her surroundings lost, was gazing straight ahead with an expression that gave Mrs. Belloc hope and even a certain amount of confidence. There was a distinct advance; for, after she reflected upon all that Mildred had told her, little of her former opinion of Mildred's chances for success had remained but a hope detained not without difficulty. Mrs. Belloc knew the human race unusually well for a woman—unusually well for a human being of whatever sex or experience. She had discovered how rare is the temperament, the combination of intelligence and tenacity, that makes for success. She had learned that most people, judged by any standard, were almost total failures, that most of the more or less successful were so merely because the world had an enormous amount of important work to be done, even though half-way, and had no one but those half-competents to do it. As incompetence in a man would be tolerated where it would not be in a woman, obviously a woman, to get on, must have the real temperament of success.

She now knew enough about Mildred to be able to "place" her in the "lady" class—those brought up not only knowing how to do nothing with a money value (except lawful or unlawful man-trapping), but also trained to a sensitiveness and refinement and false shame about work that made it exceedingly difficult if not impossible for them to learn usefulness. She knew all Mildred's handicaps, both those the girl was conscious of and those far heavier ones which she fatuously regarded as advantages. How was Mildred ever to learn to dismiss and disregard herself as the pretty woman of good social position, an object of admiration and consideration? Mildred, in the bottom of her heart, was regarding herself as already successful—successful at the highest a woman can achieve or ought to aspire to achieve—was regarding her career, however she might talk or might fancy she believed, as a mere livelihood, a side issue. She would be perhaps more than a little ashamed of her stage connections, should she make any, until she should be at the very top—and how get to the top when one is working under the handicap of shame? Above all, how was this indulgently and shelteredly reared lady to become a working woman, living a routine life, toiling away day in and day out, with no let up, permitting no one and nothing to break her routine? "Really," thought Agnes Belloc, "she ought to have married that Baird man—or stayed on with the nasty general. I wonder why she didn't! That's the only thing that gives me hope. There must be something in her—something that don't appear—something she doesn't know about, herself. What is it? Maybe it was only vanity and vacillation. Again, I don't know."

The difficulty Mrs. Belloc labored under in her attempt to explore and map Mildred Gower was a difficulty we all labor under in those same enterprises. We cannot convince ourselves—in spite of experience after experience—that a human character is never consistent and homogeneous, is always conglomerate, that there are no two traits, however naturally exclusive, which cannot coexist in the same personality, that circumstance is the dominating factor in human action and brings forward as dominant characteristics now one trait or set of traits, consistent or inconsistent, and now another. The Alexander who was Aristotle's model pupil was the same

Alexander as the drunken debaucher. Indeed, may it not be that the characters which play the large parts in the comedy of life are naturally those that offer to the shifting winds of circumstances the greatest variety of strongly developed and contradictory qualities? For example, if it was Mildred's latent courage rescued her from Siddall, was it not her strong tendency to vacillation that saved her from a loveless and mercenary marriage to Stanley Baird? Perhaps the deep underlying truth is that all unusual people have in common the character that centers a powerful aversion to stagnation; thus, now by their strong qualities, now by their weaknesses, they are swept inevitably on and on and ever on. Good to-day, bad to-morrow, good again the day after, weak in this instance, strong in that, now brave and now cowardly, soft at one time, hard at another, generous and the reverse by turns, they are consistent only in that they are never at rest, but incessantly and inevitably go.

Mildred reluctantly rose, moved toward the door with lingering step. "I guess I'd better make a start," said she.

"That's the talk," said Mrs. Belloc heartily. But the affectionate glance she sent after the girl was dubious—even pitying.

IX

TWO minutes' walk through to Broadway, and she was at her destination. There, on the other side of the way, stood the Gayety Theater, with the offices of Mr. Clarence Crossley overlooking the intersection of the two streets. Crossley was intrenched in the remotest of a series of rooms, each tenanted by under-staffers of diminishing importance as you drew way from the great man. It was next to impossible to get at him—a cause of much sneering and dissatisfaction in theatrical circles. Crossley, they said, was exclusive, had the swollen head, had forgotten that only a few years before he had been a cheap little ticket-seller grateful for a bow from any actor who had ever had his name up. Crossley insisted that he was not a victim of folie de grandeur, that, on the contrary, he had become less vain as he had risen, where he could see how trivial a thing rising was and how accidental. Said he:

"Why do I shut myself in? Because I'm what I am—a good thing, easy fruit. You say that men a hundred times bigger than I'll ever be don't shut themselves up. You say that Mountain, the biggest financier in the country, sits right out where anybody can go up to him. Yes, but who'd dare go up to him? It's generally known that he's a cannibal, that he kills his own food and eats it warm and raw. So he can afford to sit in the open. If I did that, all my time and all my money would go to the cheap-skates with hard-luck tales. I don't hide because I'm haughty, but because I'm weak and soft."

In appearance Mr. Crossley did not suggest his name. He was a tallish, powerful-looking person with a smooth, handsome, audacious face, with fine, laughing, but somehow untrustworthy eyes—at least untrustworthy for women, though women had never profited by the warning. He dressed in excellent taste, almost conspicuously, and the gay and expensive details of his toilet suggested a man given over to liveliness. As a matter of fact, this liveliness was potential rather than actual. Mr. Crossley was always intending to resume the giddy ways of the years before he became a great man, but was always so far behind in the important things to be done and done at once that he was forced to put off. However, his neckties and his shirts and his flirtations, untrustworthy eyes kept him a reputation for being one of the worst cases in Broadway. In vain did his achievements show that he could not possibly have time or strength for anything but work. He looked like a rounder; he was in a business that gave endless dazzling opportunities for the lively life; a rounder he was, therefore.

He was about forty. At first glance, so vivid and energetic was he, he looked like thirty-five, but at second glance one saw the lines, the underlying melancholy signs of strain, the heavy price he had paid for phenomenal success won by a series of the sort of risks that make the hair fall as autumn leaves on a windy day and make such hairs as stick turn rapidly gray. Thus, there were many who thought Crossley was through vanity shy of the truth by five or six years when he said forty.

In ordinary circumstances Mildred would never have got at Crossley. This was the first business call of her life where she had come as an unknown and unsupported suitor. Her reception would have been such at the hands of Crossley's insolent and ill-mannered underlings that she would have fled in shame and confusion. It is even well within the possibilities that she would have given up all idea of a career, would have sent for Baird, and so on. And not one of those who, timid and inexperienced, have suffered rude rebuff at their first advance, would have condemned her. But it so chanced—whether by good fortune or by ill the event was to tell—that she did not have to face a single underling. The hall door was open. She entered. It happened that while she was coming up in the elevator a quarrel between a motorman and a driver had heated into a fight, into a small riot. All the underlings had rushed out on a balcony that commanded a superb view of the battle. The connecting doors were open; Mildred advanced from room to room, seeking someone who would take her card to Mr. Crossley. When she at last faced a closed door she knocked.

"Come!" cried a pleasant voice.

And in she went, to face Crossley himself—Crossley, the "weak and soft," caught behind his last entrenchment with no chance to escape. Had Mildred looked the usual sort who come looking for jobs in musical comedy, Mr. Crossley would not have risen—not because he was snobbish, but because, being a sensitive, high-strung person, he instinctively adopted the manner that would put the person before him at ease. He glanced at Mildred, rose, and thrust back forthwith the slangy, offhand personality that was perhaps the most natural—or was it merely the most used?—of his many personalities. It was Crossley the man of the world, the man of the artistic world, who delighted Mildred with a courteous bow and offer of a chair, as he said:

"You wished to see me?"

"If you are Mr. Crossley," said Mildred.

"I should be tempted to say I was, if I wasn't," said he, and his manner made it a mere pleasantry to put her at ease.

"There was no one in the outside room, so I walked on and on until your door stopped me."

"You'll never know how lucky you were," said he. "They tell me those fellows out there have shocking manners."

"Have you time to see me now? I've come to apply for a position in musical comedy."

"You have not been on the stage, Miss—"

"Gower. Mildred Gower. I've decided to use my own name."

"I know you have not been on the stage."

"Except as an amateur—and not even that for several years. But I've been working at my voice."

Crossley was studying her, as she stood talking—she had refused the chair. He was more than favorably impressed. But the deciding element was not Mildred's excellent figure or her charm of manner or her sweet and lovely face. It was superstition. Just at that time Crossley had been abruptly deserted by Estelle Howard; instead of going on with the rehearsals of "The Full Moon," in which she was to be starred, she had rushed away to Europe with a violinist with whom she had fallen in love at the first rehearsal. Crossley was looking about for someone to take her place. He had been entrenched in those offices for nearly five years; in all that time not a single soul of the desperate crowds that dogged him had broken through his guard. Crossley was as superstitious as was everyone else who has to do with the stage.

"What kind of a voice?" asked he.

"Lyric soprano."

"You have music there. What?"

"'Batti Batti' and a little song in English—'The Rose and the Bee.'"

Crossley forgot his manners, turned his back squarely upon her, thrust his hands deep into his trousers pockets, and stared out through the window. He presently wheeled round. She would not have thought his eyes could be so keen. Said he: "You were studying for grand opera?"

"Yes."

"Why do you drop it and take up this?"

"No money," replied she. "I've got to make my living at once."

"Well, let's see. Come with me, please."

They went out by a door into the hall, went back to the rear of the building, in at an iron door, down a flight of steep iron skeleton steps dimly lighted. Mildred had often been behind the scenes in her amateur theatrical days; but even if she had not, she would have known where she was. Crossley called, "Moldini! Moldini!"

The name was caught up by other voices and repeated again and again, more and more remotely. A moment, and a small dark man with a superabundance of greasy dark hair appeared. "Miss Gower," said Crossley, "this is Signor Moldini. He will play your accompaniments." Then to the little Italian, "Piano on the stage?"

"Yes, sir."

To Mildred with a smile, "Will you try?"

She bent her head. She had no voice—not for song, not for speech, not even for a monosyllable.

Crossley took Moldini aside where Mildred could not hear. "Mollie," said he, "this girl crept up on me, and I've got to give her a trial. As you see, she's a lady, and you know what they are."

"Punk," said Moldini.

Crossley nodded. "She seems a nice sort, so I want to let her down easy. I'll sit back in the house, in the dark. Run her through that 'Batti Batti' thing she's got with her. If she's plainly on the fritz, I'll light a cigarette. If I don't light up, try the other song she has. If I still don't light up make her go through that 'Ah, were you here, love,' from the piece. But if I light up, it means that I'm going to light out, and that you're to get rid of her—tell her we'll let her know if she'll leave her address. You understand?"

"Perfectly."

Far from being thrilled and inspired, her surroundings made her sick at heart—the chill, the dampness, the bare walls, the dim, dreary lights, the coarsely-painted flats— At last she was on the threshold of her chosen profession. What a profession for such a person as she had always been! She stood beside Moldini, seated at the piano. She gazed at the darkness, somewhere in whose depths Crossley was hidden. After several false starts she sang the "Batti Batti" through, sang it atrociously—not like a poor professional, but like a pretentious amateur, a reversion to a manner of singing she had once had, but had long since got rid of. She paused at the end, appalled by the silence, by the awfulness of her own performance.

From the darkness a slight click. If she had known!—for, it was Crossley's match-safe.

The sound, slight yet so clear, startled her, roused her. She called out: "Mr. Crossley, won't you please be patient enough to let me try that again?"

A brief hesitation, then: "Certainly."

Once more she began. But this time there was no hesitation. From first to last she did it as Jennings had coached her, did it with all the beauty and energy of her really lovely voice. As she ended, Moldini said in a quiet but intense undertone: "Bravo! Bravo! Fresh as a bird on a bright spring morning." And from the darkness came: "Ah—that's better, Miss Gower. That was professional work. Now for the other."

Thus encouraged and with her voice well warmed, she could not but make a success of the song that was nearer to what would be expected of her in musical comedy. Crossley called out: "Now, the sight singing, Moldini. I don't expect you to do this well, Miss Gower. I simply wish to get an idea of how you'd do a piece we have in rehearsal."

"You'll have no trouble with this," said Moldini, as he opened the comedy song upon the rack with a contemptuous whirl. "It's the easy showy stuff that suits the tired business man and his laced-in wife. Go at it and yell."

Mildred glanced through it. There was a subtle something in the atmosphere now that put her at her ease. She read the words aloud, laughing at their silly sentimentality, she and Moldini and Crossley making jokes about it. Soon she said: "I'm ready."

She sang it well. She asked them to let her try it again. And the second time, with the words in her mind and the simple melody, she was able to put expression into it and to indicate, with restraint, the action. Crossley came down the aisle.

"What do you think, Mollie?" he said to Moldini.

"We might test her at a few rehearsals."

Crossley meekly accepted the salutary check on his enthusiasm. "Do you wish to try, Miss Gower?"

Mildred was silent. She knew now the sort of piece in which she was to appear. She had seen a few of them, those cheap and vulgar farces with their thin music, their more than dubious-looking people. What a come-down! What a degradation! It was as bad in its way as being the wife of General Siddall. And she was to do this, in preference to marrying Stanley Baird.

"You will be paid, of course, during rehearsal; that is, as long as we are taking your time. Fifty dollars a week is about as much as we can afford."

Crossley was watching her shrewdly, was advancing these remarks in response to the hesitation he saw so plainly. "Of course it isn't grand opera," he went on. "In fact, it's pretty low—almost as low as the public taste. You see, we aren't subsidized by millionaires who want people to think they're artistic, so we have to hustle to separate the public from its money. But if you make a hit, you can earn enough to put you into grand opera in fine style."

"I never heard of anyone's graduating from here into grand opera," said Mildred.

"Because our stars make so much money and make it so easily. It'll be your own fault if you don't."

"Can't I come to just one rehearsal—to see whether I can—can do it?" pleaded Mildred.

Crossley, made the more eager and the more superstitious by this unprecedented reluctance, shook his head.

"No. You must agree to stay as long as we want you," said he. "We can't allow ourselves to be trifled with."

"Very well," said Mildred resignedly. "I will rehearse as long as you want me."

"And will stay for the run of the piece, if we want that?" said Crossley. "You to get a hundred a week if you are put in the cast. More, of course, if you make a hit."

"You mean I'm to sign a contract?" cried Mildred in dismay.

"Exactly," said Crossley. A truly amazing performance. Moldini was not astonished, however, for he had heard the songs, and he knew Crossley's difficulties through Estelle Howard's flight. Also, he knew Crossley—never so "weak and soft" that he trifled with unlikely candidates for his productions. Crossley had got up because he knew what to do and when to do it.

Mildred acquiesced. Before she was free to go into the street again, she had signed a paper that bound her to rehearse for three weeks at fifty dollars a week and to stay on at a hundred dollars a week for forty weeks or the run of "The Full Moon," if Crossley so desired; if he did not, she was free at the end of the rehearsals. A shrewdly one-sided contract. But Crossley told himself he would correct it, if she should by some remote chance be good enough for the part and should make a hit in it. This was no mere salve to conscience, by the way. Crossley would not be foolish enough to give a successful star just cause for disliking and distrusting him and at the earliest opportunity leaving him to make money for some rival manager.

Mrs. Belloc had not gone out, had been waiting in a fever of anxiety. When Mildred came into her sitting-room with a gloomy face and dropped to a chair as if her last hope had abandoned her, it was all Agnes Belloc could do to restrain her tears. Said she:

"Don't be foolish, my dear. You couldn't expect anything to come of your first attempt."

"That isn't it," said Mildred. "I think I'll give it up—do something else. Grand opera's bad enough. There were a lot of things about it that I was fighting my distaste for."

"I know," said Agnes. "And you'd better fight them hard. They're unworthy of you."

"But—musical comedy! It's—frightful!"

"It's an honest way of making a living, and that's more than can be said of—of some things. I suppose you're afraid you'll have to wear tights—or some nonsense like that."

"No, no. It's doing it at all. Such rotten music—and what a loathsome mess!"

Mrs. Belloc's eyes flashed. "I'm losing all patience!" she cried. "I know you've been brought up like a fool and always surrounded by fools. I suppose you'd rather sell yourself to some man. Do you know what's the matter with you, at bottom? Why, you're lazy and you're a coward. Too lazy to work. And afraid of what a lot of cheap women'll say—women earning their board and clothes in about the lowest way such a thing can be done. Haven't you got any self-respect?"

Mildred rose. "Mrs. Belloc," she said angrily, "I can't permit even you to say such things to me."

"The shoe seems to fit," retorted Mrs. Belloc. "I never yet saw a lady, a real, silk-and-diamonds, sit-in-the-parlor lady, who had any self-respect. If I had my way they wouldn't get a mouthful to eat till they had earned it. That'd be a sure cure for the lady disease. I'm ashamed of you, Miss Stevens! And you're ashamed of yourself."

"Yes, I am," said Mildred, with a sudden change of mood.

"The best thing you can do is to rest till lunch-time. Then start out after lunch and hunt a job. I'll go with you."

"But I've got a job," said Mildred. "That's what's the matter."

Agnes Belloc's jaw dropped and her rather heavy eyebrows shot up toward the low sweeping line of her auburn hair. She made such a ludicrous face that Mildred laughed outright. Said she:

"It's quite time. Fifty a week, for three weeks of rehearsal. No doubt *I* can go on if I like. Nothing could be easier."

"Crossley?"

"Yes. He was very nice—heard me sing three pieces—and it was all settled. I'm to begin to-morrow."

The color rose in Agnes Belloc's face until she looked apoplectic. She abruptly retreated to her bedroom. After a few minutes she came back, her normal complexion restored. "I couldn't trust myself to speak," said she. "That was the worst case of ingratitude I ever met up with. You, getting a place at fifty dollars a week—and on your first trial—and you come in looking as if you'd lost your money and your reputation. What kind of a girl are you, anyway?"

"I don't know," said Mildred. "I wish I did."

"Well, I'm sorry you got it so easy. Now you'll have a false notion from the start. It's always better to have a hard time getting things. Then you appreciate them, and have learned how to hold on."

"No trouble about holding on to this," said Mildred carelessly.

"Please don't talk that way, child," pleaded Agnes, almost tearful. "It's frightful to me, who've had experience, to hear you invite a fall-down."

Mildred disdainfully fluttered the typewritten copy of the musical comedy. "This is child's play," said she. "The lines are beneath contempt. As for the songs, you never heard such slop."

"The stars in those pieces get four and five hundred, and more, a week," said Mrs. Belloc. "Believe me, those managers don't pay out any such sums for child's play. You look out. You're going at this wrong."

"I shan't care if I do fail," said Mildred.

"Do you mean that?" demanded Mrs. Belloc.

"No, I don't," said Mildred. "Oh, I don't know what I mean."

"I guess you're just talking," said Mrs. Belloc after a reflective silence. "I guess a girl who goes and gets a good job, first crack out of the box, must have a streak of shrewdness."

"I hope so," said Mildred doubtfully.

"I guess you'll work hard, all right. After you went out this morning, I took that paper down to Miss Blond. She's crazy about it. She wants to make a copy of it. I told her I'd ask you."

"Certainly," said Mildred. "She says she'll return it the same day."

"Tell her she can keep it as long as she likes."

Mrs. Belloc eyed her gravely, started to speak, checked herself. Instead, she said, "No, I shan't do that. I'll have it back in your room by this evening. You might change your mind, and want to use it."

"Very well," said Mildred, pointedly uninterested and ignoring Mrs. Belloc's delicate but distinct emphasis upon "might."

Mrs. Belloc kept a suspicious eye upon her—an eye that was not easily deceived. The more she thought about Mildred's state of depression and disdain the more tolerant she became. That mood was the natural and necessary result of the girl's bringing up and mode of life. The important thing—and the wonderful thing—was her being able to overcome it. After a week of rehearsal she said: "I'm making the best of it. But I don't like it, and never shall."

"I should hope not," replied Mrs. Belloc. "You're going to the top. I'd hate to see you contented at the bottom. Aren't you learning a good deal that'll be useful later on?"

"That's why I'm reconciled to it," said she. "The stage director, Mr. Ransdell, is teaching me everything—even how to sing. He knows his business."

Ransdell not only knew, but also took endless pains with her. He was a tall, thin, dark man, strikingly handsome in the distinguished way. So distinguished looking was he that to meet him was to wonder why he had not made a great name for himself. An extraordinary mind he certainly had, and an insight into the reasons for things that is given only to genius. He had failed as a composer, failed as a playwright, failed as a singer, failed as an actor. He had been forced to take up the profession of putting on dramatic and musical plays, a profession that required vast knowledge and high talents and paid for them in niggardly fashion both in money and in fame. Crossley owed to him more than to any other single element the series of successes that had made him rich; yet the ten thousand a year Crossley paid him was regarded as evidence of Crossley's lavish generosity and was so. It would have been difficult to say why a man so splendidly endowed by nature and so tireless in improving himself was thus unsuccessful. Probably he lacked judgment; indeed, that lack must have been the cause. He could judge for Crossley; but not for himself, not when he had the feeling of ultimate responsibility.

Mildred had anticipated the most repulsive associations—men and women of low origin and of vulgar tastes and of vulgarly loose lives. She found herself surrounded by simple, pleasant people, undoubtedly erratic for the most part in all their habits, but without viciousness. And they were hard workers, all. Ransdell—for Crossley—tolerated no nonsense. His people could live as they pleased, away from the theater, but there they must be prompt and fit. The discipline was as severe as that of a monastery. She saw many signs that all sorts of things of the sort with which she wished to have no contact were going on about her; but as she held slightly—but not at all haughtily—aloof, she would have had to go out of her way to see enough to scandalize her. She soon suspected that she was being treated with extraordinary consideration. This was by Crossley's orders. But the carrying out of their spirit as well as their letter was due to Ransdell. Before the end of that first week she knew that there was the personal element behind his admiration for her voice and her talent for acting, behind his concentrating most of his attention upon her part. He looked his love boldly whenever they were alone; he was always trying to touch her—never in a way that she could have resented, or felt like resenting. He was not unattractive to her, and she was eager to learn all he had to teach, and saw no harm in helping herself by letting him love.

Toward the middle of the second week, when they were alone in her dressing-room, he—with the ingenious lack of abruptness of the experienced man at the game—took her hand, and before she was ready, kissed her. He did not accompany these advances with an outburst of passionate words or with any fiery lighting up of the eyes, but calmly, smilingly, as if it were what she was expecting him to do, what he had a right to do.

She did not know quite how to meet this novel attack. She drew her hand away, went on talking about the part—the changes he had suggested in her entrance, as she sang her best solo. He discussed this with her until they rose to leave the theater. He looked smilingly down on her, and said with the flattering air of the satisfied connoisseur:

"Yes, you are charming, Mildred. I can make a great artist and a great success out of you. We need each other."

"I certainly need you," said she gratefully. "How much you've done for me."

"Only the beginning," replied he. "Ah, I have such plans for you—such plans. Crossley doesn't realize how far you can be made to go—with the right training. Without it—" He shook his head laughingly. "But you shall have it, my dear." And he laid his hands lightly and caressingly upon her shoulders.

The gesture was apparently a friendly familiarity. To resent it, even to draw away, would put her in the attitude of the woman absurdly exercised about the desirability and sacredness of her own charms.

Still smiling, in that friendly, assured way, he went on: "You've been very cold and reserved with me, my dear. Very unappreciative."

Mildred, red and trembling, hung her head in confusion.

"I've been at the business ten years," he went on, "and you're the first woman I've been more than casually interested in. The pretty ones were bores. The homely ones—I can't interest myself in a homely woman, no matter how much talent she has. A woman must first of all satisfy the eye. And you—" He seated himself and drew her toward him. She, cold all over and confused in mind and almost stupefied, resisted with all her strength; but her strength seemed to be oozing away. She said:

"You must not do this. You must not do this. I'm horribly disappointed in you."

He drew her to his lap and held her there without any apparent tax upon his strength. He kissed her, laughingly pushing away the arms with which she tried to shield her face. Suddenly she found strength to wrench herself free and stood at a distance from him. She was panting a little, was pale, was looking at him with cold anger.

"You will please leave this room," said she.

He lit a cigarette, crossed his legs comfortably, and looked at her with laughing eyes. "Don't do that," he said genially. "Surely my lessons in acting haven't been in vain. That's too obviously a pose."

She went to the mirror, arranged her hat, and moved toward the door. He rose and barred the way.

"You are as sensible as you are sweet and lovely," said he. "Why should you insist on our being bad friends?"

"If you don't stand aside, I'll call out to the watchman."

"I'd never have thought you were dishonest. In fact, I don't believe it yet. You don't look like one of those ladies who wish to take everything and give nothing." His tone and manner were most attractive. Besides, she could not forget all he had done for her—and all he could do for her. Said she:

"Mr. Ransdell, if I've done anything to cause you to misunderstand, it was unconscious. And I'm sorry. But I—"

"Be honest," interrupted he. "Haven't I made it plain that I was fascinated by you?"

She could not deny it.

"Haven't I been showing you that I was willing to do everything I could for you?"

"I thought you were concerned only about the success of the piece."

"The piece be jiggered," said he. "You don't imagine YOU are necessary to its success, do you? You, a raw, untrained girl. Don't your good sense tell you I could find a dozen who would do, let us say, ALMOST as well?"

"I understand that," murmured she.

"Perhaps you do, but I doubt it," rejoined he. "Vanity's a fast growing weed. However, I rather expected that you would remain sane and reasonably humble until you'd had a real success. But it seems not. Now tell me, why should I give my time and my talent to training you—to putting you in the way of quick and big success?"

She was silent.

"What did you count on giving me in return? Your thanks?"

She colored, hung her head.

"Wasn't I doing for you something worth while? And what had you to give in return?" He laughed with gentle mockery. "Really, you should have been grateful that I was willing to do so much for so little, for what I wanted ought—if you are a sensible woman—to seem to you a trifle in comparison with what I was doing for you. It was my part, not yours, to think the complimentary things about you. How shallow and vain you women are! Can't you see that the value of your charms is not in them, but in the imagination of some man?"

"I can't answer you," said she. "You've put it all wrong. You oughtn't to ask payment for a favor beyond price."

"No, I oughtn't to HAVE to ask," corrected he, in the same pleasantly ironic way. "You ought to have been more than glad to give freely. But, curiously, while we've been talking, I've changed my mind about those precious jewels of yours. We'll say they're pearls, and that my taste has suddenly changed to diamonds." He bowed mockingly. "So, dear lady, keep your pearls."

And he stood aside, opening the door for her. She hesitated, dazed that she was leaving, with the feeling of the conquered, a field on which, by all the precedents, she ought to have been victor. She passed a troubled night, debated whether to relate her queer experience to Mrs. Belloc, decided for silence. It drafted into service all her reserve of courage to walk into the theater the next day and to appear on the stage among the assembled company with her usual air. Ransdell greeted her with his customary friendly courtesy and gave her his attention, as always. By the time they had got through the first act, in which her part was one of four of about equal importance, she had recovered herself and was in the way to forget the strange stage director's strange attack and even stranger retreat. But the situation changed with the second act, in which she was on the stage all the time and had the whole burden. The act as originally written had been less generous to her; but Ransdell had taken one thing after another away from the others and had given it to her. She made her first entrance precisely as he had trained her to make it and began. A few seconds, and he stopped her.

"Please try again, Miss Gower," said he. "I'm afraid that won't do."

She tried again; again he stopped her. She tried a third time. His manner was all courtesy and consideration, not the shade of a change. But she began to feel a latent hostility. Instinctively she knew that he would no longer help her, that he would leave her to her own resources, and judge her by how she acquitted herself. She made a blunder of her third trial.

"Really, Miss Gower, that will never do," said he mildly. "Let me show you how you did it."

He gave an imitation of her—a slight caricature. A titter ran through the chorus. He sternly rebuked them and requested her to try again. Her fourth attempt was her worst. He shook his head in gentle remonstrance. "Not quite right yet," said he regretfully. "But we'll go on."

Not far, however. He stopped her again. Again the courteous, kindly criticism. And so on, through the entire act. By the end of it, Mildred's nerves were unstrung. She saw the whole game, and realized how helpless she was. Before the end of that rehearsal, Mildred had slipped back from promising professional into clumsy amateur, tolerable only because of the beautiful freshness of her voice—and it was a question whether voice alone would save her. Yet no one but Mildred herself suspected that Ransdell had done it, had revenged himself, had served notice on her that since she felt strong enough to stand alone she was to have every opportunity to do so. He had said nothing disagreeable; on the contrary, he had been most courteous, most forbearing.

In the third act she was worse than in the second. At the end of the rehearsal the others, theretofore flattering and encouraging, turned away to talk among themselves and avoided her. Ransdell, about to leave, said:

"Don't look so down-hearted, Miss Gower. You'll be all right to-morrow. An off day's nothing."

He said it loudly enough for the others to hear. Mildred's face grew red with white streaks across it, like the prints of a lash. The subtlest feature of his malevolence had been that, whereas on other days he had taken her aside to criticize her, on this day he had spoken out—gently, deprecatingly, but frankly—before the whole company. Never had Mildred Gower been so sad and so blue as she was that day and that night. She came to the rehearsal the following day with a sore throat. She sang, but her voice cracked on the high notes. It was a painful exhibition. Her fellow principals, who had been rather glad of her set-back the day before, were full of pity and sympathy. They did not express it; they were too kind for that. But their looks, their drawing away from her—Mildred could have borne sneers and jeers better. And Ransdell was SO forbearing, SO gentle.

Her voice got better, got worse. Her acting remained mediocre to bad. At the fifth rehearsal after the break with the stage-director, Mildred saw Crossley seated far back in the dusk of the empty theater. It was his first appearance at rehearsals since the middle of the first week. As soon as he had satisfied himself that all was going well, he had given his attention to other matters where things were not going well. Mildred knew why he was there—and she acted and sang atrociously. Ransdell aggravated her nervousness by ostentatiously trying to help her, by making seemingly adroit attempts to cover her mistakes—attempts apparently thwarted and exposed only because she was hopelessly bad.

In the pause between the second and third acts Ransdell went down and sat with Crossley, and they engaged in earnest conversation. The while, the members of the company wandered restlessly about the stage, making feeble attempts to lift the gloom with affected cheerfulness. Ransdell returned to the stage, went up to Mildred, who was sitting idly turning the leaves of a part-book.

"Miss Gower," said he, and never had his voice been so friendly as in these regretful accents, "don't try to go on to-day. You're evidently not yourself. Go home and rest for a few days. We'll get along with your understudy, Miss Esmond. When Mr. Crossley wants to put you in again, he'll send for you. You mustn't be discouraged. I know how beginners take these things to heart. Don't fret about it. You can't fail to succeed."

Mildred rose and, how she never knew, crossed the stage. She stumbled into the flats, fumbled her way to the passageway, to her dressing-room. She felt that she must escape from that theater quickly, or she would give way to some sort of wild attack of nerves. She fairly ran through the streets to Mrs. Belloc's, shut herself in her room. But instead of the relief of a storm of tears, there came a black, hideous depression. Hour after hour she sat, almost without motion. The afternoon waned; the early darkness came. Still she did not move—could not move. At eight o'clock Mrs. Belloc knocked. Mildred did not answer. Her door opened—she had forgotten to lock it. In came Mrs. Belloc.

"Isn't that you, sitting by the window?" she said.

"Yes," replied Mildred.

"I recognized the outline of your hat. Besides, who else could it be but you? I've saved some dinner for you. I thought you were still out."

Mildred did not answer.

"What's the matter?" said Agnes? "Ill? bad news?"

"I've lost my position," said Mildred.

A pause. Then Mrs. Belloc felt her way across the room until she was touching the girl. "Tell me about it, dear," said she.

In a monotonous, lifeless way Mildred told the story. It was some time after she finished when Agnes said:

"That's bad—bad, but it might be worse. You must go to see the manager, Crossley."

"Why?" said Mildred.

"Tell him what you told me."

Mildred's silence was dissent.

"It can't do any harm," urged Agnes.

"It can't do any good," replied Mildred.

"That isn't the way to look at it."

A long pause. Then Mildred said: "If I got a place somewhere else, I'd meet the same thing in another form."

"You've got to risk that."

"Besides, I'd never have had a chance of succeeding if Mr. Ransdell hadn't taught me and stood behind me."

It was many minutes before Agnes Belloc said in a hesitating, restrained voice: "They say that success—any kind of success—has its price, and that one has to be ready to pay that price or fail."

Again the profound silence. Into it gradually penetrated the soft, insistent sound of the distant roar of New York—a cruel, clamorous, devouring sound like a demand for that price of success. Said Agnes timidly:

"Why not go to see Mr. Ransdell."

"He wouldn't make it up," said Mildred. "And I—I couldn't. I tried to marry Stanley Baird for money—and I couldn't. It would be the same way now—only more so."

"But you've got to do something."

"Yes, and I will." Mildred had risen abruptly, was standing at the window. Agnes Belloc could feel her soul rearing defiantly at the city into which she was gazing. "I will!" she replied.

"It sounds as if you'd been pushed to where you'd turn and make a fight," said Agnes.

"I hope so," said Mildred. "It's high time."

She thought out several more or less ingenious indirect routes into Mr. Crossley's stronghold, for use in case frontal attack failed. But she did not need them. Still, the hours she spent in planning them were by no means wasted. No time is wasted that is spent in desperate, concentrated thinking about any of the practical problems of life. And Mildred Gower, as much as any other woman of her training—or lack of training—was deficient in ability to use her mind purposefully. Most of us let our minds act like a sheep in a pasture—go wandering hither and yon, nibbling at whatever happens to offer. Only the superior few deliberately select a pasture, select a line of procedure in that pasture and keep to it, concentrating upon what is useful to us, and that alone. So it was excellent experience for Mildred to sit down and think connectedly and with wholly absorbed mind upon the phase of her career most important at the moment. When she had worked out all the plans that had promise in them she went tranquilly to sleep, a stronger and a more determined person, for she had said with the energy that counts: "I shall see him, somehow. If none of these schemes works, I'll work out others. He's got to see me."

But it was no occult "bearing down" that led him to order her admitted the instant her card came. He liked her; he wished to see her again; he felt that it was the decent thing, and somehow not difficult gently but clearly to convey to her the truth. On her side she, who had looked forward to the interview with some nervousness, was at her ease the moment she faced him alone in that inner office. He had extraordinary personal charm—more than Ransdell, though Ransdell had the charm invariably found in a handsome human being with the many-sided intellect that gives lightness of mind. Crossley was not intellectual, not in the least. One had only to glance at him to see that he was one of those men who reserve all their intelligence for the practical sides of the practical thing that forms the basis of their material career. He knew something of many things, had a wonderful assortment of talents—could sing, could play piano or violin, could compose, could act, could do mystifying card tricks, could order women's clothes as discriminatingly as he could order his own—all these things a little, but nothing much except making a success of musical comedy and comic opera. He had an ambition, carefully restrained in a closet of his mind, where it could not issue forth and interfere with his business. This ambition was to be a giver of grand opera on a superb scale. He regarded himself as a mere money-maker—was not ashamed of this, but neither was he proud of it. His ambition then represented a dream of a rise to something more than business man, to friend and encourager and wet nurse to art.

Mildred Gower had happened to set his imagination to working. The discovery that she was one of those whose personalities rouse high expectations only to mock them had been a severe blow to his confidence in his own judgment. Though he pretended to believe, and had the habit of saying that he was "weak and soft," was always being misled by his good nature, he really believed himself an unerring judge of human beings, and, as his success evidenced, he was not far wrong. Thus, though convinced that Mildred was a "false alarm," his secret vanity would not let him release his original idea. He had the tenacity that is an important element in all successes; and tenacity become a fixed habit has even been known to ruin in the end the very careers it has made.

Said Mildred, in a manner which was astonishingly unemotional and businesslike: "I've not come to tattle and to whine, Mr. Crossley. I've hesitated about coming at all, partly because I've an instinct it's useless, partly because what I have to say isn't easy."

Crossley's expression hardened. The old story!—excuses, excuses, self-excuse—somebody else to blame.

"If it hadn't been for Mr. Ransdell—the trouble he took with me, the coaching he gave me—I'd have been a ridiculous failure at the very first rehearsal. But—it is to Mr. Ransdell that my failure is due."

"My dear Miss Gower," said Crossley, polite but cold, "I regret hearing you say that. The fact is very different. Not until you had done so—so unacceptably at several rehearsals that news of it reached me by another way—not until I myself went to Mr. Ransdell about you did he admit that there could be a possibility of a doubt of your succeeding. I had to go to rehearsal myself and directly order him to restore Miss Esmond and lay you off."

Mildred was not unprepared. She received this tranquilly. "Mr. Ransdell is a very clever man," said she with perfect good humor. "I've no hope of convincing you, but I must tell my side."

And clearly and simply, with no concealments through fear of disturbing his high ideal of her ladylike delicacy, she told him the story. He listened, seated well back in his tilted desk-chair, his gaze upon the ceiling. When she finished he held his pose a moment, then got up and paced the length of the office several times, his hands in his pockets. He paused, looked keenly at her, a good-humored smile in those eyes of his so fascinating to women because of their frank wavering of an inconstancy it would indeed be a triumph to seize and hold. Said he:

"And your bad throat? Did Ransdell give you a germ?"

She colored. He had gone straight at the weak point.

"If you'd been able to sing," he went on, "nobody could have done you up."

She could not gather herself together for speech.

"Didn't you know your voice wasn't reliable when you came to me?"

"Yes," she admitted.

"And wasn't that the REAL reason you had given up grand opera?" pursued he mercilessly.

"The reason was what I told you—lack of money," replied she. "I did not go into the reason why I lacked money. Why should I when, even on my worst days, I could get through all my part in a musical comedy— except songs that could be cut down or cut out? If I could have made good at acting, would you have given me up on account of my voice?"

"Not if you had been good enough," he admitted.

"Then I did not get my engagement on false pretenses?"

"No. You are right. Still, your fall-down as a singer is the important fact. Don't lose sight of it."

"I shan't," said she tersely.

His eyes were frankly laughing. "As to Ransdell—what a clever trick! He's a remarkable man. If he weren't so shrewd in those little ways, he might have been a great man. Same old story—just a little too smart, and so always doing the little thing and missing the big thing. Yes, he went gunning for you—and got you." He dropped into his chair. He thought a moment, laughed aloud, went on: "No doubt he has worked that same trick many a time. I've suspected it once or twice, but this time he fooled me. He got you, Miss Gower, and I can do nothing. You must see that I can't look after details. And I can't give up as invaluable a man as Ransdell. If I put you back, he'd put you out—would make the piece fail rather than let you succeed."

Mildred was gazing somberly at the floor.

"It's hard lines—devilish hard lines," he went on sympathetically. "But what can I do?"

"What can I do?" said Mildred.

"Do as all people do who succeed—meet the conditions."

"I'm not prepared to go as far as that, at least not yet," said she with bitter sarcasm. "Perhaps when I'm actually starving and in rags—"

"A very distressing future," interrupted Crossley. "But—I didn't make the world. Don't berate me. Be sensible—and be honest, Miss Gower, and tell me—how could I possibly protect you and continue to give successful shows? If you can suggest any feasible way, I'll take it."

"No, there isn't any way," replied she, rising to go.

He rose to escort her to the hall door. "Personally, the Ransdell sort of thing is—distasteful to me. Perhaps if I were not so busy I might be forced by my own giddy misconduct to take less high ground. I've observed that the best that can be said for human nature at its best is that it is as well behaved as its real temptations permit. He was making you, you know. You've admitted it."

"There's no doubt about that," said Mildred.

"Mind you, I'm not excusing him. I'm simply explaining him. If your voice had been all right—if you could have stood to any degree the test he put you to, the test of standing alone—you'd have defeated him. He wouldn't have dared go on. He's too shrewd to think a real talent can be beaten."

The strong lines, the latent character, in Mildred's face were so strongly in evidence that looking at her then no one would have thought of her beauty or even of her sex, but only of the force that resists all and overcomes all. "Yes—the voice," said she. "The voice."

"If it's ever reliable, come to see me. Until then—" He put out his hand. When she gave him hers, he held it in a way that gave her no impulse to draw back. "You know the conditions of success now. You must prepare to meet them. If you put yourself at the mercy of the Ransdells—or any other of the petty intriguers that beset every avenue of success—you must take the consequences, you must conciliate them as best you can. If you don't wish to be at their mercy, you must do your part."

She nodded. He released her hand, opened the hall door. He said:

"Forgive my little lecture. But I like you, and I can't help having hope of you." He smiled charmingly, his keen, inconstant eyes dimming. "Perhaps I hope because you're young and extremely lovely and I am pitifully susceptible. You see, you'd better go. Every man's a Ransdell at heart where pretty women are concerned."

She did not leave the building. She went to the elevator and asked the boy where she could find Signor Moldini. His office was the big room on the third floor where voice candidates were usually tried out, three days in the week. At the moment he was engaged. Mildred, seated in the tiny anteroom, heard through the glass door a girl singing, or trying to sing. It was a distressing performance, and Mildred wondered that Moldini could be so tolerant as to hear her through. He came to the door with her, thanked her profusely, told her he would let her know whenever there was an opening "suited to your talents." As he observed Mildred, he was still sighing and shaking his head over the departed candidate.

"Ugly and ignorant!" he groaned. "Poor creature! Poor, poor creature. She makes three dollars a week—in a factory owned by a great philanthropist. Three dollars a week. And she has no way to make a cent more. Miss Gower, they talk about the sad, naughty girls who sell themselves in the street to piece out their wages. But think, dear young lady, how infinitely better of they are than the ugly ones who can't piece out their wages."

There he looked directly at her for the first time. Before she could grasp the tragic sadness of his idea, he, with the mobility of candid and highly sensitized natures, shifted from melancholy to gay, for in looking at her he had caught only the charm of dress, of face, of arrangement of hair. "What a pleasure!" he exclaimed, bursting into smiles and seizing and kissing her gloved hands. "Voice like a bird, face like an angel—only not TOO good, no, not TOO good. But it is so rare—to look as one sings, to sing as one looks."

For once, compliment, sincere compliment from one whose opinion was worth while, gave Mildred pain. She burst out with her news: "Signor Moldini, I've lost my place in the company. My voice has gone back on me."

Usually Moldini abounded in the consideration of fine natures that have suffered deeply from lack of consideration. But he was so astounded that he could only stare stupidly at her, smoothing his long greasy hair with his thin brown hand.

"It's all my fault; I don't take care of myself," she went on. "I don't take care of my health. At least, I hope that's it."

"Hope!" he said, suddenly angry.

"Hope so, because if it isn't that, then I've no chance for a career," explained she.

He looked at her feet, pointed an uncannily long forefinger at them. "The crossings and sidewalks are slush—and you, a singer, without overshoes! Lunacy! Lunacy!"

"I've never worn overshoes?" said Mildred apologetically.

"Don't tell me! I wish not to hear. It makes me—like madness here." He struck his low sloping brow with his palm. "What vanity! That the feet may look well to the passing stranger, no overshoes! Rheumatism, sore throat, colds, pneumonia. Is it not disgusting. If you were a man I should swear in all the languages I know—which are five, including Hungarian, and when one swears in Hungarian it is 'going some,' as you say in America. Yes, it is going quite some."

"I shall wear overshoes," said Mildred.

"And indigestion—you have that?"

"A little, I guess."

"Much—much, I tell you!" cried Moldini, shaking the long finger at her. "You Americans! You eat too fast and you eat too much. That is why you are always sick, and consulting the doctors who give the medicines that make worse, not better. Yes, you Americans are like children. You know nothing. Sing? Americans cannot sing until they learn that a stomach isn't a waste-basket, to toss everything into. You have been to that throat specialist, Hicks?"

"Ah, yes," said Mildred brightening. "He said there was nothing organically wrong."

"He is an ass, and a criminal. He ruins throats. He likes to cut, and he likes to spray. He sprays those poisons that relieve colds and paralyze the throat and cords. Americans sing? It is to laugh! They have too many doctors; they take too many pills. Do you know what your national emblem should be? A dollar-sign—yes. But that for all nations. No, a pill—a pill, I tell you. You take pills?"

"Now and then," said Mildred, laughing. "I admit I have several kinds always on hand."

"You see!" cried he triumphantly. "No, it is not mere art that America needs, but more sense about eating—and to keep away from the doctors. People full of pills, they cannot make poems and pictures, and write operas and sing them. Throw away those pills, dear young lady, I implore you."

"Signor Moldini, I've come to ask you to help me."

Instantly the Italian cleared his face of its half-humorous, half-querulous expression. In its place came a grave and courteous eagerness to serve her that was a pleasure, even if it was not altogether sincere. And Mildred could not believe it sincere. Why should he care what became of her, or be willing to put himself out for her?

"You told me one day that you had at one time taught singing," continued she.

"Until I was starved out?" replied he. "I told people the truth. If they could not sing I said so. If they sang badly I told them why, and it was always the upset stomach, the foolish food, and people will not take care about food. They will eat what they please, and they say eating is good for them, and that anyone who opposes them is a crank. So most of my pupils left, except those I taught for nothing—and they did not heed me, and came to nothing."

"You showed me in ten minutes one day how to cure my worst fault. I've sung better, more naturally ever since."

"You could sing like the birds. You do—almost. You could be taught to sing as freely and sweetly and naturally as a flower gives perfume. That is YOUR divine gift, young lady song as pure and fresh as a bird's song raining down through the leaves from the tree-top."

"I have no money. I've got to get it, and I shall get it," continued Mildred. "I want you to teach me—at any hour that you are free. And I want to know how much you will charge, so that I shall know how much to get."

"Two dollars a lesson. Or, if you take six lessons a week, ten dollars. Those were my terms. I could not take less."

"It is too little," said Mildred. "The poorest kinds of teachers get five dollars an hour—and teach nothing."

"Two dollars, ten dollars a week," replied he. "It is the most I ever could get. I will not take more from you."

"It is too little," said she. "But I'll not insist—for obvious reasons. Now, if you'll give me your home address, I'll go. When I get the money, I'll write to you."

"But wait!" cried he, as she rose to depart. "Why so hurried? Let us see. Take of the wrap. Step behind the screen and loosen your corset. Perhaps even you could take it off?"

"Not without undressing," said Mildred. "But I can do that if it's necessary." She laughed queerly. "From this time on I'll do ANYTHING that's necessary."

"No,—never mind. The dress of woman—of your kind of women. It is not serious." He laughed grimly. "As for the other kind, their dress is the only serious thing about them. It is a mistake to think that women who dress badly are serious. My experience has been that they are the most foolish of all. Fashionable dress—it is part of a woman's tools. It shows that she is good at her business. The women who try to dress like men, they are good neither at men's business nor at women's."

This, while Mildred was behind the screen, loosening her corset—though, in fact, she wore it so loose at all times that she inconvenienced herself simply to show her willingness to do as she was told. When she came out, Moldini put her through a rigid physical examination—made her breathe while he held one hand on her stomach, the other on her back, listened at her heart, opened wide her throat and peered down, thrust his long strong fingers deep into the muscles of her arms, her throat, her chest, until she had difficulty in not crying out with pain.

"The foundation is there," was his verdict. "You have a good body, good muscles, but flabby—a lady's muscles, not an opera singer's. And you are stiff—not so stiff as when you first came here, but stiff for a professional. Ah, we must go at this scientifically, thoroughly."

"You will teach me to breathe—and how to produce my voice naturally?"

"I will teach you nothing," replied he. "I will tell you what to do, and you will teach yourself. You must get strong—strong in the supple way—

and then you will sing as God intended. The way to sing, dear young lady, is to sing. Not to breathe artificially, and make faces, and fuss with your throat, but simply to drop your mouth and throat open and let it out!"

Mildred produced from her hand-bag the Keith paper. "What do YOU think of that?" she asked.

Presently he looked up from his reading. "This part I have seen before," said he. "It is Lucia Rivi's. Her cousin, Lotta Drusini, showed it to me—she was a great singer also."

"You approve of it?"

"If you will follow that for two years, faithfully, you will be securely great, and then you will follow it all your singing life—and it will be long. But remember, dear young lady, I said IF you follow it, and I said faithfully. I do not believe you can."

"Why not?" said Mildred.

"Because that means self-denial, colossal self-denial. You love things to eat—yes?"

Mildred nodded.

"We all do," said Moldini. "And we hate routine, and we like foolish, aimless little pleasures of all kinds."

"And it will be two years before I can try grand opera—can make my living?" said Mildred slowly.

"I did not say that. I said, before you would be great. No, you can sing, I think, in—wait."

Moldini flung rapidly through an enormous mass of music on a large table. "Ah, here!" he cried, and he showed her a manuscript of scales. "Those two papers. It does not look much? Well, I have made it up, myself. And when you can sing those two papers perfectly, you will be a greater singer than any that ever lived." He laughed delightedly. "Yes, it is all there—in two pages. But do not weep, dear lady, because you will never sing them perfectly. You will do very well if— Always that if, remember! Now, let us see. Take this, sit in the chair, and begin. Don't bother about me. I expect nothing. Just do the best you can."

Desperation, when it falls short of despair, is the best word for achievement. Mildred's voice, especially at the outset, was far from perfect condition. Her high notes, which had never been developed properly, were almost bad. But she acquitted herself admirably from the standpoint of showing what her possibilities were. And Moldini, unkempt, almost unclean, but as natural and simple and human a soul as ever paid the penalties of poverty and obscurity and friendlessness for being natural and simple and human, exactly suited her peculiar temperament. She knew that he liked her, that he believed in her; she knew that he was as sympathetic toward her as her own self, that there was no meanness anywhere in him. So she sang like a bird—a bird that was not too well in soul or in body, but still a bird out in the sunshine, with the airs of spring cheering his breast and its foliage gladdening his eyes. He kept her at it for nearly an hour. She saw that he was pleased, that he had thought out some plan and was bursting to tell her, but had forbidden himself to speak of it. He said:

"You say you have no money?"

"No, but I shall get it."

"You may have to pay high for it—yes?"

She colored, but did not flinch. "At worst, it will be—unpleasant, but that's all."

"Wait one—two days—until you hear from me. I may—I do not say will, but may—get it. Yes, I who have nothing." He laughed gayly. "And we—you and I—we will divide the spoils." Gravely. "Do not misunderstand. That was my little joke. If I get the money for you it will be quite honorable and businesslike. So—wait, dear young lady."

As she was going, she could not resist saying:

"You are SURE I can sing?—IF, of course—always the if."

"It is not to be doubted."

"How well, do you think?"

"You mean how many dollars a night well? You mean as well as this great singer or that? I do not know. And you are not to compare yourself with anyone but yourself. You will sing as well as Mildred Gower at her best."

For some reason her blood went tingling through her veins. If she had dared she would have kissed him.

X

THAT same afternoon Donald Keith, arrived at the top of Mrs. Belloc's steps, met Mildred coming out. Seeing their greeting, one would have thought they had seen each other but a few minutes before or were casual acquaintances. Said she:

"I'm going for a walk."

"Let's take the taxi," said he.

There it stood invitingly at the curb. She felt tired. She disliked walking. She wished to sit beside him and be whirled away—out of the noisy part of the city, up where the air was clean and where there were no crowds. But she had begun the regimen of Lucia Rivi. She hesitated. What matter if she began now or put off beginning until after this one last drive?

"No, we will walk," said she.

"But the streets are in frightful condition."

She thrust out a foot covered with a new and shiny storm-rubber.

"Let's drive to the park then. We'll walk there."

"No. If I get into the taxi, I'll not get out. Send it away."

When they were moving afoot up Madison Avenue, he said: "What's the matter? This isn't like you."

"I've come to my senses," replied she. "It may be too late, but I'm going to see."

"When I called on Mrs. Brindley the other day," said he, "she had your note, saying that you were going into musical comedy with Crossley."

"That's over," said she. "I lost my voice, and I lost my job."

"So I heard," said he. "I know Crossley. I dropped in to see him this morning, and he told me about a foolish, fashionable girl who made a bluff at going on the stage—he said she had a good voice and was a swell looker, but proved to be a regular 'four-flusher.' I recognized you."

"Thanks," said she dryly.

"So, I came to see you."

She inquired about Mrs. Brindley and then about Stanley Baird. Finding that he was in Italy, she inquired: "Do you happen to know his address?"

"I'll get it and send it to you. He has taken a house at Monte Carlo for the winter."

"And you?"

"I shall stay here—I think."

"You may join him?"

"It depends"—he looked at her—"upon you."

He could put a wonderful amount of meaning into a slight inflection. She struggled—not in vain—to keep from changing expression.

"You realize now that the career is quite hopeless?" said he.

She did not answer.

"You do not like the stage life?"

"No."

"And the stage life does not like you?"

"No."

"Your voice lacks both strength and stability?"

"Yes."

"And you have found the one way by which you could get on—and you don't like it?"

"Crossley told you?" said she, the color flaring.

"Your name was not mentioned. You may not believe it, but Crossley is a gentleman."

She walked on in silence.

"I did not expect your failure to come so soon—or in quite that way," he went on. "I got Mrs. Brindley to exact a promise from you that you'd let her know about yourself. I called on Mrs. Belloc one day when you were out, and gave her my confidence and got hers—and assured myself that you were in good hands. Crossley's tale gave me—a shock. I came at once."

"Then you didn't abandon me to my fate, as I thought?"

He smiled in his strange way. "I?—when I loved you? Hardly."

"Then you did interest yourself in me because you cared—precisely as I said," laughed she.

"And I should have given you up if you had succeeded—precisely as I said," replied he.

"You wished me to fail?"

"I wished you to fail. I did everything I could to help you to succeed. I even left you absolutely alone, set you in the right way—the only way in which anyone can win success."

"Yes, you made me throw away the crutches and try to walk."

"It was hard to do that. Those strains are very wearing at my time of life."

"You never were any younger, and you'll never be any older," laughed she. "That's your charm—one of them."

"Mildred, do you still care?"

"How did you know?" inquired she mockingly.

"You didn't try to conceal it. I'd not have ventured to say and do the things I said and did if I hadn't felt that we cared for each other. But, so long as you were leading that fatuous life and dreaming those foolish dreams, I knew we could never be happy."

"That is true—oh, SO true," replied she.

"But now—you have tried, and that has made a woman of you. And you have failed, and that has made you ready to be a wife—to be happy in the quiet, private ways."

She was silent.

"I can make enough for us both—as much as we will need or want—as much as you please, if you aren't too extravagant. And I can do it easily. It's making little sums—a small income—that's hard in this ridiculous world. Let's marry, go to California or Europe for several months, then come back here and live like human beings."

She was silent. Block after block they walked along, as if neither had anything especial in mind, anything worth the trouble of speech. Finally he said:

"Well?"

"I can't answer—yet," said she. "Not to-day—not till I've thought."

She glanced quickly at him. Over his impassive face, so beautifully regular and, to her, so fascinating, there passed a quick dark shadow, and she knew that he was suffering. He laughed quietly, his old careless, indifferent laugh.

"Oh, yes, you can answer," said he. "You have answered."

She drew in her breath sharply.

"You have refused."

"Why do you say that, Donald?" she pleaded.

"To hesitate over a proposal is to refuse," said he with gentle raillery. "A man is a fool who does not understand and sheer off when a woman asks for time."

"You know that I love you," she cried.

"I also know that you love something else more. But it's finished. Let's talk about something else."

"Won't you let me tell you why I hesitate?" begged she.

"It doesn't matter."

"But it does. Yes, I do refuse, Donald. I'll never marry you until I am independent. You said a while ago that what I've been through had made a woman of me. Not yet. I'm only beginning. I'm still weak—still a coward. Donald, I must and will be free."

He looked full at her, with a strange smile in his brilliant eyes. Said he, with obvious intent to change the subject: "Mrs. Brindley's very unhappy that you haven't been to see her."

"When you asked me to marry you, the only reason I almost accepted was because I want someone to support me. I love you—yes. But it is as one loves before one has given oneself and has lived the same life with another. In the ordinary sense, it's love that I feel. But—do you understand me, dearest?—in another sense, it's only the hope of love, the belief that love will come."

He stopped short and looked at her, his eyes alive with the stimulus of a new and startling idea.

"If you and I had been everything to each other, and you were saying 'Let us go on living the one life' and I were hesitating, then you'd be right. And I couldn't hesitate, Donald. If you were mine, nothing could make me give you up, but when it's only the hope of having you, then pride and self-respect have a chance to be heard."

He was ready to move on. "There's something in that," said he, lapsed into his usual seeming of impassiveness. "But not much."

"I never before knew you to fail to understand."

"I understand perfectly. You care, but you don't care enough to suit me. I haven't waited all these years before giving a woman my love, to be content with a love seated quietly and demurely between pride and self-respect."

"You wouldn't marry me until I had failed," said she shrewdly. "Now you attack me for refusing to marry you until I've succeeded."

A slight shrug. "Proposal withdrawn," said he. "Now let's talk about your career, your plans."

"I'm beginning to understand myself a little," said she. "I suppose you think that sort of personal talk is very silly and vain—and trivial."

"On the contrary," replied he, "it isn't absolutely necessary to understand oneself. One is swept on in the same general direction, anyhow. But understanding helps one to go faster and steadier."

"It began, away back, when I was a girl—this idea of a career. I envied men and despised women, the sort of women I knew and met with. I didn't realize why, then. But it was because a man had a chance to be somebody in himself and to do something, while a woman was just a—a more or less ornamental belonging of some man's—what you want me to become now."

"As far as possible from my idea."

"Don't you want me to belong to you?"

"As I belong to you."

"That sounds well, but it isn't what could happen. The fact is, Donald, that I want to belong to you—want to be owned by you and to lose myself in you. And it's that I'm fighting."

She felt the look he was bending upon her, and glowed and colored under it, but did not dare to turn her eyes to meet it. Said he: "Why fight it? Why not be happy?"

"Ah, but that's just it," cried she. "I shouldn't be happy. And I should make you miserable. The idea of a career—the idea that's rooted deep in me and can't ever be got out, Donald; it would torment me. You couldn't kill it, no matter how much you loved me. I'd yield for the time. Then, I'd go back—or, if I didn't, I'd be wretched and make you wish you'd never seen me."

"I understand," said he. "I don't believe it, but I understand."

"You think I'm deceiving myself, because you saw me wasting my life, playing the idler and the fool, pretending I was working toward a career when I was really making myself fit for nothing but to be Stanley Baird's mistress."

"And you're still deceiving yourself. You won't see the truth."

"No matter," said she. "I must go on and make a career—some kind of a career."

"At what?"

"At grand opera."

"How'll you get the money?"

"Of Stanley, if necessary. That's why I asked his address. I shan't ask for much. He'll not refuse."

"A few minutes ago you were talking of self-respect."

"As something I hoped to get. It comes with independence. I'll pay any price to get it."

"Any price?" said he, and never before had she seen his self-control in danger.

"I shan't ask Stanley until my other plans have failed."

"What other plans?"

"I am going to ask Mrs. Belloc for the money. She could afford to give—to lend—the little I'd want. I'm going to ask her in such a way that it will be as hard as possible for her to refuse. That isn't ladylike, but—I've dropped out of the lady class."

"And if she refuses?"

"Then I'll go one after another to several very rich men I know, and ask them as a business proposition."

"Go in person," advised he with an undisguised sneer.

"I'll raise no false hopes in them," she said. "If they choose to delude themselves, I'll not go out of my way to undeceive them—until I have to."

"So THIS is Mildred Gower?"

"You made that remark before."

"Really?"

"When Stanley showed you a certain photograph of me."

"I remember. This is the same woman."

"It's me," laughed she. "The real me. You'd not care to be married to her?"

"No," said he. Then, after a brief silence: "Yet, curiously, it was that woman with whom I fell in love. No, not exactly in love, for I've been thinking about what you said as to the difference between love in posse and love in esse, to put it scientifically—between love as a prospect and love as a reality."

"And I was right," said she. "It explains why marriages go to pieces and affairs come to grief. Those lovers mistook love's promise to come for fulfillment. Love doesn't die. It simply fails to come—doesn't redeem its promise."

"That's the way it might be with us," said he. "That's the way it would be with us," rejoined she.

He did not answer. When they spoke again it was of indifferent matters. An hour and a half after they started, they were at Mrs. Belloc's again. She asked him to have tea in the restaurant next door. He declined. He went up the steps with her, said:

"Well, I wish you luck. Moldini is the best teacher in America."

"How did you know Moldini was to teach me?" exclaimed she.

He smiled, put out his hand in farewell. "Crossley told me. Good-by."

"He told Crossley! I wonder why." She was so interested in this new phase that she did not see his outstretched hand, or the look of bitter irony that came into his eyes at this proof of the subordinate place love and he had in her thoughts.

"I'm nervous and anxious," she said apologetically. "Moldini told me he had some scheme about getting the money. If he only could! But no such luck for me," she added sadly.

Keith hesitated, debated with himself, said: "You needn't worry. Moldini got it—from Crossley. Fifty dollars a week for a year."

"You got Crossley to do it?"

"No. He had done it before I saw him. He had just promised Moldini and was cursing himself as 'weak and soft.' But that means nothing. You may be sure he did it because Moldini convinced him it was a good speculation."

She was radiant. She had not vanity enough where he was concerned to believe that he deeply cared, that her joy would give him pain because it meant forgetfulness of him. Nor was she much impressed by the expression of his eyes. And even as she hurt him, she made him love her the more; for he appreciated how rare was the woman who, in such circumstances, does not feed her vanity with pity for the poor man suffering so horribly because he is not to get her precious self.

It flashed upon her why he had not offered to help her. "There isn't anybody like you," said she, with no explanation of her apparent irrelevancy.

"Don't let Moldini see that you know," said he, with characteristic fine thoughtfulness for others in the midst of his own unhappiness. "It would deprive him of a great pleasure."

He was about to go. Suddenly her eyes filled and, opening the outer door, she drew him in. "Donald," she said, "I love you. Take me in your arms and make me behave."

He looked past her; his arms hung at his sides. Said he: "And to-night I'd get a note by messenger saying that you had taken it all back. No, the girl in the photograph—that was you. She wasn't made to be MY wife. Or I to be her husband. I love you because you are what you are. I should not love you if you were the ordinary woman, the sort who marries and merges. But I'm old enough to spare myself—and you—the consequences of what it would mean if we were anything but strangers to each other."

"Yes, you must keep away—altogether. If you didn't, I'd be neither the one thing nor the other, but just a poor failure."

"You'll not fail," said he. "I know it. It's written in your face." He looked at her. She was not looking at him, but with eyes gazing straight ahead was revealing that latent, inexplicable power which, when it appeared at the surface, so strongly dominated and subordinated her beauty and her sex. He shut his teeth together hard and glanced away.

"You will not fail," he repeated bitterly. "And that's the worst of it."

Without another word, without a handshake, he went. And she knew that, except by chance, he would never see her again—or she him.

Moldini, disheveled and hysterical with delight and suspense, was in the drawing-room—had been there half an hour. At first she could hardly force her mind to listen; but as he talked on and on, he captured her attention and held it.

The next day she began with Moldini, and put the Lucia Rivi system into force in all its more than conventual rigors. And for about a month she worked like a devouring flame. Never had there been such energy, such enthusiasm. Mrs. Belloc was alarmed for her health, but the Rivi system took care of that; and presently Mrs. Belloc was moved to say, "Well, I've often heard that hard work never harmed anyone, but I never believed it. Now I know the truth."

Then Mildred went to Hanging Rock to spend Saturday to Monday with her mother. Presbury, reduced now by various infirmities—by absolute deafness, by dimness of sight, by difficulty in walking—to where eating was his sole remaining pleasure, or, indeed, distraction, spent all his time in concocting dishes for himself. Mildred could not resist—and who can when seated at table with the dish before one's eyes and under one's nose. The Rivi regimen was suspended for the visit. Mildred, back in New York and at work again, found that she was apparently none the worse for her holiday, was in fact better. So she drifted into the way of suspending the regimen for an evening now and then—when she dined with Mrs. Brindley, or when Agnes Belloc had something particularly good. All went well for a time. Then—a cold. She neglected it, feeling sure it could not stay with one so soundly healthy through and through. But it did stay; it grew worse. She decided that she ought to take medicine for it. True, starvation was the cure prescribed by the regimen, but Mildred could not bring herself to two or three days of discomfort. Also, many people told her that such a cure was foolish and even dangerous. The cold got better, got worse, got better. But her throat became queer, and at last her voice left her. She was ashamed to go to Moldini in such a condition. She dropped in upon Hicks, the throat specialist. He "fixed her up" beautifully with a few sprayings. A week—and her voice left her again, and Hicks could not bring it back. As she left his office, it was raining—an icy, dreary drizzle. She splashed her way home, in about the lowest spirits she had ever known. She locked her door and seated herself at the window and stared out, while the storm raged within her. After an hour or two she wrote and sent Moldini a note: "I have been making a fool of myself. I'll not come again until I am all right. Be patient with me. I don't think this will occur again." She first wrote "happen." She scratched it out and put "occur" in its place. Not that Moldini would have noted the slip; simply that she would not permit herself the satisfaction of the false and self-excusing "happen." It had not been a "happen." It had been a deliberate folly, a lapse to the Mildred she had buried the day she sent Donald Keith away. When the note was on its way, she threw out all her medicines, and broke the new spraying apparatus Hicks had instructed her to buy.

She went back to the Rivi regime. A week passed, and she was little better. Two weeks, and she began to mend. But it was six weeks before the last traces of her folly disappeared. Moldini said not a word, gave no sign. Once more her life went on in uneventful, unbroken routine—diet, exercise, singing—singing, exercise, diet—no distractions except an occasional visit to the opera with Moldini, and she was hating opera now. All her enthusiasm was gone. She simply worked doggedly, drudged, slaved.

When the days began to grow warm, Mrs. Belloc said: "I suppose you'll soon be off to the country? Are you going to visit Mrs. Brindley?"

"No," said Mildred.

"Then come with me."

"Thank you, but I can't do it."

"But you've got to rest somewhere."

"Rest?" said Mildred. "Why should I rest?"

Mrs. Belloc started to protest, then abruptly changed. "Come to think of it, why should you? You're in perfect health, and it'll be time enough to rest when you 'get there.'"

"I'm tired through and through," said Mildred, "but it isn't the kind of tired that could be rested except by throwing up this frightful nightmare of a career."

"And you can't do that."

"I won't," said Mildred, her lips compressed and her eyes narrowed.

She and Moldini—and fat, funny little Mrs. Moldini—went to the mountains. And she worked on. She would listen to none of the suggestions about the dangers of keeping too steadily at it, about working oneself into a state of staleness, about the imperative demands of the artistic temperament for rest, change, variety. "It may be so," she said to Mrs. Brindley. "But I've gone mad. I can no more drop this routine than—than you could take it up and keep to it for a week."

"I'll admit I couldn't," said Cyrilla. "And Mildred, you're making a mistake."

"Then I'll have to suffer for it. I must do what seems best to me."

"But I'm sure you're wrong. I never knew anyone to act as you're acting. Everyone rests and freshens up."

Mildred lost patience, almost lost her temper. "You're trying to tempt me to ruin myself," she said. "Please stop it. You say you never knew anyone to do as I'm doing. Very well. But how many girls have you known who have succeeded?"

Cyrilla hesitatingly confessed that she had known none.

"Yet you've known scores who've tried."

"But they didn't fail because they didn't work enough. Many of them worked too much."

Mildred laughed. "How do you know why they failed?" said she. "You haven't thought about it as I have. You haven't LIVED it. Cyrilla, I served my apprenticeship at listening to nonsense about careers. I want to have nothing to do with inspiration, and artistic temperament, and spontaneous genius, and all the rest of the lies. Moldini and I know what we are about. So I'm living as those who have succeeded lived and not as those who have failed."

Cyrilla was sileneed, but not convinced. The amazing improvement in Mildred's health, the splendid slim strength and suppleness of her body, the new and stable glories of her voice—all these she knew about, but they did not convince her. She believed in work, in hard work, but to her work meant the music itself. She felt that the Rivi system and the dirty, obscure little Moldini between them were destroying Mildred by destroying all "temperament" in her.

It was the old, old criticism of talent upon genius. Genius has always won in its own time and generation all the world except talent. To talent contemporaneous genius, genius seen at its patient, plodding toil, seems coarse and obvious and lacking altogether in inspiration. Talent cannot comprehend that creation is necessarily in travail and in all manner of unloveliness.

Mildred toiled on like a slave under the lash, and Moldini and the Rivi system were her twin relentless drivers. She learned to rule herself with an iron hand. She discovered the full measure of her own deficiencies, and she determined to make herself a competent lyric soprano, perhaps something of a dramatic soprano. She dismissed from her mind all the "high" thoughts, all the dreams wherewith the little people, even the little people who achieve a certain success, beguile the tedium of their journey along the hard road. She was not working to "interpret the thought of the great master" or to "advance the singing art yet higher" or even to win fame and applause. She had one object—to earn her living on the grand opera stage, and to earn it as a prima donna because that meant the best living. She frankly told Cyrilla that this was her object, when Cyrilla forced her one day to talk about her aims. Cyrilla looked pained, broke a melancholy silence to say:

"I know you don't mean that. You are too intelligent. You sing too well."

"Yes, I mean just that," said Mildred. "A living."

"At any rate, don't say it. You give such a false impression."

"To whom? Not to Crossley, and not to Moldini, and why should I care what any others think? They are not paying my expenses. And regardless of what they think now, they'll be at my feet if I succeed, and they'll put me under theirs if I don't."

"How hard you have grown," cried Cyrilla.

"How sensible, you mean. I've merely stopped being a self-deceiver and a sentimentalist."

"Believe me, my dear, you are sacrificing your character to your ambition."

"I never had any real character until ambition came," replied Mildred. "The soft, vacillating, sweet and weak thing I used to have wasn't character."

"But, dear, you can't think it superior character to center one's whole life about a sordid ambition."

"Sordid?"

"Merely to make a living."

Mildred laughed merrily and mockingly. "You call that sordid? Then for heaven's sake what is high? You had left you money enough to live on, if you have to. No one left me an income. So, I'm fighting for independence—and that means for self-respect. Is self-respect sordid, Cyrilla!"

And then Cyrilla understood—in part, not altogether. She lived in the ordinary environment of flap-doodle and sweet hypocrisy and sentimentality; and none such can more than vaguely glimpse the realities.

Toward the end of the summer Moldini said:

"It's over. You have won."

Mildred looked at him in puzzled surprise.

"You have learned it all. You will succeed. The rest is detail."

"But I've learned nothing as yet," protested she.

"You have learned to teach yourself," replied the Italian. "You at last can hear yourself sing, and you know when you sing right and when you sing wrong, and you know how to sing right. The rest is easy. Ah, my dear Miss Gower, you will work NOW!"

Mildred did not understand. She was even daunted by that "You will work NOW!" She had been thinking that to work harder was impossible. What did he expect of her? Something she feared she could not realize. But soon she understood—when he gave her songs, then began to teach her a role, the part of Madame Butterfly herself. "I can help you only a little there," he said. "You will have to go to my friend Ferreri for roles. But we can make a beginning."

She had indeed won. She had passed from the stage where a career is all drudgery—the stage through which only the strong can pass without giving up and accepting failure or small success. She had passed to the stage where there is added pleasure to the drudgery, for, the drudgery never ceases. And what was the pleasure? Why, more work—always work—bringing into use not merely the routine parts of the mind, but also the imaginative and creative faculties. She had learned her trade—not well enough, for no superior man or woman ever feels that he or she knows the trade well enough—but well enough to begin to use it.

Said Moldini: "When the great one, who has achieved and arrived, is asked for advice by the sweet, enthusiastic young beginner, what is the answer? Always the same: 'My dear child, don't! Go back home, and marry and have babies.' You know why now?"

And Mildred, looking back over the dreary drudgery that had been, and looking forward to the drudgery yet to come, dreary enough for all the prospects of a few flowers and a little sun—Mildred said: "Indeed I do, maestro."

"They think it means what you Americans call morals—as if that were all of morality! But it doesn't mean morals; not at all. Sex and the game of sex is all through life everywhere—in the home no less than in the theater. In town and country, indoors and out, sunlight, moonlight, and rain— always it goes on. And the temptations and the struggles are no more and no less on the stage than off. No, there is too much talk about 'morals.' The reason the great one says 'don't' is the work." He shook his head sadly. "They do not realize, those eager young beginners. They read the story-books and the lives of the great successes and they hear the foolish chatter of common-place people—those imbecile 'cultured' people who know nothing! And they think a career is a triumphal march. What think you, Miss Gower—eh?"

"If I had known I'd not have had the courage, or the vanity, to begin," said she. "And if I could realize what's before me, I probably shouldn't have the courage to go on."

"But why not? Haven't you also learned that it's just the day's work, doing every day the best you can?"

"Oh, I shall go on," rejoined she.

"Yes," said he, looking at her with awed admiration. "It is in your face. I saw it there, the day you came—after you sang the 'Batti Batti' the first time and failed."

"There was nothing to me then."

"The seed," replied he. "And I saw it was an acorn, not the seed of one of those weak plants that spring up overnight and wither at noon. Yes, you will win." He laughed gayly, rolled his eyes and kissed his fingers. "And then you can afford to take a little holiday, and fall in love. Love! Ah, it is a joyous pastime—for a holiday. Only for a holiday, mind you. I shall be there and I shall seize you and take you back to your art."

In the following winter and summer Crossley disclosed why he had been sufficiently interested in grand opera to begin to back undeveloped voices. Crossley was one of those men who are never so practical as when they profess to be, and fancy themselves, impractical. He became a grand-opera manager and organized for a season that would surpass in interest any New York had known. Thus it came about that on a March night Mildred made her debut.

The opera was "Faust." As the three principal men singers were all expensive—the tenor alone, twelve hundred a night—Crossley put in a comparatively modestly salaried Marguerite. She was seized with a cold at the last moment, and Crossley ventured to substitute Mildred Gower. The Rivi system was still in force. She was ready—indeed, she was always ready, as Rivi herself had been. And within ten minutes of her coming forth from the wings, Mildred Gower had leaped from obscurity into fame. It happens so, often in the story books, the newly gloriously arrived one having been wholly unprepared, achieving by sheer force of genius. It occurs so, occasionally, in life—never when there is lack of preparation, never by force of unassisted genius, never by accident. Mildred succeeded because she had got ready to succeed. How could she have failed?

Perhaps you read the stories in the newspapers—how she had discovered herself possessed of a marvelous voice, how she had decided to use it in public, how she had coached for a part, had appeared, had become one of the world's few hundred great singers all in a single act of an opera. You read nothing about what she went through in developing a hopelessly uncertain and far from strong voice into one which, while not nearly so good as thousands of voices that are tried and cast aside, yet sufficed, with her will and her concentration back of it, to carry her to fame—and wealth.

That birdlike voice! So sweet and spontaneous, so true, so like the bird that "sings of summer in full throated ease!" No wonder the audience welcomed it with cheers on cheers. Greater voices they had heard, but none more natural—and that was Moldini.

He came to her dressing-room at the intermission. He stretched out his arms, but emotion overcame him, and he dropped to a chair and sobbed and cried and laughed. She came and put her arms round him and kissed him. She was almost calm. The GREAT fear had seized her—Can I keep what I have won?

"I am a fool," cried Moldini. "I will agitate you."

"Don't be afraid of that," said she. "I am nervous, yes, horribly nervous. But you have taught me so that I could sing, no matter what was happening." It was true. And her body was like iron to the touch.

He looked at her, and though he knew her and had seen her train herself and had helped in it, he marveled. "You are happy?" he said eagerly. "Surely—yes, you MUST be happy."

"More than that," answered she. "You'll have to find another word than happiness—something bigger and stronger and deeper."

"Now you can have your holiday," laughed he. "But"—with mock sternness—"in moderation! He must be an incident only. With those who win the high places, sex is an incident—a charming, necessary incident, but only an incident. He must not spoil your career. If you allowed that you would be like a mother who deserts her children for a lover. He must not touch your career!"

Mildred, giving the last touches to her costume before the glass, glanced merrily at Moldini by way of it. "If he did touch it," said she, "how long do you think he would last with me?"

Moldini paused half-way in his nod of approval, was stricken with silence and sadness. It would have been natural and proper for a man thus to put sex beneath the career. It was necessary for anyone who developed the strong character that compels success and holds it. But— The Italian could not get away from tradition; woman was made for the pleasure of one man, not for herself and the world.

"You don't like that, maestro?" said she, still observing him in the glass.

"No man would," said he, with returning cheerfulness. "It hurts man's vanity. And no woman would, either; you rebuke their laziness and their dependence!"

She laughed and rushed away to fresh triumphs.